To: J...

♡ Let us claim you ipet ♡

Nyla

THEIR
LETHAL
PET

USA TODAY BESTSELLING AUTHOR
LEXI C. FOSS

Their Lethal Pet

Editing by: Outthink Editing, LLC

Proofreading by: Katie Schmahl & Jean Bachen

Cover Photography: CJC Photography

Cover Models: Lauren Skeoch & Keith Manecke

Additional Photo Manipulation (Models/Stock) & Cover Design: Covers by Sanja

Title Page Art: Sanja Gombar

Chapter Background Art: Alan Rex

Skull Art: Susan Gerardi

Rose & Moon Icon: Anna Spies

Published by: Ninja Newt Publishing, LLC

Digital Edition

ISBN: 978-1-68530-997-8

Print Edition

ISBN: 978-1-68530-350-1

AI Disclaimer: This book does not contain any elements of AI content. All art was designed by real artists, and all of the words were written by the author.

You can run and hide, little one.
But we're the monsters of the night.
And you are our chosen bride.
So be a good girl and turn the page.
I'll reward you with my knot.
Flame will let you claim his barb.
And Reaper, well, Reaper is going to test your limits in all ways.
But we'll make it good, baby.
I promise…

THEIR LETHAL PET

A MONSTERS NIGHT NOVEL

ABOUT THEIR LETHAL PET

Run. Hide. *Fight.*

It's Monsters Night, the annual event where the portals to other realms and realities open, and monsters flood the streets to search for their potential mates.

And I'm one of the candidates.

Why?

Because I broke all the rules. I fought back against the elitist system hell-bent on enslaving humankind. And f-ck if I'm going to let one of these monsters claim me. Let alone three of them.

Orcus.
Reaper.
Flame.

They saved me from a compromising situation. But that

doesn't mean I *like* them. I don't care how gorgeous they are or how well-endowed they seem to be—I kneel for no one. And I have no interest in becoming their lethal little pet.

"Try to tame me," I dare them.

"We have no interest in taming you, sweet pet," they say. "We want to make you ours."

"Ours to worship."
"Ours to love."
"Ours to keep."

WELCOME TO MONSTERS NIGHT

It started as a curse. A rumor. A hint of superstition.

But then it became *very* real.

Monsters poured out of the portals, their origins unknown, their intentions clear. For one night a year, they roamed the earth, selecting their unwilling brides and dragging them home.

Except not all the monsters went back to their own worlds.

Some stayed.

Power began to shift.

Cities were destroyed.

Humankind reverted.

Villages were created, all the mortals hiding from the dangerous beings that call our realm *home*.

And still, those portals open.

Every. Single. Year.

Allowing more monsters to flood our realm, finding their mortal mates and claiming them against their will.

Or that's the tale we've all been told.

Be good or suffer the consequences.

Follow the rules or your entries into the selection pool will increase.

Every year, sacrifices are chosen. *Sacrifices* that are then dumped into abandoned cities right before Monsters Night commences.

Offerings are what those sacrifices are called. *Offerings* meant to tempt the creatures of the night. *Offerings* put in place to ensure humanity survives this hell.

This is our reality now.

A world filled with deadly creatures and mortal survivors.

And tomorrow is the Day of the Choosing...

Will we survive another year?

Or will we become one of the Offerings for this year's Monsters Night?

Only fate can save us now...

PROLOGUE
ORCUS

"What the fuck is Monsters Night?" In all the realms and realities I've ventured to during my very long existence, I've never heard of such a concept.

"It's like Halloween," my brother mutters. "Except no one dresses up or passes out candy."

"So it's a holiday?" I translate, not following his logic.

He grimaces. "Depends on who you ask."

I stare at him. "I'm going to need a better explanation, Hades."

My brother sighs, his pitch-black eyes—the same color as my own—finally meeting mine. "Basically, these portals open, releasing creatures from various realms and realities into the mortal world. But it's only for one night a year."

I snort. "That doesn't sound like Halloween at all."

He shrugs. "Monsters roaming the night reminds me of Halloween." He scrubs the day-old stubble along his square jaw. "But I guess it's more like a mating game since the creatures infiltrate the Human Realm to find compatible brides and grooms."

My eyebrow inches upward. "And you think our

1

mother is in this *Monsters Night* realm?" That was how this conversation started—by my brother saying he thought he may have found something related to our missing Omega mother.

Hades's lips twist to the side, his gaze narrowing slightly. "I'm not sure, but I sense a presence there. One that might be hers."

"Hmm." I drum my fingers against the leather armchair, the rhythmic tap echoing through my brother's den. He takes the whole *Netherworld* vibe to the extreme in some cases, the dark fixtures and shadowy corners reminding me more of a crypt than an office.

"It's enough that we need to investigate," he continues. "But there are too many obligations and complications at present for me to pursue it further on my own. Hence..." He waves a hand at me.

"Hence the reason you're telling me about the lead."

"Exactly."

I lift a shoulder and stand. "All right. Give me the details and I'll check it out." A few hours of wandering the alternate reality will tell me if my brother's instincts are right or not.

He shakes his head. "It's not that simple."

I frown at him. "Sounds pretty simple."

"Their reality is run by supernatural beings, not humans. It's entirely unlike the Human Realm we know in our existence." His obsidian-colored eyes glitter at me. "They sensed the window portal I used to peek inside their world, Orcus. If they can sense that, they'll absolutely feel you entering their realm via a proper portal door."

"Okay, so I should come prepared for a fight?" I hedge, wondering what sort of *supernaturals* I'll be dealing with in this alternate realm.

He shakes his head. "I want you to go into their world

on Monsters Night. Your portal will be one of the hundreds opening for the mating event. You should be able to come and go without notice."

I study him for a moment, his large form half-hidden by the wooden monstrosity he calls a desk. "All right. And when is Monsters Night?"

"In two weeks," he says. "But there's more."

Of course there is.

Grumbling under my breath, I collapse back into the oversized leather chair and gesture for him to continue. "Go on, brother. Lay it all out."

"If you were less impulsive, little brother, you would see that I was already trying to do that."

I give him a look. *Little brother.* Fuck. I'm the same height and width as him. Even our wingspan is identical. "There's nothing *little* about me."

His dark gaze dances over me in amusement. "I can easily best you, *baby brother.*"

I roll my eyes. He makes it sound like I'm an infant, not four thousand years old. "Stop tempting me to kick your ass, and finish your explanation, *old man.*"

Rather than be offended, he merely smirks.

Then he clears his throat, sobers, and returns to the topic at hand. "Monsters Night will provide coverage for you to slip in and out of their reality. It'll also provide a perfect distraction to cover it all up on our end."

"Cover it all up?" I repeat.

"The last thing I need is Typhos Lucifer up my ass and asking questions," Hades grounds out. "I would prefer that he not find out what we're up to. Otherwise…" He trails off, his gaze holding mine.

Otherwise, he might find out what happened to the Mythos Fae Omegas, I finish in my mind, aware of what Hades is trying to imply.

3

Thus far, our kind has managed to keep the disappearance of our Omega Gods and Goddesses a secret.

But if that information were to be revealed, our very existence would be put in jeopardy.

"I understand," I say solemnly, all signs of my previous humor long gone. Nothing like the potential extinction of Mythos Fae kind to create a somber moment. "Tell me your plan, brother."

He nods, the intensity of the conversation deepening with each passing moment.

By the time he's done explaining the nuances of the portal, and how he plans to cover our tracks, I'm both impressed and wary. "You're asking a lot of Maliki," I tell him softly.

Hades swallows. "I know. But he's already agreed."

"Of course he has," I reply. "He worships you."

"They all do," Hades points out, referring to the Netherworld Fae, who all consider him their God.

Any fae with death-like magic, such as Corpse Fae and Death Fae, all reside within the Netherworld Kingdom and are therefore collectively called Netherworld Fae.

And my dear older brother is their chosen deity.

Probably because his soul died when he lost his Omega...

"Regardless," Hades continues, oblivious to my dark inner ramblings. "Maliki is the perfect choice. Lucifer won't kill him."

"In theory," I hedge.

"He won't kill him," Hades reiterates, the words seeming to be more for himself than for me.

Because while my brother may not want to admit it out loud, he cares deeply for Maliki. More so than most of his *playthings*.

"All right, so Maliki will be the cover story," I say,

4

returning us to the plan. "He'll tell Lucifer that he was simply helping his fellow fae feed or find mates. Meanwhile, I'll take advantage of the distraction and hunt for this mysterious aura you sensed."

He nods. "Yes."

"Excellent." I wipe my palms on my dark jeans and stand. "Then I have two weeks to mentally prepare." Not that I need it. Traversing realms and realities is nothing new to me. "If that's all..." I trail off, gesturing to the large wooden door laden with silver chains.

My brother dips his chin again, dismissing me.

Except, as I take a single step away, he says, "Oh, one more thing."

I pause and glance back at him, my eyebrow lifting in silent question. *Yes?* I ask with that look.

"Flame and Reaper will be going with you."

I stare at him. "Why?"

"Protection."

I huff a laugh. "Worried I may shop for a mate during this infamous *Monsters Night* and slaughter my competition, hmm?" I muse. "And you think a pair of Netherworld Fae will keep me on track?"

Because if that's true, then I have news for my dear old brother. Flame and Reaper are my best friends for a reason. Neither of them will try to stop me from doing a damn thing. Fuck, they'll probably *encourage* me to play.

"No, I think a pair of Netherworld Fae may help keep you unharmed in this unknown reality—one that may or may not be harboring our mother." When I simply gape at him, he adds, "The protection is for *you*, Orcus. Not for the humans or the Monsters Night creatures. But for *you*."

I grunt. "I'll be fine, but thanks for your concern."

"Reaper and Flame will accompany you," he counters. "End of discussion."

Normally, that sort of high-handed bullshit would provoke my argumentative side to come out and dominate my opponent.

But this isn't worth my time to debate.

Taking Reaper and Flame with me into a world full of human playthings—all of whom have been groomed to be potential mates for monsters of various kinds—seems like a vacation, not a daunting task.

Monsters Night, I think to myself. *Sounds like a party all right.*

I can't take a potential mate—I would need a proper Omega for that. However, playing? Yeah, I can play. Taste. Bite. *Fuck.*

Assuming I can find a human capable of handling my knot.

Unlikely, but an alternate reality poses a lot of fun opportunities.

"Don't forget your objective, brother," Hades says, no doubt seeing the excited gleam in my gaze. "Search out the potential presence. If it's nothing of consequence, then do whatever it is you want to do. Otherwise, remember what's important."

I scoff at him. "I may be a millennium younger than you, Hades, but I'm not a child. I know what's at stake."

His dark eyes glitter with understanding as he dips his chin again, a small grin playing over his lips. "Then happy hunting, brother."

I smile. "Happy hunting indeed."

CHAPTER ONE
ALINA

The Day of the Choosing

White dress.

    Flat sandals.

    Freshly brushed hair.

I study my reflection in the mirror, the woman staring back at me one I barely recognize. She looks innocent. Pure. *Matrimonial.*

All that's missing is the veil. That flimsy piece of gauzy bullshit meant to hide my face.

Maybe I should let it fall to the ground and step on it a little? I muse. *What's another broken rule?*

My tally is nearly forty for this quarter alone, hopefully guaranteeing I'll be selected for this year's Monsters Night.

Everyone thinks I'm crazy. No one wants to get on that fateful train, the one that leaves lightning sparks trailing in the wind as it heads toward Monster City.

But I know something they don't.

A secret my sister shared via a note.

9

A note she somehow slipped under my door during last year's Choosing Ceremony.

There's an Elite City, her familiar scrawl read. *Find an old map, Lina. Look for Chicago. I'll be waiting.*

It could all be a trick. A lie. A way to seduce me into volunteering for Monsters Night. But what choice do I have? Serapina is my sister. She's all I have left in this world. And she's out there somewhere, waiting for me.

I wrongly assumed she'd been captured. Claimed. No longer of this earth.

I wallowed. Cried. Mourned the loss of my younger sister, the last remaining member of my family.

Then her note appeared, inspiring renewed hope. It also left behind a taste of guilt. I'd given up on her. How could I? I knew better. If anyone could survive in this cruel world, it was Serapina.

I have to find her.

And if it all ends up being a hoax, then I'll fight until my dying breath. Slay every beast in my path. *Refuse* to submit.

This dress will look amazing covered in monster blood, I think, eyeing myself once more. *Streaks of black and red marring the too-white fabric. Hmm.*

Every year, new dresses appear for the women. Always white. Always bridal. The men are given tuxedos. It's like a fucking wedding, only none of us willingly walk down the aisle.

Well. Almost none of us.

I volunteer, I muse darkly. *Take me to Monster City. Let those creatures try to mate me. They'll soon learn I'm not worth the effort.*

Or that's the plan, anyway.

Fight. Run. Hide. *Look for an old map.*

I *will* survive. And I'll find my sister. There is no other option.

Because I can't stay here.

The men are starting to look my way with a little too much interest. I'm two-and-twenty now, the perfect age for *breeding*.

I have no parents to guard my virtue.

No older brother to ensure I'm not taken against my will.

The Village Protectors—a false title for the humans in charge of maintaining order in our mountain settlement— won't step in to intervene.

I'm alone.

Vulnerable.

And, unfortunately, my rebellious behavior over the last year only seems to have inspired more intrigue.

The men over five-and-thirty are eligible to start a family, and most of those men select women around my age to be their wives.

There's a whole process involved, one that basically removes the woman from the Day of the Choosing selection pool—if the proposal is approved, anyway.

And given that everyone between the ages of eight- and-ten and five-and-thirty are required to enter, a potential marital agreement is favorable to some.

But it does not appeal to me.

Because I don't want a husband.

Yet, for whatever reason, that seems to make me more attractive to some of these older men.

Just like Sage, I think, wincing. She's as defenseless as me, perhaps even more so.

I close my eyes, my body vibrating with nerves as I picture Sage next door. *Taking care of her mother. Preparing for today's ceremony. Hoping and praying that she survives this year's Choosing.*

She's all her mother has left. If she's selected...

11

My lips flatten, my urge to protect her making my heart beat faster. Sage is like a sister to me. We grew up next door to each other, and she's the same age as Serapina, which once made them good friends.

But with Serapina being gone, Sage and I have grown closer.

A significant portion of my extra entries these last four quarters were a result of me donating resources to her and her "outcast" mother.

And a few of my other entries were consequences of me being caught outside after curfew.

If only the Village Protectors knew my real reason for being out late all those nights...

Sage will have to take over that task once I'm gone. I've tried to prepare her, but the village security changes weekly. Unfortunately, that means her likelihood of getting caught is high. Just like it has been for me.

A few extra entries hopefully won't result in her becoming an Offering for Monsters Night, because the young silver-haired girl isn't made for that fate. She's too small. Too *innocent.*

Although, the same could be said about Serapina.

And me, I realize, taking in my five-foot-two height.

Shaking my head, I step away from the mirror as bells begin echoing through the air.

"Shit," I mutter. *I'm going to be late.*

Shivers traverse my spine, causing me to turn quickly toward the door, my veil clutched in one hand. Over two decades of training has instilled this response in my being. No matter how many times I rebelled these last twelve months, I can't quite shake the need to *obey.*

Especially today.

While the brides and grooms are the mandatory participants in the ceremony, all families are mandated to report to the town square to observe. Or rather, *celebrate*, as our Village Viscount requires.

Ice coats my veins as I think of our infamous Nightingale Village leader. He's taken three brides in the last decade, his reason being a need to procreate and ensure our people survive. As a result of his *sacrifice*, he's been granted more resources to help care for his growing brood.

Three more men have followed his example, and several others are considering the same path.

It wouldn't bother me as much if they were choosing women close to their own ages. But all three of our Village Viscount's wives are young enough to be his daughters. Hell, his latest pick could have been his granddaughter.

Not my problem, I tell myself as I wander down the dirt path that leads to our village's only road.

Except the sounds of soft steps behind me have me pausing and glancing over my shoulder at Sage's bowed head.

I wince as I think about her falling into a potential trap with these men. Her unique silver hair, bright blue eyes, and porcelain features have turned multiple heads her way these last six months.

She just turned twenty.

That makes her more than eligible in the eyes of those older men.

"We're going to be late," she whispers to me as she reaches my side and nudges me to continue walking.

"I just said that to myself a minute ago," I say back to her, my lips curling. "What do you think they'll do? Imprison me? Add another entry to that creepy-as-fuck cauldron?" The *Chalice*, as our Viscount calls it, is a sacred emblem in our village. It houses all the entries inside its eerie obsidian interior.

"*Lina,*" Sage admonishes, using my nickname.

I simply smile wider. "What, Little S? Worried they might jump out and seize me?"

Little S is my nickname for her even though we're only two years apart in age and roughly the same height. Something about her just feels so much younger to me, maybe because I still see her as the little girl who befriended my sister all those years ago.

"Yes." Her bright eyes are earnest as she answers my sarcastically phrased question. "I'm worried... worried you'll..." She swallows. "What if...? What if it's a dozen again? Like when...?" She trails off, the statement finishing automatically in my mind.

Like when Serapina was selected.

The quota of Offerings changes every year, the number one that won't be announced until our Village Viscount begins the ceremony.

A dozen Offerings were required the year Serapina was chosen. Hers had been the final name drawn out of that ominous Chalice.

Most years only demand five or six Offerings, but not that fated Day of the Choosing.

I clear my throat. "You have nothing to worry about, Sage. I'll be fine."

"What if they pick you?" she asks in a rush, her bare feet whispering over the ground as my sandals clip annoyingly. "You gave us so many meals, so much water, all at your own expense. If they choose you—"

"It'll be because I wanted to be chosen," I interject. "Don't you dare feel guilty, Sage. I used you and your mom as a cover for my own desires." I've told her this before, that I *want* to be an Offering. But she thinks I'm lying, that I'm only telling her that to make her feel better.

"Lina," she breathes, her hand finding mine as she

forces me to stop walking. "I know what you've done for us. I appreciate it. But you don't need to lie to me."

"I'm not lying," I promise her.

She shakes her head. "You are. No one wants to be chosen. No one wants to suffer Monsters Night."

"I do," I insist.

Her blue eyes harden, her characteristic softness melting away to reveal the fierce woman beneath the porcelain exterior. "Stop trying to assuage my guilt, Lina. I'm not nearly as naïve as you think I am."

Sighing, I pull my hand from hers and wrap my arm around her shoulders instead. "I'm not trying to *assuage* anything, Sage. I'm telling the truth."

She huffs, clearly ready to push me away.

And I realize this may be the last time I'll ever see her. Because if I'm selected today, I'll be immediately escorted to the *Lightrailer*—yet another stupid name created by our Viscount.

It's a train, I've wanted to correct him several times. *A. Damn. Train.*

It just happens to move very quickly.

Regardless of the name or its intended destination, the reality is that I'm leaving. Or rather, I hope to be leaving. Which means this is my chance to say goodbye to Sage, and I really don't want to leave her like this.

"Sage," I say softly, holding on to her as she tries to squirm away from me. It's a very sisterly thing to do, which instantly makes me think of Serapina and how I used to do this very thing to her whenever we argued over something trivial. Being two years older provided me with some additional strength.

At least, that's what I used to jokingly say to her.

But as Sage is proving now, age is just a number.

"Let's just go," she snaps, her fiery side out in full force.

15

She rarely shows it to anyone in public, mostly because it's not *allowed*.

Women are meant to be submissive. The perfect brides. That's all our studies teach us, anyway. Because we'll be mated to either a monster or a man in the village. Regardless, we are destined to be *owned*.

Unless we run, I think, my teeth grinding together. "There's an Elite City," I mutter, causing Sage to freeze.

"What?" She blinks at me.

"Serapina…" I glance around, ensuring we're nowhere near any buildings where recording devices might overhear our conversation. They're tricky little instruments used by the Village Protectors to spy on us. I'm not sure how they work, or what they even look like, but I've heard rumors of their existence.

However, we're nearly to the road now, the only stalls around us filled with empty bins meant for fruits and vegetables.

"Serapina left me a note last year."

Sage's eyes widen. "A note?"

I nod. "During the ceremony."

"How?"

"I don't know," I admit. "But it was her handwriting." So I have to believe it was real. To consider anything else just isn't feasible. *She's alive. I'm going to find her. We'll be together again. Somewhere. Somehow. Someday.*

"Why are you just now telling me this?"

"Because I *want* to be chosen," I stress. "I… I need to find Sera." It's a nickname I usually only reserve for my sister in private, but Sage is basically family.

Which made withholding this information hard. But I wanted to protect her.

And, if I'm being honest with myself, I wanted to protect my secret as well.

Trust has always been a hard concept to accept.

But if I could trust anyone in this village, it would be Sage. Maybe in another lifetime or in an alternate reality, that could have been possible.

Still, I need Sage to understand that she isn't to blame for my choices.

"Sera's out there and she's waiting for me. All I know is I have to search for the Elite City she mentioned in the note. *Chicago*, she called it. That's why I've accepted all the extra entries. You and Paulina don't owe me anything."

Paulina is Sage's mom. She rarely leaves their house, her outcast status exempting her from today's events. Hence the reason her daughter is here alone.

"Don't blame yourself if I'm chosen," I went on. "Please understand and believe me when I say I *want* this."

She gapes at me with wide, unblinking eyes for a long moment, the bells' echoes growing more insistent with every passing moment. "She survived Monsters Night."

"She survived Monsters Night," I repeat, nodding. "And so will I."

"By finding the Elite City?"

"Yes."

"Chicago," she echoes, causing me to nod again.

"I'll be fine," I tell her. "And so will you. Just keep your head down. Avoid the Viscount and his Barons." That's the title the other men in his circle have taken on, their status demanding respect from the other villagers.

"I don't know how to do that," Sage tells me. "They... they keep showing up at the gardens, Alina."

"Just don't do anything to draw attention to yourself." I pull her into a hug, my mouth near her ear. "Only trade entries for resources you really need. And don't break any rules. If I've learned anything this year, it's that being a rebel makes you more of a target."

For indecent offers.

Promises of false protection.

Interest that's a little too personal.

I don't tell her those things, just leave it all unsaid. Because she knows better than anyone what happens when a female is seen as weak or easy prey. Her mother is living proof of how women are punished for the sins of men here.

"Remember what I told you," I continue softly. "Wednesdays. Ten p.m. South Street by the cornfield. He'll have a flashlight in his left hand, not his right. And he only accepts smoked meats."

I've told her that a hundred times now, yet I can't help doing it one final time.

"Stay safe," I add, tears pricking my eyes. "And if you're ever chosen, look for an old map. Find Chicago."

I let go of her before she can reply, the ringing loud and overwhelming in my ears.

I don't mind drawing attention to myself by being late, but Sage needs to hide. As well as she can with that silver hair, anyway.

Swallowing, I start toward the main road once more with Sage right behind me.

She says nothing, just grabs my hand and gives it a squeeze.

I release her when we near the festivities, the veil still clutched in my opposite palm.

With a deep breath, I slide the combed ends into my dark hair.

And genuinely pray for the first time in my very short life.

Please call my name.

Please call my name.

Please call my name…

CHAPTER TWO
ALINA

THE TOWN SQUARE is deathly silent.

Not a word is spoken. I'm convinced that some of us are not even breathing.

This is the waiting period. The dreaded anticipation as our Village Viscount prepares to deliver his annual sermon.

We'll cast a prayer to the monsters for allowing us to survive among them, bless the upcoming sacrifice, and beg the Fates to choose the right Offerings.

To provide the wrong Offerings could result in the extermination of humankind. Or that's what our Village Viscount always says, anyway.

I swallow, the warm air causing my white gown to stick to my clammy skin. Summer is upon us, as evidenced by the blistering sun overhead. But that doesn't stop our Village Viscount from drawing out the ceremony.

He's standing up there in the shade provided by the overhang hovering above his stage, his podium a few feet in front of his tall, imposing frame.

There's a fan stirring a breeze near his suit-clad form,

something I can see but not hear. And I can only see it because it's causing the wisps of his long blond hair to dance around his broad shoulders.

He's one of the oldest men in attendance, his Barons the only others close to him in age. It's rare for men to make it to over fifty in our village. Too many farming accidents. Too harsh a work schedule. Too limited on basic necessities.

I curl my hands into fists as several around me sway in discomfort. We're hungry and thirsty. Overheated. *Scared*.

Except my fear is different this year. I'm no longer afraid of being chosen; I'm afraid of *not* being chosen.

My jaw clenches as I stare our Viscount down. *Screw. This.*

I'm tired of this show of power. Everyone around me has their heads bowed, their respect devout.

But I can't quite bring myself to tuck my chin. I want to stare at him, to *see* him. And I want him to see me, too.

It's a bizarre urge. A forbidden desire. An *angry* reaction.

This man has the audacity to stand up there with his *fans* while the rest of us burn.

The fabric around my face feels heavy, my overheated skin sticking to the gauzy material.

My gaze narrows. *I'm done.*

Soon, my name will be called, and I'll be free. I have to believe that or I'll scream. *There's no other option. Fate has to be on my side here.*

And if it's not, then maybe I can do something to guarantee it. Push this Viscount a little more and force his hand. Make him *choose* me. Because a defiant villager makes an excellent Offering. Isn't that why broken rules earn more entries?

Testing the theory, I push the veil away from my head

so that it's covering my hair and not my face. The men don't have to hide behind a curtain of white fluff, so why do I?

"*Lina*," Sage hisses under her breath. "What are you doing?"

"Defying the order," I reply while barely moving my lips.

A few around us stir, clearly having heard our conversation. They may not have understood the words, but the whispers were loud in this too-silent square.

The Village Viscount instantly finds me in the crowd, likely not because of my voice, but because of my movement.

He's too far away for me to properly discern his elderly features, but his attention is very clearly on me now.

What are you going to do? I demand with my eyes, even as my spine tingles with the need to submit. I've never been this bold. It feels reckless. Liberating. Terrifying.

He's surrounded by Village Protectors, the men all marked by their faceless appearances. Their hoods hide their identities. Some of them may actually be from the train behind the stage.

The Lightrailer.

It's a massive train with too-white metal siding, the pristine color reminding me of my dress.

How does it stay so clean? I wonder.

I've been in this gown for a mere three hours, and it already feels dirty. Yet that train is shockingly bright despite however many thousands of miles it's traveled.

I swallow, unease prickling my neck at the thought of boarding the Lightrailer. It's my goal. My desire. But that doesn't make it comforting.

My focus returns to the Viscount to find him still

staring at me. Or that's the way it looks from way back here. There are over a thousand people in this town square with several thousand more around us.

The village always feels small until all of us congregate. We're so spread out, some of us living closer to the center —like me and Sage—and others expanding up and down the mountains. Several people here walked four to five miles this morning to reach the ceremony.

All without water or nourishment.

Yet you continue to stand there and lord your power over us, I think, glaring at the Viscount. *Just get it over with.*

I swear he narrows his gaze in reply. Maybe it's my imagination. Maybe I'm delirious from the heat and being forced to wait. Or maybe I'm seeing him clearly for the first time.

This man isn't worthy of my respect.

It's a stark realization that sends a jolt down my spine.

For two-and-twenty years, I've feared and worshipped this man. But now? Now I just want him to say my name and let me board that train.

What if he doesn't pick me from the Chalice? I wonder. *What if I'm stuck here for another two-and-ten months?*

What if there are no Offerings this year?

Shit.

If I don't get on that train today, I—

The Viscount steps forward, causing my thoughts to grind to a screeching halt.

Er, no. That's not the cause of the screeching... It was his microphone.

Everyone in the crowd seems to fight a wince, including me. But it's not so much the sound that has me wanting to cringe as it is the fact that the Viscount is still looking right at me.

He presses his hand to his ear in a strange gesture, his gaze flicking to the train station several yards behind him as his jaw visibly moves. The barest hint of his voice travels through the speaker, the deep baritone unintelligible. He's just out of reach of the microphone. But that tone is enough to send a chill through my entire being.

Have I made a mistake? I wonder. *I've been bold. Too bold. What if there's something worse he can do to me?*

I'm no longer a sheep. I've strayed from the herd. I don't care if they put my name in the Chalice. Hell, I *want* them to add my entries.

Does that make me a target for another sort of punishment?

The way the Viscount grins as he turns his attention my way again causes the answer, *Yes,* to whisper through my mind. *Yes, Lina, there are worse punishments. Much worse.* I can see it in the way the Viscount evaluates us all now, his expression almost sinister.

How have I never noticed this before? I marvel, blinking up at him like a deer lost in a sea of wolves. *Because I've never really looked at him before.*

We were taught to bow at a young age.

Submit.

Treat our *elders* with reverence.

"They've lived this long for a reason," my mother used to say softly. "Remember that. Respect that."

Alas, I lost my respect for our Viscount and his Barons when I received that note from my sister. Or rather, I stopped caring about respect.

I've been solely focused on being selected as an Offering. My name is in that Chalice probably close to three hundred times.

But there are a thousand other men and women in this

town square now that are all eligible. Each of them has put their name in the selection pool at least once, too. Many of them will have more than one entry. It's the only way to survive here—bartering entries for resources.

"Welcome to the Day of the Choosing," the Viscount says, his hands spreading wide despite everyone else's gaze remaining on the ground. "Today we celebrate monsterkind and give tribute by selecting our Offerings."

He says that like we should all applaud.

No one does.

No one even moves.

It's like he's talking to a damn wall.

Yet he smiles anyway, clearly enjoying his podium and placement on that stage. I've never actually *watched* this part before. Never really paid attention. But the Barons behind him are grinning as well.

"For over three centuries, the monsters have been kind enough to allow us to live in harmony with their presence on this great earth. They have supplied us with the many resources we need to survive, ensured our good health, and gifted us with longevity. To thank them, we provide them with Offerings. Which makes this ceremony so incredibly important—we need to make sure we send the *right* Offerings."

He looks at me with those last two words.

Or maybe it simply appears that way since I'm the only one staring directly at him. But I can't seem to bow my head now, not even as nerves dance along my limbs and trickle down my spine. We're engaged in some sort of battle of wills that I can't afford to lose. Yet I'm not sure I can afford to win, either.

"Before we get started, I'd like to take a moment to thank monsterkind with a prayer. If you'll please close your eyes and join me in worship…" He trails off, his gaze still on me.

I don't close my eyes.

I don't even move.

And I swear I can hear his teeth grinding together from way back here.

What are you doing? I ask myself. *This is a whole new level of defiance.*

Over the last year, I've grown bolder in my rebellion, but it's all been for the sole purpose of being selected as an Offering.

However, this feels different. Necessary. And utterly insane.

The Viscount begins his prayer, the words ones I've heard uttered annually in this very square.

Except it's all different now. Because he's speaking them while staring at me. His voice sounds… deeper. Angrier. More intense.

Am I imagining it?

Shivers skate along my limbs, stirring goose bumps despite the balmy air. My stomach clenches in response to the sensation, my insides cold while sweat dots my brow.

The conflicting temperatures make me dizzy, causing me to nearly blink away from the Viscount. But then his final words anchor me in place.

"To the Fates we pray that our Offerings are of the best quality, that monsterkind is appeased by our sacrifice, and that none of our brides or grooms let us down in any way."

It's the way he always ends his sermon.

Except this time, he adds, "And if, for whatever reason, the monsters are not pleased, we will make an example of the offending Offering to ensure the monsters are never displeased again."

That causes a few members of the crowd to shift a little, their surprise evident in their not-so-subtle gasps.

What the hell does that even mean? I wonder, *still* staring at the Viscount.

But he simply smiles in response and claps his hands together. "Let's get started, shall we?" He's practically beaming now, causing every warning bell in my mind to blare with alarm.

And not just because he's finally looked away from me.

But because his last statement sounded like a threat.

One aimed directly at me.

My heart hammers in my chest, the *thud, thud* echoing in my ears.

It's loud.

Violent.

Overwhelming.

I can't think over the sound. All I can do is see. Observe. *Watch* as the Chalice is brought forward on its ceremonial platform.

It's so heavy that three Village Protectors have to wheel it across the stage.

Thud, thud.

The Viscount's mouth is moving again, but his voice sounds so far away. Like I'm ten feet underwater and he's growling from the surface.

Thud, thud.

I'm still the only one looking at him. No one else dares to disrespect him in such a way.

No one except me.

Thud, thud.

His hand goes toward the Chalice, his jawline hard as he digs deep for the name of the first Offering.

Did he say how many there will be? I wonder, my throat dry. *Do I have a chance? Hell, do I want to have a chance?*

His words linger in my head.

"We will make an example of the offending Offering." An example. An example. An example.

What does that mean?

Am I the example?

Because I'm staring at him? Or because I've drawn too much attention to myself?

I force my eyes to close, my need to take a deep breath overpowering whatever rebellious instinct overtook my senses. *Focus,* I tell myself. *Focus on the ceremony.*

At this rate, I won't even hear my own name over the beating of my heart.

If he calls my name at all, I think, swallowing. My heart pangs uncomfortably in my chest at the thought, my motivations over the last year coming to a grinding halt. *I need to go to Monsters Night. I need to find Serapina.*

But something about this feels incredibly wrong. Like I've somehow waltzed myself into a trap.

Impossible. It was Serapina's handwriting. I'm sure of it.

Except—

"Our first Offering," the Village Viscount announces, his voice finally piercing the thumping of my heart and causing my eyes to spring open. "Bartholomew Monroe."

Everyone remains still for a beat, then the crowd begins to part as a tall man with white-blond hair starts toward the stage. I don't recognize him, which isn't surprising. I really only know those who work in my garden district.

There are so many farms around here with huts that span nearly ten miles up and down the mountains on either side of the square, making it impossible for us all to regularly socialize. The Day of the Choosing is the only time we're all together like this.

Fingertips brush mine, causing me to jolt. Then I remember that Sage is beside me. She's been there the whole time. I lost sight of her presence after I removed my veil, my focus so resolute that all I could see was the Village Viscount.

His hand disappears into the Chalice once more as Bartholomew joins him on the stage. I can't see the blond man's expression, but I suspect he appears bored. Outward displays of emotion are not acceptable. Same with defiance.

The Village Viscount reads a second name, this time one of a female closer to the stage. All I can see is her dark hair since her veil and dress are covering everything else.

My nails bite into my palm as a third name is called—one that *isn't* mine.

If I could volunteer, I would. But that's not how things are done.

By the time a fifth name is called, I'm sweating for very different reasons than from the overbearing sun.

How many is he going to call?

Fuck, why wasn't I listening?

What happens if he doesn't say my name?

A sixth is chosen.

A seventh.

An eighth.

My stomach drops, my limbs beginning to shake.

He's not going to say my name.

Is that good or bad?

Bad. I need to find Serapina, I think as another part of me says, *Good. I don't want to be an example.*

"And our final Offering," the Viscount says.

Sage's palm grasps mine as he pulls one last name from the Chalice. I know she's hoping I've been spared. But I'm not. Or I am. A little. I… I'm conflicted.

The Viscount is confusing my priorities. I—

"Alina Everheart."

My name echoes across the town square as the Viscount looks right at me. And this time, I know it's not because I'm the only one staring at him; it's because he knows my name.

Shit. I shouldn't have pulled off my veil...

CHAPTER THREE
FLAME

"Let me get this straight," I drawl, propping my feet up on Orcus's coffee table as I relax against the leather couch behind me. "You want us to venture into an alternate reality where something called *Monsters Night* is celebrated in a Human Realm?"

"Rude," Reaper mutters. "Mating Night would be a kinder phrase."

"Or Fuck Fest," I offer casually.

Reaper sits forward. "Now *that* I'll attend. When do we leave?"

Orcus grunts, his irritation palpable. "We're portaling into an unknown realm to search for my mother, not play with breakable humans."

"Who says they're all breakable?" Reaper asks, cocking his head to the side. "There's a reason these otherworldly majestic creatures have chosen to visit this realm in search of mates, yes?"

"Majestic creatures," Orcus echoes with a sarcastic snort. "They could be real monsters, you know."

Reaper presses a palm to his chest, his expression one

of clear indignation as he straightens his spine. "Are you going to start calling Death Fae 'zombies' now?"

Orcus sighs and rolls his eyes. "Can you both be serious for a minute?"

"No," Reaper and I answer in unison.

Reaper chuckles and sprawls out in Orcus's office chair like he owns the room. I simply cross my feet at the ankles and tuck my hands behind my neck, my smile lazy as I gaze up at Orcus's prowling form. He's pacing his office like some sort of big rival cat. Which is humorous since he can't shift.

My inner beast purrs with contentment inside me, completely at peace among the two men I call my best friends.

Only friends, really.

Without them, I would happily live in solitary.

Alas, my jaguar rather likes Orcus and Reaper. Perhaps because they're useful.

Orcus is basically a god. And Reaper has all the shiny toys.

So much potential.

So much *death*.

"We're going to enter an unknown world via an illegal portal. I need you both focused and ready for anything to go wrong." He pauses midstep to look at me. "Maliki is going to let several Ghouls through as a cover story. You'll be too busy protecting them to get your dick wet."

I arch a brow. "You severely underestimate my ability to multitask, my friend."

"I overestimate your ability to pay attention, too," he tosses right back, causing my smile to return.

"You do," I agree, stretching my arms over my head.

It's all in jest.

I'm *very* good with details and he knows it. And

noticing details requires a certain degree of attention, something I perfected long ago.

"Flame isn't going to let anyone harm the Ghouls. And I won't let anyone harm you," Reaper drawls as a blade appears in his hand—one he starts twirling between his long fingers. "So if that's all squared away, let's talk about what you know. *Monsters Night* aside, this reality we're going into is more... dystopian? As far as Human Realms are concerned, I mean."

Orcus runs his fingers through his dark hair and collapses into the open space beside me. "Yeah, dystopian is a good adjective. I've been using the small window portal Hades created to peek at different parts of the realm over the last week, and from what I've gathered, humans are assholes."

I snort. "That's not news."

"They've set up this elitist system where certain families in society own villages and basically treat all the humans in those villages like cattle," he goes on, ignoring my side commentary. "They're literally breeding them in an effort to create perfect brides and grooms for monsterkind. It's fucked up."

Reaper stops twisting his knife. "Breeding?"

"Of course that's the word you heard in my explanation," Orcus mutters.

"I heard all your words, but only one interested me," Reaper replies, setting his dagger down on the desk. "How exactly are they *breeding* these humans?"

Orcus shoots him a wry look. "You want me to pull up a portal window so you can watch?"

Reaper's mouth curls into an intrigued smile. "As a matter of fact, I do." He cocks his head. "However, I was actually asking how they're making these humans worthier of monsterkind. Are they infusing them with special genetics? Such as... genetics that will allow a human to take a knot?"

"Or a barb?" I interject, my inner predator suddenly *very* interested in this conversation.

"I don't know." Orcus falls silent, perhaps following our train of thought to the possibilities of humans being genetically modified to be more compatible. That, no doubt, was Reaper's intention when he mentioned a *knot*. Because Reaper himself didn't have one. Only Orcus did. And it impeded him significantly when searching for appropriate bed partners.

After a beat, Orcus shakes his head. "It doesn't matter. What I'm trying to say is, the elite humans treat the non-elite like commodities more than people. It's disgusting."

"Sounds more archaic than disgusting," I say, thinking back on mortal history and the times when royals very much ruled the Human Realm. Although, I suppose that was more about an uneven distribution of wealth and resources, not necessarily about treating other humans like cattle.

"I've been focusing on one of the Elite Cities," Orcus continues. "Primarily because there are supernaturals living there among these elite humans. I'm trying to better understand their security protocols. However, they keep sensing the portal—just like Hades warned me they would."

I pull my feet to the ground and brace my forearms on my thighs. "Are they hostile toward it?"

Orcus shakes his head. "No, just interested."

"Have they tried to communicate?"

Another shake of his head. "Not yet. But I haven't stuck around long enough for anyone to try."

"Then they're not efficiently tracking your portal movements," I translate.

"No. It could be because I'm doing sporadic hits in various places, or they're just used to portals randomly appearing and disappearing. It's hard to say."

"Well, if that's true, we could slip over now instead of forcing Maliki to put his neck on the line with Lucifer," Reaper points out after listening to my back-and-forth with Orcus.

"If we create a portal door now, they'll very easily track us, and I would prefer not to deal with another world's politics," Orcus replies.

"You mean Hades would prefer to avoid another world's politics, but has no problem putting Maliki in the path of Lucifer's wrath." Reaper's no longer smiling, his irritation over Maliki's upcoming sacrifice evident. The pair of them are good friends, which means Reaper will do whatever it takes to protect Maliki.

Just like Reaper would do whatever it takes to protect me and Orcus, too.

He might be sadistic and borderline insane, but he's a good ally.

Orcus sighs. "Maliki volunteered."

"Of course he did," Reaper returns. "Maliki will do anything Hades asks of him."

"Same could be said about us for Orcus," I murmur, shrugging. "Maliki's not the only one taking a risk, Reap. We all are."

"No." Reaper points at me, the reaction causing my lips to quirk up. "We're not doing that."

"Why not?" I ask, feigning innocence. "Too intimate for you?"

"I don't know, *kitty cat*. What do you think?"

My eyes narrow. "That's a terrible nickname."

"The same could be said for *Reap*."

"That's literally your name."

"And you're literally a cat," he tosses back at me.

"I'm a fucking jaguar, *Death Fae*. Not a *kitty cat*."

He lifts a shoulder like he didn't just insult me and my heritage. "Same thing."

I stand. "Want to play with my *kitty cat*?" I dare him.

Orcus sighs loudly from the couch. "You're both going to get us all killed on Monsters Night." He says it like he's annoyed, but I can hear the amusement lurking in his tone. He knows exactly what just happened—I purposely distracted Reaper.

There's no changing Maliki's mind.

Just like there would be no changing Reaper's mind or mine about going on this mission with Orcus.

We both know the importance of finding Orcus's mother. Just as we both know what's at stake should anyone find out what we're actually seeking in this other realm.

The three of us have been in this trio of ours for well over a thousand years. We might not be blood-related, but we consider ourselves to be brothers.

Reaper ignores my posturing and simply produces another one of his infamous weapons—this one a long throwing dagger.

He doesn't release it, though. Just taunts me with it by playing the silver metal between his fingers, whirling it in a way most others could never replicate.

All Death Fae have their talents.

Reaper's talent is weapons. He can create anything he desires with magic, then use it with absolute precision. He's quite literally the perfect assassin.

"I want to see inside this other realm," he says, his silver-blue eyes on me. They're glittering in the office's low lighting, just like his silvery hair. The long, thick locks are down today, dancing around his broad shoulders and giving him a wildish appearance.

He usually ties his hair back at the nape.

But it seems he's feeling a little unhinged at the moment. It makes me wonder if he's close to the edge of a psychotic episode—something caused by all the souls he's required to eat to survive.

Unfortunately, that sort of diet comes with a downside.

One that often leads to, well, insanity.

"We won't be able to look for long," Orcus informs Reaper, drawing me back to the discussion about the other realm. "But I can bring up a small portal window. There was something I wanted to watch today anyway."

That grabs my focus. "What did you want to watch?"

"A Day of the Choosing," he mutters. "Basically the selection process for the Monsters Night sacrifices. I heard one of the elitist assholes talking about it and wanted to see what it entails."

"You're going to go to this realm wanting to murder a bunch of mortals, aren't you?" Reaper muses as I sit beside Orcus once more.

"Probably," our godlike friend admits.

"Mmm," Reaper hums as he stands and wanders over to us on the couch. Rather than sit with us, he positions himself behind us, essentially guarding our backs. "Sounds yummy."

"Only you would think so," Orcus says to him.

I don't comment. Primarily because I don't need much motivation to rid the world of dark souls. If Reaper wants to snack on them while I do it, then I'll slice and dice and give him a good, bloody meal.

Dark strands whirl around us as Reaper's chaotic energy escapes from his skin, the long ribbons ash-like in appearance. Yet the obsidian wisps don't leave an essence behind, the power all belonging to Reaper. Every day, he seems to lose just a little more control of his inky threads.

I'm not sure what's causing it.

Age, perhaps. But it more likely has something to do with him lacking a mate. He needs a soul who can provide him with balance, *anchor* him in the now rather than in the past.

Alas, he has no interest in such a concept.

Reaper has embraced his psychotic side.

Soon, there will be no pulling him back to our reality.

Ancient words whisper on the breeze as Orcus calls upon a power that is uniquely his own. *Mythos Fae*, I marvel, always impressed by the level of vitality Orcus can command. He's a god more than a fae. A being of immense strength and ability, one who can traverse realms and realities with a mere incantation.

So fucking admirable, I think, jealous of his ability to move through time and space with such ease.

I'm part Shifter Fae, part Corpse Fae. While I have my own share of talents, teleportation is definitely not one of them.

A deep voice enters the room, one that causes me to frown.

"Everheart" is all it said.

"What the hell is an Everheart?" I wonder aloud.

Orcus shrugs as he starts panning around the image to take it away from a clear blue sky and down to a field of people.

No, not a field. It's… it's kind of like a town center. There's a bunch of broken streets and pathways leading to it, the outskirts framed by wheelbarrows and old-fashioned food stands.

"I feel like we just went back in time," Reaper says quietly. "Is this the eighteen hundreds or something?"

"No, but the people living in this world seem to favor that way of life," Orcus grumbles.

The fabric of Reaper's leather jacket shifts behind my head, suggesting he just crossed his arms. "Weird."

I'm about to add my own two cents regarding the image when movement in the middle of the screen catches my attention. A woman with a translucent veil covering her dark hair starts through the crowd, causing them all to part around her like she's walking down the aisle at a wedding.

Except everyone in attendance is wearing either a bridal gown or a tuxedo.

And unlike all the other females in attendance, this one has her veil pushed back to reveal her face.

"Can you zoom in on her?" I ask without thinking, my jaguar stirring inside me. There's something about this female that seems to call to him. The determination in her expression? Her fierce eyes?

Eyes that are the color of midnight.

Shimmering.

Stunning.

And even more expressive now that Orcus has the portal focused on her.

She doesn't seem to see us, probably because of whatever magic Orcus is using to peek inside at this reality. It's a voyeuristic ability that could have so many uses. But for now, I'm content to just... follow this woman through the crowd.

"Fuck, she's beautiful," Reaper whispers behind me.

"Yeah," I agree, swallowing. "A sleek panther among a herd of sheep."

"I don't think that's the right saying." Reaper utters the sentence in a distracted way, like he's just commenting about my incorrect phrase while remaining entirely captivated by the screen. "But I'm starting to understand the appeal of this mating-night thing."

The portal shifts as she reaches the stage, causing my

lips to curl down when I realize all the other females up there still have their veils pulled down. *Why is this one showing her face when everyone else is hiding?*

"That makes nine Offerings for this year's Day of the Choosing," an elderly human announces from a podium.

No one applauds.

No one even seems to breathe.

"This is fucked up," Reaper says. "I assume *Offerings* are the humans going to the... mating fest?"

"Monsters Night," Orcus corrects him. "Yes, that's what I've gathered."

"Shit," I breathe, still watching the one called *Everheart*. Or I assume that's her name, anyway. She moved right after this elderly guy called for her. It's a safe guess, and a fitting one.

Because her gorgeous face is heart-shaped.

Everheart.

The guy in charge says something else that I miss, causing her eyes to widen slightly as she holds his intense gaze. Because he's looking right at her, and she's boldly staring back.

Everyone else is bowing their head, even the others on the stage.

But not her.

She's holding her own with her confident expression and bold stance.

A panther challenging a fellow predator, I recognize. *So fucking hot.*

But before I can see how the scene ends, the vision disappears.

"Hey! I was enjoying that," I protest.

"Me, too," Reaper grouses.

Orcus snorts. "I can't keep it open for longer than a few minutes without being noticed. But I'm glad to see your interest is piqued. Should we discuss our strategy, then, for Monsters Night?"

"Strategy?" I repeat, my heart beating a little too rapidly in my chest.

My inner beast is intrigued. He wants out. To be free. To prowl. To *hunt*.

That delicious little brunette checked all our boxes.

Maybe this mission can have two purposes. First, find Orcus's mother. Second, track down that dark-haired feline.

Everheart.

That's a name I won't soon forget.

See you soon, little panther.

CHAPTER FOUR
ALINA

MY SKIN still burns from where Sage dug her nails into my palm. It was a quick, emotional goodbye, one I couldn't return because the Viscount was all but glaring at me from the podium. I didn't want to risk him seeing me speak to Sage, let alone hug her.

So I simply let her go.

Walked up to the stage.

Past the Protectors waiting there.

And joined the other Offerings.

Except the ceremony didn't end there—not the way it should have, anyway.

Instead, the Viscount said, "As I mentioned, our quota for this year's Monsters Night is nine Offerings. But I fear one of these Offerings might be an inappropriate pick. As such, I'll be selecting a tenth, just in case."

His gaze was on me the entire time he spoke despite me being off to the side of the stage.

Then he picked a tenth name.

"Amberly Honeycutt."

Her name repeats now in my head as she joins us on

the stage, her black hair glittering in the sunlight while she keeps her head dutifully bowed.

I swallow as the Viscount grins at her. It's not a kind grin. It's a knowing one. A *lascivious* one.

"Yes, a fine replacement indeed," he murmurs away from the microphone.

Then he returns his focus to the crowd and engages in one final prayer, blessing the Nightingale Village's Offerings.

My empty stomach churns. His invocation—a promise to satisfy the monsters—sounds more like a threat than a prayer to me.

I wonder if anyone else can hear the sinister quality of his voice or if it's all in my head.

My eyes search the crowd for Sage, her silver hair something I spy almost immediately. It helps that I know where she stands in the square. Except... her hair looks a bit purple in the sunlight.

A silvery violet. I blink. *That's... strange.*

Is it a trick of the light? My exhaustion finally catching up to me? My mind officially failing me?

All options are possible.

The clearing of a throat brings me face-to-face with the Viscount, his sermon apparently done. A single arch of his white-blond brow has me instantly regretting my misplaced veil. Primarily because I can't stop myself from cocking my eyebrow back at him in return.

His jaw clenches.

My eyebrow stays arched.

And inside, I start wondering if the village will even bother hosting a funeral for me.

Although... I'm an Offering now, I remind myself. *That has to mean something, right?*

However, he threatened to make an example of the *offending Offering*.

There's no doubt in my mind that he means me.

And his expression right now confirms it.

"*Move*," he demands, gesturing with his chin toward the others, who are already exiting the stage.

I must have missed some sort of instructions. Or perhaps the Village Protectors provided some kind of silent direction for everyone to follow.

Regardless, I struggle to obey. *Moving* will require giving the Viscount my back. And I really don't want him behind me.

But perhaps it would be best for me to behave now, to be the *perfect* Offering rather than an *offending* Offering. Maybe that'll make it harder for him to punish me.

Unless it's already too late.

In which case, I'm fucked.

"*Ms. Everheart*," the Viscount says, his tone underlined with authority.

Yep. Definitely knows my name.

I've never spoken to him. And while I've been rebellious this last year, my infractions have been mostly minor. Things like being late for my shift at the gardens and throwing a rotten tomato at a Village Protector who refused to step out of my way while I was pushing a wheelbarrow.

Nothing that really earned the attention of our Viscount.

Until today. Until *now*.

I don't give him a chance to repeat his command. I simply turn, my veil fluttering behind me like a taunt.

Or maybe he sees it as a white flag. I technically obeyed him. *Finally*.

Yet it doesn't feel like obedience. My eyes are focused ahead, not downcast. My shoulders are square. And my steps are sure.

All the while, my heart threatens to take over my hearing again.

Deep breaths, I tell myself as the train rumbles to life before me. *Just hop on board and go to Monster City. Then look for Sera.*

Over a dozen Village Protectors line the train platform, all of them hidden behind their ominous hoods.

They're silent, imposing statues, but I know they're watching me, waiting to see if I'll run. That's their purpose.

It's happened before, back when I was a young girl. The Offering made it as far as the alleyway just off the square before she was caught by her hair and dragged back to the train.

Serapina was distraught after the violent display, her seven-year-old mind struggling to understand the cruelty.

Our parents were nowhere nearby to console her, leaving me to calm her down.

If only I knew then how common that would become —me being a mother to Serapina.

Because we lost our parents a year later, leaving us orphaned in the village. Fortunately, they'd saved enough resources for us to live on in their absence.

I'm still not sure how that was possible, especially now that I understand how basic necessities are handled in our village. However, it wasn't like I could ask anyone for clarification. I simply accepted what we needed to survive, guarded my sister the best I could, and...

Ended up on this train platform, I think, eyeing the extra-wide door before me.

With Protectors on either side and the Viscount at my back, I don't have a choice but to continue forward. Not that I want to stop now.

I need to see this through.

Even if the Viscount plans to make an example of me.

My spine straightens in response to the looming threat. *I will not give in to the urge to submit.* Besides, it's too late now to even try.

So I don't.

I simply board the train.

Another Protector waits inside, his arm lifting to gesture to his left.

No words, just a silent command.

Goose bumps prickle my arms, not only from his ominous presence but also from the blast of cold air that hits me as I walk.

It's *freezing* in here.

A shiver works through me, my clammy skin instantly chilled.

What is this? I marvel. *A freezer?*

There are a few in the village, mostly used to store meat. But I've never seen one large enough to walk into before.

Is this… air-conditioning? I wonder, glancing around at the too-clean interior. It's all silver and white, the hallway seemingly endless.

I've read about air-conditioning. But I've never experienced it before. That must be the source of this frigid temperature. It's… *overwhelming*. Too cold. Too foreign.

My skin continues to tingle, unused to the frosty sensation. But as I enter an opulent room decorated in golds and velvety reds, the air conditioner becomes the least of my worries.

49

All the Offerings are standing in a line, heads bowed, still as statues, as a man in elegant apparel studies them intently. Unlike the Protectors behind him, his head is exposed to reveal a shock of dark hair and slightly aged features.

His brown-black eyes snap up to meet mine as I enter, a prominent wrinkle in his brow seeming to crease even more as he pulls out a gilded pocket watch to evaluate the time.

"We're behind schedule," he tells the room, his accent decidedly unique. "That's unacceptable."

The Viscount grunts behind me. "There were a lot of names to call this year. That takes time, *Your Grace*." Those last two words are heavily laced with sarcasm, causing the one called *the Grace* to narrow his gaze.

"Yes, ten, apparently." The man slides his ornate watch back into a pocket on his embroidered vest, then rests his hand over it like he can't quite let go of the timepiece. Odd, considering it's already attached to one of his gold-encrusted buttons via a chain. "You significantly deviated from the script."

"And I'm sure you can see why," the Viscount replies, nudging me forward. "Your algorithm is inaccurate. This one is obviously not suitable."

The well-dressed male arches a single arrogant brow. "You feel it's your place to question *my* algorithm?"

"I do when it's clearly resulted in an error." The Viscount walks around to stand beside me. "It's fine, Greg. As the Village Viscount, I've made an adequate replacement. After all, I know these people far better than you do."

Greg's eyes narrow further.

But the Viscount isn't done.

"As a proper thank-you, I'll keep Ms. Everheart.

Although, it'll honestly be more of a benefit to you than to me."

"A benefit how?" the Grace asks slowly, his tone and expression telling me that he's not pleased by this conversation at all.

But the Viscount appears to be unaware of the growing tension in the room. Or maybe he just doesn't care.

I'm not sure who this *Greg* is, but his expensive appearance and stature indicate that he's someone important. However, the Village Viscount is the highest-ranking official in our village. *Maybe this guy is a leader from another village?*

"Her behavior needs to be corrected in front of the villagers to demonstrate that this level of defiance is unacceptable and will not be tolerated. Fear is always a good motivator, is it not?"

"Still not hearing how this is a benefit to me," the Grace says, his thumb stroking his watch through his textured vest.

"Fear keeps the villagers in line, Greg." The Viscount utters the words in a tone that suggests he's irritated with the other man. "It's something your father would deeply appreciate and see as a favor."

"I'm not my father."

"Oh, I'm very aware of that," the Viscount spits back at him. "So, as your elder, I recommend—"

"You are *not* my elder," the Grace interjects. "*You* are a Viscount. *I* am a Duke. And it seems rather clear to me that you're in great need of a lesson on what that means." He finally lowers his hand from his vest, his shoulders pulling back into an arrogant line.

A Duke? I repeat to myself, glancing between them. *What does that even mean?*

"Greg—"

"*Duke* Nightingale," the man corrects, his cultured tone ringing with authority in the train car. "Protector Jeffries, I want you to take Offerings One, Three, and *Nine* to their grooming appointments. They will be going to Monster City for Monsters Night."

The Viscount opens his mouth, but the Duke holds up a hand, his severe expression one that sends cold dread through my system and I'm not even the one receiving that look.

"Protector Jordan, take Offerings Two, Four through Eight, *and* Ten to the cargo hold. I'll meet you there with further distribution details." He says all of this while maintaining the Viscount's stare. "As for you, you may leave. There will be no gift this year. No bonus rations. *Nothing.* Now go."

"You can't do that," the Viscount snaps, his hand wrapping around my bicep as he gives me a violent shake. "Not over *this*. She's not an ideal candidate. You saw what she did out there."

"What I *see*, David, is an old man who needs to retire before he oversteps and loses everything he's ever been *gifted* in this life," Duke Nightingale tells him. "I suggest you take your leave before I give Protector Xavier an order to remove you from the train."

The Viscount sputters while Duke Nightingale turns toward the Protectors behind him.

"I gave two of you an order," he says, his deep tone filled with palpable irritation. "Why are you not moving?"

"Apologies, Your Grace," one of them says as he bows low before snapping to attention. "Offerings One, Three, and Nine, follow me."

The one called Bartholomew steps forward, followed

by a petite blonde female. *The first and third candidates called by the Viscount.*

Which makes me Offering *Nine*.

I attempt to move, only to be yanked back by the Viscount's hold on my arm.

"*Viscount O'Michaels,*" the Duke hisses.

But the man beside me isn't listening, his bruising grip only tightens, eliciting a wince from deep within me. *That's going to leave a mark*, I think dizzily, confused and taken aback by the vehemence emanating from him.

"This is not over," the Viscount growls against my ear.

I'm not sure if the words are for me or for the Duke, but I suspect it's the former.

As though to confirm that suspicion, he gives my bicep a final squeeze and releases me with a shove. I bite back a yelp as I stumble toward the waiting Protector and the other Offerings, my legs tangling in my hideous bridal gown.

Bartholomew catches me before I can fall, his grasp gentler than I would have expected from such a large man. Up close, I can tell he definitely worked on the farms in our village, probably wrangling cattle or handling heavy machinery.

He doesn't look at me, just helps me stay upright before letting me go.

By the time I gather my bearings enough to face the Viscount, he's gone.

And instead I come face-to-face with a simmering Duke.

"Clean her up and run her labs," he demands. "We only have a week."

"Yes, Your Grace," the Protector replies dutifully, heading toward a door with a clipped "Follow me" over his broad shoulder.

53

LEXI C. FOSS

"Oh, and, Jeffries?" the Duke calls after him. "Bruises are an imperfection. Make sure she's taken care of properly."

"Of course, Your Grace," the Protector says, inclining his head. "She'll be the perfect Monster Bride."

"I know," the Duke says, his gaze meeting mine. "Our best one yet."

CHAPTER FIVE
ORCUS

Don't do it, I tell myself. *She's just a girl. She means nothing. Just an Offering.*

There are more important things at stake here. Tasks that need to be handled. Other items to focus on.

And yet…

I can't shake the vision of that dark-haired beauty from my head. Those stunning near-black eyes are engraved in my memory.

Fuck.

I close my eyes, determined to forget her. But that only makes this craving worse. It's like she's haunting me, her features so Goddess-like that I'm questioning my own sanity.

She's a human. Not an Omega.

Maybe it was her petite frame that has my knot pulsing with this foreign need. That too-pale skin—an alarming contrast to the sun illuminating her alluring form.

I rub my temple, wishing I could somehow erase the female from my mind. But it's impossible. She's been lingering in my thoughts all fucking week. Showcasing in my dreams. Dancing around in my mind during my waking hours.

It's an obsession.

A *curse*.

I wince, my fingers curling into fists.

What is with this female? I wonder. It's like I can already feel her dainty fingers stroking my cock, her lips imprinting on my neck, her teeth sinking into my skin.

It's fucking lunacy.

"She's not mine," I say to my reflection in the mirror. "No fucking way. It's impossible."

My eyes flash red in response, overtaking the black hues and allowing my Alpha traits to shine through. I can almost hear a purr rumbling to life, my baser instincts threatening to take over.

Hunt. Mount. Claim. Rut.

My teeth grind together as I fight the urge and again tell myself that she's *human*.

I haven't even scented her yet.

Only seen her.

Yet that seems to be enough to scatter my instincts and send me into a mating frenzy.

"This is ridiculous," I mutter, shaking my head and shoving away from the bathroom mirror.

I'm naked.

Because of course I'm fucking naked.

It's too damn hot for clothes, and all I want to do is stroke myself to completion. *With thoughts of that woman staring up at me with those deep, dark eyes. Taking my cock between her plump lips. Sucking me all the way to my knot.*

A groan strangles my throat as my palm lands on my marbled wall. "*Enough.*"

I need to prove to myself that this girl is just human. *And not fucking mine.*

That voice in my head—the one demanding just minutes ago to not do this—is instantly drowned out by my whispering the portal incantation. Only, I add a subtle flare to the invocation now, one that has my magic seeking out the female tormenting my every thought.

That I'm able to bring her into view so easily is... damning. Because I shouldn't be able to do that. I should have had to search the village for her and trace her essence to wherever she is now.

However, my ancient power found her with ease.

And now that vitality is throbbing with fury.

Because she's *naked* and *exposed* and *surrounded* by a bunch of men in fucking white coats.

Her full bottom lip is tucked between her teeth, her gaze holding a mix of irritation and discomfort as the men discuss her as though she's a display animal, not a human fucking being.

It's a good thing these assholes can't see me, or they would all run screaming from the bloody room.

Actually, maybe I should let them see me, I think darkly. *Pull down the veil, give them a peek at what's coming for them.*

Because they're staring at my Omega with a little too much interest.

Not my *Omega,* a small voice whispers from the back of my mind.

But I ignore it, my possessive instincts far too loud for that inconsequential reminder to take root. Because all I want to do is reach through the small window and yank off one of their coats to give it to her.

"Definitely fertile," one of the doctors is saying, making me snort. "It's a shame she's not heading to the compound instead. She would make a fine breeder."

"Duke Nightingale made his declaration clear—she's

an Offering," another replies, his long finger pushing a pair of glasses up his nose.

The other man sighs long and loud. "A shame, really. The Duke is so consumed by thoughts of the Immortality Sector that he's lost sight of the long game."

"And what *long game* would that be?" a deep voice demands, the English tones reminding me of my own. They're regal in nature. Crisp. Borderline arrogant.

The source of the voice pushes open a door, revealing a male wearing a strangely modernized version of Regency Era attire. Or I assume that's what he's going for with his pressed slacks, flowy dress shirt, and tailored vest.

He pulls out a pocket watch and grimaces. "Never mind. I don't have time to waste on an irrelevant topic. This Offering's labs are excellent. The monsters will be pleased."

"Yes, Your Grace," two of the men reply, bowing slightly.

This must be Duke Nightingale, I deduce.

He ignores everyone in the room and continues like the others haven't spoken. "I need Ms. Everheart properly rested, groomed, and dressed, and we only have two days before Monsters Night. So give her something to help her sleep and move on to the next phase."

The Duke doesn't wait to be obeyed; he simply leaves the room.

A few of the men in lab coats exchange glances while another stares a little too long at my female's exposed breasts. "I'll handle her sleep lab," he says, his pupils flaring. "The rest of you can move on to the next set of Offerings."

No one disagrees, just nods and leaves this creep with my Omega.

She narrows her gaze at him, her lips pulling into a

tight line. But she doesn't say anything, just watches him warily as he bends to press his lips to her ear.

"You really don't know your place in this world at all, do you, Alina?" he whispers, his voice loud to my predatory hearing. "Don't worry. You'll learn soon."

She shivers in response.

"The Viscount looks forward to seeing you again," he adds before straightening his spine.

My female's eyes widen. "What?"

But the man doesn't say anything else, his focus falling on a tray of tools.

When he picks up a needle, my Omega sits up. "What did you say about the Viscount?"

He doesn't reply, simply grabs a tube connected to her arm and sticks a needle into a cross section.

She makes a move to stop him, but he easily catches her wrist and finishes upending the contents into her IV. He tsks as he moves her hand down to her side, the gesture deceptive because I can see how tightly he's holding on to her.

My fists clench, the urge to create a portal door hitting me in the chest.

This guy needs to die.

That thought only grows louder in my mind as he guides her quivering form back onto the bed, his chest far too close to hers.

"Sweet dreams, Alina," he says, his lips brushing her ear. "I doubt you'll ever sleep this soundly again once the Viscount finds you."

Who the fuck is this Viscount? I wonder. *The arse from the other day? The one who called her name from that stage?*

But before I can even process what to do, the portal begins to close.

And the last thing I see is Alina's eyes falling closed, her sweet face lost to immediate sleep.

"Fuck," I snarl, desperately wanting to pull the portal window back up. But I can't. Not without drawing attention to our realm and potentially revealing my identity in the process.

I completely lost sight of what I intended to do.

Prove she's not an Omega? That she isn't mine?

Well, I failed that particular mission. My drive to protect her superseded my purpose.

This is asinine. She's a human.

Of that I'm certain.

Yet all my instincts are firing in a way I've never experienced. However, I'm Alpha enough to know what it means.

Hunt. Bite. Rut.

Blowing out a breath, I leave the bathroom and head directly to the communications console built into the wall. "Call Reaper," I demand.

"Calling Reaper," the system confirms.

The male in question appears a beat later, his crazy silver-blue eyes dancing over me with interest. "Have you invited me over for a shag?"

I growl at him. "Does it look like I have a fucking female here to share with you?"

He shrugs. "She could be lounging about in your bed already." He sits up, revealing his own bed behind him. "Is she a brunette, perchance? I've been craving one all week. Specifically one with dizzying dark eyes and full, pouty lips."

His gaze takes on a dreamy quality that almost chases away the chaotic shadows swirling in his hypnotic irises.

"I want to spar," I tell him, cutting off his fantasy. "I need to kill something."

"You mean someone," he murmurs. "Me, perhaps?"

"You do look good dead."

He grins. "Why, thank you, Orcus. I think so, too. But you know, Flame is part Corpse Fae. He makes a pretty sexy zombie."

I snort. "I'll call him just so you can say that to his face."

"Well, now, if you do that, he'll be the one killing me, not you. Defeats the goal of your sparring plans, yeah?"

He's not wrong, but... "I'll enjoy watching someone die almost as much as I'll enjoy killing someone myself."

His eyebrows rise. "Someone has well and truly pissed you off. Care to share the details? I'll happily devour a soul for you, brother."

Brother is a term Reaper uses affectionately. Usually, I like it. Right now, I just need him to stop talking and get his tattooed ass over here. "Come over and we'll talk. I think our mission to the Human Realm just got more complicated."

Because it's not just my mother we need to find now, but potentially my Omega mate as well.

CHAPTER SIX
ALINA

Monsters Night

My eyelashes have black paint on them.

My lips are bright red.

And my hair… I… I don't even know…

Nope. There are no words to describe the feathered monstrosity on my head. I hate it almost as much as the garment suffocating my rib cage.

A corset, the lady called it. *It's the current fashion.*

Like I give a racoon's behind about *fashion*.

But apparently the monsters are into this. They want all their potential brides and grooms to be dolled up for a night out, as though we're being courted, not hunted.

I run my palms along my smooth skirt, the sleek blue fabric unlike anything I've ever touched before.

"What is this?" I asked one of the ladies helping to dress me.

"Silk," she said with a frown, her expression suggesting it should have been obvious to me.

But given that my village clothes were always made of cotton, how was I to know such a fabric existed?

It's much smoother than the gauzy bridal gowns for the Day of the Choosing. Although, I now know the name of that texture, too—*muslin*.

Useless information, really, I think, glancing at the lady behind me. She's adding some final touches to the bird's nest she's created with my hair. The ribbon she's weaving through all the feathers matches my skirt. But the whole thing is… atrocious.

I would literally die back in the village if I had to wear this. The heat alone would kill me.

Hopefully, Monster City is cooler.

Wherever Monster City actually is.

All I know is that we've been on this train for at least a week. It routinely stops for hours, then continues on for a while during the night—something I've been able to see via the windows in my quarters. It's my only glimpse of the outside. The scenery has drastically changed from the greenery of the mountains.

We've seen flatter lands.

Industrial-looking villages covered in soot and strange brick buildings.

A seaside village, which I particularly enjoyed until the infamous *lab coats* came to get me for another round of testing.

Fortunately, that seems to have been my final medical session because I slept for an unknown time after that, thanks to whatever *Mr. Threat in a Lab Coat*—Threat for short—had given me.

Not exactly the most creative nickname, but it suited the ominous male who mentioned the Viscount to me. Threat prickled my nerves the first time he entered the room, his eyes a little too lascivious for my taste. However, he stayed to himself at first, simply observing and commenting on me as though I were some sort of experiment, like everyone else did.

Until the last session.

When he finally had me alone.

And he told me the Viscount would *see me soon*.

There was something incredibly ominous about that statement. Maybe it was his tone or the way the Viscount left last week. But it sounded very much like a threat.

One that unfortunately did follow me into my *dreams*.

When I woke up back in this room, I was so disoriented that I threw up. Then breakfast arrived with a team of women, and the lady holding the tray told me to hydrate because, "It's going to be a long day."

She wasn't lying.

Three of the women bathed me.

Trimmed and painted my nails.

Put some weird products in my hair. Cut my hair. Dried it.

Literally wrapped me up in this dress.

Painted my face—which was a bizarre experience all around.

And now, thankfully, they appear to be almost done.

Which is good because all four women seem to be getting jumpy.

The train stopped an hour or so ago, the windows showcasing a wall and nothing more. It was a wall similar to the one I woke up to see earlier today, making it impossible for me to know the actual time.

I wince as one of the feather ends scrapes the delicate skin beneath my hair. I had no idea just how sensitive my scalp actually was until today. *Until these women started treating me like a damn doll.*

The lady doesn't apologize. She just digs a little more until the feather is right where she wants it.

My jaw ticks.

I'm *very* done playing dress-up.

I look ridiculous. Nothing about this outfit is logical. I'll be lucky if I can even walk.

At least they paired this hideous gown with flat shoes, I think, grateful for that part of my wardrobe.

The door opening has the woman poking me so hard I can't stop the hiss from escaping my lips.

"Why isn't Offering Nine ready?" a deep voice demands, the familiarity of it making me swallow.

Duke Nightingale.

I've seen him several times since boarding this train, but he never talks to me, just about me. However, this time, he meets my gaze in the mirror and freezes like he's as startled by my appearance as I am.

"I'm sorry, Your Grace," the woman behind me says demurely. "Her hair is… unkempt."

I nearly snort. *It's not unkempt. It's just not supposed to do whatever it is you're trying to do with it.*

The Duke blinks, his unsettled expression immediately dissolving into a bored mask. "We're out of time," he informs her. "And the monsters are not going to care if she's missing a few feathers."

"Of course, Your Grace," she says, instantly stepping away from me with a low curtsy toward him. But his focus is no longer on her, as he's returned his gaze to mine.

She takes the hint and leaves, the other ladies following behind her in a hurry.

Their nervous energy leaves a lingering chill in the air, causing the hairs along my arms to rise in response. *It's Monsters Night.*

I've known this was coming, but somehow the realization feels all the more real now. Because it's time.

Swallowing, I move to stand, only to be met with the Duke's hand as he holds his palm out for me. "Here," he says, his voice much softer than before. "Allow me to escort you."

I blink at his hand, confused by the gesture. But it's not like I can say no to him. And he doesn't give me the same vibes as Threat. If anything, the Duke seems more *fatherly* than anything else. Which is a crazy description, yet strangely accurate.

His palm feels weird against mine. Not *creepy* weird, just *different* weird. However, his sturdy grip lends me the strength and steadiness I need to stand and keeps me upright when I nearly trip over the voluminous skirts tangling with my legs.

"This dress is…" I trail off, realizing that he's really not the right one to complain to.

Yet he must know what I intended to say because he chuckles in response, the sound almost rusty in nature. "Suffocating?" he guesses. "Impractical? Difficult to breathe in?"

I gape at him, shocked that he pulled all those descriptions from my mind. But if he's going to be truthful, then so am I. "It's terrible."

He laughs outright then, his head tipping back a little and lighting up his features to reveal a much younger man underneath. "You sound like my daughter."

That has me staring at him in a whole new light. "Your… daughter?"

His amusement seems to die in an instant, his expression sobering as he stares down at me with his nearly black eyes. "Yes. I think she would like you, if she could meet you. Alas…"

69

He clears his throat and starts toward the door, only to pause midstep and look at me once more.

"I realize this all feels… intense to you. Scary, even. But trust me when I say your fate with the monsters will be a lot kinder than your fate in that village. They'll worship you, Ms. Everheart. They'll make you their queen."

My eyebrows rise. "Is that why I'm dressed in this hideous gown?"

Some of that amusement returns, his eyes crinkling a little at the corners. "You're wearing some of the finest materials money can buy, Ms. Everheart. The fashion might seem strange to you, but the monsters love it. And if I'm right about you, then you're going to impress them all."

I clear my throat. "What if I don't want to impress them?"

He simply smiles, but it's not the same smile as before. This one seems almost pitying. "You've already impressed them, Ms. Everheart. Just by being you."

I frown, not following. "That can't be true. I haven't met any of them."

"You don't have to meet them to impress them," he says, threading his arm with mine and starting toward the door again. "But you're tonight's prize. So thank you, Ms. Everheart. You have no idea what your sacrifice means to me. I hope, in turn, your future mate or mates give you everything you've ever wanted and more."

With that bizarre statement, he opens the door and we're met by two Protectors dressed in their trademark hoods.

The smiles and amusement no longer exist in the Duke's expression, his hard features set in a way that tells me any further comments will be met with a sharp reply.

It's almost like he's two people.

A father and a Duke, I think, still frowning at him. *And what did he mean by* mates? *Like more than one monster?*

While he described them as, uh, sort of enticing, I guess, I... I don't want a single mate, let alone *multiple* mates.

"Your Grace," one of the Protectors says, the voice sending an immediate chill down my spine. "Would you like us to take her to the landing platform?"

That's Threat. After hearing his statements repeat in my dreams for hours, I know his tones all too well.

Except he was one of the lab coat men, not a Protector.

So why is he a Protector now?

Were all the men in lab coats actually Protectors?

It was hard to know for sure since they always cover their features when in uniform. But this Protector is definitely *Threat.*

"No, I'll walk her there, Timothy," the Duke replies. "Then you and Protector Edvard can take over."

Timothy, I think, not bothering to listen to his placating response. *At least I was close with the T nickname.*

Duke Nightingale is quiet as he escorts me down the long train hallway, past numerous doors and seating areas, until we finally enter the room I first met him in.

But he doesn't stop there.

Instead, he continues past it to the door I entered a week ago. It's open to reveal a marble-floored platform and another train across from ours.

Everything is white. Too white. Too pristine. Too clean. Including the walls and ceiling.

It's like we've been teleported to another dimension, one painted in a solitary color.

The other two Offerings from my village stand waiting for me, their attire rivaling my own. Well, Bartholomew's

71

outfit is similar to the Duke's vest and slacks combo, only Bartholomew also has on a jacket.

Miranda—the name of Offering Three, which I learned during our first day on board—has on a dress like mine. Except hers is maroon.

This is my first time seeing both of them since that fateful Day of the Choosing. I imagine they've shared experiences similar to mine over this last week.

Bartholomew's light blue eyes find mine as I join them on the marbled platform just off the train. Everything about his gaze and expression says he's bored, but I notice the slight clench of his jaw as he looks at where my arm is threaded through the Duke's.

I'm not sure what that's about. Maybe he thinks I'm receiving some sort of preferential treatment?

"The three of you represent the Nightingale family now," the Duke says, his strange accent seeming a bit thicker. "It's up to you to fulfill the Offering requirements to the best of your abilities."

He slides his arm away from mine and slightly inclines his head in our direction.

"Thank you for your sacrifice," he continues before straightening his spine. "May you take mates of the highest caliber and make our family proud."

Turning, he faces a team of Protectors who have gathered just off the train.

"Lead them to their starting positions," he instructs them before glancing at his pocket watch. "The portals will open in six-and-thirty minutes." He meets my gaze once more. "Or, as the monsters prefer to say it, thirty-six minutes. Good luck."

With that, he returns to the train door and leaves us without a backward glance.

This is it.

Monsters Night.
Time to run.

CHAPTER SEVEN
ALINA

Oh, good. More white.

Because why would there be any other colors here?

When I think of monsters, I think of darkness. Blood. Cruel fates. Not *white*. And yet this box we're currently in —an *elevator*, I believe—is as pristine as the platform we just left.

One of the Protectors presses his palm to the wall, causing a panel to appear. "Ground floor," he says, his voice deep.

Not Timothy, I think. But that thought doesn't bring any relief with it because there are three other Protectors in this contraption with us, and one of them is Timothy.

Or rather, it sounded like him earlier.

Okay, but if it is him, what can he actually do? I ask myself. *The portals will be opening soon, and then I'll be monster bait.*

Maybe he's just trying to scare me? A final punishment from the Viscount before I'm released into Monster City?

My knees lock as the room—*elevator*—begins to move, the sensation foreign and unsteady. I nearly reach out to

Bartholomew for support but curl my fingers into a fist instead as I regain my balance.

Discomfort tugs at my ears, suggesting we're moving upward quickly.

That explains all the white walls, I think numbly. The scenery had melted into concrete sometime while I'd slept, suggesting we'd ventured underground. But the pressure on my head now tells me we were much deeper than I'd realized.

I've only ever felt this sensation one time before—when I was driven up into the mountains for my parents' funeral ceremony. There were several families involved, all of us having lost loved ones in the same accident.

My nose twitches, the scent of smoke tickling my senses. It's a sensory memory, one I know isn't real. But I swear the acrid stench of burning flesh is forever burned into my nostrils.

Not a good time to reminisce, Lina, I tell myself as the elevator dings and the world stops moving. *Focus on running.*

Because if I'm caught by a monster, I won't be able to find my sister.

I don't care what the Duke told me about potential matings and monsters being kinder than my village. All I want is to locate Serapina.

I picture her in my mind, her golden-blonde hair and crystal-blue eyes such a stark contrast to my darker features. We don't look like sisters at all apart from our smaller stature and pale skin. However, looks can be deceiving. Our souls know the truth. She's always been my other half. It nearly destroyed me when she was chosen.

But her note changed everything.

I'm here, I want to tell her. *I'll be with you soon.*

Just thinking of my purpose has my spine straightening, my head lifting, and my eyes instantly focusing on our surroundings as we step out of the elevator into a massive room with glass all around it.

Glass walls.

Glass ceiling several stories above my head.

Glass doors.

Glass *everything*.

And beyond it is… a scene I barely comprehend.

Trees intertwine with metal, creating an architectural design that's so unique I can't even begin to define the structures outside.

It's nighttime. I think. Because there are lights illuminating the streets and the remarkable buildings waiting for us beyond the glass.

Bartholomew and Miranda appear to be just as enthralled as I am as we're led through the doors, our gazes instantly following the spirals upward into the sky. I've read about *skyscrapers*. But these… these are something else entirely.

They remind me of massive trees with metal trunks and branches, decorated with green leaves. It's unworldly.

Monsterly, I correct, reminding myself of where we are. *Monster City*.

Of course the architecture here would be different from that of my village back home.

The sudden understanding dampens my intrigue, allowing my gaze to return to the street. There are a dozen or so other people here, all dressed in outfits similar to my own.

Meanwhile, the Protectors have created a line by the all-glass building I just departed from, their defensive stances making their silent command clear—*you shall not pass*.

That's fine.

I intend to find a map, not hitch a ride on a train.

"Twenty-five minutes," a feminine voice announces. I scan the crowd for the source, but I don't see anyone with a microphone. Although, that voice sounded like it came from the sky. She also said *twenty-five* as opposed to *five-and-twenty*.

Because the monsters prefer that style of telling time, I think, recalling what the Duke said right before he departed.

I glance up again, wondering if perhaps the monster is hanging off a building somewhere. Or maybe even flying above us. However, a flurry of enthusiastic chattering distracts me from my search. A trio of girls push through one of the glass doors to join us, all of them tittering at one another as they glance around with obvious intrigue.

They're dressed in corsets and gowns, like me. Although, their hair is tastefully braided over one shoulder, not piled on top of their heads like a wild bee nest.

Much more practical.

What isn't practical, however, are their giggles. They appear to be... excited.

Meanwhile, everyone else is looking a little lost.

"Are these all other Offerings?" Miranda whispers, her words seeming to be for Bartholomew, not for me.

He gives her a stiff nod. "From the other villages."

"Oh." She swallows, her blue-green eyes dancing up and down the street. "Are we...?" She trails off as she catches her lip between her teeth and glances at the row of Protectors.

They don't seem to care that she's talking. Just like they're making no move to stop the happy trio walking in our direction.

"Two blocks," one of the girls is saying as her group waltzes right by us. "That's where the Ozamique Portal opens."

"I know, Gretch," the other replies. "We studied the same maps that you did."

Maps? I think, suddenly very interested in their conversation.

"Yeah, yeah," the one called Gretch returns. "But you're hoping to seduce a Shadowfen and be taken to the Blight Realm." The slender woman shudders as she mentions the last two words. "Good luck breathing underwater."

"They have vessels," the one mutters as she flips her long black braid over her shoulder. "Or something like them."

Gretch snorts. "You're just hoping to live in some sort of glorified water palace."

"I don't think the monsters pick us based on our preferences," the third one in their party informs them both. "We're meant to suit their needs, not the other way around."

"Oh, not this again," Gretch groans, her voice growing distant with each step the girls take. "I'm so tired of this lecture, Playa. It's a mutually beneficial arrange…"

I strain my ears to hear more, but the trio has turned down another road, leaving our street entirely.

Frowning, I glance at the Protectors, wondering if they're going to go after them.

They don't.

In fact, another group walks in the opposite direction and heads down a different street, and the Protectors don't even flinch.

Bartholomew and Miranda are engaged in some sort of quiet conversation about expectations, both of them oblivious to the movements of the others.

They don't even seem to notice as another trio leaves the glass building. This one is composed of two men and one female. They all share looks with each other, nod, and go separate ways.

My lips curl down even more as they walk off with purpose and no one stops them or says a word.

Did you observe this behavior, too? I wonder at my sister. *Did you follow one of them? Find a map? Run off to the Elite City?*

It seems probable.

It also feels like a solid plan.

I take a step away from Bartholomew and Miranda, then glance at the Protectors once more.

No one notices me. Or, if they do, they don't appear to care.

I move a few more paces backward.

No comment. No retaliation. No reaction whatsoever.

Okay…

I turn around and walk toward the road the three girls ventured down. *Maybe I can catch up to them and ask about their map.*

With my head held high, I pretend to know what I'm doing and trail after the strangely eager trio.

It's not until I've turned onto the street—where I don't see any sight of the giggling girls—that I realize Bartholomew and Miranda are following me.

But no sign of any pursuing Protectors. *Good.*

Bartholomew arches a brow, his expression silently asking, *Now what?*

Shrugging, I keep walking, deciding to test the boundaries of what is and isn't allowed.

When nothing happens, I just… keep going.

And going.

And going.

All the buildings look similar with their metallic sidings mingling with greenery, only there appear to be windows, too. Lots of windows.

I pause to peer inside one, curious.

But it's too dark for me to see.

"What are we looking for?" Bartholomew asks, his deep voice low and close to my ear.

I didn't realize he was attempting to look through the glass as well, his movements oddly quiet for such a large guy. I'd almost expect the ground to shake with each step. But instead, all that muscle is encased in a sleek and stealthy package.

"Alina?" he prompts, glancing at me with his light-colored eyes. "Are we looking for a place to hide? Or something else?"

"I like the idea of hiding," Miranda says softly.

He ignores her, his focus on me.

I clear my throat. "I…" I pause.

I was about to admit that I have no clue what I'm doing, but an idea smacks me across the face in the next blink.

"Um, those girls mentioned a map…" I trail off, searching for any signs of recognition in Bartholomew's and Miranda's features. Because maybe they know something about a map, too.

Alas, all they do is stare at me and wait for me to keep talking.

Hmm. "I think finding a map might be useful," I conclude, shrugging. "Those girls seemed to know where to go, and obviously the Protectors aren't going to guide us. So…"

Bartholomew and Miranda continue watching me for a beat before the big guy slightly nods his head. "That's a good idea."

"Yeah," Miranda agrees.

I release my breath, relieved. Probably because it's nice

to have some help. And I'm glad I don't have to explain the real reason I want to find a map.

"Well, it's not in there," Bartholomew adds. "All I see is a bunch of green-skinned men with massive horns drinking at a bar."

I blink at him. "What?" He gestured at the window while he spoke, making me peek through the glass again. "I don't see anything."

Miranda follows suit, her brow furrowing. "Neither do I."

Bartholomew glances between us, then at the building beside us. "You don't see the monsters?"

Miranda and I share a look, then shake our heads.

"What about the ones in the diner over there?" he asks, pointing to another dark-windowed building.

"Diner?" Miranda repeats.

"Yeah. Where the neon sign is," he replies.

"What neon sign?" Miranda and I ask at the same time.

His brow furrows. "The giant one that says *Diner* across the—"

"Fifteen minutes," the feminine voice from overhead interrupts, sending a chill down my spine.

"Shit," Bartholomew mutters. "We need to move."

He doesn't pause to debate what we all can or can't see, just turns toward a darkened alleyway and starts walking.

The direction certainly isn't my first choice, but his vision here seems to be clearer than mine, so I let him take the lead.

He pauses every now and then to peek into windows, wincing every time. When I look, I see nothing.

My stomach churns with each passing minute, the hairs along my arms dancing on end every time that feminine voice speaks from the sky.

"Ten minutes."

"Five minutes."

"One minute."

"Fifty-five seconds."

"Fifty seconds."

Bartholomew yanks open a door to his left and steps inside. Miranda hesitates. But I don't. Being in a building sounds better than standing in this alleyway.

Although, the inside leaves a lot to be desired. It's just… empty. And way too clean, just like everything else in this city.

No dust. No cobwebs. No dirt. Just pristine floors and walls.

At least it isn't white.

"Forty-five seconds," the voice echoes through the room, making me wince.

Bartholomew glances all around like he's searching for the source, his gaze wild.

"Forty seconds."

Miranda's eyes well with tears, her stance remaining unsure in the doorway. "They're coming. They're coming. They're—"

"Thirty-five seconds."

Miranda collapses onto her knees, causing Bartholomew to run to her.

I back away slowly as he lifts her into the air, carrying her inside with hushed whispers against her ear. These two must have known one another prior to the Day of the Choosing. It's written in their body language and the way he's able to calm her now.

In another life, I might have asked questions.

But not in this one.

Not with that voice counting down over our heads.

She's going second by second now, her voice piercing

83

my every thought and weaving ominous energy through my veins.

"Twenty."

"Nineteen."

"Eighteen."

I shake my head, wishing she would *stop*. There's absolutely nowhere to hide in this large room, and I'm not entirely convinced it's truly as empty as it feels. But Bartholomew is too busy with Miranda to provide any insight. His lips whisper across her cheek to her mouth, their kiss oddly sweet in this dangerous environment.

"Ten," the voice says. "Nine. Eight..."

Bartholomew wraps his arms around Miranda and holds her close, the two of them lost in an embrace that leaves me feeling *very* out of place.

This is their moment, not mine.

I... I need to...

"Five."

Run, I think. *Hide. I can't let any of them catch me.*

"Three."

Shit!

I dart toward a hallway inside the building, hoping to find a smaller room with furniture or something to hide behind.

"Two."

There's nothing.

"*One.*"

Static electricity crawls over my arms, making me freeze as a humming sound rolls over my senses.

Then...

Silence.

I barely breathe, my ears straining to hear more.

Growls. Screams. Angry cries. I expect to be inundated with all of the above, yet... there's nothing.

My brow pulls down as I slowly glance over my shoulder, half anticipating a drooling monster to be right behind me.

But I'm alone.

No sign of Bartholomew or Miranda. No hint of sound.

Have I gone deaf? I wonder numbly. *What's going on?*

I cautiously retreat back down the hallway to find the large room completely empty.

Did they run? I marvel, looking around more frantically now. *Did they find a place to hide?*

My lips part, their names almost leaving my mouth. But I instantly swallow the instinct. *They're fending for themselves. I need to do the same.*

Turning back around, I head down the hallway with measured steps, trying my hardest not to make a sound. It's just too quiet in here. It's eerie. Like I'm lost in some sort of sequence or countdown that I can't quite hear or feel.

Energy flows across my being, the kiss of it oddly familiar.

Something is coming.

No. Not something. Someone.

I'm not sure how I know that, but the knowledge causes me to freeze once more.

A masculine scent touches my nose, demanding that I inhale.

Fir trees on a warm summer's night. Bliss.

Ohhh... I like that.

My eyes fall closed, some part of me instantly at ease. Comfortable. *Pleased.*

Want, I think. No. *Need.*

I *need* more.

To find the source.

To lose myself in—

85

A hand clasps around my throat, yanking me out of my delirious state. A scream locks in my chest, the lack of air making it impossible for me to release the startled noise.

And I stare into a pair of familiar brown eyes.

Threat.

"Thanks for making this so easy, Alina," he drawls, slamming my back against the wall.

I can't even reply, my ears ringing from the impact of my head meeting the hard surface behind me. My lungs scream in protest at the lack of oxygen, too.

It all happened so fast.

Too fast.

And now my vision is swimming with spots.

What the hell just happened?

One second I was lost to a strange scent and now... now I'm—

"Don't kill her," a deep voice demands. "The Viscount wants her untouched."

"She's fine," Threat—*Timothy*—snaps back.

"She's turning purple, T," the other guy growls. "*Let her go.*"

Timothy mutters something under his breath that I don't quite catch, and the world suddenly shifts. My knees protest, shooting pain up my spine as they crash into something hard.

The ground? I marvel, falling to my side on a wheeze as I grasp at my aching throat. I curl into a ball, only to find myself being handled once more as someone jerks me up off the floor.

I yelp, my head stinging from my hair being caught in a fist.

"Dude, what the fuck is wrong with you?" the one guy barks. "What part of *untouched* don't you fucking get?"

"He wants her virginity, Mark. He couldn't give two

shits about her actual condition beyond that," Timothy replies as he roughly positions me in his arms. "Stop worrying about me and worry more about getting us underground. We need to get on the train."

Train? I repeat groggily. *No. No, thanks. I am* not *going back.*

Some part of that thought seems to kick my reflexes into gear because suddenly I'm squirming and fighting for this guy to release me.

He hisses words at me I barely understand, my instinct to escape overriding all thought and comprehension. All I can think about is freedom. I need to get to my sister. To find a map. To *run*.

The man—*Timothy*—grunts as my knee connects with his groin, my feet somehow on the floor.

I shove myself away from him, my shoes slapping on the ground as I make a run for it.

Only for my hair to be caught in a fist once more.

I scream, *furious* at this ridiculous outfit and the impracticality of it all. *Furious* at the man grabbing for me. *Furious* at this world and the dark fate taunting my every breath.

"Let me go!" I demand hoarsely, my hands flying aimlessly. *Recklessly*. I'm a ball of fiery limbs and newly released fury.

Yet all I seem to be doing is ripping my own hair out.

My scalp burns, followed by my cheek as I'm shoved up against the wall once more.

Fingers dig into my hip, a palm wraps around my sore throat, and tears stream down my cheeks.

"Just knock her out!" a man shouts. I'm not sure which one. I'm too busy trying to break free of this impossible hold.

I won't go down easily.

I won't just allow this to happen.

I won't—

I blink, darkness overwhelming my last... last thought.

Give up, I think, finishing the phrase.

Only... only it sounds like a man's voice. Breathed against my ear. Tainting my mind. Ruining my fight. Overcoming my... resistance.

"You're going to regret that, *whore*," he says ominously.

A vicious snarl answers that comment, one I feel vibrating every nerve inside me.

Yet I'm not the one who released that sound.

Something else did.

Someone else.

He's here, I think, dizzy from a realization that I don't quite understand. But somewhere inside me, I just... *know.* Because I can *feel* him.

No.

Not just him, but *them.*

What...?

I blink.

And suddenly my blackening world resembles shades of red.

Blood.

Growls.

Death.

CHAPTER EIGHT
REAPER

"This is fucking incredible," I marvel, admiring the buildings all around me. "I hate New York City. But this…"

"Is Monster City," Flame tells me, stating the obvious.

"Indeed it is."

There are portals everywhere, but I don't give a fuck about the creatures coming and going through their magical spirals. I'm too enthralled by this realm's version of Times Square. It captivated me the moment we arrived, which was only minutes ago, yet it feels as though hours have passed.

None of the traditional skyscrapers exist here. It's all metal and greenery with a few splashes of windows. No billboards. No obnoxious human pedestrians. No taxis. No cars at all. Just open air, tall, environmentally friendly buildings, and hints of parks on every street block.

"I can smell the ocean," I say, ignoring whatever Orcus

and Flame are discussing. "No overpowering stench of garbage or human ruin. Just... life." So fucking bizarre. "It makes me want to destroy some shit."

Because I can't feed on *life*.

Hmm.

I dance around, looking for a potential meal.

Humans scatter about, their fear an aphrodisiac that makes my stomach growl with hunger. Where there is fear, there is a cause. And those causes typically make a fine meal.

Except all I see is supernatural creatures prowling about, their good intentions tainting their scents. *Too sweet. Too good.*

I frown. "There's not a single dark soul here," I tell Orcus, more shocked by that than I am by the impressive architecture. "Not a single being worth killing."

But Orcus doesn't appear to be listening to me.

His eyes are ruby in color, his dark orbs completely overtaken by the Alpha within, as he scans the crowd, his nostrils flaring.

"What is it?" Flame asks softly.

"*Omega*," Orcus replies, that word underlined in a growl unlike any I've heard from him.

Flame and I share a glance.

Orcus's mother is an Omega. However, his expression and demeanor suggest it's not his mother he scents now, but another female entirely.

He takes a step forward, then pauses and abruptly turns right, his growl intensifying.

Flame and I immediately take our positions at his back, our centuries of friendship clicking into gear as our protective natures take over.

Orcus's steps grow faster with each passing second, his

inner Alpha in complete control now. I've never seen him like this. However, he's been acting strange these last few days. I chalked it up to this mission, but now I'm wondering if it was something more. Something related to this *Omega* he appears to be currently hunting.

A potential mate? I question, shifting into a jog as Orcus takes off down a side street.

"And he thought we would be the ones distracted by our purpose here," Flame says to me conversationally.

I snort. "We're never letting him live this down."

"Never," Flame agrees.

If Orcus hears us, he doesn't reply. He's too busy sprinting down the alleyway between buildings.

Flame and I pick up speed, our gazes searching everything while Orcus remains dead set on chasing the Omega calling to his Alpha soul.

Strangely tinted windows, I think, noting the various creatures standing behind them. They seem to be observing our chase with interest. *Why are you all hanging out in there instead of out here?* I want to ask them.

But there's no time.

Orcus is practically flying now, his wings clearly threatening to break free from his back. I can sense it in the way he's propelling himself forward, his ethereal nature blinking in and out of view.

"Fuck," I mutter, realizing I'm about to lose my best friends. Because if he goes into angel mode, then Flame is going to let his panther out, and I'll be the only one left running on two legs.

There are lots of things I can do. Alas, flying and shifting are two abilities outside the realm of my possibilities.

My lips part, Orcus's name nearly leaving my mouth as

a delicious scent almost knocks me on my ass. *Dark souls. Three of them. Sinful. Decadent. Like chocolate-covered strawberries.*

I blink. *That* is new.

Dark souls usually remind me of smoke, not dessert.

My nose twitches, my senses firing as Flame growls beside me. I'm too lost in my thoughts of a mouthwatering meal to focus on the cause of his irritation.

Focus, I try to tell myself. *You can eat* after *helping Orcus.*

Except every step is bringing me closer to the sweet fragrance of impending death, causing my mouth to salivate with *need*.

Energy swirls along my arms, my tattoos slowly unwinding to taste the air around me. Wisps and strands twirl, power unfurling from inside me to stroke everything and everyone in our path.

Orcus disappears through a doorway, only to come to an abrupt halt.

I growl as I run into his back, my hunger reaching a peak. *Seek. Destroy. Devour.*

Flame grips me by the nape and throws me against a wall, his jaguar very much in his gaze.

I leap forward, grabbing him by the collar of his leather jacket. "*What*—"

"Let me go!"

My eyelashes flutter, my head slowly turning as my ears attempt to locate the source of those three words. Despite the hoarse quality of the voice, I know it belonged to a woman. One who appears to be struggling nearby.

One that makes Orcus growl low, his fury a palpable whip that makes me release Flame and take a step back.

My inky strands slowly come back to me, thoughts of a meal instantly replaced by a need to find the woman who uttered that demand.

"Just knock her out!" someone shouts, drawing my focus down a long, dark hallway.

A hallway that Orcus is already striding toward.

Flame glances at me, his irises allowing me to see his jaguar. He's livid, and I doubt it's because I shoved him.

No. It has everything to do with the *whimper* that followed the *knock her out* suggestion.

"Give up," another voice says with a sneer that has my eyes narrowing.

Another whimper follows.

Orcus's wings burst from his back, his responding growl one that vibrates the walls all around us.

However, the soon-to-be-dead soul ahead of us must not hear him because he says, "You're going to regret that, *whore.*"

I snarl at the sight unfolding before us of a man with his hand wrapped around the throat of a beautiful female.

A female I instantly recognize.

Because she's been haunting my dreams all week.

The dark-haired woman from the village.

I could *never* forget the determination and strength highlighting her stunning eyes.

Except her expression right now exudes *pain* and *fear*. And *that* is not acceptable.

Flame leaps around Orcus to grab the guy with his palm wrapped around our woman's throat. A crack follows as the human male is thrown against a wall, his body instantly going limp.

There are two other men in the room.

Two black souls.

Two humans who do not deserve to live.

I stalk toward them while Orcus crouches down to gather the female into his arms, his purr a foreign sound that almost distracts me from my task. *Almost.*

Fear pours off the men I'm hunting.

And the cowards turn to run.

But my deadly strands are waiting for them, my tattoos unfurling in an instant to unleash every ounce of my lethal strength.

I wrap them up in my cords and *squeeze*.

Screams follow.

Delicious fucking screams.

And I drink in every bit of vitality these assholes give me, reveling in their sweet deaths as I swallow their souls down... down... *down.*

They're husks of human shells when I'm done, their darkness no longer a burden for this world to carry. That privilege is now mine.

I feel them inside.

See every sordid deed they've ever committed.

And lock them away in a box where they'll exist until my dying breath.

Enjoy purgatory, I think at them, pleased to be their executioner and their punisher. *May you rest in hell.*

I turn then, determined to end the third man. The one who *dared* to touch *our* woman.

Although, she's not ours, *is she?* I think, my head slightly clearer now that I've fed.

I blink at the woman, noting the way Orcus is cradling her in his lap and humming against her ear, his wings nowhere in sight. The only evidence he even released them is in the tattered state of his shirt.

Is she his *mate?* I wonder, noticing the way he's staring down at her with uncharacteristic reverence in his gaze. *His Omega?*

My teeth clench. *Why does he get to have her and I don't?*

Wow, wait. No. What the fuck was that? Since when do I even want a mate?

Sex? Yes. Always.

A mate? No. My soul is far too destroyed to entertain the possibility of a *mate*.

And yet…

I cock my head to the side. *She is very pretty.* I scent the air. *And she smells like strawberries.*

My eyes widen. *Wait…*

I glance at the man Flame has hoisted up against the hallway wall, his grip unrelenting as he growls at the man.

He's waiting for me to come feed. To end the man's life and devour his soul.

But the flavor… the *fragrance*… it's coming from the girl.

Only, her soul isn't black at all. It's pure. White. *Beautiful.*

And I want to taint it with my touch. *Lick* her.

Bite her.

I shake my head in an attempt to see reason. This isn't like me at all. Bondage while fucking? Yes, fucking please. Biting? No. Biting equals mating.

Licking is okay.

Nibbling is approved.

Biting… no. Unacceptable.

And yet, my mouth waters with the urge to sink my teeth into her sweet flesh and taste her delectable blood. Bind our souls. *Marry* us for eternity.

I take a step back and grab my nape. *This realm is fucking with my head.*

"Reaper?" Flame growls. "You have five seconds before I kill this asshole myself."

"No," Orcus interjects, his tone soft despite the growling purr rumbling in his chest. "Alina has the first right of kill. He hurt her. She chooses his death."

97

I hear Orcus's words and understand them. Hell, I even *agree* with them.

But all I can focus on is the fact that he knows her name.

Alina.

It's beautiful, just like her. Soft, yet strong. Short, while packing a punch.

I can see the evidence of her fight, the scratch marks practically engraved on her assailant's face.

"You're right," Flame says without releasing the human he has pinned to the wall. "How would you like him to die, little panther?"

I blink at him.

First, Orcus knows her name.

Second, Flame has already given the girl a nickname.

And I... I have nothing.

No. That's not true. I have weapons. *Thousands* of weapons.

I grin, my tattoos already unfurling again as I move toward Orcus. He doesn't take his eyes off the female. I can't blame him. She's hypnotizing.

She's also gaping right back at him.

And now at me.

I don't sense fear from her, just confusion.

"Who are you?" she asks, looking between us, then focusing on my inky strands. "*What* are you?" She shifts her attention to Flame. "And what...? What do you mean...? How would I want him to *die*?"

"He hurt you, little panther. He doesn't deserve to live," Flame explains with a shrug.

"No, he deserves pain," I add.

"A great deal of pain," Orcus agrees gruffly. "But it's your choice, Alina. Do you want to kill him?"

"And if you do, can I interest you in any weapons?" I

ask her, already forming several within my strands in hopes of impressing her. "A hand knife to slit his throat, perhaps? Or a sword to sever his head completely?"

Her eyes widen.

"I can also create a gun," I tell her. "If you prefer a longer-range method."

"Too quick," Flame mutters.

"While I agree, it's her decision," I reply, smiling at her. "So what it'll be, pet? What's your weapon of choice?"

CHAPTER NINE
ALINA

I… I must be dead.

It's the only explanation.

This man—this hauntingly *beautiful* man—is drenched in blood and offering me *weapons*.

No. That's not quite right.

I thought it was blood. But it's… it's… too dark to be blood.

Is that smoke? Black ribbons? Wisps? I can't define them. But they're clearly attached to this man, yet my mind can't seem to comprehend how. Nor can I understand how those ethereal appendages magically created the knife and the sword.

Both items glint in the low light as the beautiful man waits for my reply.

Actually, all three of them are waiting.

And all three of them are ridiculously good-looking, I think, swallowing. *Why does that suddenly matter? Since when do I notice looks? Also, why am I in this big guy's lap? And is he… vibrating?*

So many questions.

Too many thoughts.

I touch my throat, wincing at the soreness, and try to swallow. I somehow managed to force out my questions before, but now... now I'm just tired. Confused. *Yet oddly not scared*.

Actually, I feel safe.

It's ridiculous. But something about the guy holding me makes me feel protected in a way I can't explain. Maybe it's his size? He's huge. Like, six and a half feet tall. And I'm pretty sure he has wings. At least, he had them before. But not now. They disappeared.

Is he like an angel of death? I wonder. *Do I feel safe because I'm dead and he's my escort to the afterlife?*

If that's true, then why am I still in this weird building?

And why would the figments of death pin my killer up against a wall?

I blink at Timothy. He looks terrified.

The guy holding Timothy, however, seems bored. He's simply watching me and waiting for a verdict.

On how I want Timothy to die.

Do I want Timothy to die?

I glance at the other dead men, their eyes forever frozen in horror.

Horror at what the hauntingly beautiful man with the smoky wisps did to them.

I swallow. *Why do I feel so calm?* I wonder. *Shouldn't I be scared? Screaming? Alarmed by what these men—specifically the one with the* weapons*—can do?*

Maybe I hit my head a little too hard when Timothy shoved me up against the wall before.

That would explain my lack of a reaction to these three obviously intimidating men, the fact that one of them apparently knows my name, and also the strange sensations I'm feeling in response to the big guy's *vibrating*.

The haunting one tilts his head to the side, his silver-blue eyes assessing. "I can demonstrate a few other options, if you like?" he offers, his words making my brow furrow.

Then I realize what he means—*weapon options*.

Because he's offered to give me something to *kill* Timothy.

And I'm back to wondering how I feel about his death. My fingers absently stroke my throat as I consider the man who threatened me.

His words about the Viscount tumble through my mind, his intentions pretty clear.

But he hadn't tried to kill me.

Just wanted to take me to the Viscount.

Although, he did mention how my physical condition wouldn't matter, that the Viscount just wanted my...

I shudder, unwilling to think of the *term*. Because that isn't something I want to give to *him* or anyone else.

Well... I glance at the beautiful men around me. *Well, maybe not* anyone *else. But...*

I shake my head, trying to clear the inane thought from it, and immediately regret the action. A groan escapes my lips, my sense of balance instantly distorted.

Definitely hit my head too hard... Ugh.

I cover my eyes with my palms, my stomach suddenly churning with the need to purge whatever it can.

Only, I haven't eaten in... I don't know how long. And after all the preparations and walking and everything else, I'm just *done*.

I'm tired.

I'm lost.

I'm confused.

And all I want to do is curl into a ball against the vibrating warmth beside me and forget everything.

Forget the Viscount.

Forget the train.

Forget the Choosing.

Forget Monsters Night.

Forget—

My eyes fly open. *Monsters Night.*

Apparently, I'd already forgotten about it, too wrapped up in this situation to think it through, but now... *now* I understand.

"Monsters," I breathe, my gaze swinging from the haunting one to the vibrating one to the bored one. "You're monsters."

I blink.

Oh, crap.

What the hell is wrong with me? I knew they weren't human. The one has tattoos that basically melt off his body into smoky ribbons. The other has feathers and *vibrates.* And the third, well, actually he looks pretty normal. But he's holding Timothy like he weighs nothing at all.

"You know, I take offense to that," the haunting one informs me as the weapons vanish. "If anyone is a *monster* here, it's that dark soul over there." He points at Timothy. "I can practically taste all his sins, and trust me, he's the definition of *monstrous.*"

"Monsters are what the humans call otherworldly beings in this realm, Reaper. I'm sure she's not trying to insult you," the vibrating one says softly. "Right, Alina?"

I snap my gaze to him, his black eyes rimmed with a reddish hue that's distinctly inhuman.

"How do you know my name?" I ask, very aware that the question is pretty inconsequential compared to the many others I could ask. But it's the second time he's said my name, and I'd really like to understand how he knows it.

Those red-black eyes study me for a long moment

before he says, "I saw you through a portal window and overheard someone else say your name."

"A portal window?" I repeat, blinking at him.

"It's exactly what it sounds like," the haunting one—*Reaper*—tells me. "Orcus was using it to check out this reality before we ventured into it. However, it seems that's not all he was checking out." He gives the man holding me a knowing look.

Orcus, I think, committing the name to memory along with *Reaper*.

"She's an Omega," Orcus says, causing my frown to return.

A what?

"Yes, I've gathered that from your purring," Reaper drawls, his inky strands whirling around him as though dancing with his words. Except, the smoke slowly starts to disappear into his skin, etching dark swirls into his arms.

Wow, I think, temporarily mystified by the phenomenon. *That's... so pretty.* I have the strangest urge to reach out and touch the tattoos. *Are they smooth? Warm? Will they move beneath my fingertips?*

But the source of my admiration steps away from me and back toward the two dead men, firmly returning me to the present.

He killed them.

He's a monster.

They're all monsters.

"Let's see," Reaper muses, squatting by the bodies. "You planned to zip-tie her wrists and shove a ball gag into her mouth. How unoriginal."

"What were they planning to do with her after that?" Orcus asks, his vibrations morphing into a growl that elicits a shiver from deep within.

And it's not a shiver born of fear, but of something else entirely.

What is happening to me? I wonder, dizzy all over again. *Why do I like that sound? It should be terrifying, not* enticing.

"Take her on the train and give her to someone..." Reaper trails off as he fishes something out from the pile of death, his head cocking to the side. "The Viscount?"

Orcus releases another deep rumble, causing me to squirm. He instantly stills, his purring reigniting as he says, "Sorry, little one. I'm not trying to excite you, just comfort you."

Excite me? I gape at him. *What the hell does* that *mean?*

And what does he mean by *little one?* I'm short, yes. And, well, a lot smaller than him. But I am *not* little.

I'm about to say as much when Reaper throws something over my head.

"Catch," he says with the motion, causing the one by the wall to instantly reach for whatever it is that's heading his way. "Might as well do to him what they planned to do to her."

"I've always enjoyed your brand of punishment," the dark-haired one says, amusement coloring his tone. His accent is similar to Reaper's, making them both easy to understand.

However, Orcus... his lilt reminds me of the Duke. Although, that's the only similarity between them. Orcus is much taller and wider, and he's dressed in jeans and a leather jacket rather than an embroidered vest and slacks.

Because he's a monster, not a man, I remind myself once more.

He certainly looks *like a man, though,* another part of me argues. *He smells nice, too.* Like clean, fresh air. I inhale deeply, feeling like I can really breathe for the first time in my life.

It's… strange. Alarming. Oddly soothing. And just so *confusing*.

I want to nuzzle into his broad chest and beg him to deepen that rumble of his, all while breathing him in and losing myself to his embrace.

He must be hypnotizing me, I realize. *Seducing me with his monster… something. Prowess?*

I try to pull away from him, but my body literally refuses. For the first time in my life, I feel safe, and I appear to be clinging to that sensation.

It's a lie, I tell myself as Reaper moves across the room, his sleeveless black shirt allowing me to see all the beautiful tattoos swirling along his muscular arms. *It's… it's a trick. I need to run. I need to—*

"Don't forget the zip ties," he says, interrupting my thoughts as he hands some string-like plastic things to his friend. "And make them tight. Because that was their plan for Alina."

The dark-haired guy snorts as he yanks Timothy's arms behind his back and secures his wrists. A full-body wince goes through Timothy, his yelp muffled by the gag.

"Ankles, too," Reaper says, eyes narrowed.

"Is that all they planned?" his friend asks. "To tie her up and take her to the Viscount?"

"No, they intended to play with her once the Viscount finished with her." Reaper utters the words with a growl, his gaze returning to the dead men. "I should have made them suffer, but their black souls were too tempting to draw out the meal." He looks back at Timothy. "I won't be making that mistake again. Once Alina decides how to kill you, I'll show her how to make it last."

I startle at his words, the reminder that these men want me to *kill* Timothy anchoring me in the present once more. "I don't…" I swallow. "I don't…"

I don't want to kill him, I say in my mind. But for some reason, I can't utter the words out loud. Maybe because my throat is sore.

Or maybe because part of me—a very small, very dark part of me—wants to hurt him like he hurt me. Maybe not *kill* him, but scare him a little.

Which is depraved and wrong.

And so very unlike me.

Maybe all the rebelling over the last year has addled my brain.

Or, more likely, these *monsters* have altered my perception of reality.

Why am I still sitting here? I push upright, only belatedly realizing I pressed my palm against a solid slab of muscular man to do so. *Wow, he's hard. And hot. Sooooo hot.*

Stop it, I tell myself. *Get up. Run.*

The commands cause my spine to stiffen, but my legs don't budge. Meanwhile, my hand… it stays against the masculine wall behind me.

Closing my eyes, I steal a deep breath.

And immediately regret it because it's full of that fresh-air scent, making my limbs automatically relax. Couple that with his soothing rumble, and I feel lightheaded, like I need to curl up and sleep.

Safe.

Warm.

Claimed.

My eyes widen with that last thought. *I need to go. These monsters are…*

Well.

They're…

I don't know what they're doing, but whatever it is, it's dangerous.

"I have to go," I blurt out, finally voicing a proper thought aloud.

My hands and legs finally get the memo as I push away from the vibrating wall of muscular flesh and crawl several feet away.

Except I'm stopped by a pair of vibrant eyes that flash purple in the light. I swallow as the man tilts his head to the side, sending all his dark hair falling over one side of his forehead.

I hadn't seen much of this one's features before, his back having been presented to me as he'd held Timothy up against the wall.

But he's no longer holding the other man.

No, now the dark-haired one is crouched on the floor before me, granting me a perfect view of his stunning face.

He's as gorgeous as the other two, yet something about him is even more intimidating. More… *untamed.*

He's too perfect. Too handsome. Too symmetrical.

His cheekbones are sharp, his jawline intense, yet his eyes are dusted with thick black eyelashes. They remind me of how mine looked with all the paint on them in the mirror earlier. Only, his appear to be natural.

I thought Reaper was beautiful, but this man… this man is beauty incarnate. Meanwhile, Orcus is the masculine one, with all the hard lines and brute strength. And Reaper… Reaper is still haunting in an undeniably attractive way.

Snap out of it, Lina, I tell myself. *You need to go.*

"Where do you want to go?" the beautiful man before me asks, either hearing my thought or maybe responding to something I said. *Did I speak out loud? Or did I…? Did I already say I want to go?*

I can't remember.

I can't seem to function at all.

Yet I hear myself whispering, "Chicago." It's such a strange response, one I don't fully understand until the city name slaps me across the face. "*Chicago.*" To find Sera. "I need a map."

That's what I'm supposed to be doing. Not ogling these monsters. Not fighting off Timothy. But hiding until Monsters Night is over and searching for a map.

Well, I didn't hide very well, I realize, wincing.

"Chicago?" Reaper repeats. "Are you craving some pizza, pet? Because I'd be down for a quick stop in Chicago for some deep dish."

I blink and glance up at where he's standing behind his dark-haired friend. "What?" Nothing he just said makes any sense.

He stares back at me, his lips curling down before he groans and looks at Orcus behind me. "Fuck, tell me there's pizza in this realm. I may prefer this version of New York City, but without pizza, it'll be a complete bust."

"You literally just ate," the dark-haired one says, glancing over his shoulder. "There's no way you're hungry."

Reaper gives him an affronted look. "I am *always* hungry for pizza."

"You know where Chicago is?" I interject, focusing on the fact that he'd repeated it back to me with some familiarity and ignoring all the talk about… *pizza.*

"Of course I know where Chicago is," he replies to me, his head cocking to the side in a way that he seems to favor. "But if you don't want pizza, then why are you interested in Chicago?"

My lips part, the truth almost leaving my mouth. Only it comes out on a yelp as the world abruptly shifts around me.

I suddenly find myself in the air, clutched in the arms

of the dark-haired one, with Reaper and Orcus standing in front of me, giving me their backs.

"Chicago is the Elite City," a cultured tone says from somewhere I can't see. "I imagine your human is looking for it, or perhaps someone within it."

Orcus and Reaper stiffen as someone materializes from the shadows. Their bodies are blocking the figure from my line of sight, making it impossible to discern any prominent features. But the voice was masculine, not feminine.

"Which is interesting," the newcomer goes on. "Villagers don't typically know about the Elite City, let alone the former name for it."

Orcus folds his arms, causing his leather jacket to stretch across his broad shoulders. Whatever vibrations he'd been emitting before are gone, but the one holding me seems to have taken over in the rumbling department. Except his is... different. Softer somehow. Quieter.

I glance at him, curious. However, his eyes are on his friends, or maybe even the other guy. I can't see anything more than muscular backs and the beautiful face of the man holding me.

How did I even end up here?

"Who are you?" Orcus demands, his tone making me shiver. There's something very powerful in that voice. Something deadly. Yet, inside, all I do is tremble in response.

Some twisted part of me *likes* that voice.

"A Monster City Emissary," the cultured one replies. "You may call me Jones."

"I don't feel much like calling you anything," Reaper drawls.

"And that's your prerogative, sir," Jones murmurs. "Regardless, I am here with a message from our Queen."

"Queen?" Orcus repeats. "Queen of what?"

"The Queen of Monster City, sir." There's a pause before Jones adds, "She sent me here to personally welcome you all to Monster City."

CHAPTER TEN
FLAME

My BEAST GROWLS from deep within, not liking this *Emissary* one bit. He's an outsider. An intruder. A creature of unknown origin. And everything about him smells *wrong*.

Alina shifts slightly in my arms, her dark eyes showcasing a myriad of emotions.

She's not scared, but she's not comfortable either.

The bruise on her throat becomes more apparent as she stretches her neck in an attempt to see around Orcus and Reaper. I nearly growl at the sight, ready to turn around and rip her assailant's head from his body.

But that would require setting my little panther down and leaving her temporarily unguarded.

Not an option.

Not with the potential threat standing a mere ten feet away.

His green eyes blink, displaying a pair of double eyelids that are distinctly inhuman. Although, the rest of him is every bit mortal-esque. Two legs. Two arms. Standard torso. However, the green eyes paired with his dark skin is a striking combination. As is the shock of white hair on top of his head.

"Our Queen wishes to meet with you," Emissary Jones goes on, his odd gaze flicking to me before returning to Orcus. "She's arranged a suite for you in her tower, should you opt to remain in our realm for an extended visit."

My jaw ticks at the request. Mostly because this doesn't sound like a request at all. It's a veiled offer to play nice with the local politics. A way of saying, *Yeah, we know you're here. We also know you don't belong here. But we'll let you stay, if you agree to our terms.*

"And if we opt not to extend our visit?" Orcus asks, his tone bored. However, I can feel his power whirling around him, preparing to strike should the need arise.

Jones doesn't respond right away, his gaze instead choosing to take in the corridor—including both of the dead bodies and the bound human weeping a few feet to my right.

"It is actually illegal to kill humans in Monster City," Jones says conversationally, his focus shifting to Reaper.

The Death Fae merely shrugs. "Black souls are fair game in our realm."

Jones gives a short nod. "Yes, well, you're visiting our realm. The rules are different here."

"So the Queen wishes to bestow judgment upon us?" Orcus interjects, his tone telling me he has one eyebrow arched at the unknown supernatural. It's a challenge. *And what? You think we'll just... cooperate?* is what he really means.

However, Jones simply laughs in response. "Oceans, no. The circumstances are understandable."

Oceans? That's a new one. Maybe this guy is some sort of water creature.

"That said, understanding often requires a conversation," he goes on, his tone no longer amused. "So should your realm wish to maintain good status for future returns, I would very much recommend taking the Queen up on her offer."

And there it is—the political reason for this "request."

Orcus's jaw has to be clenching right now, something I can't see from behind him but know he's doing. Because he *hates* politics. That's why he leaves Hades to run the Netherworld. His brother has a natural knack for handling conversations like this one.

Meanwhile, Orcus is more of an enforcer type. Just like me and Reaper.

We don't dance around with fancy words and bullshit *conversations*. We act. We fight. We *kill*. Hence the reason Reaper delivered justice to those assholes without even blinking. And I would have done the same to the bastard on the floor had Orcus not pointed out Alina's right to choose her assailant's death.

"Where's the Queen's tower?" Orcus asks, his voice carefully controlled.

"Toward the center of the city," Jones replies with a smile. "I would be happy to escort you there."

Another demand veiled as an offer, I think, not liking this guy one bit.

But if our realm wants to *maintain good status*, we'll have to take him up on the offer. And given that our work here hasn't even begun, we need to play nice.

Plus, we have Alina to consider now. While she's currently content in my arms, I know it's the pheromones dulling her reactions. She was practically drunk on Orcus's Alpha scent, and now she's eagerly inhaling mine.

The poor sweetling has no idea what's happening to her.

I can't help my animal's reaction to her any more than

she can help her reaction to me, but at least I understand this attraction thriving between us.

It's a natural response to a compatible mate, something I've never experienced before. However, I grew up witnessing it between others and have spent over a millennium searching for someone who calls to my beast the way Alina is doing now.

Orcus is different, yet similar. His Alpha soul requires an Omega, and apparently he's found that in this little human.

How that's possible, I don't know.

But the Omegas of his kind have all gone missing. Finding one in this realm only furthers the importance of following this world's rules.

"We would be honored to be the Queen's guests," Orcus says as though he's just come to the same conclusion as I have.

Jones grins like he's just won a prize. "I thought you might feel that way."

Reaper snorts, not bothering to hide his distrust or dislike of this creature. If it offends the other man, he doesn't show it.

Instead, he adds, "If you'll leave the human there, I'll see to it that he's properly contained. You can discuss your wishes for him with Queen Helia. Again, given the circumstances, I'm sure she'll understand your desire to rid our world of his *black soul*." Those last two words seem to be aimed at Reaper.

The Death Fae simply snorts again, clearly unimpressed.

"Fine," Orcus agrees. "Lead the way, Emissary Jones."

I readjust Alina in my arms, preparing to carry her to wherever we're going. Her corset seems a bit tight, making me concerned about her comfort. Her skirts are also rather bulky, but she appears to be too lost in her thoughts to focus on her physical condition.

If I were to guess, I would say she's trying to clear her head. Some part of her has to know that she's acquiescing a little too eagerly. It's very unlike the woman I observed through that portal window, the one who held her head high as she approached the stage.

She'd been practically daring fate to fuck with her.

Now, however, she's simply submitting to her future.

Unfortunately, the pheromones won't dissipate. If anything, they'll only intensify.

But there are ways to help her regain control of her own mind. Once we're alone, we'll help her voice her thoughts. Consent is vital in a mating. And while her body might be practically rolling over in acceptance right now, I'm certain the woman inside her is screaming in protest.

This is too fast.

Too foreign.

Too overwhelming.

She's not like me and Orcus. She hasn't spent her whole life searching for a compatible soul. Patience will be key here.

Patience and understanding. As well as a hint of seduction. And maybe some light petting.

My inner jaguar purrs in delight at that last bit, his desire to pet and lick an all-consuming need that has me tightening my grip on Alina. Her eyes find mine in response, those dark orbs full of confusion.

"I know this doesn't make sense to you," I tell her softly as we start walking down the hallway. "But I'll try to help you understand."

She swallows, her gaze slipping to my mouth before slowly traveling back upward. "H-how? How will you help?"

"By answering any questions you ask," I say. "And giving you time to adjust."

Because now that we have her, we won't want to let her go.

She's too unique. Too perfect. Too *ours*.

We'll do whatever we can to ensure she doesn't reject us. I don't even need to talk to Orcus to know he feels the same way.

Reaper, however, may feel differently. He would never force himself on Alina. But his mating instincts vary from mine and Orcus's. I'm not even sure if he feels a pull toward Alina. He might be completely indifferent.

Although, the way he went after those dark souls makes me wonder. He usually revels in his kills by drawing out the meal and prolonging the torture. However, he ended those assholes in a blink, then instantly shifted his focus to *her*.

Alina.

The gorgeous little rebel in my arms.

She's looking around in a daze, an adorable frown marring her brow. There are supernaturals everywhere, most of them smiling and talking animatedly to humans. There are a few mortals who appear frightened, their eyes darting from side to side as creatures of the night speak to them in gentle tones.

This certainly isn't the *fuck fest* I pictured when Orcus told me and Reaper about Monsters Night. The scene now reminds me of the bride mixers that Lucifer has hosted for his eligible Hell Fae. Everyone is being courteous, not pushy. Just chatting like one would on a date.

Only, this is no ordinary dating game. These creatures will claim their potential mates by the end of the night and drag them back to their home realms. Fortunately, most of the humans look accepting of that fate.

Unless they're drunk on pheromones, too, I think, glancing down at Alina. She probably wouldn't protest if we took her back to the Netherworld in this state.

But I suspect that once her sense of reasoning returned, she would very likely hate us for it.

Which makes prolonging our stay here a benefit.

Because I want a willing mate, not a resentful one.

Her pretty eyes dance around, taking in the unique scenery as we make our way back to the city center. *Times Square*, I recognize. Except it's nothing like the Times Square of our Human Realm. No billboards. No flashy lights. Just large tree-like buildings littered with glass windows.

Clean energy.

Clean streets.

Clean *everything*.

The tower Jones leads us to is no different. He's at the front of the group, giving Reaper and Orcus a grand tour, having explained the city layout while we walked. I've not listened to a word, but I start paying attention now as we move through a security checkpoint.

"This is just a precaution," he explains. "Queen Helia values the privacy of her guests, so only those invited into the Queen's tower may enter."

"And are those who enter also permitted to leave?" Reaper drawls, his tattoos whirling along his arms in clear agitation.

My panther paces inside, feeling that unease and forcing me to take in every angle of the lobby. *Cameras. Everywhere. Guards, too.*

Power hums through the three-story room, causing the hairs along the back of my neck to dance. I'm starting to understand why Hades insisted his brother take me and Reaper with him to this realm.

However, Orcus remains the epitome of nonchalance,

his shoulders relaxed, his spine straight, his hands loose at his sides.

Of course, he has the ability to create a portal on a whim and take us home in a flash.

I suppose if I possessed that talent, I would also feel pretty at ease in this situation.

"You are allowed to come and go as you please," Jones answers Reaper, his grin displaying a pair of dimples as his double eyelids flicker strangely. "But you will be asked for an eye scan before you leave, just so security can identify you upon your return."

"Hmm," Reaper hums, taking in the men near the scanning machines.

I can already hear him saying, *That's never going to happen.*

Because I feel the same way.

But we'll jump that hurdle when it appears.

Jones doesn't seem to notice our resistance, instead opting to continue with his tour by pointing out the various tower amenities.

"There are five restaurants on the main level," he informs us, gesturing to an archway with inviting confetti decorating the metallic siding. "The menus are extensive and feature anything from traditional human fare to dehydrated bone to orc stew."

"What about dark souls?" Reaper asks, being his usual sarcastic self. "Is that on the menu? Or do I need to go retrieve the one we left tied up in that building?"

Jones blinks at him. "I will... talk to the chef about your needs and see what we can prepare."

A chuckle tickles my chest, causing Alina to look at me with her inquisitive gaze. "Dark souls can't be prepared," I whisper to her. "They can only be consumed during active death."

Her nose crinkles. "Oh."

"Stop scaring her, Flame," Orcus tells me.

"I'm not scaring her. I'm just explaining the situation and why I find it amusing that Jones here thinks his chef can properly meet Reaper's needs." I stare down at Alina once more. "It's impossible. He's insatiable and impossible to satisfy."

"Now that's just not true," Reaper interjects, a hand covering his heart. "I'm certain Alina would satisfy me just fine."

"Stop," Orcus cuts in before I can respond to that. "Take us to our room. We'll learn about your amenities later."

His authoritative tone has Jones swallowing, his vibrant eyes bouncing between the three of us before looking at Alina. "Consent is important in Monster City."

"Another rule?" Reaper drawls. "And what happens when one is taken without consent?"

"Reaper," Orcus warns.

"What?" he asks with false innocence. "Those dark souls were trying to take Alina without her consent. But this guy says it's illegal to kill humans. So what punishment should they have received for their actions?"

Death, I think. *No other option.*

"That's a conversation for Queen Helia," Jones says, his tone indicating his discomfort. But after a beat, he clears his throat and smiles. "I'll just show you to your room. She can tell you about our other amenities, like the rooftop recreation area, the underground pool, and our other dining establishments."

He wanders over to the elevator bay while Reaper smirks at his back. "More dehydrated bones and orc stew?"

Jones presses the button before replying, "Yes, actually. As well as lava drinks, catermines, and bulbas fruitas."

I have no idea what those things are, and I know Reaper doesn't either, yet he smiles widely and gives Jones an enthusiastic nod. "Can't wait to try them, old chap."

This time, my chuckle reaches my throat and escapes through my mouth. Reaper's take on an English accent—which Jones has—is *atrocious*.

But the *old chap* doesn't appear to care or notice. He simply escorts us into the elevator and peeks over at Alina again.

However, her gaze is on my lips, something I definitely don't mind. I smile down at her. "Comfortable, little panther?"

Her nose scrunches. "Why do you keep calling me that?" Her voice is like music to my ears, the raspy quality from earlier seeming to have diminished a bit. However, her wince tells me her throat still hurts.

Definitely deserved death, I think, recalling the assholes who tried to hurt her. If Helia disagrees about the main assailant, then we might have a problem during this future *conversation.*

But that's a problem for later.

Right now, I have a sweet little panther's question to answer. "Because you remind me of a panther."

"A big cat?"

"A lethal cat," I correct her. "Sly. Beautiful. Sleek. *Strong.*"

Her brow furrows, providing me with a glimpse of that adorable little frown line again. "But you don't know me."

"Maybe not," I agree. "But my jaguar senses his equal in you."

"Jaguar?"

"Yes. My inner beast. My other half." I dip my head down so our faces are close as the elevator doors open on some unnamed floor. "I'm part Shifter Fae."

"Shifter Fae," she echoes. "I don't know what that means."

"It means I can shift into an animal," I explain. "Specifically, a black jaguar."

I give her a moment to digest that information as I step into the hallway.

Orcus gives me a disapproving look, likely because he thinks I've ignored his order not to *scare* her. But Alina needs to know these things about us to understand us. And I don't see any issue with revealing details about myself. That's my choice, not his.

"Shifter Fae," she says again, glancing at Orcus and Reaper.

"No, I'm the only Shifter Fae here," I tell her, not wanting her to think Orcus and Reaper are the same. "They're different types of fae."

"Fae." She seems to be tasting the word on her tongue.

"Yes. Fae," Reaper affirms. "*Not* monsters."

Jones glances at him with interest, but Orcus steps into his view. "Which room is ours?"

The Emissary clears his throat, obviously uncomfortable with Orcus's dominance. "This way, sir."

I swear the guy skips a little, like he's forcing himself to walk when all he really wants to do is run. Orcus often has that effect on others.

Alina studies the metallic walls as we wander down the corridor, her gaze occasionally drifting upward. I follow her glance to see what she's intrigued by and notice the vine-like lights decorating the ceiling. It's actually rather pretty.

The pattern continues all the way to the end and stops at a double door with a sign hanging above it that reads, *Guest Suite 4747.*

Jones gives us the code and steps aside for Orcus to key it in.

The Alpha doesn't hesitate, but I tighten my grip on Alina, ready to sprint away at the first inkling of trouble.

Except all that greets us inside is a stunning view of Monster City through a huge glass wall.

In front of it is a living area with tons of cushions and ornate furniture, the setup seeming to sink into the plush carpeted floor.

"There's a kitchen and dining area to the left," Jones says. "The main master suite is to the right. I believe the accommodations will suit your party size."

"Oh?" Reaper slips inside, his tattoos swirling menacingly along his arms as he disappears from my view.

Jones clears his throat once more. "There's information inside on how to ring for room service. I'm sure your human is hungry."

"Alina," Orcus says. "*Our human* is named *Alina*."

"Right. Yes. Of course, sir." Jones gives an awkward bow. "I'll just leave you all to be acquainted. Queen Helia will be in touch sometime tomorrow. Oh, and, if you need anything else, dial zero."

With that, he steps away.

And basically jogs down the hall.

"He started off so confident," I muse, my attention slowly returning to Orcus. "I wonder what scared him off." I pair the fake innocence in my tone with a batting of my eyelashes.

Orcus grunts. "Bring Alina inside and set her down. I need you to sniff out any bugs in the room."

He doesn't wait for me to agree, just follows Reaper's path and leaves me in the doorway with Alina.

"I realize this is all probably overwhelming, but you're safe with us," I promise her. "And if at any point you need a moment, just say it. We'll give you whatever you need. Okay?"

She swallows.

Then she nods.

But I can tell by the glimmer of uncertainty in her gaze that she doesn't believe me.

I don't blame her. If I were in her position, I wouldn't believe me either.

Trust takes time.

It's also best acquired through actions, not words.

Orcus's surveillance request is going to have to wait. Once Alina is settled, I'll sweep the room for listening devices.

First, I'll see to Alina's comfort.

We'll start with food.

Afterward, I'll help her remove this archaic dress.

And then, I'll brush her pretty hair. Because this tousled mess on her head looks very uncomfortable.

"Let's find the menus," I tell her. "I'm starving."

CHAPTER ELEVEN
ALINA

A Shifter Fae.

The term rolls around in my head as I study Flame's profile, his long eyelashes fluttering as he blinks.

Flame, Orcus, and Reaper.

They haven't actually confirmed their names or even really introduced themselves to me. But I've gathered their names through their conversations with each other.

Flame's currently talking to Orcus about the room, saying it's clean.

I'm not sure why this is such an important discussion. The cleanliness of the suite rivals that of the entire city, which is all very *pristine* to me. But apparently Orcus has strong sanitation values.

Fae, I think, studying him now. His sturdy jawline. Long, dark hair tied at the back of his nape. Strong shoulders. Chiseled cheekbones. Muscular forearms.

He lost his jacket at some point, leaving him in just a T-shirt, jeans, and boots.

Flame is similarly dressed, only his shirt is long-sleeved.

And Reaper is still sporting that sleeveless shirt, his

tattoos on full display as they writhe along his arms. He seems particularly agitated, his long legs eating up the marbled floor of the kitchen as he paces back and forth near the dining area.

"It's possible their bugs are undetectable," Flame says, drawing my attention back to his conversation with Orcus. "But I'm not picking anything up on the scanner." He hands a small chip to Orcus as he says that, causing my eyes to follow the movement.

"You guys are pretty serious about sanitation," I muse aloud. "You'd hate my village."

Orcus frowns. "What?"

I shrug. "It's full of bugs and dirt."

He stares at me for a long moment, like he's struggling to understand my words.

"They're talking about listening devices," a voice says by my ear, making me jump. I glance back into a pair of hypnotic silver-blue eyes.

Reaper.

A second ago, he was pacing beside the dining table.

Now, he's right behind me, his lips curled into a smirk.

Fae, I tell myself again. *A very* fast *fae.* But not a Shifter Fae like Flame. "What kind of fae are you?" I blurt out, alarmed and impressed by his speed.

"A Death Fae," he tells me. "Or, in human terms, the Grim Reaper."

My brow furrows. "The Grim Reaper?" I've never heard that term before.

"They probably don't know that name in this realm," Flame says as he lounges in the chair beside me. "The Grim Reaper is like an angel of death in our Human Realm."

"Basically, I escort souls to the afterlife," Reaper adds. "Which is why my kind is often associated with the Grim

Reaper. However, Death Fae actually focus on dark souls and devour their essences rather than take them to wherever their souls would otherwise go."

"Oh." My nose scrunches as I ponder everything he's said. "What are dark souls?" He's mentioned that term a few times, once in reference to Timothy and again when talking to that Emissary about food.

"Those who have committed heinous acts," he replies, his gaze turning distant as he starts pacing again.

"All souls begin white and innocent, but each sinful deed colors the aura," Orcus says, his tone soft. "The darker the soul, the worse their transgressions."

"So your kind eats the souls of bad people?" I ask slowly, piecing it all together.

Orcus smiles. "My kind? No. But yes, that's basically what Death Fae do. Only, Reaper also likes hunting dark souls in the flesh and introducing them to their fates earlier than expected."

"Before they can do anything worse and hurt more innocents," Reaper growls.

Orcus and Flame both glance at him, their expressions exuding an understanding that I don't quite grasp.

There must be a story here, I realize. *A reason Reaper hunts dark souls while they're still alive.*

I shiver.

I don't think I'm quite ready to hear whatever reason accompanies that need.

"I'm a Mythos Fae," Orcus says, drawing my attention back to him. "Not a Death Fae."

"I see." I glance between him and Flame and the still-pacing Reaper. "And what's a Mythos Fae?"

"A God," Flame drawls. "Or a Goddess. At least as far as human conception goes."

"And most other fae," Reaper mutters as he pauses

midstep, his gaze drifting toward the foyer. A low growl fills the air, the sound emanating from his chest.

Then a buzzing noise echoes through the room, causing him to disappear and reappear by the door.

My eyes widen in response to seeing him move. Because *that* was definitely not human.

However, it wasn't very monster-like either.

Fae, I remind myself. *They're... fae.*

And not all that scary.

Well, maybe a little deadly. Especially Reaper. Except he opens the door with a wide grin and joyfully shouts, "Pizza!"

Flame rolls his eyes.

Orcus just shakes his head.

And the guy in the doorway clears his throat. "Uh, yes. It was ordered by Mr. Flame?"

"Mr. Flame?" Reaper repeats before glancing at the Shifter Fae. "Is that your new superhero name?"

Flame snorts. "Only if we're calling you Grim Reaper going forward."

Reaper no longer looks amused. "No."

"Pity," Flame drawls.

Orcus sighs audibly and stands. "Here. I'll take that." He moves toward the guy holding a huge tray and plucks it from his grasp with a murmured "Thank you."

The tray no longer looks big now that Orcus is holding it. He's dwarfed it entirely, and yet the contents fill the entire table as the various plates are distributed among the four place settings.

Flame picks up my empty glass—he poured me a water when we first entered the kitchen and dining area, saying it would help my throat. He was right.

He refills the contents and brings it back to me, then grabs the seat across from me with Orcus beside him.

Reaper reclaims the chair next to me and scoffs at my plate. "Chicken and broccoli?"

"And mashed potatoes," Flame says.

"Why?" Reaper asks, sounding offended. "We're in *New York City*. Pizza is obviously the requirement for everyone, and yet..." He glares at the hunk of meat in front of Orcus. "Filet mignon and"—he shifts his focus to Flame—"is that *salmon*?"

Flame merely smiles. "Not all of us have your refined tastes, Reaper."

"Clearly," the Death Fae grumbles before flipping open a box to reveal some sort of thin, cheesy pie.

Pizza, I think, somewhat intrigued.

He grabs a slice and folds it before shoving a corner into his mouth.

My eyebrow lifts a bit at the display, primarily because I've never seen an adult eat with his hands before. That's usually something a child would do.

Reaper's silver-blue irises meet mine as he chews and swallows, his silvery eyebrow inching upward in response to my silent observation. "Want a bite?" he asks.

I blink at him. "I, um, no. I... I've just never seen food like that before."

"You've never seen a pizza?" He looks alarmed. Then he shoves my untouched plate into the middle of the table before rotating his chair toward me. "Open your mouth."

"What?"

"You heard me. *Open your mouth*."

"Reaper," Orcus says, a warning in his tone.

"Stay out of this, Alpha. This is between me and our pet." His intense focus goes to my mouth. "Now part those pretty lips for me, and I promise you'll be rewarded."

I have no idea what to do. No one has ever spoken to me like this.

What is he going to do? I wonder as my mouth obeys his command. *Why am I allowing this?*

Because I'm curious.

Because I… I kind of like this.

It's a startling realization, one that has my lips parting even more.

"Such a good girl," Reaper whispers before tearing off a small piece of his pizza and setting it on my tongue. "Now enjoy your reward and don't forget to swallow."

Something about his tone feels sensual. Or maybe it's his words. I can't quite determine the cause, but my skin heats a little in response.

Then my mouth explodes with flavors, making me forget all about his words.

Oh my monsters…

I've never tasted anything like this. So savory. So rich. So *greasy*.

I… I'm not sure if I like it, love it, or hate it. It's just so different. Exquisite yet nauseating. Flavorful and too much at the same time.

It's only a small bite, but I savor it, my mind struggling to decide how I feel about this creation.

Only for the moment to end too soon as I automatically swallow.

Reaper stares at me expectantly. "Well? What do you think?"

I swallow again, the cheese a bit thicker than I realized. "I…" I clear my throat. "I don't know."

His eyebrows shoot upward. "You don't know?"

I grimace. "It's… it's flavorful?" I state lamely.

He snorts. "*Flavorful*, she says." He flashes a look at Orcus and Flame that I don't quite understand. It's too quick for me to even guess because in the next instant, he's focused on me once more. "That's fine. When we go to

Chicago, we'll try pizza again and you can tell me what you think then."

I gape at him. "Chicago?"

"Yes. You mentioned wanting to find it, right? I assume that means you want to go?" He takes another bite of his pizza while he waits for me to reply.

But Orcus interjects before I can even attempt to puzzle through a response. "*Reaper.*" It's just one word— the Death Fae's name—but it's enough to scatter goose bumps down my arms.

Because he uttered it with a growl.

Something inside me squirms in response, his dominance a palpable presence that leaves me unsettled.

"What?" Reaper demands, his eyes locking with the other man's. "She mentioned needing to find Chicago, presumably to go there. We're obviously going to take her, yeah?"

"Our only plans right now are to meet with this Monster City Queen and satisfy this realm's political protocols," Orcus replies, that growl still rumbling through his words.

But Reaper appears to be unfazed, because he simply snorts. "Right. Political bullshit aside, Alina's an Omega."

Orcus remains silent, his gaze narrowing slightly.

What's an Omega? I wonder. Orcus mentioned it before as well, but I have no idea what it actually means.

"Look, all I'm saying is, if our pet wants to visit Chicago, then Chicago is on our agenda. Ergo, it's fair game for discussion." He picks up his pizza to take another bite, completely uncaring of the tic that seems to have formed in Orcus's jaw.

Flame clears his throat. "How about we focus on our meal for now? Alina needs to eat. Then I'm sure she would like to shower off all that hairspray and makeup.

We can discuss further plans after she's properly cared for."

He gently nudges my plate back toward me and gives me a soft smile before returning to his own food.

Reaper and Orcus say nothing.

Meanwhile, my stomach growls, and I realize I don't have much of a choice here. I need to eat, just like Flame said.

So I do.

But with each bite, I keep marveling over Reaper's comments regarding Chicago.

He wants to help me find Chicago? Why would he do that? Do I want that?

Up until a few hours ago, the thought of monsters terrified me.

However, these guys weren't very monstrous.

Well, maybe Orcus is, I think, taking in his size again. *But he doesn't scare me.*

No, his growls do something else entirely.

I shiver and shovel more food into my mouth. I barely taste it, my body working on autopilot.

This is crazy.

They're fae.

What am I even doing here?

What if they can help me find Chicago? Can I trust them?

I barely know them.

But they've been nice so far...

I grab my water and take several gulps, the thoughts making me dizzy. *Just take this one minute at a time,* I tell myself. *Finish eating. Then... then...* "A shower would be good," I blurt out, recalling Flame's words. "Can I do that now?"

Because I would love to get out of this dress. It's too tight for me to eat much more anyway.

And my hair… *Ugh.*

Not to mention all the paint on my face.

Yeah, a shower sounds beautiful right now. Even if it's too hot or too cold. I just want to feel like me again.

That'll help me get my head on straight. Bring back my ability to focus. Reset my goals and desires.

Yes.

A shower.

Right now, please.

CHAPTER TWELVE
FLAME

"She's overwhelmed," I tell Orcus and Reaper as I enter the dining area. "And rightfully so, given the situation."

Alina hid it well, though.

The moment she mentioned wanting a shower, I set my fork down and escorted her into the room to help her prepare for it.

She was shy at first, her teeth snagging her bottom lip. But when I made it clear that I was just in there to make sure she had what she needed, she relaxed.

"I'm going to find you something to wear" were my final words to her. "If you need anything else, or help with your dress, just let me know."

She visibly exhaled when I stepped away.

I spent a few minutes in the bedroom, talking on the phone with the concierge about clothing options. And when Alina didn't call for anything else, I left the room.

I pull out the chair beside Orcus and collapse into it.

Neither he nor Reaper comments on my statement regarding Alina's emotional state, so I shift focus to my other news. "They're bringing up some outfits for all of us since we didn't exactly pack for an extended stay."

"Is it going to be a bunch of Regency Era bullshit?" Reaper asks.

I shrug. "I don't know. And I don't care. I'll wear my fur if I have to."

Reaper grunts.

Orcus just leans forward, his fingers steepling together on the mostly empty table—apparently, they cleaned up while I was helping Alina.

"She's an Omega," he says, his tone filled with awe despite him stating the obvious. "But she's human."

That last part explains his amazement.

Because Mythos Fae are immortals. They're Gods, not humans.

"You're absolutely certain she's an Omega?" I ask him.

"I sense it in her soul," he tells me. "But I guess I won't be sure until I breed her."

"Oh, let's add that to our agenda," Reaper suggests eagerly. "Chicago pizza and breeding our pet. Yes. Excellent vacation."

Orcus cuts him a look that would wither most fae.

But Reaper merely smiles. "Tell me you wouldn't enjoy everything I just said, and I'll shut up."

The Alpha's jaw clenches, his lips flattening into an ominous line. However, he doesn't comment. Because he can't. He would relish everything Reaper just mentioned.

And so would I, I think, glancing at the closed bedroom door.

The three of us are not new to sharing women with one another. Although, it's never been quite like this. And it's always been a two-on-one situation, not a three-on-one.

Will Alina even like that? I wonder. *Will she want any of us at all?*

Orcus could play his Alpha card, saying she's one of his kind and therefore his mate. However, he hasn't given any indication of his intention to do that.

My inner beast could attempt to do the same. All it would take is a single bite to make her mine.

Yet I don't feel the possessive need to keep her to myself. If anything, I like that she might have all three of us. It would ensure her protection for eternity.

Assuming she has the capability of becoming immortal, I realize, frowning. "I don't understand how she has an Omega soul as a human. That can't be a genetic manipulation, right?"

"Are you suggesting her scent has been altered?" Orcus asks, his tone interested rather than irritated.

"Maybe," I admit. "I don't know. It just seems strange that she can have the soul of a fae without actually being one."

"And not just any fae, but a godly fae," Reaper adds, his playful demeanor having disappeared behind a mask of seriousness. To others, his abrupt emotional shifts might feel like whiplash. But I'm used to Reaper's mercurial nature.

"I won't know until I knot her," Orcus says.

"Bringing us beautifully back to my agenda-planning discussion," Reaper murmurs, his eyes lighting up in excitement. "First, we handle the political bullshit. Then, we'll go to Chicago for pizza and to please our pet. And afterward... we fuck."

"She's not a pet, Reaper," Orcus tells him. "She's a potential mate."

The Death Fae blinks at him. "Yes, that's what I said."

"No, you keep calling her a *pet.*"

Reaper arches a brow. "Yes, and...?"

"I'm saying she's more than that."

Reaper blinks again. "There is nothing more important than a pet." He looks at me. "Tell him, Flame. Pets are cherished."

I sigh and shake my head. "I think it's his pet name for her."

"Yes," Reaper says. "That."

"It's belittling," Orcus tells him.

"No, it's not," Reaper argues. "It's cute. *And* she likes it."

"How do you even know what she likes?" Orcus demands.

"How do you know what she doesn't like?" Reaper counters, folding his arms. "Just because she's your *little one* and Flame's *little panther* does not mean she *likes* either of those names. So I'm trying *pet*. And I happen to enjoy it a great deal. Just as I happen to enjoy her, too."

Orcus looks ready to throttle Reaper—which is fascinating since Orcus is typically the patient one of our trio—but all three of us are distracted by a strange sort of roar from the bedroom.

Reaper is instantly on his feet.

Orcus and I are right behind him.

Only for us all to freeze as an adorable growl follows that roar. A very *feminine* growl. *Like the kind made from a little panther,* I muse.

"Oh, shit. Did she just… *growl?*" Reaper asks, glancing back at us.

"Yeah," Orcus breathes. "Yeah, she did."

"*Fuck,*" Reaper groans. "Oh, hell, I hope she does that around my cock sometime soon."

Reaper's crass comment goes straight to my dick, causing me to harden just as the door opens to reveal a disheveled-looking Alina. Her pretty, dark eyes instantly find mine as she heaves a furious sigh.

"Can you please help me?" She trails off and gestures at the tangled mess of fabric around her torso. "I... I don't..." She grinds her teeth, her expression filled with a heartbreaking mix of irritation and desperation.

I'm moving toward her before she can say anything else, already understanding what she needs. "Reaper, can you get us a knife?"

He clears his throat, likely trying to recover from his fantasy of Alina growling around his shaft. "Uh, yeah. What kind? Throwing dagger? Paring knife? Carving blade? A cleaver? Something thicker, like a butcher's tool?"

I glance at him in exasperation. "Something that'll slice through fabric like butter."

He nods, his tattoos writhing along his forearm to his wrist as metal glints at the end. Within a few seconds, he's holding a very sharp-looking blade. "This'll do?"

"You are not using that on Alina's dress," Orcus interjects. "Make him some scissors instead."

Reaper frowns but creates the item in his opposite palm and holds them both out to me. Only, Orcus grabs the one he prefers first and hands me scissors with a pointed look. "Hurt her and I hurt you."

I roll my eyes. "My claws are sharper than both of those toys."

"My promise still stands," the Alpha tells me.

"I'll only hurt her in ways she'll like," I counter, turning toward the wide-eyed female in the doorway. "Come on, little panther. Let's get you out of that monstrosity."

It's a purposely chosen term, one that has her nostrils flaring. "I didn't choose it."

"I have no doubt that's true," I tell her as I close the door behind us and lead her through the bedroom to the bathroom. "All right, go stand in front of the mirror for me." I could technically do this by the bed, but I want her to be able to see what I'm doing. We have to develop trust, and this seems like a good way to do it.

She swallows as she does what I request, her eyes meeting mine in the reflective glass.

"I'm going to work on snipping through the ties of your corset. You might want to hold the top against your chest while I do this so it doesn't fall down." Not that I would mind catching a glimpse of her tits—in fact, I would *love* to see her tits—but I strongly suspect she's not ready for that.

She's still caught up in the confusion of the moment. She's also not built like we are. My jaguar knows she's compatible, and he's ready to mate her right fucking now. He doesn't care that we've just met. He knows what he wants, and he's very happy to take it.

Orcus's Alpha instincts are likely saying the same thing.

And Reaper, well, he often follows the needs of his dick and doesn't give a shit about the potential repercussions of his impulsive actions.

But Alina needs time. Trust. Compassion. And comfort.

So I demonstrate that I understand each of those things now as I gently cut through the laces of her corset.

Her palms flatten against her chest, holding the fabric to her body while I loosen it from behind. Her skirts seem to be held up by buttons along her ass, but I'll handle those when I reach them.

As I cut through the final lace, the corset splits, revealing her back. *Not quite the same as the Regency Era,* I think, admiring her pale skin.

"Your skirt is going to be a little trickier," I inform her, my voice slightly lower than I intended. But I can't help my physical reaction to her. She's stunning, and my inner animal is eager to taste her.

"O-okay," she says, shivering.

"If you want, you can try it on your own again," I suggest. "Now that your torso is free, I mean."

She swallows, her midnight irises holding mine in the mirror once more. "I... I would prefer your help." The words leave her in a whisper, an array of goose bumps pebbling down her arms.

My tongue feels a bit thick, so I nod rather than reply, and unfasten the top button of her skirt. The fabric parts to show a hint of white lace beneath.

Fuck me, I think. *If this is what I think it is...*

I pop another button.

Yeah, that's what I think it is.

Definitely *not* a Regency Era item, but a much more modern one. *And fuck, it's translucent.*

I have to bite back a low growl as each button displays more creamy skin decorated with lacy lingerie. It fits her beautiful backside perfectly, the virginal white far more of a turn-on than I could ever have expected.

Black and red have always been my preferences in the bedroom.

But Alina... *fuck*, she looks good in this. Too damn good.

My fingers flex, my claws scraping at my senses. My beast is raging inside at just the small glimpse of lace.

Settle down, I demand.

He snarls back, his feral nature threatening to come out to play.

I close my eyes and steal a deep breath while my fingers work. After several seconds of regaining control, I allow my lashes to flutter open and find Alina still staring at me in the mirror. "Are you okay?" she asks, her unease instantly dampening my growing arousal.

"Yeah," I tell her. "My jaguar..." I trail off, debating

how to phrase this without scaring her. "He's very interested in you." There's no point in hiding the attraction. She deserves to know the truth. "I'm just trying to control him."

She swallows again. "Oh. And, um, by 'interested,' you mean...?"

"He wants me to kiss you," I say, taming down the actual desire coursing through my veins. It's still an honest reply, just not as intense as saying, *He wants me to mount you and bite you.* I'm sure he would also enjoy kissing her, too.

"I... I see." She clears her throat, her fingers seeming to clutch the fabric a little tighter.

"I'm not going to," I promise her. "Not yet, anyway."

Her eyes widen a little. "So you plan to kiss me?"

I pop the final button, causing the skirt to fall along her legs to the floor. She's left standing in those fucking lace panties and her unfastened corset. "I plan to do a lot more than kiss you, little panther," I inform her, my voice even deeper now. "But not until you tell me you're ready."

I force myself to take a step backward. "I know Jones already said Monster City values consent, but so do I. Orcus and Reaper feel the same way, too. None of us will touch you without your permission. Just remember that, okay?"

Because I can see the fear brewing in her gaze.

As well as a hint of interest.

She's intrigued, but she's also intimidated.

I don't need to know her to be able to see the innocence written all over her. I doubt she's ever felt a man's touch. From what little I've seen, I can tell this society seems to frown upon sexual experience, preferring to preserve the virginity of their *Offerings*.

Such a flawed concept, I think darkly. *I want a willing and wanton woman, not a terrified little virgin bride.*

But I'll teach Alina.

Slowly. Purposely. *Thoroughly*.

And in the end, she'll be a fucking wildcat in bed.

That rebellious nature of hers will absolutely come in handy, too.

"Enjoy your shower," I tell her softly. "If you need anything else, I'll be out in the living area with Orcus and Reaper." I turn, then pause at the door. "Oh, and they're bringing up some clothes. I'll leave some on the bed for you when they arrive."

I go to leave one more time.

Just to stop again.

"Let me know if you want any help with your hair." My voice is gravelly again, forcing me to clear my throat. "I'd be happy to brush it for you."

My jaguar purrs inside at the notion, very pleased by the idea.

He's easily placated. Fucking, sunning, and grooming are three of his favorite pastimes.

With a nod, I finally leave.

And commit the image of her standing there in her lacy panties to memory.

CHAPTER THIRTEEN
REAPER

Sleeping on the floor sucks.

But Orcus captured the couch while Flame offered to guard the room by shifting into his jaguar form near the foyer doors.

Meanwhile, our pet has taken over the giant-ass bed in the other room.

I don't mind her sleeping there. Hell, I want her there. She deserves the comfort. But the mattress could easily fit five men Orcus's size, making it overkill to give the petite female the entire bed to herself.

"It's the gentlemanly thing to do," Orcus said last night.

What part of me is considered gentlemanly? I nearly demanded. But I could tell by his tone that he wasn't going to listen to practicality. The Omega has him by the knot, and he's no longer thinking clearly.

Stretching my arms over my head, I wince as my back cracks. *This is ridiculous*. I could have slept in that bed without Alina even noticing me.

Assuming I kept my hands to myself, anyway.

Which… I probably wouldn't have.

Those smooth curves of hers are pretty fucking delicious. And the way she growled last night… *Fuck.* I'm getting hard just thinking about it.

I'm not one who typically craves women. I fuck them. Ensure they're pleased with the experience. And move on.

But Alina is something else. She's special. *An Omega.* I'm not particularly drawn to that aspect of her, though. I'm more intrigued by the conflict I can sense in her soul.

She's a sweet little rebel.

One I want to corrupt with my darkness.

Tempt into sin.

Roll in the shadows with and introduce to my brand of pleasure.

Thinking of that, along with her delicious little growl, has my cock ready to play.

Alas, she's asleep.

Sighing, I roll to my back and glare at the high ceilings overhead. *I am definitely* not *asleep.*

I drum my fingers against my chest, my gaze dancing around the room, searching for a distraction. The suite only has one shower. Granted, it's big enough for a party of five or six—*just like Alina's bed.*

There seems to be a theme here.

I'm guessing the Monster City Queen purposely put us in this room to accommodate our group size.

Which has me wondering how common our sort of dynamic might be here. Are there other trios of monsters who roam the realm and take one mate?

Is that what we're doing? I wonder, glancing at the couch. *Are we all going to claim her?*

Sharing isn't new to us. But this is a different type of sharing.

A pet, I muse. *Hmm.*

But does she even want to be ours?

I frown, uncertain of how to answer that.

It seems counterproductive to have a wall between us. How is she supposed to know us if she's sleeping in another room, away from her potential mates?

I sit up, tempted to rouse Orcus and demand that he join me in waking our pet. But I'm not sure he would agree with my idea. He's the only one who insisted on giving her space.

Well, technically, Flame insisted on that, too.

So, fine. They gave her space. And I... I'll just... pop in to check on her.

My body evaporates into the shadows, my ethereal ability tied to my affinity for spirits and death.

I might not be able to travel dimensions the way Orcus can, but transporting myself into the bedroom isn't difficult.

The bed comes into view, followed by the rest of the modern fixtures and plush amenities.

I only glanced in here last night when checking the space for potential threats. It's a pretty nice suite, but my focus is on the dark-haired beauty curled into a ball near the edge of the oversized mattress.

Fuck, it would be so easy to just slide into the opposite side of the bed. She definitely wouldn't notice.

But I'm not all that tired now.

No. I'm... *captivated*.

Our sweet pet looks so innocent like this, so fragile. It makes me want to take out those two souls who threatened to hurt her, and kill them all over again.

Because how could they harm her?

She's fucking stunning. So damn perfect. *So mine.*

Gods, that claim is a visceral response from deep

within, my soul suddenly feeling oddly at ease by her mere presence.

I take a step forward, drawn to her in a way I can't quite explain.

She's so soft and corruptible. My inky strands begin to unwind, the urge to touch her consuming me.

Just one stroke, I tell myself. *Right there against her porcelain cheek.*

My smoky wisp gently does what I say, sending an electric jolt through my body.

I want more.

So. Much. More.

But I want her awake when I truly touch her. Awake and willing.

And more than happy to submit.

A growl threatens to rumble in my chest, causing me to take a step backward.

I need a shower. A cold one.

Or maybe a hot one…

She was the last one to use the shower. That means it'll smell like her. All sugar and spice.

Yes.

I don't walk to the shower; I teleport there and inhale her natural fragrance. It reminds me of strawberries and cream, an intoxicating combination that's slightly tainted by the peppermint shampoo she must have used earlier.

I find the bottle and consider throwing it away.

But that scent will actually smell good on me.

I make a mental note to find something more appropriate for our pet's next shower as I strip out of my boxer shorts. All my other clothes are on the floor of the living area, near where I slept last night.

I turn on the overhead sprays—of which there are five

—and grin when warm water instantly comes from the pipes.

"Excellent." I step under the showerhead closest to me and groan as the droplets hit my shoulders. It's the perfect pressure. But while it eases my muscles, it does nothing to help with the stiffness below. If anything, I'm somehow harder now.

Probably because I can smell Alina everywhere.

She spent a lot of time in here last night.

Did you touch yourself, darling? I wonder as I tip my head back to dampen my hair. *Did you think about Orcus's knot?*

I've never met an Omega before, but from what I understand, their sexual appetites are impressive. Especially when they go into heat, something Orcus said might happen now that Alina has met an Alpha.

Everything seems so uncertain as far as her origin is concerned, her mortality confusing the Mythos Fae Alpha greatly.

I don't really mind the bizarre situation, though.

I just want to play.

Particularly with a beautiful little dark-haired vixen.

Fuck, she'll look so good on her knees for me. Taking my cock between those plump lips. Swallowing me down. *Growling* like she did last night.

I can practically see it all happening right in front of me, the fantasy feeling all too real.

Gods, she'll be so damn amazing. I can practically feel her mouth around me. Sucking. Pulling. Teasing my tip with her teeth.

I groan, my forehead falling to the tiled wall. *More,* I think. *Take me deeper. Take me all the way in. Accept me. Accept us. Accept this.*

The words are a chant in my head as I force my hands to

move. And not in the way I want to move them. Instead, I wash my hair. Soap up and rinse off my body. All while my dick begs me to finish the fantasy. To grasp the base. To *pump*.

But I want to live in this moment for a little while longer. To indulge in the vision of Alina naked. Tits covered in suds. Eyes wide as she stares up at me from her kneeling position. Lips quirked up just a little before she licks my bulbous head.

Yes, pet. Just like that, I think as I stand beneath the spray once more. *Keep doing that and I'll have to claim you.*

I stare down at where I wish she were kneeling, then eye my aching cock.

My tattoos are swimming along my skin, engraving power into my being through their thick and inky strands.

Mmm, I hum, willing the vitality to go to my groin, wanting to see my intended mate's claim.

The tattoos swirl into a cursive-like script, drawing her name along the side of my shaft. *Alina.*

"Fuck, that's perfect," I breathe, loving the way my pet's name looks on my skin. But it's not long enough to span the whole surface. So I tell the ash-like brand to add a skull to the end.

My lips curl. *Fuck yeah.* That dark mark symbolizes my pet's future as a Death Fae's mate.

I trace my finger along the tattoo, half in love already.

She's so fucking mine, I muse, wrapping my palm around my base to give myself a good, harsh pump.

The ink beneath my hand pulsates in response, telling me it's there to stay. Because my soul *likes* the thought of mating this pretty female.

When I agreed to venture into this realm, I would never have guessed this was possible.

But I'm not complaining.

I'm embracing it.

And soon, Alina will, too.

"My pretty little pet," I moan, picturing her tongue tasting the inscription on my dick. In my mind, she smiles, loving that she's marked me with her essence. Because this will be permanent the moment our bond is complete. My cock will belong to her.

And her pussy will absolutely belong to me.

"Oh, I'll share you," I tell my imaginary version of her. "Let them claim you, too. But you'll be mine in every way that counts."

I brace my forearm against the glass, my breathing coming in heavy pants. I'm so damn close. So worked up over a figment in my mind. So *ready* to claim this woman that I hardly know.

It's insanity.

And I'm so fucking here for it.

"*Alina,*" I growl, my grip practically bruising my tender flesh as I pump myself harder. And harder. And *harder*.

I picture her choking. Begging me for air, yet trusting me to let her breathe.

Gods, she'll own me like this. Destroy me in the best way. *Devour me like I devour souls.*

It'll be so depraved. So fucking delicious. "And you'll swallow every damn drop."

I can't help the growl escaping me, the feral sound echoing in the shower walls.

Alina will be mine. *Ours.*

Because I'm already hers.

Her name pulses on my dick as my balls tighten, a roar ripping from my lips as I come all over the glass. So much fucking cum. Gods, it would have drowned my pet. Made her truly choke. I'll have to remember that before our first time.

She's human.

Fragile.

Mine to protect.

And I will. I'll ensure she's guarded always. Kill anyone and everyone who tries to hurt her. And make her my Godsdamn queen.

I blow out a long breath, the vestiges of my orgasm finally subsiding enough for me to calm down. At least a little. But that tingly feeling is still very much there, tugging at my abdomen and demanding another release.

This female has me so fucking worked up.

Swallowing, I lift my forehead away from my arm—I don't even know when it fell there—and blink into the dimly lit bathroom.

A pair of wide eyes stares back at me through the glass, Alina's lips parted in shock as she takes in my nude state.

I tilt my head, my hand still running up and down my cock while she watches.

She says nothing.

She also doesn't make a single attempt to leave.

It makes me wonder how long she's been watching me. *Hopefully long enough to be impressed,* I think, my lips tilting up a little.

"Good morning, pet," I tell her, my voice low. "Have any nice dreams? Because I just enjoyed one hell of a fantasy myself."

Her mouth parts even more, this time on a yelp before she runs out of the bathroom.

"Was it something I said?" I call after her, right as the door slams.

I chuckle and turn to finish washing myself off.

The little darling can run. She can even try to hide.

But she won't get far.

You're ours now, pet. For better or for worse. Till death do us part.

CHAPTER FOURTEEN
ALINA

Oh my monsters. Oh my monsters. Oh my monsters!

I don't know what just happened.

Okay. That's... that's not true. I... I heard a noise and went into the bathroom to see what it was. And found *him* standing there like a God in the showers. All muscular lines, sculpted physique, and... and *monster dick.*

I've never seen a man's *member* before. However, I'm pretty sure Reaper's is way too big to be natural.

It was also covered in tattoos.

Tattoos I couldn't quite make out.

But wow.

Wow.

I... I don't know what to do. Or think. Or—

"Alina?" Flame calls as he knocks on the door before opening it. "Are you all right? I heard you yelp."

Of course he heard that. But he obviously didn't hear what Reaper said right before I yelped.

"Good morning, pet. Have any nice dreams? Because I just enjoyed one hell of a fantasy myself."

I shiver, his voice rolling through my mind in

combination with that beautiful memory of his naked form.

Monsters, I didn't know men could look like *that*.

Of course, he's a fae. Not a human. Not a normal man. A *fae*.

But if fae look like that…

No. I shake my head. *Focus, Lina.*

"What's wrong?" Flame asks, likely interpreting my head shake to mean something. "What happened?"

What had he asked me? If I was all right? Am I all right?

Not really.

"I'm fine," I manage to force out. "I… I was just startled." *By Reaper's monster dick.*

His expression as he stroked himself was so intensely beautiful that I couldn't stop staring. The minute I realized he was in the shower, I should have left. But I… I couldn't. I'd been captivated by his strength.

And his words, I think, recalling what I overheard.

"My pretty little pet."

"Oh, I'll share you. Let them claim you, too. But you'll be mine in every way that counts."

"Alina," he said then, making my lips part. Because I thought he caught me staring. But no. He was *talking* to me. *Thinking* about me. While he pumped himself to completion.

"And you'll swallow every damn drop" was his final statement before his expression contorted with ecstasy. His growl vibrated the room, making my legs squeeze together in response.

I can still feel the impact of it now, my inner thighs hot and damp from his *demonstration*. I'm aware of what goes on down there, my hands and fingers having explored the many ways to make myself orgasm.

But Reaper's orgasm was a whole new level of rapture.

"Alina?" Flame prompts, reminding me that he's still in the room.

Orcus is looming behind him in the doorway, his dark hair wild around his shoulders, suggesting he just woke up.

Because they all slept in the living area, I think, swallowing.

I offered to take the couch. It made a lot more sense for me to sleep out there while they slept in here, but Flame and Orcus weren't interested in discussing alternative arrangements. And I didn't feel comfortable enough debating it.

So I took the bed.

Woke up to that strange sound.

And found a naked Reaper with his hand wrapped around his cock in the shower.

"What startled you?" Orcus asks, drawing my focus to where he's standing in the doorway.

Shirtless.

In just a pair of tiny black shorts.

Boxers, my brain tells me. *He's wearing boxers.*

And only boxers.

Just like Flame.

Fae… Beautiful. Fucking. Fae.

I'm surrounded by hot, hard men. Perfectly sculpted. Muscular. Toned. *Holy fae.*

My throat works as I try to swallow, my legs suddenly feeling like jelly.

This is overwhelming.

I've barely even seen a man without a shirt on, and now this? *Three* gorgeous men in their underwear?

Oh, but one was naked. *Very* naked. And hard. And stroking…

I take a wobbling step back. *Pull it together, Lina,* I snap at myself.

But outwardly, all I want to do is whimper.

My lower belly pulls tight with a sensation I recognize from my own self-explorations.

Arousal.

And who can blame me with all this man meat on display?

Why do they need to be so damn good-looking? And where are their clothes?

I grab my shirt and look down, remembering that I'm wearing one of the items originally meant for them. But the nightgowns the concierge brought for me resembled translucent dresses, which I had no desire to sleep in. So I'd taken one of the oversized T-shirts instead.

Now I'm sort of wishing I would have worn that just to give these guys a dose of their own medicine.

Of course, that would have left me more vulnerable and exposed and—

"Alina." Orcus's deep voice cuts through my mind, his gaze intense as he prowls toward me. "Did Reaper touch you?"

I blink at him, confused. "What?"

"Did Reaper touch you?" he repeats, only a foot away from me now.

There's a strange softness to his voice, yet it's edged with dominance. Like he's demanding that I reply without actually issuing the command. "N-no. He was in the shower."

"Thinking about her, but not touching her," Reaper drawls as he joins us in the bedroom.

My cheeks flame in response, my gaze locked on Orcus so I don't have to see Reaper again.

Because all I'll be able to picture is his hand wrapped around that giant cock.

Ohhhh, thinking about it anyway now…

"You all right, pet?" Reaper asks. I may not be looking at him, but I can definitely hear the smirk in his voice.

"I'm fine," I mutter back to him.

"Good. Shower's all yours when you want it," he says as he saunters by me in nothing but a towel.

I hate that I look.

Hate that he's tempting me.

Hate that I can't seem to stop my eyes from trailing a bead of water down his strong back.

This is... I don't... I clear my throat and spin toward the bed.

Which isn't a good place to look either because now I'm wondering what all three of these guys would look like sprawled out over the covers.

"Can you all please put some clothes on?" I ask, exasperated.

Reaper chuckles.

Meanwhile, Flame mutters, "I did put clothes on."

And Orcus just... *vibrates.*

My shoulders instantly relax at that low rumbling sound, my eyes suddenly heavy.

"Cheater," Reaper says. But I barely hear him, my focus entirely on that soft, repetitive *purr.*

A strong chest meets my back, the bare skin burning through the thin fabric of my shirt. "Just using my gifts," Orcus murmurs, his voice making me want to melt into his heat.

What is he doing to me? I wonder, drunk on the feel of him.

And his *scent.*

So refreshing.

I inhale deeply, reveling in the moment and forgetting whatever we were discussing. It doesn't matter. Just that soothing rumble and the crisp aroma of a morning breeze. Woodsy. Clean. Addicting.

"She's going to fall asleep standing up," Reaper says, suddenly in front of me.

I blink at him, startled by his unexpected appearance. Because he literally just materialized out of thin air.

His silver-blue eyes flash, his lips curling seductively at the corners. "Is she going into the famous Omega heat?" he asks, a hint of excitement in his tone. "Does that mean we can fuck before Chicago? Because I am absolutely down for changing up the agenda."

What? I stare at him, my foggy mind slowly picking through what he just said. *Fuck* is a powerful word. However, it's *Chicago* that captures my interest.

Serapina.

My eyes widen and I try to take a step back, but I'm met with a masculine wall. So I spin to the side and shake my head, needing to clear it. "I need to find a map" stumbles from my lips.

How much time have I wasted?

What day is it?

Can I even leave?

So many questions. Too few answers.

Orcus moves in front of me, blocking my path before I can even try to move. "You don't need a map, Alina. We know where Chicago is. But getting there may be difficult."

My brow furrows. "You know...?" I shake my head again. They already told me they knew of Chicago. But I can't remember if they confirmed knowing how to get there. Regardless, I'm more caught up in that final sentence. "Why would it be difficult?"

"Because it's hundreds of miles away, and I have no idea what transportation looks like in this reality," he tells me. "However, I can ask about it when I meet with the Monster City Queen."

"You're... you're going to ask her about Chicago?"

"Yes," he answers without hesitation.

"Why?"

He lifts one big shoulder and lets it fall. "Because you keep mentioning it. So now I'm curious about what's in Chicago."

I gape at him. "Maybe it's not a good idea to ask her about it."

"The Emissary already mentioned it," he reminds me. "I'm pretty sure the Queen is going to ask me about it since it sounds like it's not normal for the humans of this world to know cities by their old names."

Right. Yes. The Emissary did say something about that.

I nibble my bottom lip, my gaze falling to his collarbone. *Is any of this going to cause trouble for my sister?* I wonder.

Hopefully not. I haven't mentioned her at all. And I never said how I knew about the city's name.

But it sounds like this big fae might actually be able to help me learn more about Chicago and how to potentially get there.

That's good, right?

I lift my gaze to his dark one once more. "Okay. Thank you for asking."

He nods, then cocks his head to the side, his eyes crinkling. "Want some breakfast, little one?"

It's an abrupt conversation change.

It's also accompanied by that endearment again. *Little one.* I don't feel *little*, but I definitely must seem little to him.

However, he's also called me an *Omega*—a term Reaper just used a few minutes ago, too.

I stare up at Orcus, aware of his substantial height, and

ignore his inquiry about food. Primarily because I'm tired of being distracted. I have so many questions in my head, yet I keep forgetting about them.

Because these men keep doing things like taking off their clothes.

And stroking themselves in the shower.

And vibrating.

And—

I clench my jaw, then narrow my gaze at Orcus. "What's an Omega?"

There. I asked a good question. And given the flare of his nostrils, it was the *right* question.

"How about we discuss it over breakfast?" he says, clearly trying to negotiate.

"I'm not hungry, and I would like an answer now, please," I tell him.

Flame chuckles from somewhere in the room. I'm not sure how I already recognize that it's him, but I do. "There's my little panther," he says, confirming I'm right about him being the one who laughed.

"What gift are you going to use now?" Reaper drawls from behind me. "A growl to make her submit?"

Orcus looks over my head at the other man. "I don't need to growl to make her submit." His eyes return to mine. "Nor do I have any intention of making her do anything. If she wants answers, I'll provide them."

"Can you provide the answers directly to me rather than talking about me like I'm not in the room?" I sass at him, a bit irritated by the third-person phrases.

Flame laughs again, clearly pleased.

Even Reaper chuckles this time.

Orcus, however, doesn't look as amused. But he doesn't appear to be angry either.

"An Omega is a type of fae," he says. "It can refer to

various fae species, like Fortune Fae, some Shifter Fae breeds, and a handful of other fae races. But as it pertains to my kind, Mythos Fae Omegas are extremely rare. In fact, they're thought to be extinct."

I frown at him. "But you called me an Omega."

"Yes."

My brow creases even more. "I don't understand."

He palms the back of his neck and nods. "Honestly, neither do I. But my soul recognizes yours."

"As an Omega," I say dumbly. "As what type of Omega?" I attempt to clarify. Because maybe he means I'm some other kind of fae.

Except I have no idea how that's possible. I was born in the village. And I certainly don't feel otherworldly.

"A Mythos Fae Omega."

Right. Now I'm just... utterly lost.

Orcus must see the confusion on my face because he says, "I think we need to start with how the Omegas of my kind went extinct. Then we can talk about your Mythos Fae Omega soul and what it might mean."

CHAPTER FIFTEEN
ORCUS

ALINA SITS ON THE COUCH—THE one I spent last night tossing and turning on—and tucks her legs under her. She's still dressed in just an oversized shirt, which is driving my inner Alpha wild. Because I'm pretty sure she's not wearing anything under it.

I settle beside her but leave a few inches between us to ensure her comfort. I also put on a pair of pants and a T-shirt prior to exiting the bedroom, as did Reaper and Flame.

All three of us would have been fine staying in our boxers, but it seemed our intended mate was overwhelmed —and a little turned on—by all the skin on display.

I would be more pleased with that if our conversation hadn't ventured into painful territory.

Flame hands me a cup of black coffee before sitting in the chair catty-corner to the sofa. Reaper is still in the kitchen working on his own drink, as well as one for Alina. He's into the fancy shit and said he wanted to make something special for "our girl" when we entered the living area.

I'm guessing it's one of his famous cappuccinos. It's a good thing the room came with the right equipment—a full coffee machine in the kitchen—or Reaper might have gone on a rampage searching for one.

I take a sip of my coffee, needing the scalding liquid to help anchor me in the moment. This is not going to be a fun conversation, but it's a necessary one. Especially if she's what I think she is.

After another burning swallow, I clear my throat and set my cup down on the coffee table before us. "Right, so, I guess I'll start by explaining fae kind."

"Professor Orcus, ladies and gentlemen," Reaper interjects from the kitchen.

I ignore the jokester and continue.

"There are over a hundred fae realms in our world. Each realm is unique, meaning they're typically inhabited by a specific fae type. And there's a variety of fae, including vampires, shifters, elementals, dragons, and so many more. In short, it's a vast universe of supernaturals."

"There's also a Human Realm," Flame adds softly. "It's similar to your world, except it's a little more current."

"And they don't know supernaturals exist," Reaper says as he appears in front of Alina.

She doesn't jump at his teleportation antics, just blinks up at him. Almost like she knew to expect him. And maybe she did after he startled her in the bedroom.

Reaper hands her a mug, his lips curling. "I drew you a present."

Her brow furrows, causing me to glance over and see the foamy skull decorating her cappuccino. "Er, thank you," she tells him.

Reaper practically preens in response. "Now try it. Tell me it's amazing. Because I know it is."

Alina looks from the cup to him and back again.

Rather than reply, she takes a sip. After a beat, she takes a second sip, and her eyes jump up to his once more. "This *is* good." She sounds surprised, suggesting her reaction is genuine.

"Obviously," Reaper drawls. Then he disappears, leaving her smiling against her cup.

It's a pretty smile, one I hope to see more of.

But I doubt I'll earn many happy moments throughout our conversation. It's too serious for that.

"So, as I was saying," I begin again. "There are lots of fae types and fae realms. And within those realms, there are kingdoms with even more potential variations."

That last bit is new information, but she nods, listening while sipping her cappuccino.

"We live in the Netherworld Kingdom," I go on. "And that's in the Hell Fae Realm."

Her nose scrunches, like she's considering the information. But she doesn't comment.

"The Hell Fae Realm is home to those of mixed fae origins. For example, Flame has a Shifter Fae mother and a Corpse Fae father, so he's a mixed breed. Which, by definition, actually makes him a Hell Fae."

"But I prefer to be called a Shifter Fae because my animal half is much more dominant than my corpse half," Flame inserts before setting his coffee mug down. "The fae lore is complicated enough. Basically, just understand that there are several variations of our kind."

Alina remains silent, but I can tell she's a little overwhelmed by all the definitions.

So I back up a little.

"As I said, we're from the Netherworld Kingdom. It's basically where all the Death Fae and Corpse Fae live."

She nods a little. "Okay. What about your kind?"

"Mythos Fae have their own realm," I tell her. "But

over the last few thousand years, we've drifted away from it. Nowadays, most Mythos Fae choose to live in other realms," I explain.

Her brow crinkles. "They do? Why?"

"Because our Omegas died."

Or that's what many of my kind believe, anyway.

But I'll get to that in a second.

"Without Omegas, Alphas like me can't properly procreate," I go on, trying to help her understand. "We also can't take a non-Omega mate. And eternity is a long time to live alone. So most of my kind have ventured to other realms to stave off boredom."

She stares at me, her cappuccino no longer seeming to interest her at all.

I can't really blame her. It's a heavy topic.

"However, there are some of my kind who believe the Omegas are not really dead," I inform her softly. "And those Alphas haven't stopped searching the realms for traces of their existence."

Reaper chooses that moment to return to the living area, his own cup carefully cradled in one hand. But he doesn't attempt to speak or draw attention to himself. He simply sits on the floor across from us, his expression serious.

He might be the reckless one of our trio, but he understands how important this is. And he's respecting my right to explain my history to Alina.

"My brother and I are among the Alphas who believe our Omegas are still alive somewhere. We've been hunting for over a thousand years, scouring realms and searching for alternate dimensions. Our powers are creation-like in nature, providing us with the opportunity to traverse worlds in a way few others can."

I pause, waiting for her to react to that information.

She doesn't. Perhaps because she hasn't realized that if I possess this ability, then she might as well.

If she's a real Mythos Fae Omega, that is.

She certainly fucking smells like one, I think, recalling her arousal from earlier.

The urge to throw her on the bed and taste her nearly knocked me on my ass. But millennia of discipline afforded me a moment of much-needed control.

Alina isn't ready for my knot.

But if I'm right about her Omega soul, then she might be soon. *Very* soon.

I clear my throat for what feels like the thousandth time today—the fire burning in my soul is fucking dehydrating my insides—and force myself to stay on track.

Where was I?

Dimension travel.

Portals.

Right.

"The, uh, reason we ventured into your world is because my brother found something while scouring dimensions via a portal window. That something was an Omega presence."

Her eyes widen a little. "M-me?"

I shake my head. "No. He thought he sensed our mother, who is also an Omega. But I think he may have just picked up on the presence of Omega souls. I won't know until we properly hunt each aura."

She shivers, the term *hunt* having caused her nostrils to flare. "More potential mates?"

My lips almost curl.

She probably doesn't realize it, but a hint of annoyance colored those words.

Omegas are notoriously possessive of their Alphas, and they do not like competition.

Maybe it's just wishful thinking on my part, but I'm almost positive that her Omega soul forced that question to leave her mouth.

She's testing me.

And my Alpha spirit very much welcomes the challenge.

"Potential mates for other Mythos Fae," I tell her. "Not for me. I've already found my intended."

"*Our* intended," Reaper corrects with a growl. "She's my mate, too."

I glance at him, somewhat surprised by his bold claim. He's never been the settling-down type, but I suppose it only makes sense for him to feel a connection to my Omega. I've been bonded to Reaper for a long time, our friendship a natural one that has grown over the last one thousand years.

Flame, too.

The three of us are basically brothers.

So of course we're all drawn to the same female.

We'll create an extremely powerful circle together, with Alina being our center.

Although, she's currently frozen in her seat, her eyes wide. "M-mate?"

"*Intended* mate," Flame interjects, his voice soft. "It means that we intend to court you, Alina. Nothing more. You won't be forced. You don't have to feel the same way. We're simply laying out our intentions because none of us believe in hiding our natures."

"But you barely know me," she rushes out, her cappuccino cup rattling in her hand. "I... But... Oh." She blanches. "Monsters Night. Mates. I..."

I take the cup from her before she can drop it, and gently set it down on the table. "Alina—"

"No, I get it. Monsters Night is all about brides and grooms. But it happens... so fast? I just... I didn't..."

"We didn't attend Monsters Night to hunt for a mate," I tell her.

Her brow creases. "What?" she asks, like she didn't hear me.

So I repeat my statement before adding, "We used Monsters Night as a cover to sneak into this realm. We didn't come here to find a mate; we came here to find the essence my brother originally detected in this realm. But then my soul sensed you..."

"We also saw you briefly before we even came here, almost like Orcus's dimension power was locked on to you when creating the portal window," Flame adds.

I nod. "Yes. I found you easily a second time, too." Something Flame and Reaper just learned last night.

Fortunately, neither of them gave me too hard a time about it.

"My soul has been drawn to yours from the moment I first saw you," I go on, wanting her to know the full truth. "I suspected you might be an Omega then, but I thought it was impossible. Then we arrived and I immediately felt your presence. I also... sensed your distress."

It'd been in her scent. A slightly sour note to an otherwise beautiful bouquet. My inner predator had roared, furious that something or someone was harming our ideal mate.

"All thoughts of our mission fled the moment I scented you. I had no choice but to find you. However, none of us originally came here with the goal of taking a mate. And like Flame already said, we're merely speaking our intentions. That doesn't mean we expect you to instantly accept us."

"We're more than happy to work for it," Flame adds with a smile. "Trust takes time."

Reaper snorts. "One night in bed with us and she'll be begging for eternity. I personally think that's a quicker solution to the whole courting scenario, but fine. Delayed gratification has its perks."

Rather than wait around for a reply, he blinks out of sight and reappears in the kitchen.

Alina's cup seems to have magically gone with him.

If she cares, she doesn't show it. Instead, she's too busy gaping at me, and then at Flame, and then me again.

"What if I'm not really an Omega?" she finally asks. "What if...? What if it's just a fluke or something? I'm human. I was born in a village. I have human parents. I... I can't be a... a *fae*."

I'm pleased that she's referring to our kind as *fae* now, not *monsters*.

"It could be a genetic manipulation," Flame tells her. "From what we've gathered, the humans in your realm have been, well, *altered*, for lack of a better term, to suit supernaturals."

"What does that even mean?" she demands, her voice going up an octave at the end. "Altered how?"

"We don't know," I interject. "But when I meet with the Monster City Queen, I plan to ask her about that, and Chicago."

Alina stares at me like she did the first time I mentioned my plans for talking to the Monster City Queen about Chicago. It's a look that says she still can't believe I plan to ask about that. But beneath the surprise, there's a hint of hope.

She wants to trust me.

She just isn't sure if she can.

If I'm right about her being an Omega, her soul

already has faith in me to protect her unequivocally. Because that's what Alphas do—they protect Omegas.

Which is why so many of my kind have lost themselves in other fae realms. We *failed*. Our Omegas are gone. Our purpose left with them. Now, we're forced to survive without our other halves. Live in a world where our Alpha souls are starved for a connection that doesn't exist.

Only, my salvation is seated beside me.

Watching me.

Studying my eyes.

Swallowing.

My Omega. My purpose. My heart.

"If I'm right about you"—which I have to hope that I am—"then your Omega instincts will likely start to show themselves now that you've found a compatible Alpha."

Her soul would have been in hiding, locked in self-preservation mode. But now that she's with me, her inner Omega should feel safe enough to come out and play.

"We'll know in the next few days," I tell her. "It could be small things, like feeling possessive over me"—something I think she's already shown some evidence of, but that could also be chalked up to wishful thinking—"or the urge to nest."

"Or going into heat," Reaper calls from the kitchen. "Personally, I'm looking forward to that part."

Alina glances at him, then back at me. "What does that mean?" she asks in a whisper.

"That you're going to be horny as fuck and beg us all to satisfy you for days," Reaper answers, having appeared right behind the couch, his lips near her ear.

She jumps, then squirms in an adorable way that betrays her flustered state. "Stop doing that," she scolds him.

"But I brought you another treat," he tells her, holding out a cupcake.

"Where the fuck did you get that?" I ask him. Reaper can conjure weapons of every kind, his sole purpose in life being to *kill*. "That better not have poison in it." Because that would be the only type of *food* he should be able to magically produce.

He gives me an affronted look. "I would *never* hurt our pet. What kind of Death Fae do you think I am?"

"A psychotic one," I tell him.

His lips curl. "True. But no, this isn't poisoned. I simply stole it from the kitchen downstairs."

"When did you…?" Flame trails off. "You know what? Never mind. I don't even want to know how you found a *kitchen* or when you managed to sneak off there."

Reaper simply shrugs. "Our pet is hungry, so I went hunting. Cupcake?" he offers her again. "It's strawberry. Reminds me of you." The Death Fae has literal hearts in his eyes, creeping me out a little.

"Um." Alina gingerly takes the cupcake from his long fingers. "Thank you?"

He smiles. "You can thank me properly later."

"Reaper," I growl.

"What?" he asks me. "You have your way of wooing her; I have mine. And if I do say so myself, my way is much more direct."

He vanishes again, leaving me rolling my eyes in his wake.

Reaper's completely gone now, suggesting he's shadowed off to explore the kitchen in more depth. Hopefully, he doesn't make too much trouble. We still need to meet with the Monster City Queen, and I would prefer we not piss anyone off before that happens.

I run a hand over my face and blow out a breath. "I

should try to follow up with that Emissary about when the Queen might be available to meet."

"Try phoning the concierge," Flame suggests. "They've been uncharacteristically helpful for a Human Realm hotel."

"Probably because it's run by supernaturals, not mortals," I reply before looking at Alina once more. "Are there any other questions you want me to answer before I make this call?" We've already discussed a lot. But I want to make sure she's okay before I step away.

She's still studying the cupcake Reaper gifted her, her tongue peeking out to lick her bottom lip. "I... I have a lot to think about."

"Yes," I agree. "And you can ask any questions you want, anytime you want. We'll always answer truthfully."

She nods, but I can see that she's retreated a bit into her own mind, her eyes still on the pink icing.

I glance at Flame, asking him with my gaze to keep an eye on her.

He dips his chin, his quiet way of saying, *On it.*

There's still a lot for us to go over—such as what a *heat* means, as well as other Omega traits—but we'll broach those topics later.

When Alina is ready.

For now, she can enjoy Reaper's *treat.*

And I'll focus on the Monster City Queen.

CHAPTER SIXTEEN
ALINA

Strawberry cupcakes are amazing.

It took me a while to finally eat the one Reaper brought me this morning, but once I did, I became *obsessed*.

I've now had four of them.

Four cupcakes.

All of them brought to me by a grinning Reaper.

While he might be a bit terrifying, he's also kind of… sweet.

He's lounging on the floor now with his arms tucked behind his head and his long legs crossed at the ankles, his eyes closed. He muttered something about having a nap in his new bed before lying down, then didn't say anything else.

Flame is in the same chair from earlier.

And Orcus is taking a shower.

It's quiet. We've eaten twice. Talked a little bit more. Admired the view from the windows. And discussed possibly seeing more of the city.

Because apparently the Monster City Queen can't meet with the fae until *next week*.

"She's otherwise indisposed at the moment, sir," Emissary Jones said in the doorway a little over an hour ago.

"Otherwise indisposed when she's the one who requested this meeting?" Flame replied, his incredulity clear in his tone. "Does that mean we're free to go?"

The Emissary cleared his throat. "Our Queen kindly requests patience. She values the opportunity to meet with you and is willing to offer whatever amenities you might require, in an effort to extend your stay."

"And if the *amenity* I require is freedom?" Reaper drawled.

"You're more than welcome to wander the tower—as I believe you've already done several times now—or venture into the city. Our Queen simply asks that you remain within our municipality until your meeting."

"And if we don't want to stay here?" Orcus asked, his arms folded over his chest. He didn't sound upset or even interested, just bored.

"Then I fear the relations between our two dimensions may not remain as amicable as we all might like."

The words vibrated through the room, causing all three men to stare at the Emissary for a long, tense moment. Even Reaper wore a serious expression, one that bordered on intimidating.

But Emissary Jones didn't startle. He simply stood there, clearly waiting for some sort of verdict from the three fae.

"Please thank the Queen for her ongoing hospitality," Orcus finally said. "Perhaps your concierge could provide a map or a list of local activities for us to enjoy during our visit?"

Emissary Jones grinned. "Yes. I definitely think that could be arranged." He bowed then and took his leave.

All three men studied the door for a beat before exchanging glances.

"We need to remain on friendly terms," Orcus said. "There are more Omegas here. I can feel them. We can't leave until we learn more, and we might need to return."

Flame and Reaper nodded, while I sat on the couch—a spot I seem to have claimed—and pondered what that meant.

Some part of me *hated* that Orcus wanted to find the other Omegas. It was a part I didn't understand.

A part that still feels miffed now, an hour *after* the conversation.

Does he want to take these other Omegas as mates?

No. He already said he didn't.

But what if he changes his mind after he finds them?

Who are they? What are they?

Am I really one, too?

The questions all swirl inside my head, making me dizzy.

If I had another cupcake, I would eat it.

Instead, I... stare at the table and continue to volley thoughts back and forth.

"Little panther," Flame murmurs. "Want to go for a walk?"

I blink and glance at him. "What?"

He cants his head toward the suite door. "Want to go explore with me?"

"Us," comes a groggy voice from the floor. "If you're going out, so am I."

"You've been *wooing* her all day with your damn cupcakes and that cappuccino. It's my turn to romance her," Flame tells him, his gaze returning to mine. "If you want to go."

Reaper grumbles something from the floor but doesn't protest.

And I suddenly find myself very interested in Flame's version of *romancing*.

I probably shouldn't entertain it.

But what else am I going to do? Sit here and stew in all my uncertainties?

No. I don't want to think anymore. I just want to do something. Be distracted.

And hey, maybe we'll find a proper map while we're out wandering.

Granted, these fae say they know where Chicago is, and Orcus also promised to find out more about it from the Queen.

Can I trust him? Can I trust any of them?

They haven't given me a reason not to thus far. However, we've really only just met. *But…*

I push to my feet, tired of second-guessing myself and beating up my brain with all these churning thoughts. "Yes," I tell Flame. "I would like to explore."

He smiles. "Excellent." He hops up out of his chair with an elegant grace that I can't replicate. But I join him in standing anyway.

His violet gaze runs over my shirt and jeans—an outfit I changed into earlier, after my second cupcake—and nods. "Just need some shoes. Let me grab them."

He disappears into the bedroom, presumably heading toward the closet.

"Are you sure you don't want to join me for a nap instead?" Reaper asks, gazing up at me from the floor. "Maybe a little cuddle in the bed?"

"If you want to sleep in there, you can," I tell him.

His silver-blue irises sparkle. "Yeah? You don't mind?"

Something about the way he says that seems like it

might be a trap. But I really don't see any problem with him resting in there. "No, I don't mind."

He grins. "Beautiful. Thank you."

He disappears before I can respond to his obvious excitement, his propensity for teleporting about no longer fazing me very much. Primarily because he seems to do it every few minutes.

I'm partly hoping he'll return with another cupcake.

But Flame is who I see next, a pair of boots in his hands. He holds them out for me. "Let me know if these don't fit and we'll call the concierge again."

I take the boots and see some socks tucked inside. Something about that makes my lips curl. Maybe because it's a thoughtful addition.

Sitting down again, I slip the items onto my feet while Flame watches, his gaze on my hands. Goose bumps prickle the back of my neck, his observation stirring something inside me.

It's not a sexual look but a protective one. Like he's making sure the boots don't harm me.

When I'm finished, his eyes slowly travel up my body to my face, a flicker of black overtaking the purple irises. It's there and gone so fast that I almost think I imagined it.

"Shall we?" he asks, a smile in his voice.

My lips curl in response, a flutter of excitement touching my chest. It's accompanied by a sensation of relief, too. *I'm not trapped. I'm free to leave.*

Something about that is instantly gratifying. The fae haven't exactly made me feel like a prisoner, and they've certainly seen to my every comfort, but deep down, I've felt a little caged in.

Because I've spent the last week being told what to do, where to go, and how to dress.

And I was sort of forced to come here, too. Not by the fae, but by the Emissary.

Flame holds out a hand, which I accept, and he leads me out of the room to the elevator.

It's not until we're downstairs and nearing the exit that I finally say, "Don't we need a map?" The Emissary said he would provide us with one, but we haven't received it yet.

"Nah. This might be a different version of the city I know, but the street layout seems to be similar to this area in our Human Realm." He holds open the door for me, a pair of dimples flashing in his cheeks. "Besides, getting lost might be kind of fun."

I'm not sure I agree with his definition of *fun*, but his enjoyment is infectious.

So I reply with a small smile and step through the door. "Let's go get lost."

CHAPTER SEVENTEEN
ALINA

FLAME'S FINGERS link with mine, his palm warm as we walk. It's a lot less crowded than last night, the streets practically vacant.

Which reminds me of what this place looked like when I first arrived.

On our way to the tower before, I saw several humans and what I assumed were monsters—although, most of them looked human—talking and walking around. I'd been in a bit of a daze, though, my mind consumed by the fae.

Still, everything had seemed almost normal.

Except for the outfits.

But now, it's like when I was wandering with Bartholomew and Miranda, searching for a place to hide.

Did they survive? I wonder, a slight chill swirling down my spine despite the warm air. *Were they taken by monsters?*

"Alina?" Flame asks, pausing beside me, his head tilting to the side. "If this is making you uncomfortable, we can go back."

I swallow and look up at him. "I, no. I'm okay. I... I

was just thinking about two of the others I came here with. I'm wondering if they're okay."

He studies me, then dips his chin in acknowledgment. "I imagine it's pretty strange for you, all of this." He waves around the city with his free hand. "If I'm honest, it's strange to me, too."

"It is?"

He nods again. "Yeah. This does not happen in our world." He pauses, considering that for a moment. "Well, actually, a version of it is happening in our realm right now. But it's quite different, and it involves other fae, not humans."

His world sounds interesting. "So your world doesn't require Offerings?"

He snorts. "No. Not mortal Offerings, anyway. There are definitely a few fae realms with unique gifting practices, and I know some of the Mythos Fae like a variety of tributes, but it's nothing like this. Our humans don't even know fae exist."

Reaper had said as much earlier. "But your kind visits the humans?" I ask, clarifying.

"In secret," he says. "And there are a few fae who actually live among them, but the humans have no idea."

"However, you live in the Netherworld." That's the realm Orcus mentioned, the name one I committed to memory. "What's it like there?"

"It's very different from this," he says, glancing at the metal architecture as we resume our walk. "We don't have skyscrapers or greenery like Monster City. Instead, it's a bit darker. No sun. Only three moons that cycle around a thirty-six-hour clock, not a twenty-four-hour one. The sky is always clear. Lots of stars."

My brow crinkles. "No sun?"

"No sun," he echoes.

"How do you grow food?" I wonder.

"We don't. Our gargoyles conjure it." He waggles his brows at me. "They're crafty little creatures who are born in our kingdom, but they come and go as they please. However, they pay homage to their birthright by bringing back food. Pretty sure Reaper was raised by them rather than proper parents."

That last part seems to be uttered in humor.

But I'm too stuck on the word *gargoyles* to think about Reaper being raised by them. The term makes me shiver. "Are gargoyles monsters?" I ask.

Flame laughs, his hand squeezing mine. "No, little panther. Definitely not. They're, like, two feet tall, and they're harmless." He pauses for a moment. "Well, maybe not *harmless*. They're made of stone. Getting stepped on by one would suck."

"And they bring you food?"

"Yep. They stock our shelves. It's basically their way of giving us gifts." He shrugs. "We don't need food the way some fae do, so it's a treat more than a requirement."

"What about humans in your kingdom?" I wonder aloud. "Other mates?"

"We don't have humans in the Netherworld," he tells me. "Only other fae and creatures like the gargoyles."

"Oh." My brow furrows. "So when you go back…" I trail off, swallowing. I'd almost said something foolish. *So when you go back, what happens to me?*

A ridiculous thought.

I don't plan to go back with them. Heck, I don't even *want* to go back with them.

Not that it matters, anyway. They're not planning on leaving anytime soon. Orcus said there are other Omegas in this world. He insinuated that they intend to stay here and hunt them all.

But what happens when they're done? a small part of me whispers.

Does it matter?

I'll be in Chicago by then, right?

"When we go back," Flame says softly, his hand squeezing mine again. "We'll figure something out."

I blink at him, but he's staring straight ahead, his focus on something toward the end of our street. I'm about to ask what he means by *figuring something out*, when his mouth curls into a stunning smile, his excitement palpable.

"Oh, fuck, this is amazing," he says, beaming. "I was wondering what Central Park would look like in this realm, but I would never have guessed this." His steps quicken, causing me to almost jog along beside him. "It's like a jungle."

My eyes widen as the *jungle* comes into better view, the trees stretching impossibly high into the sky. "Wow," I breathe, gaping at them. "I… I didn't know trees grew like this." Back home, they were all tall, but they were nothing like this. I can't even see where they *end*.

"They don't do this in the Human Realm in our dimension. This has to be influenced by magic or something." He looks around as though trying to find the source. "Are you okay with exploring a little more?" he asks, glancing at me.

I nod. "Yeah." I wouldn't mind seeing these trees up close.

His smile is infectious again as he pulls me toward what appears to be an entrance carved into the middle of a massive tree trunk.

Wow, I think, studying the smooth wood inside as we pass through it. *This is… almost magical.*

Or maybe *unnatural* is the better term.

Except, everything around us feels dreamy. It's stunning. Green. *Alive*.

There are flowers inside, too. All of them decorating the colossal giants around them, the colors a vibrant splash against the green and brown.

Colors I can see because of the twinkling lights all around, I realize, noting the fluttering flickers dancing in the air. *Are they bugs? Or something else?*

None of them come close enough for me to see, their focus seeming to be on highlighting the flowers.

"This place is giving me Midnight Fae vibes, only it's a lot more colorful," he murmurs. "My animal is begging me to set him free and go for a run."

His exhilaration has me smiling right along with him. This all feels like a fantasy. Unreal. Like I'm dreaming.

Maybe I am.

He's a gorgeous fae, holding my hand, pulling me into this alluring, otherworldly jungle of trees and exotic flowers.

In the middle of a city.

But he said something about a park. "Central Park?" I repeat, thinking out loud. "They have this in your world?"

He chuckles. "No. Well, yes. They have Central Park. But it's nothing compared to this. It's a beautiful green space in the middle of New York City. However, this is like the Amazon, only even more intense." He tilts his head back, his eyes falling closed. "And it smells amazing."

I try to scent whatever it is he's enjoying, but all I pick up on is the heady aroma of nature—trees, flowers, *fresh air.*

That last bit makes me frown a little.

Because it reminds me of Orcus.

I glance behind me, like I expect him to be there. The

scent increases just a little as I do it, except I don't see him. And he doesn't exactly seem like the type to hide.

"Everything okay?" Flame asks.

"I…" I return my focus to him. "I thought I sensed Orcus."

Flame's lips twitched. "Yeah, you probably can. Omegas and Alphas are linked like that, typically through scent." He releases my hand to stretch his arms over his head, causing his shirt to ride up a little. "When we mate, you'll be able to sense me, too. And we'll be able to talk via our minds."

My eyebrows lift. *When we mate?*

But he doesn't seem to notice my reaction, as he's too busy rolling his neck and showing off all that masculine strength. "I'm going to have to come back out here for a run."

That's a much safer topic, I decide, clearing my throat. "Why can't you go on a run right now?" I blurt out, latching on to this conversation so I don't lose myself to my thoughts.

"Because it would require me to undress and shift," he says, shaking out his arms. "And I'd be leaving you alone."

"I could try to jog alongside you?" I offer lamely.

Flame stares at me for a long second, his dimples seeming to deepen. "Really? You would do that for me?"

"I… I would try?" I'm not in great jogging shape, mostly because I wasn't allowed outside for prolonged periods in the village.

My skin was too *fair* for farm work, thus they placed me in the fruit market instead.

I admit that aloud to Flame and add, "They would penalize me with more required entries if I burned my skin. Primarily because lotion was a premium item, not a basic resource item." I clear my throat. "But anyway, yeah, I'll try to keep up with you so you can run."

I also kind of want to see his jaguar.

How does that even work? Does it take time to shift? Do his bones break?

That last thought has my eyes blowing wide. "Wait, is turning into your animal painful?"

I think he was in the middle of saying something because his mouth is slightly open and he looks a little mystified by my random commentary.

But his surprise melts into another handsome smile. "No, sweetheart. It doesn't hurt. Rejecting him is actually more painful than shifting."

"So you're in pain right now?" Because he made it sound like his jaguar was clawing at him to go for a run. And he's clearly *rejecting* that need at the moment.

Flame cocks his head a little. "Well, slightly. But—"

"Then you should shift," I tell him. "Let your jaguar out. I don't mind. I'll try to keep up. It'll be fine." I'll probably fall on my ass and make a complete fool of myself. But I've experienced worse.

Like what Timothy did to my throat yesterday, I think, shivering. *That was definitely worse.*

And I have bruising around my neck to prove it.

Why am I even thinking about that? My mind appears to be everywhere except where it needs to be—which is right here, in this magical jungle with Flame.

"Please shift," I tell him. "I want to see your, uh, cat."

He snorts. "It's a lot bigger than a mere *cat*, Alina."

"Then show me," I dare him, feeling bold despite my babbling idiocy. "Let me see it."

One of his dark brows wings upward. "A challenge?"

I fold my arms. "I'm waiting." I'm not sure where this

boldness is coming from, but I'm thankful for its return. Mostly because I thought this side of me had disappeared over the last week.

However, the part of me who stood up to the Viscount is now challenging the Shifter Fae.

And if the amusement in Flame's expression is anything to go by, he approves.

"All right, little panther," he murmurs, lifting his finger to draw a circle in the air. "Turn around."

My brow furrows. "Why?"

"Because I have to undress to shift." His hand drops to the top of his jeans. "Unless you want to watch?"

Now who is challenging whom? I wonder, swallowing.

"Right." I spin around. Because I am *not* ready to accept that challenge.

Reaper's nude state is still freshly ingrained in my mind. Adding a naked image of Flame to my head would probably make me physically combust.

Or melt.

Or go insane.

Or all of the above.

The sound of a zipper being drawn down causes the hairs to dance along my arms. *He's undressing.* Which, of course, I knew he was going to do. But the realization that all I have to do is turn around to *see* him is…

Well, it's tempting.

Very, very tempting.

What is it about these fae that has my head so lost in the clouds? I've never been like this before. I've always been focused. Goal-oriented. Determined to succeed in whatever I set my mind to.

But with them, I find myself wanting to follow their lead.

To submit in their presence.

To indulge in whatever this burning sensation is that's blossoming between us.

I don't know them.

They're mon… I trail off, unable to complete the thought.

Because they're not monsters. They're fae. And so far, they've been pretty amazing.

They've taken time to explain things to me. They gave me the big bed. They helped me find normal clothes. They've given me food, introduced me to cupcakes, and have said repeatedly that they wouldn't push me into anything.

Yet, all the while, they've made their stance known— they want me.

I don't understand why or how, especially with them barely knowing me, but I'm starting to realize that it's different for them.

They're not human. They… they simply *know*.

And maybe, on some level, I know, too.

Is that why I can smell Orcus, even now?

Why I want to turn around and watch Flame?

Why part of me is hoping Reaper will still be in the big bed when I get back?

I swallow. *Or perhaps—*

A nose bumps my leg, causing me to jump and turn around.

And lay eyes on the most beautiful black animal I've ever seen. "Oh, *wow*," I say, meeting a pair of bright green eyes. Not purple. Not black. But cat-green.

I've seen village cats before.

But they were nothing compared to this giant, masculine beast.

His sleek coat resembles the night, his paws massive and attached to long, strong legs.

He bumps me with his nose again, a soft purr emanating from him.

Like Orcus's rumble.

Only, Flame released a similar sound, too. While carrying me last night.

Because he's a black jaguar.

His animal had been purring for me then.

Just like he's purring for me now.

I squat before him, wanting to see him better. And he instantly rubs his cheek against mine, his eyes closing with the movement.

A giggle escapes me, his soft fur a nice texture against my skin. It's also so unexpected, so *unbelievable*, that I can't help but laugh again.

For over two decades, I've had nightmares of monsters taking brides. And never, in a single visual, have I pictured *this*—a beautiful jaguar nuzzling me.

It was always grotesque beings with sharp claws and fang-like teeth.

Granted, Flame has both of those traits, but they're more majestic on him. More... alluring.

I slowly reach forward to scratch his ears, earning me an even deeper rumble from his chest. He leans into my touch, his eyes closing again as we both lose ourselves to the moment.

"You're very handsome," I tell him softly.

He preens in response, bumping me again. Then he goes back onto his haunches and starts stretching. I watch his massive paws, noticing the way his sharp talons dig into the earth. Then he stands again and shakes his fur out. With a low growl, he turns toward the trees and takes a few steps.

When I don't follow, he glances back at me expectantly.

Right. I said I would jog with him.

Swallowing, I pick up his clothes and shoes from the ground—something that just seems natural to do—and start after him.

CHAPTER EIGHTEEN
FLAME

MY JAGUAR PURRS WITH *WANT*. He wants to bite his intended mate, make her ours, then pin her to the earth and *claim* her.

Most Shifter Fae mate other Shifter Fae.

But I'm a half-breed.

And my jaguar doesn't seem to care at all that Alina is a human. He's addicted to her sweet scent, that delectable mix of strawberries and cream, a dessert we both long to taste.

She's walking alongside my beast, my clothes tucked under one arm while her opposite hand brushes my coat. My jaguar practically melts beneath her fingertips, each stroke a hypnotic caress that soothes his chaotic energy and calms my inner fire.

I feel at peace.

Like I've finally found the rest of my soul.

She's ours, I think, sure of it. She may be human, but there's something in her that's decidedly fae. Whether that's her Omega soul or something else entirely, I don't know. But it's there.

This woman was destined to be ours.

My jaguar wants to sink his canines into her soft flesh and leave behind his mark.

But I hold him back.

She's not ready to accept us yet.

And that's okay.

I'll take her gentle strokes and admiring looks for now.

We walk for at least an hour, her hand on me most of the time. She doesn't comment on carrying my clothes, just holds them like it's the most natural thing in the world.

When we reach a particularly large tree, my animal pauses and I know what he intends to do a split second before he does it.

He leaps onto a branch, his tail swishing with victory as all four paws connect where he expected. Then he practically smirks in response to Alina's startled yelp. Because that yelp is now paired with a look of awe.

Show-off, I tell him.

He preens again, pleased with impressing his chosen mate.

Alina giggles, the sound one I commit to memory. It's the second time she's made that sound tonight, and each occurrence has made me feel like a king.

I love that she's happy. No sign of fear. No sign of stress. Just... pleased with our walk. With *me.*

"Well, if you're going to rest up there, then I'll just rest down here," she says, picking a spot beside the tree trunk to drop my clothes before plopping down beside them.

She leans back against the bark, her legs stretched out and crossed at the ankles.

"This is perfect," she breathes, seemingly pleased. "I only wish I had a book or something."

My animal's ears twitch at that. *A book?* I would ask her if we were mentally linked. *What do you like to read?*

I'm guessing this realm hasn't offered her much in the way of literature.

From what Orcus observed, the humans are still educated—primarily to appease potential supernatural mates—and the academic levels vary by village.

I'm not sure how many villages he found while peeping about the world, but it was enough for him to notice trends. Such as teaching habits amongst the humans.

Alina closes her eyes, her face the picture of peace.

My animal watches her closely, his tail lazily swaying off the branch while he rests his big head on his front paws.

Minutes pass and her breathing evens out, indicating that she's fallen asleep.

It's quick. But it suggests she needs the rest. I'll give her a few more minutes to fall into a deeper sleep, then I'll jump down, shift, and carry her home. She can nap against my chest.

My cat remains alert, observing our little panther while she rests.

The rise and fall of her chest is hypnotic, and the way the breeze teases her long, dark hair has my jaguar itching to play with her silky strands.

It's perfect.

A beautiful moment in time.

I sigh inside, content.

This is—

My jaguar stills, his ears straining as the whisper of footsteps catches our attention. Our nose twitches, a familiar scent making my beast growl as we pounce onto the ground.

Strigoi.

It should be impossible. The portal to the Netherworld closed last night, and Strigoi were not on the invitation list.

Yet, I know that smell. They reek of the Morpheus Realm.

It's a metallic fragrance, one denoting their vampire nature. Only, these are no ordinary vampires. They feed on *dreams*.

Like the dreams of my *mate*.

My beast growls again, louder now, and prowls forward. I shift as we walk, needing my voice. By the time I reach the path they're hunting on, I'm back in my human form.

Both men freeze the moment they see me, their eyes widening in shock.

Because yeah, they recognize me.

Just like I recognize *them*. "What the fuck are you two doing here?" I demand.

Sebastian Sanguinis and Cage Van Drakken.

Fuck, if Lucifer catches wind of this, he's going to lose his Godsdamn mind. These two are rival Strigoi heirs, both of them coming from vastly different royal families.

Royal families that *hate* each other. Primarily because they're both eligible for the same throne—the Strigoi King's throne. Technically, Sabre is next in line. But Cage could challenge him for it. And from what I've heard, the Van Drakken family is urging him to do so.

Like vampires, Strigoi are extremely dedicated to their family covens. Consorting with outsiders is frowned upon.

Yet here they are, waltzing hand in hand down the path.

Well, they were waltzing.

Now they're just frozen and gaping at me.

"Flame?" Sebastian—who prefers to be called *Sabre*—says, blinking at me like I might not be real. Considering they live and feed off dreams, it's possible he thinks he's lost in one.

But that dream is about to become a nightmare.

Because Orcus is going to fucking kill these guys.

"What the fuck are you doing here?" I repeat. "*How* are you even here? Maliki should have closed the portal by now." And we were well beyond Monsters Night hours at this point, too. Which is why the streets were so clear before.

"Flame?" Alina calls, causing both men to glance over my shoulder toward the female I now sense behind me. "What's...?" She trails off. Probably because she sees the two intimidating men on the path.

They're both tall, broad-shouldered, and aristocratic in nature. But the hint of red flickering in their eyes reveals the predators inside, especially as they study her now.

Because they were just fucking dreamwalking in her head.

"Keep looking at her," I dare them. "See what happens."

Sabre is the first to glance away, his dark eyes meeting mine. The red is entirely gone now, confirming he's no longer linked to the dream plane.

Good.

Because if he spent another minute there, I might kill him. Mainly because my mate is probably the one who lured him there.

"Apologies, Flame," he says. "We didn't realize she was yours."

Cage clears his throat, his focus shifting toward me as well. "Yes, sorry. We... we were just wandering."

"In a realm you have no business being in," I say, my tone a show of dominance. Not because I have any royal status to stand on, but because I represent a very different level of power. Godlike power.

Sabre and Cage are high enough in rank to know that Orcus is Hades's primary enforcer.

Just as they both know Reaper and I are Orcus's seconds-in-command.

"How did you get through the portal?" Maliki was only supposed to let Ghouls through. But Ghouls and Strigoi both share the Morpheus Kingdom, so I suppose word of the portal could have spread to a few Strigoi, which means there might be more of them meandering about.

Fuck.

This is a mess.

"Maliki helped us escape," Sabre says, his spine straightening. "He told us about the portal and offered us a way out. We took it."

My eyebrows wing upward. "He told you about the portal?"

Sabre nods. "He knew we've been searching for a way to escape our fates and told us about this realm. Said how the portal would only be open for an hour or two and that it would likely be closed off and never used again."

"Clearly, he was wrong," Cage drawls.

"Clearly, he didn't tell you the actual purpose of the portal," I correct. Which was to provide a cover for our mission here in this realm. At least Maliki did that right. But he shouldn't have let these two Strigoi Princes *escape* into this world. "You can't stay here."

Sabre releases Cage's hand and folds his arms. "That's not what the Queen's Emissary said."

"Jones?" I ask, already wary about where this conversation is headed.

"No. Emissary Sheila." Sabre's brow furrows. "Who's Jones?"

"No one that matters," I mutter, running my fingers

through my hair. "Let me guess, though—you're staying at the Queen's tower?"

Cage nods. "They gave us a suite. She wants to meet with us next week. Until then, they're providing everything we need, including sustenance."

Great, I think. *This is... just fucking great.*

But it's honestly not my problem to deal with. Orcus will have to tell Hades, and Hades will talk to his cousin Morpheus. And they'll figure out how to handle these two rebel Princes.

Princes who are supposed to hate each other, I think, eyeing their closeness. *Yet that's clearly a lie.*

I shake my head and turn toward Alina, saying, "I need to get you back to the tower."

Only, she doesn't appear to hear me at all.

Because her gaze is on my abdomen.

Then it slowly lowers to my pierced cock.

Her eyes widen.

Her lips part.

And even in the dark, I can see the blush coloring her cheeks.

Despite the situation, I smile. Because that look on her face is worthy of a responding grin.

She's intimidated, probably by the bulb she can see near my base. Or perhaps by the piercings, too. Or maybe the size. Or all of the above.

But a strong sense of interest underlines that intimidation, and that interest is something I can work with.

I saunter toward her, forgetting the Strigoi at my back, and press two of my fingers to her chin to draw her gaze up to mine. "You can touch it later," I tell her softly. "After we get back to the tower."

She swallows. "I... I didn't... I don't... I mean... I..."

She snaps her mouth shut, her pupils fully dilated as she gapes up at me.

"You did," I tell her. "You do. And it's fine. I want you to touch me. Just not in front of these two assholes. They've already seen enough of you."

Cage and Sabre both snort.

I ignore them and lean down to press a kiss to Alina's fiery cheek. "I'm going to go grab my clothes," I tell her. "If one of them comes near you, knee them in the balls."

While I can't see them, I sense both Cage and Sabre rolling their eyes. They might have snuck into this realm, but they're both honorable men. They won't harm Alina in any way. And not just because she's mine, but because she hasn't consented.

Still, they are in for a world of pain when their God finds out about their little adventure.

Or maybe Morpheus won't care at all.

He's often lost to his land of dreams, too deep in his mind to care what his worshippers are doing in his kingdom. He leaves all the political management to the *Kings*, just like Hades does.

And those Kings report to Lucifer, the King of the Hell Fae Realm.

But the Gods are the ones who bestow gifts upon the kingdoms, basically functioning as an entity for everyone to pray to.

It's a different kind of governance.

One Cage and Sabre should probably fear, considering they've just earned their Almighty's judgment.

Not my problem, I tell myself again as I step around Alina to go find my clothes by the tree.

When I return to her, she still hasn't moved. But she's staring at the Strigoi with interest. They are obediently not looking back at her, something that appeases both me and my beast.

Except I don't like the way our little panther is admiring them. "They won't be joining our mate-circle, Alina," I tell her.

She blinks away from them to look at me. "What?"

"I know they're beautiful, but you're going to be too busy with me, Orcus, and Reaper to even think about them." I palm her cheek. "I promise the three of us will do everything in our power to be enough. To make you *ours*, not theirs or anyone else's."

She licks her lips, her gaze darting down my body in a brief glance before flicking back up to my face. "Okay," she says, not bothering to fight my claim.

I'm very aware that I'm being possessive.

Fortunately, she doesn't seem to mind.

Pleased, I kiss her other cheek, then thread our fingers together again. "Good girl," I whisper against her ear. "Thank you for exploring with me."

She gives me a small smile. "I enjoyed it."

"I did, too," I tell her, giving her hand a squeeze. Then I face the two Strigoi. "Follow us." It's not a request but a demand. "Orcus is going to want to talk to you."

CHAPTER NINETEEN
ALINA

Dreamwalkers, I think, shivering.

That's what the two men in our suite last night were.

Strigoi is the formal name for their kind.

They were intimidating, handsome, and almost regal in nature. Quite different from Reaper and Flame, but somewhat similar to Orcus. Only, I could tell Orcus was the dominant one in the room, and not just because of his impressive size.

The Strigoi had bowed to him the moment they laid eyes on him in the suite, clearly recognizing him as the superior being.

But then the three of them had spoken as though they existed on a similar level of status.

It was fascinating to observe, at least while I remained to hear their conversation. But when discussions turned to something about *Hell Fae Bride Trials*, I excused myself to rest.

From what little I gathered, the two Strigoi were being forced to compete for brides they had no interest in taking. Thus, it seems they didn't venture into this realm to select mates during Monsters Night either. They only came here to escape their fates at home.

I could understand that to an extent.

They felt they had no other choice.

I also felt that way about coming to Monster City, only for very different reasons.

And things here have not turned out the way I expected them to. Not in any way, shape, or form.

I shiver, my mind instantly drifting to picture Flame's *form*.

Followed by Reaper's *form*.

My thighs clench, my insides turning to molten lava. Because *holy fae*, they're stunning. Flame wasn't even aroused, yet his size was... impressive. And so very unique.

Did Reaper have a bulb at the base? I wonder, trying to picture his long length. His hand kept stroking it, keeping me from ogling every inch at once. But I don't remember there being any jewelry or rounded knots.

Flame, however, had both.

It had taken me a moment to understand *what* I was seeing in his shaft, the glint of metal unexpected. But then I realized it was a bar. Right through his dick.

Plus a ring.

I wanted to ask him why he decorated himself in that way, but I couldn't form the words. There also hadn't been an appropriate time. The minute we returned, Orcus, Reaper, and Flame engaged in deep conversation with the Strigoi, their discussions all about their home world.

Maybe I can ask today, I think.

"You can touch it later," Flame told me. "When we're back at the tower."

Well, we're back at the tower now, I want to tell him.

Only, he's nowhere near me.

I'm in this big bed alone again, while the guys sleep in the other room.

Biting my lower lip, I consider what to do.

Can I wake Flame? Ask my questions?

But how would I even start?

So, about your dick...

I almost laugh.

Except just the thought of his *dick* has me squirming again in the bed. A frustrated growl escapes me as I squeeze my legs together, my thighs slick with *need*.

I'm not wearing panties again. Primarily because the ones the concierge sent up are practically lace, which makes them nonfunctional.

Besides, the shirt I'm wearing hits just above my knees.

Only it's ridden up a little now.

Probably from all my writhing in the bed.

I just can't help it. These fae have me all worked up.

And they've been so *kind* to me.

I never anticipated any of this, especially not my attraction to them. But it's growing stronger every minute we're together.

Is this the Omega stuff Orcus was talking about?

Everything feels so different now. So *hot*.

I bury my face in my pillow and groan, my hand curling into a fist to keep from touching myself.

"You know, when you invited me to sleep in this bed with you, I had no idea you were such a fidget," a deep voice murmurs from behind me.

I freeze. "Reaper?"

A palm finds my hip, a hot chest suddenly meeting my back. "Yes, pet?"

Oh, fae. I didn't realize he was in here with me. "I thought you were out in the living area."

He grunts softly, his thumb drawing a lazy circle

against my shirt. "After being invited to sleep in here with you? Like there was ever a choice."

"I... I didn't invite..." I trail off, recalling our conversation before my walk with Flame last night.

I told Reaper he could sleep in here.

He asked if I was sure, and I had an inkling then that he was asking me something else. Something nefarious.

Yet I told him I was sure anyway.

So now... now he's in bed with me.

And from what I can feel, he's not wearing a lot of clothes, either.

"Do you want me to go?" he asks softly, his lips near the back of my neck.

I swallow, unable to answer.

Because I don't know what I want anymore.

But I like the way his breath feels against my nape. And I really like how hard he feels against my back.

His fingertips flutter down my thigh to the edge of my shirt. "Or maybe you would like my help?" he offers, his touch causing goose bumps to pebble along my arms and legs.

He pauses, like he's waiting for me to stop him.

When I don't, he starts to venture up under the fabric, the heat of his fingers a brand against my bare skin.

"Alina," he exhales, his mouth almost touching my neck. He shifts a little to run his nose along my throat, hovering over my throbbing pulse. "Is your heart racing out of fear or arousal?"

I swallow again, my thighs tensing. "Both," I admit.

"Hmm," he hums, placing a gentle kiss against my sensitive skin. "An intoxicating combination with your strawberry sweetness."

I'm not sure what that means.

And in the next instant, I'm too distracted to care.

Because his knuckles just brushed my damp sex.

"No panties?" he says, his voice deepening with the words. "Fuck, pet. That just makes me want to reward you more."

Reward? I repeat to myself as his knuckles whisper across my sensitive flesh once more.

"You're so wet," he groans, his mouth against my neck. "What were you thinking about, naughty girl?" He nibbles my pulse as his touch ventures higher to my recently waxed mound.

That had been part of my grooming preparations for Monsters Night. I hadn't understood it at the time. But with how sensitive everything is now, I'm starting to see the benefit of being bare down there.

"Talk to me, Alina." His words are a hot kiss to my senses. "I want consent before I touch you."

You're already touching me, I want to point out.

But I don't.

I *can't*.

Because I'm too lost to the heat blossoming between my thighs.

His featherlight strokes are so different from my own, his teasing caress somehow bolder. More enticing. More *intense*.

Yet he's barely done anything at all. Just a few brushes here and there, and now he's simply resting his palm against my mound. Unmoving. Tempting. *Hot*.

"Reaper." His name is barely audible, my throat seeming to close before I'm able to say more.

"Mmm, my name sounds good in that breathy tone," he murmurs. "Say it again, pet. Say it and tell me what you want."

I... I don't know what I want.

No one has ever touched me like this.

LEXI C. FOSS

I've only ever been alone.

What does he want me to say? What should I ask him to do?

"I…" I swallow, my nerves fraying at the ends. His palm is a brand against my mound, his fingertips so close to where I need them. *Lower.* "Please go lower, Reaper." The request feels foreign on my tongue, yet right. "More, please. Touch me… more."

Fae, I don't even know what I'm saying. But… but I *need* this. Him. His fingers. His—

A moan slips from my mouth as his fingertip caresses the sensitive bundle of nerves at the top of my sex. *My clit,* I think, familiar with the term from an anatomy class. I'm also familiar with how it feels.

But this is…

This is sooo much better.

It's electric.

It's fire.

It's intensity personified.

"Is this what you need, pet?" he asks against my ear.

"Yes," I hiss, pushing into his hand. "*Fae,* yes…" I'm not sure when I started saying *fae* instead of *monster,* but I don't care.

All that matters is Reaper's touch. His finger gliding through my damp folds. His palm against my clit.

Ohhh…

The sounds escaping me are ones I've never heard before. But I can't stop. Everything is burning. My insides. My thighs. My *core.*

"Fuck, you're so tight," Reaper says as his finger slides into me. "We're going to have to prepare you to properly take us, pet." He kisses my thundering pulse. "Don't worry. I know just what to do."

His hand moves against me, sending jolts of pleasure

216

up my spine. I twist and push and ride the waves of rapture overtaking my body. It's growing. Mounting. Turning into an eruption that's borderline frightening.

A scream rips from my throat as the climax hits, my legs shaking in response as my lower half *burns*. It's so damn hot. So incredibly powerful. So electrifying.

I feel *alive*.

Yet I can hardly breathe.

And Reaper… he's still touching me. Stroking me. Inside and out.

I grab his wrist.

But he doesn't release me.

It's maddening. I can't… It's too sensitive. It's…

I gasp, my orgasm seeming to tumble into a second as Reaper masterfully plays my body.

All with one hand.

Two fingers.

His thumb.

Fae…

His name leaves me on another scream, my back arching as I lose myself to this dark oblivion. I'm panting. I'm shaking. I'm *crying*.

But I don't want it to stop.

I want to live in this blissful state for eternity. It's overwhelming in the best way. And it's so much better than being *alone*.

Reaper's caress is deeper. His fingers are more skilled. And the pressure he applies to my sensitive bud is *everything*.

"One more, pet," he says, his teeth dragging across my earlobe. "I need you to give me one more."

I don't know what he means.

I'm still coming.

I haven't stopped.

Or maybe I have and I just can't feel any semblance of sanity anymore.

Whatever it is, I'm lost to it.

My nails dig into his wrist as my hips press back into his. A shudder works through me. *He's so hard. So big. And right there.*

I'm tempted to reach out and touch him, to feel the cock I saw yesterday in that shower.

But Reaper does something to my clit that has me seeing stars.

Did he just pinch me? I marvel.

It hurt for a split second before rapturous energy stole my breath.

And now… now I'm flying.

All while Reaper murmurs praise in my ear.

"That's it, beautiful."

"You're doing so well."

"Keep riding my hand."

"Just like that, pet."

"Fuck, you're amazing."

"I'm keeping you forever."

I shiver, that last statement sounding like a dream and a threat all wrapped up in a seductive male voice.

Warmth bleeds through me, my chest aching from the sensual onslaught.

I need to breathe.

To stretch my tingly limbs.

To fall into a deep slumber.

But just as my eyes close, I feel Reaper's fingers against my lips, his touch wet as he paints my mouth.

My eyes fly open. *Is he…?*

"Taste yourself," he whispers, confirming my suspicions as he pushes his fingers inside to touch my tongue.

I tremble, the sinful flavor one I've never indulged in.

"Describe it to me," he demands. "Tell me what your pussy tastes like, pet."

I quiver, his wicked request doing something to me.

I want to obey him.

And more, I want to *entice* him.

Return the favor of his words with sensual ones of my own.

I suck his fingers deeper into my mouth and twirl my tongue around the tips, a soft groan rumbling inside me. Then I slowly release him and tilt my head so I can see him from the corner of my eye.

It's so early that the sun hasn't risen yet.

But his silver-blue irises are practically glittering in the dark.

"Sweet," I tell him softly. "I taste sweet. Like the strawberry cupcakes. But there's a subtle hint of something tangy, too."

He grins. "A perfect treat." He catches my chin before I can react and pulls me into a kiss.

My back is still to his front, but he's balancing on his elbow and leaning over me so I'm not straining my neck.

Which is a good thing, as this is my first kiss. Maybe he knows that. Maybe he doesn't. Regardless, he's making sure I enjoy it.

He doesn't rush. He simply presses his lips to mine for a long, sensual moment.

Then his tongue gently slips into my mouth to tentatively deepen our embrace.

I shiver, goose bumps dancing along my nape.

Because I can feel his restraint. It's written into the hard lines of his torso and the taut muscles pressing up against me.

His body resembles granite.

Inflexible and stiff.

Yet he's also hot. *Like lava rock.*

His grip on my chin disappears, his fingers traveling to lock in my hair as he pulls me even tighter against him.

His kiss is hungrier now, his tongue sliding deeper into my mouth as he silently demands that I accept this new pace.

I learn from his movements, mimic them as I can, and allow him to guide me into this erotic dance.

It feels good. It feels *right.*

Like the pleasure below, I never want it to end.

Alas, after what feels like hours of passion, Reaper pulls back, his gaze catching mine. "You're right, pet. You do taste like strawberry cupcakes."

He brushes his lips against mine again, leaving me eager for more.

"I can't wait to dine between your thighs, Alina. It'll be fucking divine." He kisses the edge of my mouth. "But you're going to need something to eat before we try that. Because once I start, I won't stop until you pass out. And even then, I'll probably keep going just so I can watch you come again the moment you regain consciousness."

My eyes widen.

I'm not sure if that sounds glorious or terrifying.

"Stay right here, pet. I'll go grab your reward for being such a good girl for me."

I blink at him. "The orgasms weren't my reward?"

He chuckles. "No, darling. Those orgasms were for me. The cupcakes will be for you."

I'm not given a chance to react to that.

Because in the next instant, he's gone.

CHAPTER TWENTY
ORCUS

I SIT across from my brother in his lair, my ankle propped up on my opposite knee. His long fingers are steepled on his massive desk, his dark eyes inflamed with hope. "An Omega."

That's all he says.

But it's also all he needs to say.

"Yeah," I confirm. "An Omega."

He swallows, his usual stoicism melting in the face of this information.

I came here to tell him about the Strigoi Princes running around the alternate reality. However, our conversation quickly evolved when Hades picked up on Alina's scent.

The Strigoi were a minor announcement—a pesky little nuisance, really—compared to my discovery.

"You're absolutely certain?" he presses.

"You scented her on me before I even had a chance to mention it," I point out. "But..." My jaw clenches, some part of me hating that I have to express doubt about the situation.

Alas, my position requires me to be thorough.

And to be thorough, I have to voice my concerns.

"She's mortal," I tell him.

He frowns. "That's impossible."

"I know." I clear my throat. "But her scent and her soul…" I don't need to finish that statement. Hades understands.

Alina is broadcasting herself as an Omega.

"However, there are some genetic manipulations going on in this dimension," I continue, needing to tell him everything. "The humans have worked for over three centuries to create perfect mates for their Monsters Night."

While I don't know much—as a result of not meeting the Monster City Queen yet—I share what I've learned based on observations, as well as what I've sensed within the dimension itself.

By the time I'm finished, Hades appears less enthused. "So it's probably a manufactured scent," he concludes, referring to Alina.

"Maybe," I admit. "However, my Alpha soul doesn't think so."

He studies me for a long moment. "Tread carefully, brother. I understand your hope. But hope is a dangerous illusion."

My brother isn't wrong.

Hope is like a fucking drug. Just the hint of an Omega essence rendered me obsessed with Alina, making it no coincidence at all that I picked up on her presence in Monster City.

Of course, I already knew she was heading there.

And after observing her on the train, I knew I had to find her.

But there's something about her. Something addictive. Something *special*.

A human with an Omega soul.

"I'm aware of the impossibility of this situation," I acknowledge out loud. "We'll know her true nature if she goes into heat."

When, my Alpha corrects. When *she goes into heat.*

My knot throbs with the thought, my cock more than ready to satisfy the Omega for days—*weeks*—or however long it takes.

I swallow, my throat suddenly dry. "I need to return," I tell Hades. Emissary Jones gave me permission for this visit, the concept of which still rankles my nerves.

Gods don't need permission to do anything.

Yet, I played my part in this political charade and phoned the concierge with the *request* before opening a portal back home.

"Flame and Reaper will be staying behind with Alina, just in case your Queen requires a show of faith that I'll return," I told Emissary Jones.

"Our Queen will appreciate that," he replied.

I thought he was done, ready to hang up the phone.

However, the Emissary continued speaking.

"Typically, portals are only allowed on Monsters Night. But we do have a few beings with clearance to travel at will."

I wasn't sure how he wanted me to respond to that, so I replied with a mere "I see."

"While you do not have that clearance," he went on, "I have authorization to allow this as a one-time courtesy. But do return, sir. Otherwise, our Queen may see your disappearance as a sign that your realm does not wish to cooperate with ours."

With that, he finally hung up the phone.

And I pictured throwing the device at the wall.

Except the *phone* was a translucent screen that hovered above the desk, making it impossible to destroy.

So I took a steadying breath instead, told Reaper and Flame to guard Alina, and left.

"I'll talk to Morpheus about the Strigoi situation," Hades says as I stand. "I want an update again after you talk to this *Monster City Queen*." His eyes narrow with the title. "In all my observations of that realm, I've not seen her, which I now suspect might be purposeful."

I nod, agreeing with that assessment. "Her Emissary mentioned our portal windows, suggesting she knew about us all along."

"So it seems," Hades muses. "I look forward to learning more about her."

"Likewise," I admit. "Along with a great many other things." Such as the genetic manipulation going on in the realm and how that might be altering certain scents. I also want to ask about the Elite City in Chicago for Alina.

And maybe learn why she's so interested in it, or how she even knows about it.

"I'll tell the Strigoi to behave," I tell my brother. "Otherwise, I'll be in touch."

Hades nods. "I'm sure Morpheus will want to have a word with them." He considers for a moment. "Or not." He shrugs. "Regardless, not my problem. But I will be talking to Maliki about it."

The way my brother's eyes darken with that last statement says he's already planning out exactly how he intends to handle that particular conversation.

If the slight smile taunting his lips is anything to go by, he's going to enjoy it.

Poor Maliki, I think. According to my brother, the Death Fae is currently in Lucifer's custody—which was to be expected for creating an illegal portal in the Netherworld. But Hades fully anticipates Maliki to be released back to him for punishment soon.

Which is likely what my brother will enjoy.

Fortunately for the Death Fae, he likes pain.

"Speak soon," I say to Hades before stepping out of his office and teleporting to an old dungeon in the Mythos Fae Realm.

I reentered my reality here earlier, just in case anyone attempted to follow me. Not that I think anyone could, but the new dimension is still an unknown entity. Best to trap any unexpected guests here than to lead them straight to my brother's lair.

Besides, this realm is out of Lucifer's jurisdiction, making it impossible for him to feel the manifestation magic used to create a portal big enough for me to walk through. Little portholes didn't require enough energy for the Hell Fae King to sense.

Alas, I can't fit through a porthole.

I suppose, technically, I could have just come here initially to create a connection to the other dimension rather than go under the cover of Monsters Night. However, venturing into a new world—especially an alternate universe—came with a myriad of potential consequences.

Exploring and testing the magical limits of the unknown beneath the veil of an accepted practice—like opening portals on Monsters Night—made the most sense.

Of course, I'm not done testing those limits yet.

Hence the reason I'm creating a portal in an old mirror, deep underground in this old crypt-like jail cell.

These haunted catacombs make my skin crawl, primarily because I can feel the old Mythos Fae spirits writing in wait down here, searching for an opportunity to escape.

But they're forever incarcerated underground, punished for their sins and blamed for what happened to our Omegas.

I won't allow them to absorb my power or use me as a vessel. Not that they can reach me anyway. They're all trapped in Pandora's Box—a magically secured prison, guarded by its creator, Ares.

Ignoring the chilly sensation inching up my arms, I call forth the mirrorlike doorway. It opens with ease, my mind and soul already locked into the manifestation energy associated with this particular domain.

I step through the mirror and out into the middle of the living area of the suite, and freeze.

Slick.

My eyes widen, my focus instantly on the bedroom door.

Omega. Slick.

The portal shatters behind me, the glass disappearing before it can hit the floor, and my feet move before my brain can catch up with the motion.

Only for Flame to step right into my path, his expression severe. "Don't. She gave him consent. I heard it."

"What?" I don't understand his words. Why is he stopping me from going to my Omega? She's *wet*. She's *ready*. And *fuck*, is that her *moaning*?

I teleport around Flame, ready to charge in and take what's rightfully mine.

My hand is on the knob when something hard and heavy tackles me to the ground, drawing a growl from my chest. "What the fuck?" I demand, curious about the two-hundred-plus-pound jaguar on top of me.

He snarls in my face.

I snarl back.

And we grapple across the ground as my Omega moans again from behind the door.

I'm going to fucking kill this Shifter Fae if he doesn't let me go to her. She's in need. She's *begging*. My knot pulses in response, ready to fill her. To rut her. To *breed* her.

Mine, my Alpha purrs. *Fucking mine.*

But a pair of jaws around my throat forces me to freeze. Flame has me pinned, his teeth digging into my skin and drawing blood.

"You have a death wish, *half-breed*," I growl at him.

I swear the cat fucking chuckles on top of me.

"Get off of me, Flame."

He doesn't.

And my Omega stops moaning.

My ears strain to hear her, my body so fucking primed that if I could teleport to her without risking my throat, I would. But the damn jaguar's fangs would probably slice me open along the way, turning me into a less-than-handsome sight for my betrothed.

Oh, I'd heal.

However, I doubt my Omega would like the sight of all the blood running down my chest.

"Taste yourself," I hear Reaper say, making my lips curl down.

What?

At first, I think he's talking about my blood.

But then I realize... he's not in the room with us.

He's... he's with *Alina*.

My eyes round.

"Describe it to me," Reaper goes on. "Tell me what your pussy tastes like, pet."

Ohhhh, fuck.

Those words. The vision accompanying them. The realization that he's playing with our Omega. *The sound of her gorgeous acceptance…*

"Sweet," she says, the softness of her voice displaying no signs of disquiet or discontent. She's pleased. *Aroused,* even. "I taste sweet. Like the strawberry cupcakes. But there's a subtle hint of something tangy, too."

I groan, my mouth watering at the description.

I want her slick on my tongue, coating my lips, *drenching* my throat.

And then I want to sink deep into her sweet heat and claim her.

Mark her.

Bite her.

Breed her.

The latter is an instinctive response to finding my Omega after so many millennia of searching. I want her pumped full of my seed, pregnant with the next generation of Mythos Fae, and resting tenderly in an Omega nest filled with children.

I don't even care that some will be Reaper's or Flame's kids, because they'll all have Mythos Fae blood running through their veins.

They'll all be products of *her.*

My Omega. *Our* mate.

Flame slowly eases off me, likely noticing that the fight has fled from my limbs, and returns to his human form. "Your Alpha's an asshole," he says, touching his jaw.

I hadn't even realized I'd hit him.

But I don't apologize.

Mainly because his teeth marks are still in my neck. "The same could be said about your fucking cat," I mutter.

"Call him a *cat* again and see what happens," he dares me.

I snort. But I know better than to taunt his beast. He's a fierce creature, one who could easily bite my head off. Literally.

Fortunately, it would grow back.

Because Mythos Fae can't die.

Hence the prison I just left. Pandora's Box is the only item that can trap a Mythos Fae's essence.

I push up off the floor to a seated position, my gaze returning to the quiet bedroom. Reaper murmurs something to Alina that I don't listen to; I want to give them their privacy.

"She gave consent?" I confirm again.

But of course she did.

While Reaper is a lot of things, he isn't a rapist. He values consent, just like the two of us.

"Eagerly," Flame replies. "She basically begged him to touch her."

"That she did," Reaper murmurs as he appears in the room, wearing a pair of low-slung gray sweatpants. "I'm off to fetch our pet a few cupcakes. Want anything from the kitchen while I'm there? Something strawberry-flavored, perhaps?" He waggles his brows.

Flame flips him off.

I just sigh. "I'll be fine with coffee." Because I haven't slept and could use the caffeine. Not that it would do anything for me physically, but mentally, I would enjoy it.

Reaper just grins like he's won a prize, which I suppose he has, and vanishes.

Flame stares at the door, his dick pointing toward it as though to signal its owner on which direction it would like to go.

I almost tell him to put on a pair of fucking pants, but I see the boxers he shredded in his shift lying a few feet away from him.

He obviously didn't have time to remove them before pouncing on me.

Running my palm over my face, I say, "I'm going to drink some coffee, then talk to the Strigoi." They gave me directions to their room last night. "Go take care of your barb, then see if Alina needs anything."

Flame rolls his head toward me, his violet irises resembling a burning flame. "There will be no *taking care* of this. I'm going to be hard until I finally mount her."

He stands, his movements agile, and bends to grab his shredded shorts.

"But I'll check on her after I find some pants," he adds, glancing around the room.

I watch as he pulls on a pair of jeans, wincing when he does up the zipper. Primarily because I know exactly how he feels right now. My own knot is pulsing against the confines of my pants, demanding release.

And after hearing those delectable sounds from the other room, I doubt my cock will ever be soft again.

Not to mention the lingering scent of slick, I think, inhaling deeply.

It's not as potent as before, but it's still there. Heady and sweet. A beckoning fragrance that dares me to steal a taste.

Soon, I promise my inner Alpha. *Soon.*

CHAPTER TWENTY-ONE
ALINA

I STARE AT THE BED. I have the strangest urge to roll across the mattress, despite my freshly cleaned state. Like I want to absorb the memories Reaper imprinted there and ensure they never leave my mind.

Because *wow*.

He made me feel alive. On fire. Awake in a way I've never been before.

It's strange yet liberating.

I press my palm to the spot on the bed I slept on, the space where Reaper made me fall apart.

I can still smell the aftermath of our time here.

I like it, I decide, smiling as I head toward the closet to find something to wear. Except the moment I enter, a new scent swirls around me. Something decidedly masculine and fresh.

Orcus, I breathe, inhaling deeply and spinning around to find him. Only, he's not there. No one is. Just me and that alluring cologne.

There's a hint of cedar in here, too. *Flame?* I think, dizzy from the combination of fragrances. The mixture of

Flame's and Orcus's essences reminds me of a clear mountain day, of wandering in the woods. I close my eyes, picturing it all in my mind.

Fresh air.

Fir trees.

And a campfire…

That last bit has my nose crinkling. It's the ideal addition, but the scent doesn't come from Flame or Orcus.

It's Reaper, I realize. *Oh, fae…*

Collectively, it's… it's *everything*.

I want to live here, amongst this scent. It's the fragrance of a perfect day.

Bending, I find the sources of the enticing combination and carry it out into the bedroom. It's an unusual desire, but I can't seem to stop myself. I need to pair this alluring cologne with the perfume Reaper and I created on the bed.

So I do.

I just… drop it all on the bed.

Then stare at it.

And frown.

This isn't right at all.

The aroma is fine. It's flawless, in fact. But the organization…

No. It needs… hmm.

I pick up a towel, one that has Flame's scent on it, and set it by the pillows. Then I grab a shirt—*Orcus's*—and carefully lay it over the towel.

Nodding, I snatch up a robe and inhale. *Smoky tendrils. Ash. Campfire.* That's definitely Reaper. I set the fabric on top of the others and knead it all into a wall of sorts along the back of my pillow and the pillow beside mine.

Tapping my chin, I realize something is still missing and glance down at the cotton wrapped around my torso.

I rip it off my body and curl it around the wall I've

created, making something that almost looks like a long body pillow.

When I lean forward and inhale, I smile. "Perfect." But I need more.

Glancing around the room, I frown, realizing I don't have anything else to pad the bed with. Only my sheets, and those... those are where they should be.

Frowning, I slip off the bed and turn toward the closet again.

And freeze.

Because Orcus, Flame, and Reaper are all standing inside the door, gaping at me.

I stare back at them, blinking.

"Is she building a nest?" Reaper asks, gesturing to the bed.

"Yeah," Orcus replies, swallowing.

"Cool," Reaper says, nodding. "I very much approve of the whole naked part of the experience."

My eyes widen as I glance down, suddenly remembering that I took off my towel to... to... do whatever the hell I was just doing.

"So when does the heat part begin, again?" Reaper drawls as I dive into the bed and pull the blankets over me.

Like, all the way over me.

Covering my head.

And holding on to the comforter for dear life.

What the heck is wrong with me? What was I even doing? And why—why—*does it still smell so good in here?* I groan, my nipples hardening at the fragrance engulfing me from head to toe.

Because it's them.

These fae.

These *men*.

I'm practically drunk on their cologne, the vision of a

perfect day hitting me once more. *Wandering the mountain side. Heat on my shoulders and arms. Trees swaying in a gentle breeze.*

I whimper, lost to the daydream and mortified at the same time.

"Alina," Orcus says softly, the mattress shifting as he joins me on the bed.

Only, he's not lying down; he's sitting. And he's not touching me either.

I wait for the others to join us, but it's Orcus's cologne that overpowers the room. *Did they leave?* I wonder. *Or are they still watching from the doorway?*

Oh, fae. Heat creeps up my neck. *How long were they watching?*

I can't even remember when I took off my towel or why I felt compelled to do so.

"I don't know what's happening to me," I say aloud, *hating* how scared I feel and sound. It's not me. I'm strong. I fight. I *rebel.*

But this… this isn't normal. This is… it's *them.* It's the fae.

Yet it all feels so right, too.

I want to scream and pull out my hair. To curl into a ball and cry. To jump out of the bed and *yell.* The competing needs cause my stomach to churn.

"Do you want me to explain it?" Orcus asks me, his voice holding a hint of that rumble behind it. The *purr.*

He's purring.

Everything in me stills as my senses lock on to that gentle rumble, my body instantly relaxing beneath the soothing vibration.

Oh, I like that sound.

"Yes," I whisper, pleased with his purr and his voice. I want more. I *need* more.

He represents a salvation I didn't realize I needed. A protection I didn't know I craved.

I just want to curl up beside him and revel in the serenity of his embrace.

But he doesn't touch me.

He doesn't even move.

And something about that irritates me.

Why isn't he holding me?

"I've told you that I believe you have an Omega soul," he says, causing me to blink.

What? This again? That's not what I want to discuss. I simply want him to purr and hold me. Why—

"I think meeting me has freed that soul. And now you finally feel safe enough to be yourself. But you've spent… How old are you?"

My eyes flutter at the unexpected question, yet somehow my mouth knows exactly how to reply. "Two-and-twenty."

He says nothing for a long moment, then clears his throat. "Your Omega soul has been in hiding for over two decades, forcing you to cope without that part of yourself. But now, the two halves of your being are joining, which I imagine is a very confusing experience."

Understatement of the millennium, I want to tell him. But I'm too busy trying to digest his words while battling my instinctual need to yank him under the covers with me.

His purr would be so nice in here, part of me is thinking.

I'm losing my mind is another thought.

And lastly, I can't help wondering, *My two halves are joining? What the heck does that even mean?*

So yeah. *Confusing* is an understatement. Yep.

"I've known Omegas in the past," he goes on, causing my heart to skip a beat.

Some part of me does not like the way he phrased that.

That part of me has my eyes narrowing as I demand, "Known how?"

Because it'd better not be intimately, the part of me thinks, scowling inside.

It's… it's disconcerting. Like another entity is voicing that comment, not me. And yet, I feel it deep in my soul that I would *not* like him knowing another Omega *intimately*.

"As in, I've been around them," he says, a hint of amusement in his tone.

My hands fist in the comforter as I yank it off my face, needing to see him. Because there is nothing funny or amusing about this conversation.

But the minute our eyes meet, my blossoming ire dies.

Red irises stare down at me. Red and bold.

And there are no signs of amusement in his expression.

There are also no signs of anyone else in the room. It's just us. *Me and the Mythos Fae Alpha.*

His purr intensifies, or maybe it's just louder now that I've come out of my cocoon of blankets. Whatever the cause, I'm thankful for the rumbling vibration because it instantly soothes me.

Orcus reaches out a hand to brush some of my wayward hair out of my face, his palm cupping my cheek.

"I've never been with an Omega before," he tells me. "You'll be my first and my only, Alina."

I swallow, uncertain of how to reply to that.

"That possessive instinct you feel, it rivals my own for you. That's part of the Alpha-Omega bond. Our souls are tying themselves together. Every moment, we grow closer. And as we grow closer, your Omega traits will strengthen."

"I don't feel very strong right now," I admit in a whisper, hating how vulnerable I've become over the last few days. "I feel weaker, Orcus. And I'm… I'm losing who I am?"

The rebellious girl from the village.

The one determined to find her sister.

What happened to her? *Where did I go?*

"I'm supposed to be going to Chicago right now," I tell him. "I didn't want a mate. I only wanted to be chosen for Monsters Night so I could…" I trail off, my throat working as I wince.

But really, what would it matter if I voiced the truth?

These fae already said they would take me to Chicago.

Why not admit that I want to find my sister?

The old Alina would tell him, I think. *The old Alina would be strong and state her purpose.*

I want to be that old Alina again.

I want to be *me*.

Not this… this purr-loving, scent-obsessed *Omega*.

I start to push away the sheets, determined to get up and leave.

Except the moment the cold air touches my breasts, I remember that I'm naked and immediately pull the blankets up once more.

Only this time, I don't whimper or groan. I *growl*.

Because I'm frustrated.

Because I'm *vulnerable* again.

Because I'm so tired of not being able to do what I want.

"I've been forced to do what the Protectors demanded for years. Forced to adhere to the village rules. But then I broke them. Well, some of them. And I made it to Monsters Night by *choice*. I'm not weak."

"Omegas are not weak either," Orcus replies, drawing my attention to his full mouth. "Omegas are strong.

They're able to handle an Alpha's strength and then bring him to his knees. Omegas have all the power in my world. That's why we're lost without them."

"But... but I'm obsessed with *scents* and your *purr* and..." I shake my head. "I don't understand it, Orcus. I don't understand what's happening to me." I get the whole Omega-soul-coming-out part. It's what that actually entails that has me feeling so lost.

I try to explain that last part to Orcus aloud, but I feel like I'm just rambling.

Because I'm not me.

I'm not—

"You were building a nest," he says, interrupting my thoughts. "A nest is a safe place for an Omega to mate with her Alpha. Or, in your case, your mates. Because I suspect that whatever you and Reaper did earlier triggered a need inside you. And you reacted to that need by starting your nest."

I blink at him. "A nest."

"Yes." His lips curl a little. "Think of it like a safe haven, one you control and own. You decide who enters it. How they enter. Where they lie. It's your space for you to direct as you desire."

My nose crinkles. "I don't know what to say to that."

He lifts a shoulder. "You don't have to say anything at all. I'm just trying to help you understand the instinct. You were building a nest with your mates' scents because your inner Omega feels safe with us."

I picture the beautiful mountain afternoon again and note how secure and warm and happy it makes me feel.

That's what their scents represent, I realize. *Harmony. Utopia. A place of contentment.*

"As for my purr, you like it because Alphas purr for

242

their mates. It's a sound I will only ever make for you. And Flame actually purrs, too. But his is a little different. However, the same principle applies." Orcus lowers his palm from my cheek, his irises a hypnotic swirl of red and black.

I study his eyes and his sharp cheekbones. This close, he doesn't seem so big. Which is strange because he's actually huge. However, there's a softness to him that lessens his intimidating size.

"I can growl, too," he adds, showcasing the ability by adding a slight rumble to his words. "Growls excite Omegas and inspire a mating lust." He utters that part without the added sound effect. "It causes the Omega to produce... slick."

I'm staring at his mouth again while he speaks, a part of me wishing he would growl again. Because I rather liked that sound. "What's slick?" I ask, paying attention despite being somewhat distracted by his beautiful lips.

"The lubricant between your thighs."

My gaze jumps back up to his. "Wh-what?"

"Growls make you wet," he clarifies. Not that I needed it. My question was rhetorical, primarily because I didn't expect him to say *that*. "*Very* wet."

I shiver. "O-oh."

Amusement flirts with his eyes as he studies me. "A lot of your Omega instincts revolve around mating, Alina. That's what Alphas and Omegas do. But there's nothing weak about it. Your body is built to take my brute strength. And my heart was created to love you for eternity."

His palm finds my cheek again, his stare suddenly very intense.

So intense that I can barely breathe.

Because he's looking at me like I'm his world. His everything.

"You're my life now, Alina," he breathes. "My forever. And that, my sweet Omega, makes you the strongest one of us all."

CHAPTER TWENTY-TWO
ALINA

ORCUS'S EXPLANATIONS stay with me over the next few days, his voice in my head helping me to better understand my foreign instincts.

Unfortunately, though, understanding them doesn't make them go away.

No.

They're just getting stronger.

As evidenced by the growing pile of clothes surrounding the perimeter of the bed.

If it bothers Reaper, he doesn't show it. He's joined me the last couple of nights and woken me with orgasms every morning.

Well, almost every morning.

Today, he appears to be missing.

So I go to shower on my own, a little disappointed in our break in routine.

Not that we have a set schedule or anything.

Except, the last handful of days have followed a similar sequence—morning orgasms with Reaper, cupcakes for breakfast, afternoon learning sessions taught by Orcus with some group meals tossed in, and evening walks with Flame.

It's been… nice. Exceptional, even.

So where is Reaper? I wonder as I wrap a towel around my midsection. He's the only one who has slept in the bed with me, probably because I haven't invited the others to join.

But they also haven't asked.

If they did, I… I might say yes.

The warmth spreading through my veins is one I finally understand. It's arousal, but a far more intense version brought on by my no-longer-dormant Omega side.

Yesterday, Orcus finally explained to me what the *heat* experience is that Reaper keeps mentioning.

"It's about procreation. You'll become insatiable, and it'll take all three of us to satisfy you," he told me, his accent somewhat thicker as he spoke the words. "And by the end, you will likely be with child."

Pregnant, I think now, my palm pressing to my belly. *Why doesn't that scare me?*

It should.

I've never desired children.

But that was when I thought I would have to raise them in this world or couple with one of the men in my village.

With the fae, I… I don't know. It doesn't sound all that bad, being with them.

"Do you want a child?" I asked Orcus yesterday.

"I do," he answered without hesitation. "But I want a mate more."

I frowned at him. "What do you mean?"

"I mean, if you don't want children, or if you're not ready for children, we won't rut you. We can satisfy you in other ways." He smiled then, like he was thinking of those other ways.

But I was too caught up on the word *rut*—which he said a few times during our conversation—to focus on those other ways.

I want the fae to rut *me,* I think now. *Is that crazy?*

I stare at myself in the mirror.

It doesn't feel very crazy. In fact, it feels like the most natural thing in the world.

Maybe it's because I'm all hot and bothered from my missed session with Reaper. Maybe it's just fate.

Maybe I should stop overthinking things and go find that Death Fae, I think, my gaze narrowing in the mirror.

Why should he be the one who gets to start our morning fun? And why hasn't he asked me to touch him back yet?

I run my fingers through my damp hair and step into the bedroom, determined to find the man on my mind and demand some answers.

But when I reach the living area, all I see is Flame in his jaguar form.

He's lounging on the foyer marble, his big head having lifted when I entered. His green eyes blink at me. And I blink back.

"Where's Reaper?" I ask him.

He stands and stretches, his sleek form displaying all those impressive muscles. Then he prowls toward me, still in cat form.

I watch him, waiting for him to shift, but he doesn't. Instead, he comes right up to me and rubs himself against my leg.

My fingers automatically find his soft fur, my lips quirking up at the sides.

"Good morning to you, too," I say as he nudges me

back into the bedroom. "Are you going to cuddle me instead of Reaper?"

It's not exactly what I was looking for, but I wouldn't mind curling up in bed with Flame's jaguar. He's so soft and warm and powerful. That last part is very evident as he guides me toward the bed and practically knocks me down onto the mattress.

A gasp leaves me as I land unceremoniously on my ass, his big body crowding mine.

"What are you doing?" I breathe as I scramble backward onto the bed, a soft laugh catching in my throat. Because his jaguar is clearly feeling playful.

Except, as he climbs onto the bed, there's nothing playful at all in his eyes.

Especially not as his snout disappears under my towel to touch the apex between my thighs.

My mouth drops open, stunned.

Only to be even more surprised as the massive jaguar starts crawling up my body and begins shifting into a man.

Flame.

By the time his snout would have reached my face, he's fully changed into his human form.

And *very* naked on top of me. "Hello, little panther," he murmurs, a purr underlining his voice as he draws his nose along my cheek. "You're smelling particularly sweet this morning."

I shiver, my thighs clenching around his in response to his sensual rumble. It's different from Orcus's, which always seems to relax me.

Flame's purr can be soothing, too. But as I'm learning right now, it can also be extremely sexual.

His lips ghost across my jaw, his movements hypnotic and new. He's only kissed me on the cheeks a few times, the chaste touch nothing compared to the seductive predator on top of me.

"Reaper and Orcus are talking with the Emissary," he tells me softly. "It seems Orcus might finally meet the elusive Queen today."

I still. "She's ready to meet?"

Flame nods, his mouth going to my neck. "That's the working theory, yes." He nibbles my pulse. "We might get some answers today. But until then... I vote that we play."

"Shouldn't you be there with them?" I ask, confused as to why Orcus and Reaper left him behind. I'm not surprised that I'm not on the invitation list; I'm a human.

Or sort of a human, anyway, I think, still confused by this "Omega soul" that's taking over my life.

"Reaper and I drew blades, and I won." Pride colors Flame's tone, his lips curling against my neck. "So I chose to be here with you while they handle the political bullshit."

"Drew blades?" I repeat, not understanding what he meant by that.

"It's a game we play—whoever draws a sharp toy the fastest wins." He goes to his elbows on either side of my head. "I partially shifted my hand while he conjured a dagger. It was almost a tie, but Orcus declared me the winner."

I just stare at him. "That's a game?"

He grins. "Yeah, kitten, it's a game. And since I won, my reward is playing with you."

Kitten? I think. *What happened to "little panther"?* My brow furrows. "I'm not a kitten."

Flame chuckles and nods. "Little panther it is, then."

"Madam panther," I tell him, then frown. "No. Little panther is fine." *Madam* makes me think of the elderly matrons of my village. *Little* is... well, I *am* smaller than all these fae, so I'll accept the adjective since it's said endearingly, not condescendingly.

"As you wish, little panther," he murmurs. "Any other demands you would like to issue this morning? I'm yours to command."

I arch a brow. "You are?"

"Always."

Hmm. That could be a dangerous proclamation, especially in my current mood.

Reaper seems to have trained my body to expect orgasms every morning now. He's clearly woven some sort of sensual spell over me.

Or maybe it's my *Omega* side making me feel so hungry for a man's touch.

Regardless, I have a naked Shifter Fae on top of me.

A sexy-as-sin Shifter Fae, I think, clarifying with an internal grin. *A sexy-as-sin Shifter Fae who says he's mine to command.*

And he's hard, too.

Not just all those muscles, but between my legs. I can feel his heat through the thin fabric of my towel.

His face was just down there in jaguar form, I remember, shuddering. There's no doubt in my mind that he could smell my arousal, not to mention *see* it.

All our walks have been sweet, his patience with me appreciated. But I want more than holding hands and chaste kisses on the cheek.

I want *him.*

Fae, I want them.

These males are my addiction. It's… it's like I'm alive for the first time in my life. And I'm fully embracing the refreshing experience.

They don't want to hurt me; they want to protect me.

Cherish me.

Make me their *mate*.

Three fae, one sort-of-Omega.

Not a bad existence. In fact, it sounds like an amazing one.

"Should I be scared?" Flame asks, his eyes studying mine.

I blink up at him. "What? Why would you be scared?"

"Because you're taking an awfully long time to come up with your next command."

Oh. I lick my lips. "Right, yes, you should probably be…"

"Yeah?" He arches a dark brow, his violet irises radiating sinful intent. "Do your worst, little panther. Tell me what to do."

The dare makes me even wetter between my thighs, my mind reeling with foreign concepts and ideas. Most of them have been put there by *Reaper*.

"Someday soon, I'm going to lick you down there, pet," he said to me yesterday. "I'm going to nibble this swollen little clit of yours while you come, then bring you to completion again on my tongue."

My insides clench at the memory, my desire to feel Reaper's mouth down there making me hot all over.

Fae, what would that be like?

Would Flame show me?

He observes me through his thick lashes, his handsome face scant inches from mine. How can I ask him to kiss me down there when our lips have not even met yet?

Maybe it's tame, but I want to start by feeling his mouth on mine. By learning his tongue. By experiencing his brand of passion and understanding what he likes.

Not necessarily to compare him to Reaper, but just to know Flame.

To know both my fae men.

Oh, just the thought of having them both has my legs tensing all over again. I *need*. I *burn*. "You have to kiss me, Flame. Please. I—"

His mouth silences my ramblings, his lips gentle against mine.

At least… at first.

But after a few seconds, that gentleness melts into something hotter, something *coaxing* in nature.

It's subtle, yet I can feel him mastering me with soft, enticing strokes. Telling me what he wants with a silent sweep of his tongue. And taking command the moment I part my lips.

Fae… He's all sensual grace.

A slow seduction.

A purposeful embrace.

A flawless kiss.

I shouldn't be surprised. Everything about Flame is perfect, from his handsome features, to his stunning jaguar, to his gentlemanly mannerisms.

But there's nothing gentlemanly about this kiss now.

His tongue dominates mine as he *purrs.*

Oh, that rumble. It's… it's so hypnotic. So commanding.

"I love your purr," I say against his mouth. "It… it makes me tingle all over."

He grins. "It should. That's my jaguar's mating call. He uses it to soothe you, but also to seduce you." He draws his nose along my cheek to my ear. "Is it working, little panther? Does it make you want to spread your legs for me?"

"My legs are already spread," I tell him.

"Mmm, but not wide enough," he replies, his palms skimming down my sides. "This towel is also in the way."

"Then maybe you should remove it," I suggest, feeling oddly bold and a whole lot needy.

"Is that another command, my panther queen?"

I quiver, liking that new endearment. *Queen* makes me sound powerful, not weak. It's a title of distinction. Although, I'm not quite sure I've earned it.

But if he feels I'm his *panther queen*, then I'll accept it. "Kiss me again," I beg him, having lost whatever topic we were discussing. I wasn't even sure why we began talking to begin with. I want more of his tongue, more of his mouth, more of his *passion*.

And he gives it to me.

Oh, how he gives it to me.

His kisses are more sensual than Reaper's, but both of them are equally potent. Addictive. *Lethal* to my brain cells.

Because I no longer know up from down or left from right. Not that directions matter right now.

"Flame," I breathe.

"Alina," he returns, his mouth wet against mine. "Tell me to taste you. *Please* tell me to taste you." He kisses me again before I can reply, his purr intensifying with the motion. "My jaguar wanted to lick your sweet pussy so fucking badly, but I pulled him back. I need your consent. I want your *command*."

My thighs squeeze his, my insides weeping with the need to obey his request while issuing a demand of my own. It's a strange combination, this feeling of being empowered yet knowing deep down that I'm actually submitting.

He wants to *lick* me.

He's telling me to command him to do so.

And I want nothing more than to utter that demand.

"Taste me," I say to him. "Taste me everywhere, Flame."

His violet gaze is tinged with ebony flecks, something I've learned that indicates his animal is close to the surface. He's part beast, yet all man.

He wants my consent—which I've provided. And I can see the relief that consent has given him.

Something settles in him.

A refined predator takes control.

And dark intent flashes in his blazing gaze.

I quiver in anticipation, expecting him to rip the towel from my body. But he doesn't.

Instead, he kisses me again.

But this kiss is far more intense than the last one, even more *dominant*. Like I've just unleashed something inside him. Granted him permission to do whatever it is he really wants to do.

Allowed his jaguar to lead, I realize. I'm not sure how I know that, but I do. And I'm both terrified and thrilled by it.

He growls. Purrs. Growls again.

Then fists the fabric between us and yanks it open.

Almost fully black eyes stare down at my exposed breasts, his tongue flicking out to lick his bottom lip. "I'm going to devour you, Alina." His voice is deep and low and filled with warning. "I need you to pick a safeword."

My brow furrows. "A what?"

"A safeword," another voice says as Reaper appears beside us on the bed, his head propped up by one hand. "A word that'll tell him, well, *us*, if we've gone too far."

I gape at his lounging form, surprised by his sudden appearance. And also stunned by his explanation. "Can't I just say *stop*?"

"No," they both reply in unison.

"Sometimes, you may tell us to stop when you really mean for us to keep going," Reaper adds. "So we need a word that actually means stop. A word that'll yank us out of the moment and force us to check in with you."

"Not that we won't be doing that the whole time," Flame says, his eyes more violet again in color. "It's just a precaution in case our beasts take it too far."

"It's also a way to demonstrate your power, Alina," Reaper tells me with a smile. "No dominant man wants his woman to safeword him. Knowing you can stop it all with one word gives you complete control, even when you might feel like you have none at all."

Flame nods, agreeing with Reaper.

If he's bothered by his friend's interruption and unexpected appearance, he doesn't show it. Actually, he seems quite at ease with Reaper's presence.

Because they want to share me.

A shiver works through me at the knowledge of their desire. *I think I want them to share me, too.*

"So what'll it be, pet?" Reaper asks, his lips curling into a sinfully enticing smile. "What's your safeword?"

CHAPTER TWENTY-THREE

REAPER

FLAME DOESN'T BOTHER to ask why I'm here and not with Orcus. Probably because he assumes the Alpha dismissed me or said I was no longer needed.

Alas, it's none of the above.

Emissary Dickwad Jones told me I couldn't attend the meeting with his beloved Queen Bitch.

I debated arguing.

But a look from Orcus had me shrugging again. He could take care of himself.

And in the interim, I could take care of Alina.

So I teleported back here to play with my pet and very happily landed myself in the middle of a threesome.

Now she just needs to give a safeword so we can properly begin.

I've spent the last few days slowly warming her up, which I did for her benefit as much as mine.

Orcus might be fine with just talking, and Flame might be satisfied with his evening strolls, but I needed to touch our pet. To taste her. To *know* her.

And I think she needed my brand of training, too.

She's going to be a free spirit in bed. She just needs to let go of her insecurities and spread her invisible wings.

"Chicago," she whispers, making me frown.

"Orcus is meeting with the elusive Queen soon. They'll discuss it," I promise her.

"N-no. I... I was picking my safeword. *Chicago*."

"Oh." I smile. "Chicago it is."

"Chicago," Flame echoes, acknowledging the safeword. "If for some reason you can't speak, hold up two fingers or tap twice." He demonstrates with his hand while Alina gazes up at him with wide eyes.

"Why wouldn't I be able to speak?" she asks, sounding alarmed.

"Oh, darling pet," I muse, sitting up to pull off my shirt. "The things we're going to teach you..."

Starting with what I can do with my ethereal strands.

"You were about to taste our pet, yes?" I say to Flame.

"Yes," he confirms, his gaze going to her beautiful tits. "My jaguar wants to lick every inch of her."

"Understandable. She's delicious." My tattoos writhe as I say the words, the smoky tendrils slowly seeping out of my skin and swimming through the air toward our female.

She sees them but doesn't say anything, just watches as I wind them around her wrists. I apply some pressure to guide her arms over her head, causing her lips to part in surprise. Then I bind her hands together and loop a strand around the headboard to secure her.

"Taste her," I tell Flame. "Make our girl scream."

Alina parts her lips like she wants to object, but all that comes out is a moan as Flame sucks one of her rosy nipples deep into his mouth.

He groans around the dainty bud, his free hand going

to her opposite tit to squeeze the rounded flesh. She fills his palm beautifully, proving that her body was made for him —for *us*.

I've touched those perky breasts, too.

But I haven't licked them yet.

One of my strands wanders down to stroke the underside of her boob as Flame switches his mouth to her opposite peak.

The sounds coming from Alina confirm how much she likes this, making me wish I would have pushed her a little harder in our experimentations. Because those noises she's making are fucking divine.

I unfasten my jeans, my cock throbbing behind the zipper. But I don't free myself entirely.

I'll wait for Alina to do the honors.

Until then…

I lean down and absorb her moans with my tongue. She instantly returns my kiss, her mouth eager against mine.

This is a kiss I know, a kiss I've *taught*.

Our little pet is such an excellent student.

I reward her skills by deepening our embrace while Flame feasts on her tits like a starved man. He's driving her crazy, making her hips pump upward in a demand for more.

Flame responds by pinning her to the bed with his lower abdomen, his growl vibrating through the air.

She whimpers against my mouth, making me grin. "Feeling needy this morning, pet?" I lick her lower lip. "Did you miss my hands on you?"

"Yes," she says, trying to arch again.

Flame releases another rumble. "Don't rush me, little panther. When I said that I intended to taste every inch of you, I meant *every inch*."

Her pupils blow wide, her lips parting on a pant.

So I distract her once more with my mouth while Flame continues feasting on her gorgeous tits.

By the time he starts to move south, Alina has tears in her eyes. She's all worked up and needy, and all Flame has done is kiss her nipples and curves.

Her arms strain as she tries to reach down, no doubt to touch herself between her thighs.

I tsk, my strands tightening around her wrists. "No moving, pet. This is for Flame."

And very much for her, too.

But that's all part of the lesson.

She's learning. We're teaching.

I suck her bottom lip into my mouth and gently bite down. "Just relax and feel," I tell her. "You'll love it."

She shudders, her hands curling into fists against my restraints. I love her fight. And I love the way she moans as Flame nibbles his way down her torso.

"You're doing so well," I whisper, kissing her cheek and then her ear. "Just let us worship you, pet. Let us please you."

"Reaper," she whispers. "*Flame.*"

He chuckles, drawing my gaze down to where he's just licked her clit.

Alina strains against the bindings as he does it again, another delicious sound leaving her beautiful mouth. My dick throbs in response to Flame dragging his tongue down her slick folds and back up to her sensitive little nub, his slow movements drawn out with purpose.

He's fucking licking her like a bowl of cream.

Strawberry cream, I think, groaning at the sight. I can't wait to fucking taste her like that.

"*Ohhh*," Alina moans, her gorgeous figure straining as Flame devours her pussy.

I smile, enjoying the show of hedonistic passion. "He's going to make you come so hard, darling. So fucking hard." I trace my finger around her damp nipple, loving the way the pink has turned red from Flame's mouth. "And then I'm going to make you come again."

Alina visibly reacts to both my words and Flame's tongue, her skin pebbling with goose bumps.

I lean down to lave her stiff peak, then sink my teeth into her flesh.

Not hard enough to make her bleed, but hard enough for her to yelp.

A blade forms in my shadows, my bite inspiring a hint of bloodlust. I won't hurt her. But I will make things a little more interesting.

I flip my hand, allowing the dagger to slip into my palm, then show Alina the knife. "This is about trust," I inform her softly. "About introducing you to our desires while provoking deep-seated needs of your own."

I go back onto my elbow beside her, the weapon still in my grip as I lightly drag the tip along her arm and up to her bound wrists.

"You know your safeword," I remind her as her nostrils flare, her chest rising and falling as her eyes track my movements.

The conflict in her features has my groin tightening in response. She's afraid of what I'm going to do, yet utterly lost to the sensations Flame is provoking between her splayed thighs.

"Just relax and feel," I tell her again. "The hint of fear only heightens the experience. It sharpens the senses, makes you experience every second of pleasure and potential pain."

She swallows, her pulse racing so hard I can practically see the throbbing point in her neck. "Reap—" She gasps, her eyes flicking down to where Flame is watching her, his dark eyes demanding her attention.

"I'm the one between your legs, sweetling," he says. "If you want to come, you'll say my name. Otherwise…" He nips her, drawing another gasp from our pet.

"*Flame…*" She's practically panting now, confirming that slight hints of pain definitely do it for her.

"Flame what?" he taunts her. "What do you want me to do, little panther? Tell me."

I hum in approval and continue to drag the tip of my blade up and down her arm while I watch her fight for her words.

She's so worked up that she looks ready to scream in both pleasure and frustration.

It's an intoxicating sight.

A state I'd like her to stay in for just a little longer.

Because once she tips over the edge into oblivion, she's going to experience the most mind-blowing pleasure of her life.

"I… I need your fingers…" she manages to say. "Please, Flame. Your mouth. Your… your *everything*."

"Mmm, don't tempt me too much," he replies softly. "I don't think you're ready for my barb just yet."

Alina's pupils dilate, the term one that seems to intrigue her.

But before she can ask about it, Flame returns to his task and her eyes roll into the back of her head.

My ethereal strands warm as she tries to move again, my binds holding her in place so she can't grab Flame or accidentally jolt beneath my blade.

A blade I draw down.

Down.

Down.

To where her shoulder meets her neck.

And then gently place it against her throat before leaning in to kiss her once more.

She freezes beneath me, her body straining not to move despite the pleasurable assault Flame is unleashing below.

The threat of my knife has her momentarily stunned. She's barely even breathing.

Sweat dots her brow, her lips still against mine, her eyes wide.

Then Flame must do something with his teeth or his tongue, because she trembles violently, indicating that her orgasm is fast approaching.

"*Fae*," she breathes, the term beautifully applying to both of us.

And then she screams.

My weapon disappears, primarily because I don't want to accidentally harm her—which would be too easy to do with how fiercely she's thrashing against my restraints.

This orgasm is nothing compared to what I've unleashed on her with my hand, and I fucking love that. Because *this* is what pleasure should feel like. An intense moment of insanity where nothing and no one else matters, just the moment and the overwhelming sensations rippling through one's body.

I lean back to admire the show, my cock weeping with the expectation of being next. I've delayed my gratification all fucking week.

No more.

Today, Alina is going to touch me.

And if the look in Flame's eyes is anything to go by, he fully intends for her to touch him, too.

But rather than rush it, he continues to lick her.

Driving her onward.

Forcing her to prolong her ecstasy.

All while preparing her to do this again.

Only it'll be me between her thighs next, something I tell him with a look.

He doesn't fight me.

He knows how to share.

When it's time, we'll switch.

And perhaps switch again.

Prime her. Pleasure her. Then show her how to return the favor.

"Such a good fucking girl," I say against her ear. "So beautiful and carefree." I kiss her thundering pulse. "Now let's do it again, pet. Only this time, you're going to come on my tongue while Flame sucks your tits."

She moans, the sound resembling a slight protest. This is where *stop* might come into play. But unless she says *Chicago*, I won't let up.

And she doesn't.

All she screams is my name. Flame's name. *Fae.*

Over and over again.

While I dine between her thighs. Feast on her breasts. Fuck her with my tongue. Kiss the fucking life out of her. And worship her with my hands.

Flame moves in tandem with me, working our pet to the brink three times before finally watching her fly with a satisfied grin on his face.

It's magical.

It's hypnotic.

It's borderline *addicting*.

I could play with her for eternity and never once want to stop.

Because this female is ours.

Our mate.

And I know exactly what I'm going to do to her.

I'm going to teach her how to handle our brand of darkness. Show her how to properly defend herself, not just against us but against others as well. Mold her into a sensual threat. Groom her to embrace her Goddess-like status.

And train her to become…

Our lethal pet.

CHAPTER TWENTY-FOUR
ORCUS

Emissary Jones steps out of the elevator on the fifth floor, his expression giving nothing away. "The Queen will be ready for you at noon sharp. Just use the code we discussed, and the elevator will take you up to the penthouse suite."

With that, he walks away, already very aware of my mounting impatience.

Primarily because he called to demand that I join him in the lobby, just to promptly dismiss Reaper and then say, "The Monster City Queen would like to meet in two hours."

"That message could have been conveyed over the phone," I informed him dryly.

He shrugged. "Perhaps, but our Queen likes to ensure her rules are followed."

"Meaning our *obedience* this morning was a test," I translated.

The Emissary smiled. "Our Queen would also like me to treat you to breakfast." He gestured toward a hall that led to one of the tower's many dining rooms.

"A request or a command?"

"What do you think?" he asked.

"I don't think you have any interest in dining with me," I replied. "Which means you're following orders."

"As I said, our Queen likes her rules."

"Hmm." *Or power plays*, I thought.

But I indulged him anyway. I need the Queen to play along and give me the information I require. And I also want our dimensions to have a peaceful relationship with one another. It'll make traveling between them easier.

Thus, I'm forced to play this political game.

Alas, I still have twenty minutes to kill before I can key in the code Jones gave me for the Queen's penthouse.

I originally considered returning to my suite to wait, but I selected a different floor instead.

Now I step off onto that floor and head straight for the Strigoi's rooms.

I knock and wait.

And wait.

And wait.

I'm about to try again when Cage answers the door in a towel, his long blond hair damp and dripping down his bare chest. Sabre is behind him, tying a robe around his middle, the two of them having clearly just been showering together.

Studying them has my jaw clenching.

I've spent the last century thinking these two hated each other. Their families are rival royals, both vying for the same throne.

And these two Princes are the primary heirs.

"You both put on quite a show in public," I concede aloud, forgoing greetings. "When Reaper told me you two fuck in private, I almost didn't believe him." But Flame said he found these two holding hands in the park.

They also ventured into this world together, suggesting friendship.

Or romance.

Whatever it is, I'm annoyed because I didn't pay enough attention to pick up on it. Details are important, and if I've missed such a significant one when it comes to royal families in my world, then what other details have I missed?

Fortunately, Reaper and Flame notice things I miss.

As evidenced by Reaper's lack of a surprise that Cage and Sabre were here together. "Maliki probably let them through. He and Cage are old friends." The Death Fae shrugged then and went into the kitchen to search for something.

Apparently, he didn't find Cage and Sabre's relationship to be all that important. Otherwise, he would have said something about it previously.

But I definitely don't share his lack of regard.

"You're both going to ignite a war between your families," I tell them. "I'm just glad I don't have to deal with the fallout." That'll be Morpheus's task. "Anyway, I merely wanted to let you know that I'm about to meet with the Monster City Queen. If she gives permission for me to open a portal, then I'll create one for you to return to the Morpheus Realm."

I didn't request this initially, as it seemed clear the Queen wanted to meet with the Strigoi as well. But as the higher-ranking fae from our world, it makes sense for me to take the meeting and negotiate terms.

Sabre clears his throat. "And if we don't want to return?"

I stare at him for a long beat. "That'll be for you and Morpheus to discuss." My only job here is to see that he and Cage are safe. If Morpheus gives them permission to stay here—which I highly doubt he will due to their royal positions—then they can remain. "You would also need permission from the Monster City Queen."

Which she may or may not give.

I have no idea what to expect from this woman, other than the fact that she has a fondness for rules and power plays.

Sabre looks a little pale, likely from the realization that he'll have to discuss his future with his God. Of all the Mythos Fae to upset, Morpheus is honestly one of the better ones to piss off. Mainly because he's constantly lost to his dreamy state of being and very rarely cares what those are doing around him.

However, he won't like that Sabre and Cage have inconvenienced him by forcing him to leave his dream world.

So he won't exactly be kind with whatever punishment he gives them.

Unless he decides that he just doesn't care.

Mythos Fae are mercurial. Sometimes they want to cast judgment, sometimes they want chaos, and sometimes they just do not give a fuck.

That last bit is how I feel right now.

I don't care that these Strigoi are here. It's a minor inconvenience on my part. They can do whatever the hell they want.

Morpheus can judge them, kill them, leave them be, or just eat popcorn while the Strigoi Royal Court falls apart. His domain, his rules.

Maybe this Queen is a Goddess, I think. *Her domain, her rules, hmm?*

Blowing out a breath, I rub my hand over my face. "I'll mention your request to the Queen, too. Just so you know if it's even an option for you to stay here before you talk to Morpheus."

I don't know if Morpheus will be around to talk to them, though. I haven't tried reaching out to my brother since the other day.

"Just… don't go anywhere. I really don't want to have to track you down, yeah?" I tell the Strigoi.

Sabre still looks pale, but that could just be his vampire-like coloring. It's the middle of the day, which might be weakening him here. Fortunately, though, the Queen gave him a suite with blackout curtains. And there are no windows in the hallway, either.

"There's nowhere for us to go," Cage replies, his blue eyes flashing. "But we won't be returning to the Morpheus Kingdom."

I arch a brow, somewhat impressed by his display of a backbone. It takes serious courage to stand up to a Mythos Fae, especially when his kind worships my kind.

"Again, that's a discussion for you and Morpheus," I tell him. "I'm not going to force you to do anything other than answer to him." Because I want nothing to do with any of this.

Cage doesn't seem fully satisfied by my response, but I'm not sure what he expected me to say. I can't grant him clemency. It's just not my place.

Sabre winces, causing me to frown. "Are you all right?" I ask him. He's still pretty pale, and I doubt I scared him that much with my words.

"He just needs more blood," Cage says, wrapping his arm around his lover's back. "Maybe you can ask the Queen for that, too?"

I nod. "I'll see what I can do." *And add it to my long list of items for the Queen.*

273

I'm not sure when I became an ambassador between realms, but I'm hoping this job is temporary.

Because I'm not cut out for this diplomatic bullshit. *Fucking rules. Fucking power plays. Fucking meetings.*

"I'll be back," I inform the Strigoi, my voice holding a touch of a growl to it. My frustration has very little to do with them and everything to do with the Queen waiting upstairs.

Glancing at my watch, I see that I still have about ten minutes.

Rules. Rules. Rules.

You know what? Fuck your rules.

I stalk off toward the elevator, deciding to let this Queen know who she's dealing with.

Punching the button, I call it to me. Only, when it opens, it's to reveal a man in a crisp suit.

No. Not a man. Something far more powerful than a man.

He studies me with glass-like eyes, his gaze running over my leather jacket and jeans before returning to my face, a frown marring his brow.

I move back on instinct, not because I wish to bow to this creature, but because I need more room to defend myself, should it come to that.

"You must be Orcus," he says, stepping out of the elevator. His height rivals mine, placing him well over six feet tall.

However, his aura is similar to those of the Strigoi.

Another dreamwalker? I wonder, studying him closely. *From another realm, perhaps?*

"Who are you?" I demand.

"Cain," he replies.

"*What* are you?" I add, noting that his accent is rivals my own.

He smiles. "Are you always so demanding of those you just met?"

"Only potential threats."

Amusement shines in his glass-blue eyes. "I'll take that as a compliment."

"You shouldn't," I inform him. "I don't like threats."

"Ah, well, then you and Helia are going to get on famously," he drawls. "I almost wish I would have stayed for the meeting now."

"Helia?" I repeat.

"The Monster City Queen," he tells me, catching the elevator door before it can close. "She's ready for you, by the way."

I cock a brow at him. "Are you here to escort me up?"

He laughs, though the sound lacks humor. "I'm not in the habit of escorting anyone anywhere, Orcus. But unless you want an Emissary to come find you, I recommend heading up to see Helia. The Emissaries around here are all about punctuality and rules."

He lets his arm fall then and starts down the hallway.

I stop the door from closing this time and stare at the man's back, half-tempted to ask where he's heading.

But given that he didn't answer my question about his supernatural type, I doubt he'll give me that information either.

Besides, it's not really my business.

All I want to do is to get this meeting over with.

I step into the elevator.

Key in the code.

And steel my spine.

Time to find out what kind of creature becomes a Monster City Queen.

CHAPTER TWENTY-FIVE
ALINA

I BLINK INTO THE DARKNESS, bliss swimming through my veins.

This is where I exist now.

This delirious world that smells like evergreens and ash, with a hint of refreshing air mixed in. It's… it's my safe haven. My happy place.

A soft purr rumbles against my ear.

Something hard nudges my lower belly.

Lips whisper across the back of my neck.

A palm squeezes my hips.

Male voices murmur over my head.

Yes, this is my utopia, I decide, nuzzling into the source of the purring. *Warm. Masculine. Flesh.*

So hard. So muscular. So *enticing*.

I squirm, causing a thigh to brush the tender apex between my legs. A moan leaves my mouth, followed by a chuckle from one of my fae.

"Insatiable," Reaper says, suggesting he's the one who just chuckled. "Fucking perfect, pet."

"Fucking perfect indeed," Flame agrees, his deep voice

a rumble against my ear. Because it's his chest I'm resting on.

No.

Shoulder.

Which is why I feel his dick against my lower belly.

Hard. Insistent. Throbbing.

My hand wanders on instinct, my desire to feel him overtaking my sense of reason.

He's naked. He's aroused. And he's pressed up against me.

This is allowed, right?

His hiss of a reply has me wondering if maybe… maybe it's not allowed.

But he wraps his hand around mine in the next second, his fingers guiding mine to encircle his pulsing flesh. It's hot against my palm, his thickness making it difficult for me to fully grasp him.

"Gods, Alina, that feels good," he says, pushing into my hand.

"I have no idea what I'm doing," I admit in a whisper. "I've never done any of this before."

"It's okay, pet." Reaper's breath is warm against my nape. "We'll teach you."

Flame releases my hand to grab my chin and guides my gaze up to meet his. "Just do whatever comes naturally to you, Alina."

I swallow and slide my grasp upward to the barbell decorating his shaft. "Did this hurt?"

He chuckles. "Not really, no. But we'll need to remove it before I fuck you."

My brow furrows. "Why? Will it hurt me?"

"No, it'll hurt me," he says, deepening my frown. "You're my mate, Alina. I'm going to want to use my barb on you, and I can't do that with my piercings."

Piercings, I repeat to myself, my fingers venturing higher to fondle the ring dangling from his head. "What's a barb?" I ask while touching him.

"It's... it's something that'll connect us during our climaxes." His voice deepens with the words. "It will pulsate inside you, prolonging your ecstasy while I fill you with my seed."

"It's for breeding," Reaper adds. "Just like Orcus's knot."

"O-oh." I... I don't know what to say to that.

"It's also for pleasure," Flame assures me. "My barb is ribbed in a way that intensifies the vibrations."

I draw my finger over the tip. "So you have to remove the piercings to use it?"

He nods. "Otherwise, the barb will rip through them."

That doesn't sound comfortable. "Why did you pierce it if you have to, you know, take it out?" I ask, still playing with the metal ring.

"Because I've never had to take it out before," he tells me. "My barb is for my mate and no one else."

My eyes widen, understanding slowly overtaking my lust-induced mind.

"You'll be his first," Reaper whispers like he's reading my thoughts. "He's fucked before, but never like this. Same with Orcus." He kisses a path along my neck, his palm sliding up and down my side. "You're changing everything for us, Alina. *Everything.*"

I shiver, my hand squeezing around Flame's bulbous head. "What about you?" I ask, my head tilting back so I can try to see the man behind me. "Do you have a barb?"

His lips curl. "Only cats have barbs."

Flame growls against me. "*Big* fucking cats."

"House cats, too," Reaper tosses back, making Flame growl even more.

But his growl dies when I run my hand back down his length, searching for the barb. Only, I don't feel it anywhere, causing me to look at him once more. "Where is it?"

"It'll come out during sex," he tells me. "And it's not the same as a cat's barb. It's…" He pauses, searching for the right words. "Real jaguars have barbs, but they usually hurt. Shifter Fae jaguars, like me, are not traditional animals. We're, well, fae. And fae like to fuck. Hence…"

"Hence, his barb is pleasurable," Reaper drawls. "We've already covered that. I believe our pet was asking about my cock now."

He's right; I was.

I twist my neck to see him again. "So you don't have a barb."

"I do not."

"A knot?" I guess, but suspect he doesn't have one of those either. Primarily because only Orcus has been mentioned in combination with the term *knot*.

"No knot."

"Okay." I wait for him to say more, but he doesn't. "Well then, what do you have?"

"Why don't you turn around and find out?" he dares me.

A few days ago, I would have hidden.

But today… today I'm feeling bold. Rebellious. *Strong.*

Like I'm me again, I marvel, giving Flame's shaft a gentle squeeze before releasing him. Then flip to face a smirking Reaper.

Flame instantly presses himself flush with my back, his cock hard and demanding against my ass. He grabs my hip bone to hold me in place, his lips finding my shoulder and trailing a path up to my neck. "When you're done playing with Reaper, I would love to feel your tongue against my piercings."

I shiver. *Oh, fae…*

I want to taste Flame.

But I also want to finally feel Reaper.

I can do both, I realize, my blood heating despite all the pleasure I've experienced this morning. *I don't have to choose.*

"I turned around," I tell Reaper.

"Yes, you did," he murmurs. "Now all you have to do is *find out.*"

My brow furrows, my brain having trouble processing what he means.

But then I recall what he told me to do—*"Turn around and find out."*

My gaze drifts over his chiseled chest and abdomen to his jeans, noting the unfastened top button. But the rest of him is all zipped up, hiding his lower half from view.

I reach for his pants, then dart my eyes back up to his in an attempt to judge his expression. His silver-blue irises give nothing away. But his lips… his lips are still tilted upward in an enticing smile.

So I tug the zipper down.

His pupils flare in response.

He's excited. He wants this. However, he's holding himself back.

For me, I realize. *He's allowing me to set the pace.*

Oh, he'll push me. He proved that with the knife earlier—which was an experience I will never forget.

Even though the blade scared me, I liked how it made me feel. Because while I knew Reaper was dangerous, deep down, I also knew I was in control. If I used my safeword, I had no doubt in my mind that he would listen to me.

Maybe trusting him was crazy.

But at this point, I'm just embracing fate.

And right now, that fate is staring down at me expectantly. "Are you going to touch me, pet?" he asks. "Or should I just bind your wrists again?" His tattoos move as though preparing to do just that while his focus goes to my lips. "I don't need your hands when I can use your mouth."

Emboldened, I tug at his pants, trying to yank them down his muscular thighs. But I'm on my side, making it difficult to do with one hand.

He doesn't help me.

Just watches as I struggle.

I narrow my gaze. "Take them off, Reaper."

Amusement flashes in his eyes. "That's hot. Command me again."

"Follow my first command and I will," I counter.

He gifts me with a smile. "All right, pet." He disappears from the bed, causing me to gasp.

"*Reaper*," I growl. "That's not—"

He returns to his same position, sans pants, and cocks a brow. "That's not what?" he asks.

But any thought of a retort or a reply vanishes at the sight of his beautiful, naked form.

His tattoos are still moving, the dark swirls shifting on and off his torso and running up and down his arms. However, his thighs are bare.

And his cock… is tattooed, too. Only it's not swirls. It's…

"Is that my name?" I ask, stunned.

"Yep."

No explanation or elaboration. No hesitation, either. Just… *Yep.* "What…? What does that mean? And why is there a skull next to it?"

"You're a Death Fae's mate," he says simply. "*My* mate. And you know what a good mate would do right now?"

I blink at him. "I… No?"

"A good mate would trace the tattoo on my shaft, preferably with her tongue."

Flame chuckles behind me. "I think Reaper would like you to thank him for his tribute, little panther."

"I don't need a thank-you, but I would love a blow job," Reaper says, his dick seeming to strain toward me while he speaks.

I'm guessing a "blow job" is something sexual, based on his physical reaction. And given that he requested I lick his dick, I'm going to assume said "blow job" involves my mouth.

"He wants you to suck his cock, little panther," Flame whispers against my ear, his words making my belly flip. "Do you want to taste him?"

I swallow, my eyes tracing each letter of my name. "I do," I admit, my fingers reaching for Reaper. "Yes, I do."

Because I want to feel him. Know him. *Savor* him.

Just like these fae have done to me.

"I want to taste both of you," I say to them.

"Then do it, pet," Reaper dares me. "Lick me."

CHAPTER TWENTY-SIX
ALINA

I DON'T IMMEDIATELY CAVE to Reaper's demand. Instead, I wrap my palm around his base and give him a tentative stroke.

He's not as thick as Flame, but he's long. *And hot.*

Flame kisses my shoulder again, then drags his teeth along my skin to my pulse, where he gently bites down. "Push him to his back, little panther," he instructs me. "Then straddle him so he can feel your sweet heat against his cock. It'll drive him crazy."

My heart skips a beat at the thought of pressing my intimate flesh to Reaper's. Yet, as I follow Flame's command, I realize how natural it all feels. My thighs automatically part over Reaper's hips, my core meeting his shaft in a sinful kiss. It's... it's where I should be. With him. With *them.*

I lean down to press my lips to his, needing him to feel what I feel. To experience this intensity. To understand that I *belong* here.

His arms wrap around me, his skin a brand against my lower back.

I shift on top of him, painting him with my arousal.

It's… it's just so intuitive. I want to share this part of me with him, to claim him with my body.

But I still want to taste him.

So I do what Flame did to me—I start exploring Reaper's body with my tongue and my mouth. I work my way down his torso, pausing to trace his rippled abdomen with my lips, and continue to his hardened flesh.

My succulent aroma is all over his skin, creating an erotic experience as I taste the moisture on his tip. That part was all him, the saltiness combining with my essence to produce an intoxicating flavor that I need more of.

"Fuck, pet," Reaper groans, his fingers weaving through my hair as I take more of him into my mouth. "Try to swallow your whole name. Yeah, just like that. *Fuck*."

Another hand goes to my nape, this one hotter and belonging to Flame. He's right beside me, his thumb circling my pulse. "That looks amazing, little panther," he tells me. "You're taking so much of him into your beautiful mouth."

I pull back up to breathe, then go down again, my throat instantly soothed by the feel of Reaper gliding in deep.

"Grab his base," Flame whispers. "Give it a squeeze and hollow your cheeks."

I do what he says.

"So good, sweet panther," he praises me. "Look at Reaper. Do you see that fire in his eyes? *You* created that. And now you're stoking it with that talented mouth."

A shiver traverses my spine, my lips nearly curling.

Because he's right.

Reaper looks like he's positively burning for me.

I'm doing this to him. Me. I'm driving him crazy, just like he's done to me.

Realizing that only emboldens me more.

I run my thumb along his throbbing shaft, tracing one of the thick veins while I torture the tip with my tongue.

Then I suck him down again.

He curses.

His grip tightens.

His muscles strain.

And so I do it again.

Teasing him. Laving him. Sucking him. Swallowing around the head.

I even pause to trace my name with my tongue, just like he requested earlier.

Then I return to my task, all while Flame is whispering praise into my ear, his palm never leaving my nape.

Reaper is panting, his jaw clenching as his grip tightens even more in my hair. It almost hurts. But I like it. I like it because it shows me how close he is to losing control.

"Don't stop," he tells me. "Don't fucking stop."

I obey, but I love knowing that I technically don't have to, that I can pull away whenever I want to and leave him in this tormented state.

However, I don't want to do that to him.

I want to make him fall apart.

I want to give him pleasure like he's given me.

"That's it. Fuck, yeah, just like that." He pumps up into my mouth, forcing me to take more of him. "Gods, I hope you can swallow, pet…"

"Take a breath," Flame murmurs against my ear. "You're going to need it."

I follow his advice and am glad I did. Because in the next instant, Reaper growls and something hot hits the back of my throat. I swallow on instinct, my stomach tightening with desire.

I've never tasted anything like this.

It's salty and smoky and tinged with my sweetness.

And so, so good…

My throat works around him, taking every drop as I absorb Reaper into my very soul. *He's mine. My Death Fae. My mate.*

It's a foreign concept.

A strange sort of understanding.

But I know deep down that he's my destiny.

By the time he's done, I'm dizzy with the need to breathe, yet I can't stop hoping for more of that delicious flavor. This sense of *purpose*.

Reaper says my name.

Flame does as well.

But I don't stop. Not right away. *Not yet.*

I suck him down one more time, then twirl my tongue around the tip before pouncing on Flame. Because I need to know if he's the same. I need to feel connected to him, too. I need his soul to brush mine, to ground me in this moment for eternity.

He catches my hips as I slide on top of him, amusement curling his lips. "Ready to play, little panther?"

"Yes," I say, bending to kiss him with a renewed ferocity.

My blood is on fire.

My body damp.

My core *clenching* with desire.

I need these fae. These men. *My mates.*

Everything is moving so quickly, my world spinning with passion and *want*.

I can't stop it. I don't want to stop it. I embrace it.

Flame's body is hard beneath my tongue, his muscular

planes similar to Reaper's yet somehow more pronounced. Maybe it's his sleek shifter form, or maybe he's just a little bulkier than the Death Fae.

I don't care. I adore both of them equally.

And they're both mine, I realize, dizzy all over again. *How do I have two mates?*

No.

Not two.

Three…

I'm missing my fresh air. Yet his cologne is still here, swirling around me, taunting my inner spirit, telling me I'm his, too.

My refreshing mountain hike, I think, feeling at ease and needy at the same time.

Flame curses as I draw my teeth against his throbbing flesh, his palm finding my nape again as he holds me in place. "Tongue the ring," he begs me. "Explore it, little panther. And, fuck me, use your teeth again. Yeah, sweetling. Just like that."

I suck on the metal, then draw my touch down to the bar and lick the tip of it against the underside of his shaft. I'm about to tug on it with my teeth when I feel Reaper behind me, his palms skimming up my inner thighs to widen my stance.

"I want to see how wet this makes you, pet," he tells me as he repositions my lower body over his face. "Sit."

The command sends a spike of lust up my spine and forces my body to obey.

Fae… I'm straddling his face.

My sex is against his mouth.

His tongue is prodding my entrance. His fingers, too.

I'm going to suffocate him, I think, trying to move.

But a slap to my ass has me pressing down into his face in response.

"He can breathe," Flame says, his voice strained. "And if he can't, he'll happily die between those thighs. Now focus on sucking my cock, Alina."

Oh, fae... Between Flame's demand and Reaper's tongue, I'm a shaking mess.

I'm not even sure I can climax again.

But the heat brewing inside me suggests I might be able to. Especially if Reaper keeps doing *that*.

I swallow, the action reminding me of the metal against my lips. I'm not even sure how to begin navigating this for Flame, but I'm excited by the challenge.

He wants me to suck his cock? I'll suck. I'll play. I'll *fondle*.

A hiss escapes him as I close my mouth over his thick head, my tongue flicking his ring along the way. Then I take him all the way down to the bar piercing at the center of his shaft.

I'm so full that I'm not sure I can take any more.

However, I'm suddenly determined to try.

I wrap my hand around his base, just like he told me to do to Reaper, and force more of him into my throat. It's dangerous. I can't breathe at all like this. I... I might choke. And the piercings are an addition that I'm not sure I'm ready to handle.

Yet I try anyway.

I do it for him. For me. For *us*.

And I'm rewarded with a squeeze against my nape as he says, "You're so fucking good at this, my panther queen. A fucking Goddess."

Reaper hums in agreement against my clit, then sinks his teeth into my flesh, making me yelp around Flame's cock.

"*Fuck*, do that again," Flame demands.

I'm not sure who he's talking to, but I realize he means

Reaper when the man between my legs bites me again. This time I scream because it *hurts*.

Only for him to lave the pain away with his tongue.

My thighs quake, my insides ablaze with renewed desire.

I'm sweating. Panting. Sucking. Nearly choking. Exploring with my tongue. All while fighting the urge to fall apart on top of Reaper.

It's the definition of insanity.

The best kind of insanity.

A world of eroticism.

I feel empowered. Cherished. And *used*.

It's… it's amazing.

Flame pumps himself into my mouth while Reaper plunges his tongue into my core. They're fucking me from different angles, the sensuous dance drawing me into a euphoric state of existence.

We're creating something powerful, our mingling scents reminding me of a strawberry field hidden deep on a mountain side.

I want to revel in that existence, live there for the rest of my life, and join myself with these fae.

"Use your teeth, little panther." Flame's deep voice pierces through my mind, driving my actions. "Fuck, sweetling. Keep doing that."

I'm not biting him, but I'm applying more pressure as I drag my mouth up and down his thick manhood. He's so hard that I can feel his pulse through the silky skin. It's beating against my tongue, demanding more. Demanding that I keep going. Demanding that I swallow him whole.

So I do.

All the way down.

As deep as I can possibly go.

"*Fuck.*" He arches into me, hitting the back of my throat. "Make her come, Reaper. *Now.*"

I swear the Death Fae between my legs smiles, but I don't have a chance to think much of it because he bites me so hard in the next instant that I tumble over the cliff into a world of pain-induced pleasure.

I don't understand what he did, but that bite... that bite... *is intoxicating.*

"Fuck, yes," Flame groans, his cock driving in and out of my mouth. "I'm about to join you, little panther. Try to swallow for me, sweetheart."

I don't know if I can.

I'm swimming in ecstasy.

And now he's going to drown me with his essence.

I try to relax my throat for him, but my body is too keyed up from the orgasm to listen to me. Dark spots dance in my vision as he explodes in my mouth, his flavor different from Reaper's. His seed still has that hint of salt, but it's headier. Thicker. More decadent.

I'm instantly hit with another climax, and I'm not sure if it's from Flame's intense flavor or Reaper's skilled mouth.

Or both.

But I'm overcome with it all, grinding on top of Reaper's face while drinking from Flame.

It's all so much. Too much. Those dark spots are getting bigger. I've forgotten how to breathe. I can only swallow and writhe.

I'm barely aware of the men moving until I'm cradled against Reaper's chest, his strong arms holding me while Flame kisses me. My body is still shaking, my insides tightening and spiraling and sending shocks of pleasure to every nerve ending.

How...? I want to ask.

But my mouth is busy with Flame's, his tongue gently caressing mine while Reaper kisses my neck and shoulders. "You're doing so good," he says against my ear. "Just ride it out, pet."

I whimper, not sure what he means. *Why am I still shaking?*

Flame's palms are on my cheeks, his mouth soft and commanding at the same time.

Reaper's hands stroke my back.

We're a tangle of limbs, all of us naked and hot and sweaty.

The heady aroma of sex tinges the air, my sweetness potent and ripe.

By the time I stop trembling, I'm practically coated in the fragrance. It's everywhere. In me. On me. All over them.

I gasp as Reaper's teeth bite into my shoulder just hard enough to anchor me without breaking the skin.

Then Flame pulls back to stare into my eyes. "You're amazing, Alina."

"Fucking phenomenal," Reaper echoes.

I blink at the Shifter Fae, unable to form words. My throat hurts, not just from taking his thrusts but also from *screaming*.

Yet I don't even remember making a sound.

My fingers flutter up to my throat as though searching for answers. But my wrist is caught in Flame's grasp as he brings my hand to his mouth. "Thank you, little panther."

Reaper snorts. "You're thanking her like we're already done." His palms continue to soothingly stroke my back, his lips at my ear once more. "You can rest, pet. I know Flame's cum can be potent. But once the aftershocks die down, we're doing this again."

"She needs to eat first," Flame tells him, a hint of dominance in his tone. "I'm also pouring her a bath."

"You just want to brush her hair."

"Of course I want to brush her hair. I've been dying to brush her hair since the moment we first saw her," Flame tosses back at him, making my lips curl a little.

"You want to brush my hair?" The words come out raspy, my vocal cords clearly damaged.

"She needs some soup," Flame informs Reaper. "How about you work on that while I groom her?"

Reaper sighs. "Fine. But once we formally mate her, this will no longer be an issue. She just needs a little immortality boost to help her recover."

Flame grunts but doesn't say anything as he takes me from Reaper's arms.

Immortality? I repeat to myself. *Is that what will happen when they mate me?*

I'm not sure how to feel about that.

Happy? Scared? Relieved?

Because it means I can truly keep them for eternity.

Live like this for the rest of... *forever.*

That... that doesn't sound all that bad. Actually, it sounds pretty amazing.

As does letting Flame brush my hair, I decide, gazing up at him from where he has me cradled in his lap. "I—"

A glass of water appears as Reaper's nude form comes into view. He's standing next to the bed. "Drink that before you speak, pet."

I don't bother arguing, mostly because I'm parched.

He stands there and observes as I drink every drop, his expression satisfied at the end. "Good girl." He takes the glass. "I'll bring more into the bathroom." He looks at Flame. "Go groom our pet. Lunch will be ready when you're done."

CHAPTER TWENTY-SEVEN
ORCUS

"I HEAR YOUR INTENDED MENTIONED CHICAGO," Queen Helia says, her long nails drumming along the armrest of her chaise lounge.

She's not what I expected. Oh, she's regal and clearly used to being the most powerful being in the room, but she's relaxed in a way I didn't anticipate.

It seems her obsession with rules isn't quite as intense as what Emissary Jones led me to believe.

"I'm sorry for all the formalities and the runaround, God Orcus. My Emissaries are protective of me," she said shortly after I arrived.

My eyebrow inched upward at the title. "You're aware of what I am?"

She shrugged. "I sense origins. Power. Portals. It's all within my realm of knowledge." She stepped forward, extending her hand. "I'm Helia, Queen of Monster City. But please don't worry about the distinction. I wouldn't dare to ask a God to address me as his Queen."

All expectations of hating the woman on sight ended in that moment.

Instead, I accepted her gesture and joined her in the opulent seating area of her suite, where she served some sort of red alcoholic punch.

Reaper would tsk at me for trying it, but it wasn't like poison would work on me.

"It's fascinating," she continues now, bringing me back to our ongoing conversation. "Humans of this time are not acquainted with old city names. I don't suppose your intended mentioned how or where she heard about Chicago?"

"She hasn't. She's only said that she needs to find Chicago." I lean forward in my chair—an oversized beige leather monstrosity that pairs well with the gold fixtures of the room—and brace my forearms against my thighs. "What can you tell me about the Elite City?"

Thus far, we've primarily focused on inner-dimension relations. She hasn't given my world express permission to remain here, and I haven't requested it. *Yet.*

I suspect we won't reach that part of the conversation until she's done feeling me out.

Which is precisely what she's been doing since I arrived.

I can feel her energy caressing mine, searching for any and all weaknesses.

Unfortunately for her, she won't find any.

"In order to understand the Elite City, you first need to understand our history here." She picks up her crystal wine glass and brings the decorated rim to her plump lips.

It's a seductive move, one I suspect is another test of sorts.

She's a beautiful woman, with long, athletic legs and a model-esque form. If she were a Mythos Fae, I would guess her to be an Alpha like me. She's too tall to be a Beta or an Omega, and she's too bold to be anything other than an Alpha.

But her skin gives her away as being something entirely other.

At first glance, she appears to be dark-skinned. However, the sunlight streaming in betrays the violet shimmer coating her otherwise black complexion.

It's a trait that's extremely evident now when the sun catches her hand as she returns her glass to the table.

"The first portal opened in this realm over a thousand years ago, but for many centuries, monsterkind visited in secret. That changed when we realized some of the humans were actually compatible mates." Her long legs shift along the chaise as she angles her body toward me and props her head up on her elbow.

"I assume this discovery led to the establishment of Monsters Night?" I prompt her, not interested in whatever sexual game she's trying to play with me.

"In a roundabout way, yes. But it took us over two centuries to perfect it. We're now in our three hundred and thirteenth year, and we've more or less perfected the process. However, it took collaboration with the humans to get to where we are. Which is how the Elite City comes into play."

Helia delves into a history lesson regarding how the monsters first approached a particular sect of humans.

They were mortals of certain bloodlines and beings with strong influence over their constituents—basically royal families, politicians, and other high-ranking members of human society. The monsters offered them boons in exchange for helping them manufacture ideal monster mates.

"Places like the Elite City were created to house these

families and now, their descendants," she goes on. "Within the city walls, there are sectors. Each sector comes with more power and gifts, with the ultimate layer being the Immortality Sector."

"Of course," I reply, not at all surprised that humans are willing to barter with monsters for such a precious gift. "Humans always want to live forever."

"Exactly," she says. "And they're willing to do anything and everything in their power to achieve it. Including sacrificing other humans to the cause."

My stomach tightens with unease, certain that I'm not going to like the direction this conversation is headed in.

"You see, each Elite family owns a village of humans. Your intended, for example, is from the Nightingale Village. Duke Nightingale, a human, oversees the breeding and maintenance of the crop in that village. He then reviews ample data and statistics every year to decide who is and isn't chosen for Monsters Night."

It takes serious effort to school my features and not react to my intended being referred to as a *crop*, like she's an animal, not a Goddess.

However, Helia's commentary about the *breeding* does interest me.

Because it's clear that humans in this world have been infused with some supernatural traits, thus making them even more compatible.

Although, her words suggested it may have actually been a natural evolution, not a manufactured one.

"When you say *breeding* and *maintenance*, what do you mean exactly? Is Duke Nightingale pairing specific humans together to increase the potential for compatibility with otherworldly beings?" I ask, interrupting whatever Helia had been about to say.

She smiles. "Basically, yes. Which is the beauty of our

program here. The humans are competing with each other to manufacture the highest-quality monster mates. So yes, they are prearranging matches based on genetic markers known to be compatible with beings from other realms."

I arch a brow. "And that's all they're doing?" I can't help the incredulity in my tone.

Alina's an Omega. There's no way humans just happened to create her with normal mortal genetics.

"Well, that's what they're supposed to be doing. But humans are prone to cheating. And cheating has severe consequences, as some Elite families have discovered the hard way."

Her lips purse as darkness flirts with her features. It makes me wonder what she's not telling me.

Is Alina a result of said cheating? Or is she thinking about something else entirely?

Helia blinks, her dark expression clearing in an instant. "Well, that all said, the breeding process is overseen by the Elite families. They decide how they want to create their ideal Offerings; we just provide them with general accommodations to help facilitate the process."

Helia starts talking about the breeding compounds utilized by the Elite families.

Apparently, the Nightingale Compound is right outside of former-day Chicago.

"Most ideal children are born there, then placed with adequate families in the village," she explains. "Of course, that practice varies by Elite family. Some choose to do it the old-fashioned way, too. We, as in monsterkind, don't tell them what to do. We simply reward them for a job well done and remind them of their task when they fail to meet our expectations."

She elaborates a bit, saying how the reward structure is based on how well the village's Offerings do during

Monsters Night. Higher-ranking supernatural matches earn higher rewards.

Offerings who fail to match, however, fall into the *reminder* category. Which I assume relates to some sort of punishment system to keep the Elite families in line.

"If Alina Everheart proves to be your ideal mate, then Duke Nightingale will be handsomely rewarded," she adds. "You're a God from a brand-new dimension. There is no one in this city who is higher ranking than that. Not even me."

"So it's all about which mates are chosen and by whom," I translate.

"Yes. And you being from a new dimension makes your match even more profitable. Particularly as we hope to establish a potential partnership between our worlds."

"What kind of partnership?"

"We'll get back to that," she tells me, waving it away with those sharp nails of hers.

Yes, I think. *We will.*

"What I'm trying to explain is, the humans compete with each other to create the best Offerings. The Elite City your intended is interested in houses the Elite families who manage our villages. I can't imagine why she would want to go there. She shouldn't even know that the Elite City exists."

That much I've already gathered from what she and the Emissary have said. "I'll have to ask more about it later," I say, reiterating that I don't know why Alina mentioned Chicago.

And even if I did know, I likely wouldn't share the information with Helia.

It's not any of her business why my Omega wants to find the Elite City.

However, I do want to ask Alina about it, primarily for my own knowledge.

"Are we allowed to venture into the Elite City?" I inquire, curious as to what boundaries this Queen may try to impose upon me and my fellow fae. I also want to shift the conversation away from my Omega. She keeps using Alina as an *example*, and it's making me uncomfortable.

"If we come to amicable terms between your dimension and mine, then yes, you can venture anywhere you want. Personally, I would recommend Monster Island or Monster Isle. The Elite City is mostly populated by humans, and as you seem to have found your mate, you'd probably be bored there."

I don't comment on her suggestions. While playing peekaboo with the portal window, I caught sight of both those places—Monster Island was in the Pacific Ocean, and Monster Isle was formerly known as the Isle of Man.

I may visit them later to search for other potential Omega souls. But for now, I would focus on the Elite City. *For Alina.*

"As you can imagine, we've adopted the Monsters Night process all over the world," Helia continues. "Each location has a monster ruler, except for the villages. Villages have Viscounts, who report to the Elite families. In most cases, the Viscounts are the only ones who know about the Elite families."

She turns thoughtful, her gaze narrowing.

But after a moment, she shakes her head and picks up her glass once more. "Anyway, once your realm is in good status, you and your kind can venture wherever you'd like. I'll just add that it's considered common etiquette to let the local leadership know if you intend to visit."

I nod. "Then we should discuss your terms for good status."

"Oh, the terms are quite simple. We request that your dimension only visit one night a year—on Monsters Night —and only for the allotted time. Anyone wishing to remain in our realm will need to request permission from the leadership of their chosen locale. For example, if one wished to stay in Monster City, he or she would need to talk to me. And we ask that you refrain from any and all violence while on our soil."

"I assume you're referring to the humans we killed," I drawl.

She shrugs. "We're more concerned with monster-on-monster violence, but yes, harming humans is frowned upon. However, it's my understanding that you had just cause?"

"We did. And we want access to the third human so we can continue delivering our judgment."

Her dark brow arches. "Your soul eater's mental torment isn't enough for you?"

I assume *soul eater* refers to Reaper.

Because of course he's been visiting the human.

I can practically hear him saying, "They said we couldn't kill him. They said nothing about delivering other forms of punishment." He would follow that up with a shrug, adding, "I'm still following the rules."

Typical Reaper.

Regardless of his antics… "Alina deserves the right to kill the man for trying to harm her," I say to Helia.

The human hurt our intended mate.

The human will suffer.

"This is not how we typically operate, but given the circumstances, I can offer him to you as a gift. However, I want something in return."

My eyebrow lifts. "A boon for a boon?"

"It's how things are done here, and thus far, I've offered you and your mates several boons."

Reaper and Flame are technically not my mates, but I don't correct her.

Instead, I focus on the insinuation that I owe her a great deal for her *boons*.

"We remained here as a courtesy, Queen Helia. While we appreciate your hospitality, it's not a gift or a boon when partnered with a mandate. We did you a favor by respecting your meeting request when we could have very easily vanished."

Not exactly true—we needed to remain here.

But she isn't aware of that.

Her dark eyes flash as she studies me, her energy whirling dangerously around my aura. "I think we both know we stand to win more by creating a partnership. Becoming enemies would be… a disappointment."

"I agree," I tell her. "But understand that your definition of a boon does not match my own. So whatever you intend to request from me needs to be an appropriate trade."

She dips her head, her wine glass twirling in her fingers. "Fair enough." She sets the drink aside again and sits up, her thin heels clacking loudly on the marble floor. "I would like to invite you and your mates to a dinner."

I stare at her. "You want us to attend a dinner?"

She nods. "As a boon, yes."

I'm instantly suspicious. "Why?"

"Do I need a reason?"

"If you're asking me to sacrifice something, then yes, you do."

"All I'm asking for is the sacrifice of time, God Orcus." She smiles. "It will just be an intimate gathering between mates."

My lips flatten. "We don't share. And we don't swing."

The Queen throws her head back on a laugh that booms through the room. Whatever monster type she hides beneath her skin is intense. That sound alone proves it.

"Don't worry, darling. Orgies are no longer my thing." Her eyes are dreamy as she adds, "I'm a two-mate kind of woman now, and those positions are very much filled."

"Then what's the purpose of this dinner?"

"To form an alliance and to appease our mates," she says cryptically. "Do you agree to the boon or not?"

Reaper and Flame are going to fucking kill me.

But alliances are important.

And we need to remain on good terms in this realm. *So...* "I agree."

She smiles. "Excellent. My mates will be pleased."

Meanwhile, my two best friends will be fantasizing about how best to slay you, I think. *But as that's their version of pleasure, I suppose I could say the same.*

Alas, I refrain from voicing that out loud and focus on more important items.

Like *rules.*

"Just so I'm clear, if I want to travel within this realm, I'm allowed," I say. "However, if I want to stay somewhere, I should provide notice of my intent."

"Yes. Although, the transportation offerings vary by region. My territory, for example, specializes in trains. But, as you may have gathered, my jurisdiction primarily stretches between the Elite City and Monster City. It also goes as far north as former-day Boston, and as far south as Nightingale Village, which is near where Asheville used to exist in the olden days."

She talks about a few other locations, such as the

boating system near Monster Island, and something about ferries in Monsters Isle.

I listen politely, but I don't really care about standard transportation mechanisms. They won't be needed.

"What if I want to portal home?" I finally interject, more interested in any potential restrictions that may forbid me from venturing between dimensions. "Emissary Jones mentioned that I needed a higher rank to portal at will."

She nods. "Portals between realms are frowned upon outside of Monsters Night. We don't want beings coming and going without prior authorization. It has the potential to upset the balance we've created here."

"While I respect that, I'm not someone who can remain grounded in a single realm," I tell her.

"Yes, I suspected as much." She taps her chin. "All right, while you're in my territory, you can portal at will. But any other beings from your world—not including your mates—are only allowed to visit this realm on Monsters Night. Violation of that term could result in a breaking of our new alliance."

"Only within your territory?" I ask, clarifying that point.

"I can only grant permissions within my own kingdom. Should you wish to be allowed universal portaling rights elsewhere, you'll need to confer with the local King or Queen."

"So in the Elite City…?" I trail off, arching a brow.

"Oh, the Elite City King is a dear friend of mine. If I grant you portal rights, he'll honor them as well. But anywhere else? Yes, you would need permission."

"I see." While inconvenient, it isn't the worst requirement. "As for my fae remaining in this realm, there are two Strigoi in the building who have expressed an interest in staying. Are you saying they need to return to my world?"

My voice is neutral as I ask the question. I really don't care either way, but I told Cage and Sabre that I would inquire about their options.

"You mean the dreamwalkers?"

"Yes. We call them Strigoi." Because they're more than dreamwalkers. They're strongly related to vampires, hence their need for blood.

"Interesting." She considers for a moment, like she's truly intrigued. "Hmm, well, they're no longer under my jurisdiction. Cain has already escorted them to the Elite City."

"What?" *The guy in the suit from earlier has my Strigoi?*

She blinks at me. "When I mentioned their existence to Cain, he came to learn more about their talents. And I felt the three of them leave shortly after our conversation began. I assume that means he intends to keep them."

"He can't *keep* them. They're under my protection."

"Well, I'm afraid you'll have to take that up with Cain."

I pinch the bridge of my nose. "Which, let me guess, requires approval from the Elite City King?" Since I'll have to visit fucking Chicago to track this asshole down.

"Well, normally, yes. But in this case, Cain is the Elite City King." Her lips curl. "I'm sure he would love for you to visit."

I'm sure he won't want me to visit at all.

Because when I find him, I'll unleash Reaper on him.

Trying to keep our Strigoi. Who the fuck is this guy? And what the fuck is he?

I run my hand over my face. This meeting has gone on long enough. "I need to inform my men of this development."

"Of course," she murmurs. "I'll send you an invitation for dinner at a later date. Until then, feel free to keep the suite."

"Thank you," I tell her.

But we won't be needing it much longer, I think. *Because all four of us will be heading to the Elite City. Tonight.*

CHAPTER TWENTY-EIGHT
FLAME

"YOUR HAIR IS SO BEAUTIFUL," I murmur as I draw a comb through Alina's damp strands. She's lounging in my lap in the bathtub, her body practically humming with content.

Or maybe that's just my purr whirring through her that I'm sensing.

It's no longer a sexual rumble, but a soothing one, similar to the one Orcus emits in her presence.

My jaguar is momentarily satisfied.

Yet my cock is still hard against Alina's bare ass.

I'm pretty sure I will forever be aroused in her presence, and I'm not the least bit displeased with that fact.

"Thank you for brushing it," Alina whispers. "It feels nice."

I kiss her neck. "I'll happily brush your hair every day for the rest of our lives."

She shivers, her body melting into mine even more. "For... for eternity, right?"

I smile. "Yeah, little panther. For eternity."

"Once we mate?" she clarifies, obviously having heard Reaper's comments about her pending immortality.

"Yes." I set the comb aside and clasp her chin to guide her face backward so our eyes can meet. "How do you feel about that?" I imagine it's a bit overwhelming for her.

Although, she was born in a world where supernaturals taking mates is considered normal, so perhaps it's not all that unexpected.

"I... I feel relieved," she whispers. "I like being here with you. With Reaper. With Orcus, too. You all make me feel safe and warm and..." She trails off, her nose scrunching.

"And?" I prompt her.

"Needy," she admits, squirming a little in my lap.

I chuckle, my arm banding around her lower belly while I keep my opposite hand on her chin. "Fae have quite the sex drive, my panther queen. It's okay to feel needy. I think it's pretty clear that I feel similarly." To showcase my point, I press my cock against her ass.

She blushes fiercely in response.

It's adorable.

"Mythos Fae Omegas are even more sexually charged than most," I add. "Or that's what Orcus has said, anyway. Reaper is quite excited about it."

Alina's cheeks turn redder. "I'm not sure how to respond to that."

"You don't have to respond at all." I release her chin to palm her cheek. "But I wouldn't be sad if you wanted to kiss me again instead."

Her lips curl a little, then she leans into me and slowly turns around in the water to face me.

It's a massive whirlpool-style tub, making it easy for her to move and straddle my hips.

Of course, this position presses her hot center to my throbbing shaft.

Which just makes me want to devour her all over again.

But I don't want to push her. So instead, I simply kiss her. It's a tender embrace, one I allow her to lead with her tongue.

She's hesitant at first, then grows bolder as she presses her tits to my chest. I slide forward to allow her legs to wind around my back, our sexual position exciting my inner beast. He's practically feral for her.

However, I still have my piercings in. Thus, I can't fuck her yet.

Although, that could be quickly remedied.

Her pussy grinds against me, her breathing coming in a sweet pant as she presses herself even closer to my chest. "Flame," she exhales.

"Alina," I return, my teeth grazing her lower lip. "Tell me what you need, sweetheart."

She quivers, her long, dark lashes parting to reveal her big, beautiful eyes. "I just want to be near you."

"Then be near me," I tell her. "I'll be whatever you need me to be, little panther."

Her arms tighten as she hugs me and buries her face in my neck. I wrap myself around her in kind, my nose going to her freshly washed hair. We showered before getting in the tub, mostly so we could just soak and relax in the whirling water.

I'm happy about that decision now, as it's clear she needed it.

"This is all so different from how I thought Monsters Night would go," she says near my ear, her voice low. "But the Duke said something about how my fate with the monsters would be a lot kinder than my fate in the village. He said my future mate, or *mates*, would worship me."

I'm not sure who this Duke is that she's referring to, but... "He wasn't wrong," I say aloud.

"He, uh, didn't mention the *breeding* part, though," she adds as she pulls back to study my face. "What... what does that mean, exactly?" Her brow furrows. "I mean, I know what the term means. But... for us. You want... children?"

I run my thumb across her bottom lip. "Yeah, I do." I slowly return my gaze to hers. "Do you?"

She swallows. "I didn't before, back in the village. The men there repulsed me. The idea of creating a family with them..." She blanches, her expression telling me everything I need to know about that concept.

"But now?" I prompt. "How do you feel about the idea of receiving my barb? Knowing what it might create?"

Her pupils dilate a little. "I don't know," she admits softly. "I..." She frowns. "It's strange. I know it should intimidate me, especially with how fast everything has changed. But I don't fear it?" She phrases it as a question, like it confuses her that she's not afraid.

"That's not the same as wanting a child," I point out.

She considers me for a moment. "I think it's too new for me to determine my true feelings. I just know that it no longer repels me like it did in the village. Instead... the notion feels pleasant. Like it's something I want to embrace."

I nod. "It's a big change for you to accept," I acknowledge out loud. "For me, Orcus, and Reaper, we've all been searching for our mate for so long that this doesn't feel sudden or unexpected at all. There's simply no alternative for us. No competing desires. There's just you."

"Just me," she repeats with a breath.

"Just you," I echo. "I know it's overwhelming, but what you experienced with me and Reaper today? That's only a taste of what we can offer you."

Goose bumps pebble down her arms despite the warm water, her lower half pressing intimately into mine. "Only a taste?" Her throat works as though she's thinking about said *taste*. "I... I don't know if I can handle more..."

I chuckle. "We'll see, won't we?"

Because I can smell her approaching heat.

While I might not be a Mythos Fae, I am a Shifter Fae. And my jaguar is all Alpha. He's content at the moment, simply observing through my eyes and patiently waiting for his chance to truly pounce.

It'll be intense.

Powerful.

Mind-blowing.

And Alina is going to love it.

There's just one part that concerns me—her stance on children. While she seems to consider it a pleasant prospect, it lacked the excitement I'm used to hearing in a fae's voice when speaking about faelings.

Granted, she wasn't born a fae; she's human.

Which is why I need her to understand what's going to happen during her heat. Orcus has explained it as well, but her consent—her *willingness*—is vital.

Moving too fast could push her away, and I would never forgive myself if that happened.

She's our mate. Our world. Our destiny.

She needs to know that we won't force her to do anything that she's not one hundred percent comfortable with doing. Her consent before her heat is imperative. Because once she loses herself to the need to procreate, she won't be of sound mind to make decisions for herself.

It'll be up to us—her mates—to ensure her wishes are respected.

"When you go into heat, your body is going to lead your every instinct," I tell her softly. While I might not be a Mythos Fae, I am familiar with Shifter Fae heats. And from what Orcus has said, the process is very similar for the Omegas of his kind.

"Meaning?"

"Meaning your mind won't be in control," I explain. "You'll be consumed by the need to fuck. And you're going to beg us to fill you with our seed. To breed you. To create a life together."

It'll be an innate need that she hopefully won't regret after it happens.

Unless the mortal part of her—the one staring incredulously at me right now—reacts otherwise.

"I realize it's a lot," I whisper, my fingers combing through her damp strands. "We're trying to ease you into it."

"I know," she says, her voice equally soft. "Thank you."

My mouth curls. "Don't thank me for doing the right thing, sweetheart. Your comfort will always come first. No matter what." I press a kiss to her lips, my smile growing as I hear her stomach rumble with a need to eat. "And speaking of comfort, it's time for lunch."

Alina doesn't protest as I pull her out of the tub and wrap her up in a fluffy towel. She's still a little dazed from our conversation, or perhaps her dreamy state is from the multitude of orgasms she's had today. Regardless, it's cute.

I comb her hair again—because I want to.

Then find a robe for her to wear. It's too big and hits her at midcalf, but she's comfortable and that's all I really care about.

I grab one for myself as well—the fabric not nearly as

oversized on my taller frame—and guide her out into the suite to where Orcus and Reaper are deep in discussion.

They pause when we enter, Orcus's gaze instantly going to Alina. His hard expression melts almost immediately, his dark eyes flickering with glimmers of red as the Alpha inside him admires his chosen Omega.

"You look pleased," he murmurs, devotion underlining those three words. "Like a queen."

"Because she's fucking magnificent," Reaper says, winking at her. "Which reminds me…" He vanishes into the kitchen and returns with a tray. "Six cupcakes for six glorious orgasms." He presses a kiss to her cheek. "Such a good pet."

Her cheeks pinken.

But rather than comment, she plucks a cupcake from the tray and peels off the wrapper to begin eating it.

"Six?" Orcus echoes, sounding impressed.

"She had four," Reaper amends. "We had one each. That's six."

Alina's face is bright red now.

I just shake my head with a laugh and kiss her opposite cheek. "Just safeword him if he starts to bother you," I tell her, making her eyes widen.

"She has a safeword now?" Orcus asks, no hint of jealousy in his tone, just mild curiosity. "Care to share?"

"Chicago," Reaper replies as he sets the tray of cupcakes down on a nearby table.

Orcus frowns at him. "I'm getting to that. I want my question answered first."

"No, that's the safeword," Reaper clarifies. "But yes, we also need to discuss our plans. You tell them what's happening, and I'll go get the nest packed up."

My eyebrows lift as Reaper vanishes once more, presumably to *pack*. "What's going on?"

"We're going to Chicago," Orcus says, causing Alina to pause midbite. "The Elite City King kidnapped our Strigoi, and I need to go find out why." His irritation is palpable, and an emotion I share.

I gape at him. "Why the fuck would someone kidnap our Strigoi?"

"I haven't the faintest clue what's going on," Orcus admits. "And the Monster City Queen—*Helia*—wasn't much help. But she gave me permission to portal, so that's what we're going to do."

"Permission," I repeat with a laugh. "I bet you took that well."

The look he cuts me confirms my assessment. "We'll eat lunch and then go find a safe location to make camp. I didn't trust the supernaturals here before, and I really don't trust them now."

A fair opinion. "All right." My arm is still around Alina's lower back, so I give her hip a squeeze. "Looks like we're going to Chicago."

Her eyes are round, her lips smeared with strawberry icing.

I lean in to lick some of it off her mouth, desiring a taste.

She blinks. "Chicago."

I frown, pulling back. "What did I do?"

"No." She shakes her head. "I mean... I was saying the city, not the..." She growls a little, the sound causing my inner predator to perk up with interest. "I need a new safeword."

I can hear Reaper chuckling from the other room.

"I agree," Orcus says. "But you don't have to pick one right now."

He's right, I think. "We can ask again before our next session," I say out loud.

"Okay." She swallows, her eyes telling me she likes the sound of having a *next session*. But there's also a hint of something else in her gaze. An emotion I can't quite define.

Is it related to why she has interest in Chicago? I wonder. *Are you going to finally tell us why you want to go there?*

Alas, she doesn't.

Instead, she blinks again, finishes her cupcake, and grabs a second from the tray.

Orcus clears his throat, his gaze having been on her mouth. "Let's eat," he says, his voice gruff. "Then we'll talk more about this Elite City and what else I learned from Helia."

CHAPTER TWENTY-NINE
ALINA

I'M NOT sure what to be stunned by more—my orgasmic morning, the information Orcus shared about the Elite families, or the magic unfolding before me right now.

Not only did Orcus create a mirrorlike doorway that led to another part of the world, but he's also currently renovating an old cabin.

When we arrived, it was basically a pile of wood.

Now… now it's… *it's a home*.

We're right on the water—a place called Lake Michigan, according to Flame. "It's a good home base while Reaper goes to scout the Elite City," he added. "We're close enough that Orcus can get there quickly if needed, yet far enough away to go undetected."

"In theory," Orcus inserted. "We're only about an hour north of the city, and the magic in this realm is… unique."

I suspected he said that last bit because of everything he learned from Helia. From what I gathered, she impressed him. And he wasn't sure how he felt about it yet.

Particularly as his Strigoi were taken during the meeting.

"She obviously knew what was happening, making me wonder if the whole meeting was just a distraction," he told Flame earlier after lunch.

"Maybe. However, why would someone want the Strigoi?" Flame asked again. "I realize they're royals, but that can't mean much of anything here."

"I don't know," Orcus grumbled.

"I'll find out," Reaper offered.

Which was how they devised the plan of making Reaper the city scout.

"He's a literal shadow," Flame told me afterward when he picked up on my concern. While I knew these fae could take care of themselves, I didn't like the hint of danger involved in their Elite City espionage plan. "He'll just pop in, look around, and pop right back."

Well, he *popped* off about an hour ago, and none of us have heard a word from him.

I gaze up at the moon overhead, my lips twisting to the side.

It's pretty here. But that doesn't help soothe the pang of discomfort growing in my lower belly.

Reaper should be back by now, I think. *Where is he?*

That sense of unease merges with another emotion, one that has my heart skipping a beat. *Hope.*

I might find my sister soon.

Except my elation is paired with a troubling sensation, one driven by guilt.

Because these fae males are the only reason I'm here.

And they have no idea I even have a sister.

They've done everything to support me, to protect me, to *teach* me, and I've held myself back.

Why?

Why can't I just tell them?

It's not that hard. It's not even that big a secret, is it?

322

As soon as Reaper returns, I'm telling them, I decide.

They might be able to help me find her.

Orcus lands a few feet away from me, his massive wings unfurled to reveal thousands of silky black feathers. His long, dark hair is wild from the wind, and his red eyes are focused on his project ahead.

He places his hands on his lean hips, his muscular arms rippling with the movement.

Actually, every part of him is rippling.

Because he's shirtless.

Wearing just jeans.

Boots.

And wings, I marvel again. *Fae, I just want to pet him…*

He's gorgeous and completely oblivious to my ogling his stunning physique. Although, Flame notices the moment he walks out the door, his gaze knowing as he brings me a bottle of water.

"Enjoying the show?" he asks me.

I take a drink before I reply, "It's… it's impressive."

"Hmm," he hums, winking at me.

Orcus's attention, however, remains on the cabin.

"What's he doing?" I whisper, not wanting to disturb him. Of course, he doesn't even seem to realize I'm standing here.

"Manifesting," Flame drawls.

I glance at him. "Okay… And that means…?"

He grins. "Hey, Orcus, our girl wants you to explain your powers to her."

I gape at him.

He presses a kiss to my cheek. "I'll be inside playing in the new kitchen."

I'm not given a chance to reply. He just leaves.

And Orcus turns his red eyes my way.

I swallow, his presence even larger than usual with his

giant wings and bulging muscles. He's been flying all around the area, doing whatever it is he's been doing.

Manifesting.

Right. Yeah. Makes total sense.

"I'm a Mythos Fae Alpha." He says it like that explains everything. "We specialize in creation."

He steps toward me, his palm reaching for my face. I stop breathing as he tucks a strand of hair behind my ear. Only, he smiles as he pulls his hand back to reveal a black rose with gold tips.

I gasp at it, shocked by its unnatural beauty. "How...?"

He hands it to me as he says, "I pictured it in my mind and brought it to life." He looks at the cabin again, his wing stretching as he makes a gesture with his hand.

My eyes widen as a set of three bushes sprout up from the ground, all of them blossoming before my eyes.

Several minutes pass as the buds turn into leaves and the stems morph into black rosebuds.

Black roses with gold tips.

He just created dozens of them on the bush.

"That's... amazing," I breathe.

He shrugs. "You won't be as impressed when your Omega talents come to fruition. You'll be able to bring new souls into the world; I can merely manifest soulless items."

I blink at him. "I'll be able to... *what?*"

A hint of black edges the crimson in his irises as he stares at me once more. "You'll create life, Alina. There is no greater gift."

Create life.

Like... like... "You mean children?" I ask, my brow furrowing.

"I mean powerful beings," he corrects me. "But yes, they will come to us in the form of children." His palm goes to my belly. "You'll grow them here. I can't imagine a greater gift."

My lips curl down. "You're saying my having a baby is a better gift than being able to build a cabin with my mind?" I ask, incredulous.

He matches my frown with one of his own.

"You have no idea how unique and beautiful a gift it is that you can bring more Mythos Fae into the world, Alina. We haven't experienced the birth of a faeling in over two thousand years." He lifts his hand away from my belly and clasps my nape, pulling me to him. "It's a miracle."

"So is creating a cabin in under an hour," I mutter.

He tilts his head. "Perhaps I wasn't clear." There's a hint of humor in his tone. "Manifestation magic applies to all Mythos Fae. Alphas, Omegas, Betas—everyone can create soulless objects. But only an Omega can birth a new soul."

My lips part, then close, and then part again. "So you're saying I'll be able to create a cabin?"

He chuckles. "Perhaps not at first, but one day, once you've honed your abilities, yes. I'll even teach you when you're ready, if you'd like."

I'm gaping again.

Primarily because he's telling me all of this like it's just... normal. As though humans become immortal beings with wicked powers every day.

Yet the part he's in awe of is me having a baby.

I palm my belly. *Is it really that big a deal?* I wonder.

Then I think about what he said, about how there haven't been any Mythos Fae faelings—which I assume are fae babies—in over two thousand years.

Except, I might be able to create one.

He's staring down at my hand with a reverence I can feel, his wings fluttering in the night breeze. "What if I'm not the Omega that you think I am?" I ask him. "What if...? What if I can't...?"

The question floats away on a breeze, my heart panging at the prospect of not being able to create a child. It's a pain unlike anything I've ever experienced, like my soul is crying from within.

I could lose my fae, I think. *I... I could lose everything.*

However, it's not just the thought of my fae abandoning me that leaves me feeling bereft. It's the thought of not creating a life.

I... I want this, I realize with a start. *I well and truly want this.*

Not just my fae, but everything we can experience together.

A future. A child. A *family.*

Orcus's hand cups my cheek, drawing me back to him. "If we can't produce a faeling, then we move forward as a mate-circle without children."

He utters the words with ease, but I sense the underlying longing in his tone. Mainly because my own soul is weeping at the prospect of failing. It's an unacceptable notion, one I don't want to embrace.

But I have to consider it.

Because there's a very real possibility that I won't be able to create a soul. *This could all be a fluke.*

"If I can't conceive, then I'm not a real Omega," I whisper to him. "Right?"

"If you can't conceive, it's not because of what you are or what you are not. It's because the Fates have not chosen us for that path," he tells me.

My stomach churns again, some part of me adamantly refusing to accept such a future. *I want this. I want them. I want a family.*

"If that's our destiny, then I accept it, Alina," Orcus

goes on, oblivious to my inner turmoil. "Mythos Fae might not have true fated mates, but you're still mine. I can feel it in my soul. We were meant to find each other, to mate each other, and to create a powerful circle together—with Flame and Reaper."

I swallow, tears suddenly blurring my vision. "You really believe that." It's not a question but a statement.

"No, Alina. I don't *believe* anything; I *know* it." His thumb brushes my pulse, his opposite arm coming around my waist. "You're my Omega. You're Reaper's pet. You're Flame's little panther. And together, you're *ours.*"

His wings come around me as he leans down to press his mouth to mine, his kiss so vastly different from any I could have anticipated.

It's soft.

Tender.

Borderline *sweet*.

Like he's sealing a promise with his mouth, vowing to keep me for eternity no matter what happens.

I'm his Omega. His other half. His *soul mate*.

My belly flutters with the realization, my heart thundering in my chest.

Orcus is mine.

I know it deep within my being, my insides *burning* with the knowledge.

It's like something is awakening within my soul. Something big. Something… overwhelming.

My mind spins, all the emotions of today swirling together to create an inferno of all-consuming confusion. I feel dizzy. Hot. *Alive*.

Orcus's mouth stills against mine, causing me to growl against him.

It's an unexpected sound, one born from somewhere deep inside. I don't understand it. But I embrace it.

And I bite his lower lip.

Because I want more. A stronger kiss. More passion. *Dominance.*

"Alina," he whispers, a hint of raw emotion underlining my name.

My eyes narrow. *Speaking is not kissing.*

I nip at him again. But he doesn't respond the way I desire, causing me to pull back and stare up into his crimson gaze.

My Alpha is playing hard to get.

A game, I realize, suddenly intrigued.

"Fuck," he says.

Mmm, the end reward of winning the game, I think, even more intrigued now.

"Is she...?" Flame's deep voice caresses my ears, causing me to glance at the male in the doorway. His violet gaze is tinged with black as his jaguar stares me down.

I stare right back, challenging him in a way I don't quite understand. Yet it feels natural. *Will he join our game, too?* I wonder.

Except I'm not sure what *game* we're actually playing.

Yet somewhere deep down, I'm determined to win.

To run. To hide. To make them hunt.

I blink. *What?*

My stomach twists again while Orcus says something I don't quite hear.

Flame's jaguar growls, the feral sound one that inspires excitement within me, not fear.

But Orcus's wing cuts off my view of Flame, his accented voice drawing my focus to his lips. "This is my game to win," he tells Flame.

If the Shifter Fae replies, I don't catch his response. I'm too focused on Orcus's intense jawline to hear him.

Game. Game. Game.

Run. Run. Run.

The words play through my mind, overshadowing whatever Orcus says next. I just see his mouth moving. His bottom lip is swollen from my bite, the sight hypnotic. I want to lick him. But I also want to make him work for it.

Such a strange urge.

But it's driven by that voice in my head, the one saying, *Run. Hide. Make them hunt.*

I shiver.

The impulse rolls over me, *through* me, heating my veins and causing me to take a step backward.

Orcus's nostrils flare, his gaze capturing and holding mine. "I'll give you a head start, little one," he tells me, his voice low and seductive. "Hide well. Make me work for it. Or I'll take you against a fucking tree."

My thighs clench at the visual his words paint in my head. *Orcus hoisting me in the air, his hips pinning mine, his wings flared out behind him as he drives into me. Over and over again. Making me scream.* Knotting *me.*

It's so vivid, so specific, that I'm frozen in place before him.

Because I have no idea where these urges are coming from.

Except… that's not true. I do know. *My soul. My inner Omega.*

Is it true? Am I really… a Mythos Fae?

It shouldn't be possible. It sounds insane. And yet, I can feel the truth of it in my core. The very knowledge that's driving me to know what to do next. The voice telling me to *run.*

On an intellectual level, I understand what's happening to me, what *will* happen once I'm caught.

Orcus will claim me.

Then Reaper and Flame will claim me, too.

All three of my fae.

And my heat will consume me.

Render me incapable of making sound decisions, just like Flame and Orcus have warned me it would do. I'll have to trust them to see me through it, to take care of me, to ensure my wishes are respected and met.

It's impossible for me to truly know what I want, especially with all the chaos boiling inside me. But I do know what I desire. *These fae. These mates. A future with them.*

If that includes a faeling... then yes, I want that.

A little miracle, I think.

No, I don't just want that. I *need* that.

Why do I keep fighting this? Who cares if it's moving fast? This is the right path for me. The only *path.*

These men are my destiny as much as I'm theirs.

I lock my gaze on Orcus once more, aware that he hasn't started to count yet. He's giving me time to comprehend our game, to welcome my Omega into my heart, to finally embrace who I am meant to be.

He's a good Alpha.

The kind of Alpha who will always take care of me.

And I *want* to be his Omega.

I want to be Flame's little panther.

Just as much as I want to be Reaper's pet.

I'm theirs and they are mine.

"You'd better find me, Alpha," I say to Orcus, my voice holding a sultry note to it that I've never heard before.

"Oh, I'll be doing more than simply finding you, Omega," he replies, his wings tucking behind his back but not disappearing. "Now... *run.*"

CHAPTER THIRTY
ORCUS

FLAME'S JAGUAR looks ready to rip my throat out. "We need to find her. *Now.*"

I snort at him. "I love you like a brother, but this is my game." Which I've already said twice. "I'll hunt her when she's ready to be hunted."

Which should be any second now.

My inner Alpha is pacing, causing my feathers to strain against my back.

I want to seek.

To bite.

To *claim*.

But I want to give my Omega the head start I promised her.

This is the mating dance between Mythos Fae. *A hunt.*

She wants me to prove that I'll always find her.

And I want her to prove that she knows how to properly nest.

The way Alina melted into her Omega role, allowing the instincts to overtake her, is further proof of who she is meant to be—who *we* are meant to be together.

Flame growls again, not liking that our intended mate is running through a forest full of unknowns.

However, I just spent the better part of the evening putting up protective shields everywhere. I could smell Alina's impending heat, her pheromones making it decidedly difficult to focus. It didn't help that she kept eyeing me with obvious interest, watching the way my wings moved as I sent energy cascading all around us.

Oh, she thought I was too consumed with my task to see her.

But I fucking noticed.

The only part of my manifestation that feels undone is the nest inside, but Alina will fix that soon.

Once I find her. Mount her. Claim her. And knot her.

My dick throbs in response, my body more than ready to take our Omega and fuck her into oblivion. However, my soul calls for patience.

Soon. Very soon.

Our Omega is hiding.

This is her way of accepting our bond. If she didn't want me, she wouldn't play. But she wants to be hunted.

It's primal.

It's instinctual.

It's erotic as fuck.

My muscles clench, my legs demanding that I *chase*.

Flame looks ready to do just that, but a look from me holds him in place. I respect him as a fellow Alpha, despite our different fae breeds. However, I'm still his God.

Which means I'm in charge, and I'm claiming that right tonight.

The clenching of his jaw tells me he's not pleased, but he's conceding.

I won't let anything happen to our mate. He knows that. Just as he knows I need this.

And so does Alina.

She's embracing her Omega soul. I felt her acceptance the moment she bit me.

Consent isn't always verbal.

Sometimes actions say everything.

"I'll bring her back," I promise Flame. "But I need this. *She* needs this."

He gives me a stiff nod, the man inside him clearly understanding me. His animal, however, is a different story entirely. His jaguar scents Alina's arousal, bringing his feral nature to the surface.

But it's my turn to play with our mate.

Reaper and Flame have already had their taste.

Now it's time for me to introduce her to my tongue.

And my knot.

"Update Reaper when he returns," I add. He's only been gone for a little over an hour. I don't expect him to return for at least another two or three.

Whatever he found in the Elite City will have to wait.

Alina is our priority right now.

"Be ready, Flame. When I bring her back, she's going to need us. *All* of us."

The Shifter Fae nods again, his jaw clenched.

I lean my head back to inhale, my eyes falling closed as Alina's strawberry-like aroma taunts my inner Alpha. *Mmm, she's ready.*

Her natural perfume has blended with the woods, creating an enticing fragrance that has my wings stretching wide before disappearing at my back.

I want to find her the old-fashioned way.

No magic.

Just pure, masculine *drive*.

I stalk forward into the trees, following the sweet scent of Omega need. *Strawberries. Cream. So much fucking cream.*

It's her slick. Her desire. Her demand for my damn cock.

My knot throbs.

My balls tighten.

My wings threaten to burst from my skin once more.

And my steps quicken.

This is a fantasy come to life. A dream I thought I would never experience.

Hunting my Omega mate.

I inhale deeply once more, my body vibrating with hedonistic determination. *Find. Rut. Knot.*

My Omega is quiet, telling me she's hiding, just like I told her to.

Nesting.

It's an important skill, one she'll use to protect herself and our young.

Mmm, but that scent can't escape me. Alina Everheart is mine. My intended. My *mate.*

"I'm not sure if it was wise or naïve to hide so close to the cabin," I muse, spinning toward her resting place. She's slipped behind a pair of bushes, the subtle color of her blue jeans barely visible through the leaves.

I step forward, half expecting her to dart out of her spot and run. But she doesn't move.

So I crouch, ready to pull her out, and realize… she's not there.

I reach in and grab her jeans, yanking them out from the branches with a chuckle. "I stand corrected," I say to no one in particular. "Clever indeed."

Standing again, I scent the air, searching for her sweetness.

The jeans—which are covered in her slick—distract my senses. The realization that she's pantless also distracts me.

My lips curl, though, my Alpha impressed with our Omega's quick wit.

I create a portal back to the cabin and throw her jeans through it. Flame catches them, his reflexes on point. "Our Omega is very good at this game," I tell him through the mirrorlike door.

Then I close it and focus on her fragrance once more.

Mouthwatering, I think, loving her decadent perfume. *Fuck, the things I'm going to do to her...*

I pick up my pace, more determined now than ever to find my Omega and reward her with my tongue.

That determination strengthens when I find her tank top hidden in another pair of bushes.

Followed by her bra.

And finally, her panties.

Either she's only wearing shoes, or she's left those for me to find next.

Flame growls when I send him the final item of her outfit—the soaked underwear—and starts issuing a demand when I shut the portal once more.

It's a demand I don't need.

Our Omega is *naked*.

Not only that, but she's naked *and* wet.

"Oh, I'm going to knot you so fucking hard, little one," I tell her, aware that I have to be close to wherever she's hiding. "You're going to need that new safeword." Not that she'll even know to use it when her heat hits.

She'll be so damn needy that she won't care how we fuck her.

Which makes it all the more imperative that I observe her limits now.

Because she hasn't completely lost her senses yet—as evidenced by how well she's hiding from me.

An Omega in the throes of her estrus would be lying

337

out in the open, legs spread, and begging her Alpha to fuck her. Not cleverly nesting in the woods.

"Sweet Omega of mine," I coo at her. "I'm so fucking proud of you right now."

I creep forward, my nose leading me to a thick tree. Either Alina's behind it, or she's left me her shoes to find.

Given the strong aroma of strawberries, I'm certain it's the former.

"Hello, little one," I say, voice soft. "Care to reveal my prize?"

The prize being her naked form.

She doesn't respond.

"Hmm, I see." I step around the tree and grin when she takes off running down a nearby path. Her dark hair trails in the wind behind her as her long, shapely legs move quickly through the underbrush.

I give her a few seconds, then sprint after her, my inner Alpha more than ready to take our mate to the ground.

She's running in her shoes—an intelligent choice I mentally applaud—but the rest of her is utterly exposed, which creates quite a show. Hips swaying. Tits bouncing. Hair swinging.

My Omega is fucking *perfect*.

And I can't wait to see her swell with our future child.

I don't care if it's my seed that does it, or Flame's or Reaper's. The babe will be Mythos Fae because of Alina's blood.

A miracle, I think, the word one I voiced earlier as well. Because that's exactly what we might create together. And even if we don't, Alina is still a miracle unto herself. An Omega soul in a human form.

Not human for much longer, though, I muse as I close the distance between us. The moment I bite her, she'll become a fae.

And that bite will mate us for eternity, too.

Mine, mine, mine, my steps say as I pound the earth in her wake. *Mine, mine... "Mine."*

She screams as I snag her by the waist, taking us both to the ground below.

Her nails scrape along my chest and shoulders while we wrestle across the dirt, her growls ferocious and borderline feral.

I catch her wrists and hoist her arms over her head, pinning her hands to the ground beneath one of my palms.

She snarls, her hips bucking up into mine, only she's no longer fighting me. She's trying to draw me closer—as evidenced by the way her athletic legs wrap around my hips and pull me into her.

I give in to her silent demand, relaxing into her splayed thighs, and place my lips at her ear. "I need your new safeword, little one."

"Monster," she breathes, arching into me.

I pull back, needing to see her beautiful eyes. "Monster."

She nods. "Because you, Reaper, and Flame aren't monsters. You're fae. You would have to do something to make me very uncomfortable for me to say otherwise."

A shudder runs through me. The thought she put into this... it further demonstrates how perfect she is for us.

It also proves that she's still very much coherent, despite her mounting heat.

"Monster it is," I say, my wings unfurling once more at my back to cocoon us on the ground.

She gazes up at me in wonder, her black eyes rimmed with intrigue. "You're going to claim me."

"I'm going to claim you," I echo back at her, giving her a chance to voice her safeword if that scares her.

But she doesn't.

339

She simply stares back at me expectantly.

I lean down to kiss her softly, extending the moment just a few seconds longer, but the way her mouth parts for mine tells me she's more than accepted our intertwined fates.

She wants this—she wants *us*.

Knowing that has me thrusting my tongue into her sweet little mouth, my inner Alpha demanding that I do this right.

Alina moans, her slick center practically soaking my jeans as she grinds her pussy against my hard cock.

She doesn't seem to care that there's a barrier, her body so pent up with need that she's willing to endure the roughness for a little friction between her legs.

I kiss her harder, my hand pushing her wrists into the ground as I move against her in kind.

Fuck, I need more. So much more.

My wings rustle as I shift to unbutton my pants. The zipper practically undoes itself, my hard dick forcing its way out like it can't take another moment inside my jeans.

Alina gasps as my arousal meets her damp flesh, her eyes going wide and instantly looking down. "Oh, fae, that's…"

"A knot," I say for her as I lift up to finish removing my pants and shoes. While I'm kneeling between her legs, I help rid Alina of her footwear as well, leaving her gloriously naked beneath me.

Her midnight irises are glued to my knot, her mouth wide like she's inviting me to fuck her there first.

But the hint of fear taunting her scent tells me those lips are agape for very different reasons.

She's intimidated.

And rightly so.

There's a notable size difference between us, one she's certainly taking into account right now.

Yet another sign she's nowhere near lost to her estrus. Otherwise, she'd be begging me to cover her with my wings and mount her into oblivion.

"Remember what I told you before, Alina. Your body was made to handle mine. Just like my heart was made to love you. We're meant for each other, but you have to trust me to take care of you. Can you do that?"

She swallows, her gaze slowly rising to mine. "That… is going inside me?"

I grin. "Yeah, Alina. And you're going to love it."

Her expression radiates incredulity.

"Don't worry, baby. I'll warm you up properly first." I grab her knees to spread her legs wider, needing her to accommodate my shoulders. "We'll take it slow. And I'll check in with you along the way."

Because the last thing I want to do is hurt her.

"Okay," she whispers. "I trust you."

CHAPTER THIRTY-ONE

ALINA

I TRUST YOU.

Sera is the only other person in this world I've ever said those three words to. She's the only one I've ever felt I could truly trust.

But when I spoke my heart to Orcus just now, I meant it. I trust him. I trust Flame. And I trust Reaper.

These fae are mine just as much as I'm theirs.

Orcus smiles down at me, his hard body illuminated by streams of moonlight coming in through the branches. He's positively stunning, his muscular physique chiseled in all the right places.

And his wings.

Dear fae, *his wings.*

He resembles an angel of the night, his black plumes reflecting the moonlight and giving him an intimidating glow.

But I'm not afraid of him.

Or his giant cock with the large bulb at the base.

Fae, that's never going to fit. His girth rivals Flame's, but Orcus is longer. His head is also… thicker.

I doubt I can even wrap my hand around him. However, before I can try, he crawls over me and cages me beneath his strong body.

Then he kisses me.

Really kisses me.

His tongue masters mine, telling me to submit without words. So I do. I simply accept him. Accept *this*. And allow him to lead me into a sensual dance.

He's gentle in a way I didn't expect, his palms stroking up and down my sides before moving to my breasts.

"Gods, all I want to do is worship you," he breathes, his fingers pinching my nipples as he begins kissing a path down my neck. "You have no idea how long I've waited for you, Alina. I refuse to rush this. I'm going to take you slowly. Thoroughly. Make you beg me to come. And only then will I give you my knot."

A tremble works through me, my body coming alive beneath his hands and his mouth. He's so hot and *dominant*. I can feel him holding back, his aggression on a tight leash. He's all Alpha male, and I'm the one who was built to handle him.

But true to his word, he eases me into it.

Kissing. Licking. Nibbling.

Fae, I'm on fire for him.

Every inch of me is consumed by his need, my limbs shaking as he focuses his attention on my breasts. He sinks his teeth into one while he palms the other, his tongue chasing away the sting of his bite. It didn't break the skin, but it was close.

"Harder," I whisper, wanting to feel his claim. He explained to me the other day that he'll need to bite me to properly connect us, yet he's teasing me now, dragging his teeth along my skin and eliciting goose bumps in his wake.

"Just deciding where I want to mark you, Omega," he murmurs before capturing my other peak with his mouth.

My legs squeeze around his, sweat beading along my limbs. He's driving me crazy on purpose. First with this hunt, then fighting me on the ground, and now this… being gentle, yet in charge. It's a quiet dominance, one he's allowing to simmer as he gradually introduces me to his preferences.

"*Orcus*," I hiss when he nips me again, his tongue quickly soothing the sting.

He chuckles, the sound a vibration I feel between my thighs. Then I realize it wasn't a chuckle but a responding *growl*.

"Ohh," I moan, writhing beneath him as the rumble echoes through my fevered form. My sex practically weeps for him, my insides clenching with need. "*What* is that?" I ask, breathing heavily as the reverberations drive me mad with *want*.

"A mating growl." That thrumming sound underlines his words.

I nearly whine, the vibrations almost too much. Yet they're not enough either. I need more. I need *him*. I need—

A gasp escapes me as he sinks his teeth into my breast once more, this time breaking the skin. Stars burst behind my eyes, blackening my vision as pleasure unlike anything I've ever experienced rolls through my being.

It's not an orgasm.

It's something else entirely.

An awakening.

My soul… *rejoicing*.

Orcus's tongue is suddenly in my mouth, the taste of my own blood acting as an aphrodisiac as he kisses me to completion, helping me through the rapturous waves assaulting my being.

I grab a fistful of his long hair, holding him to me as I return the embrace, my tongue dueling his in a passionate battle fueled by my need to claim him in kind.

I don't think; I act, biting down and drawing blood from his *tongue*.

He growls.

I growl back.

And our bodies intertwine in a new dance, this one more feral in nature as he spins us. His wings flatten against the ground, creating a feather bed as I straddle his hips. He's so hard against me. So *hot*. I dig my nails into his chest and sit up to press myself even more against him. It feels right. Perfect. Like our bodies were made for this.

Like I was made for him, I marvel, realizing how right Orcus was when he said that.

I grind down on top of him while energy swirls around me, my skin suddenly shimmering despite the darkness.

"Fuck me," Orcus breathes. And I'm not sure if that's a demand or a reaction to what's happening to me. Maybe both.

His hands are on my hips, his grip borderline bruising. But I don't care. Because I can take it. I feel… invincible. Unbreakable in a way I can't even describe. I just know… I'm no longer human.

I'm an Omega.

And I'm your Alpha, a voice answers in my head. Masculine. Deep. Accented.

Because it's Orcus.

He's in my thoughts and I'm in his. Thousands of years of history are suddenly at my fingertips, making me dizzy.

His longing. His search. His loneliness. His

determination. His hope. His *love*. It all washes over me in a tidal wave of confusing emotions, drowning me in Orcus's mind, in his very being.

I shudder, collapsing on top of him, only to be caught up by his mouth again, his hands suddenly on my face.

He's spun us once more, putting me on my back as I absorb our bond, our connection, our *future*.

Lips brush my skin. My breasts. My lower belly. Then I feel his tongue between my thighs, circling my clit and sending shock waves through my *soul*.

He's pleasuring me. Mastering me. Possessing me. Yet underneath it all, I hear his restraint, hear him acknowledging my wants and needs while putting my comfort first.

He's a good Alpha. A good *man*.

My mate, I marvel, my hand in his hair again as he slides a finger inside me. *My… mate.*

Yours, he agrees, sucking on my flesh. *And you're mine.*

He punctuates that with another thrust, causing me to squirm. His hands are big, making his intrusion one I definitely feel deep inside despite it only being one finger.

No. *Two.* He added another. Preparing me. Ensuring I'm stretched. I can hear it all in his mind while I feel it down below.

It's intoxicating, this whirlwind of mingled thoughts, feelings, and sensations. Because Orcus's yearnings swirl inside me as well, his intention to knot me making me squirm beneath him.

I want him inside me.

Truly. Completely. *Fully.*

I don't know how it will feel. I don't know if I'll love it or hate it. But I don't care. I want him there, filling me, pumping in and out of my body, and gifting me with his pleasure.

LEXI C. FOSS

His seed.

Oh, fae... This could be it. We might create a life together.

Except I hear deep down in his mind that I'm not quite in the throes of my heat yet. Which makes this a warm-up. A way to slowly introduce me to what's to come.

Fae, if this is just an introduction... I shudder, my legs spread wide to accommodate Orcus's every intention.

He's destroying me in the best way. I can feel my orgasm mounting, the tightening of muscles driving me that much closer to the edge.

So close, I think. *So clo—*

Orcus stops, his mouth going to my hip bone to lay a gentle kiss.

I snarl at him.

He growls back, worsening the ache below and stirring a fresh wave of damp heat.

Slick, I hear him say, the word a moan inside his mind. *Fucking decadent.*

I'm a wet, sobbing mess of *need.* "Orcus," I say, unable to stop the plea in my voice. "*Please.* I... I need..."

"Mmm, you need a knot," he finishes for me. "I know."

Yet he doesn't give it to me.

He just keeps *playing.*

Three fingers now. In and out. Twisting. Stretching. Penetrating.

His tongue taunts my clit. Swirling. Sucking. Licking.

I'm panting, tears streaming from my eyes, because every time I almost fall over the edge, he *stops* again. His name leaves me on a frustrated scream, my body pent up in a way I've never experienced before.

He promised to make me beg.

I'm begging now.

348

Both with my voice and inside my mind.

Still, he tortures me with his hands and his mouth, drawing it out, reducing me to a mindless mess of *need*.

"Almost ready," I hear him murmur, my mind barely functioning enough to hear him. "Gods, you're so beautiful like this, Alina. All sensation and desire. Like a fucking sex Goddess."

I think I grunt. Maybe I moan. I don't really know. But his name leaves me again, a final plea. He's driving me insane. I'm going to black out at any moment from this blinding *need*. It almost hurts, the pain of being brought to the brink over and over again, only to be coaxed back down…

I…

I don't know how to breathe anymore. How to move. How to properly process *anything*.

The world feels so far away that I barely notice him crawling up my body, his body as damp as mine as he settles over me.

My arousal—the taste of it—touches my tongue as he kisses me deeply, his growl vibrating every inch of my body, claiming me to my very soul.

He reaches between us, his thumb brushing my abused clit and drawing a hoarse scream from my mouth.

Then I feel the head of his massive cock at my entrance.

I don't even care that it's going to rip me apart. I welcome it. I welcome *him*.

"Please," I whisper. "*Please*, Alpha."

That's my Omega side taking over, begging him to truly claim me. I embrace it. I embrace my *soul*.

Everything feels… right.

Aside from my emptiness below.

I need. I want. *I demand.*

349

"*Orcus.*" It's a snarl of sound, one that I punctuate by drawing my nails down his muscular arms.

His wings are around us, his eyes glowing red in the dark. "*Alina,*" he returns in a similar voice.

Then he punches his hips forward, drawing a very different kind of scream from my mouth. One that's part torment, part surprise, part *elation*.

Oh... fae!

I... I can't breathe.

He's... the size of him... the... the...

I swallow, his mouth suddenly there as he kisses me through the intrusion, coaxing me with his tongue and soothing me with his growls.

No. Not growls. His purr...

A quiver rolls down my spine, my body instantly relaxing into his, my innate sense of trust overtaking every other urge I could have conjured.

No more screams. No more tears. Just... a sublime existence.

Except my clit is still throbbing, my insides clenching, my lower belly *burning*. I say his name again, only this time it's a request. "Knot me," I whisper. "Please, knot me."

He smiles against my mouth. "I would love nothing more, my sweet Goddess."

Orcus doesn't give me a chance to reply, his wings feathering out around us once more as he begins to move.

Really move.

I swear my eyes roll into the back of my head, the feel of his knot at my entrance a tease of what's to come. Because he's too wide at the base to fully enter me, but I know from his mind what will happen when he climaxes.

When *we* climax.

That bulbous organ will shoot inside and force me to take every last inch of his long cock.

It'll hurt in the best way.

I dig my nails into his biceps in anticipation, my lower half clenching around him in silent demand. All while he kisses me.

Loves me.

Cherishes me with his tongue.

I lift my hips to meet his thrust, my body moving on instinct. His mind helps guide me, too. When I twist a certain way, he mentally groans. When I squeeze him with my walls, he *growls*. Being inside him like this... it's the best way to learn. To know. To *understand*.

And he uses that same method on me, his hand disappearing between us again so he can stroke my clit.

I'm so swollen that his touch borders on pain, but I embrace it, knowing that this time... this time he's going to let me fall apart.

In fact, he's going to mandate it.

Every punch of his hips drives me closer to the edge, his thumb applying just the right amount of pressure.

Please, please, please, I think, hoping he won't play with me anymore and allow me the gratification I crave.

His pace quickens, his movements harsh yet thorough, striking me deep inside.

It's almost punishing, his feral side peeking out at me more and more with each thrust.

I can feel his control slipping, hear his mind falling apart.

Yet somewhere deep within, he harnesses it, his need to please me first slamming through his animalistic instincts and forcing him to focus on what matters.

Her, I hear him saying to himself. *This is for her.*

Fae, I don't know about that, I think back at him. *It feels like it's for us.*

If my words register, he doesn't show it. His attention is on making me feel good.

His movements slow, his shaft sliding almost all the way out before slamming back into me.

Over and over again.

I squirm, pant, and feel the tears welling once more.

Then he pinches my clit…

And my world…

Explodes.

I can't… I can't see. Or hear. Or focus. There's just this overwhelming quake consuming my existence. Rumbling. Throbbing. Quivering through my limbs.

Then a sound pierces through my bubble, my mind belatedly catching up to the present as my screams echo through the fog.

So much. Too much. Fae… fae… Orcus!

Pain shoots through my lower abdomen, followed by an intense rupture of ecstasy, one that thrives through my veins, setting every part of me on fire.

I'm crying.

I'm screaming.

I'm… I'm *drowning*.

A whirlpool of sensation takes me under, flooding my insides with the most intense orgasm of my life.

And it doesn't stop.

It. Just. Keeps. Going.

Orcus's purr helps soothe some of the insanity, but I'm… I'm lost… to this… sea of bliss. I may never surface again.

The overwhelming tide pulls me back out to the dark waters of lust, drowning me once more.

Then Orcus's rumbles anchor me again, reminding me of where I am.

He's on top of me, still inside me, still coming, his *knot* lodged deep within. He's emitting that soft, calming sound, his fingers combing through my hair as he kisses my cheek. My chin. My neck. Warm words leave his mouth, all of them sounding like a prayer.

He's praying… *to me.*

Thanking me.

Worshipping me.

Loving me.

I feel his emotions, his bliss, his *pleasure.*

Fae, it's so much. It's too much.

I'm locked around him, my legs refusing to release his hips.

And still, I'm riding the rapturous waves of my climax.

It goes on and on and on until I'm an incoherent mess of moans. Words are impossible. Thoughts no longer exist.

I'm simply… a ball of nerves.

Writhing.

Pulsing.

Being.

"Rest," I hear Orcus whisper. "We'll be here when you wake. And then the fever will begin."

Fever? I think dizzily.

But I'm suddenly too exhausted to ask.

So I lean into him.

And give in to the urge to sleep.

CHAPTER THIRTY-TWO
REAPER

ORCUS's massive black wings are the first thing I see when I reappear near the lake.

The freshly renovated cabin is the second item.

And Alina's naked body cradled against Orcus's chest is the third and final sight—something I would have noticed first had Orcus been facing me when I landed. However, he turned as he sensed me, thus allowing me to spy the sleeping beauty in his arms.

One inhale is all I need to know that she's come into her Omega heat.

I didn't expect to sense it like this; Death Fae don't have estrus cycles. But I can smell Alina's sweet strawberry fragrance from all the way over here. It's enough for me to shadow toward them rather than walk, my gaze on her blissed-out face.

"Rest," Orcus says to her in a whisper. "We'll be here when you wake. And then the fever will begin."

Fuck fest, I want to correct him. *And then the* fuck fest *will begin.*

But I refrain.

Instead, I simply smile at Alina's responding sigh, her limbs going limp in his arms.

"So you knotted her," I say, not guessing, just knowing. "And how was it?"

He looks at me. "A private affair."

I arch a brow. "Don't tell me you're thinking of keeping her to yourself now, Alpha. You might be my brother, but I will fucking fight you on this."

He snorts. "I wouldn't dream of keeping her away from you and Flame. She's chosen you, too. But what Alina and I share... will remain ours. Just as I'm sure you'll have things you share with only her, too."

Like cupcakes, I think, the thought one that comes automatically. "True." I reach forward to tuck one of her sweaty strands of hair behind her ear. "You worked her hard."

"Yes," he admits, giving me nothing more. "When she wakes up, she'll be lost to her estrus."

I smile. "About fucking time."

He snorts again and turns toward the door where Flame is waiting, his expression dark. Based on the way his eyes are narrowed at Orcus, I'm guessing he wasn't invited to the knotting show.

I understand his disappointment.

But I'm certain we'll be given another opportunity to watch.

Leaning forward, I press a kiss to our girl's forehead. "Mmm, you smell like strawberries and sex, pet. A delicious dessert." One I fully intend to enjoy after the dinner of dark souls I just consumed.

"She should wake up comfortably," Flame says, walking toward us. "I'll take her."

"You just want to groom her again," I drawl. It's such a catlike thing to do.

He doesn't deny it, just pulls her from Orcus's arms and carries her inside. Flame's shoulders instantly relax along the way, suggesting the nearness has helped calm his inner beast. But I suspect he's going to unleash his feral side during the heat.

Our beautiful pet is in for one hell of a ride.

"When will she wake up?" I ask, eager to begin.

"Soon." Orcus folds his arms over his bare chest and spreads his wings when I take a step forward, my intention having been to follow Flame.

I arch a brow at the naked Alpha. "Yes?"

"Tell me what you learned."

My teeth grind together. Of course the big guy wants a report of what I've seen. "If she wakes up while I'm talking, I'm ghosting in there," I tell him. Because what I have to share isn't nearly as important as our pet's needy pussy.

"I suggest you speak quickly, then," he says, arms still folded.

I blow out a breath and palm my nape, my body pent up and ready to play with Alina, not engage in a serious discussion with Orcus about Strigoi royals. "They're fine," I inform him. "Cain didn't kidnap them. They went willingly."

Orcus arches a brow. "You spoke to them?"

"Yeah. Well, I spoke to Cage. Sabre was, uh, busy." An image of blood and chaos rings through my head, causing my lips to curl. "They were having one hell of a party. It's not often I enjoy reconnaissance, but in this case, it was delicious." I glance at the cabin door. "Not as delicious as strawberries and cream, though."

"A party?" he repeats.

"A massacre, a party." I shrug. "Same thing. Lots of bad souls to eat." I tilt my head. "It's strange, though. The

357

darkness doesn't feel all that... dark? Like the voices are quiet. I can feel them, seek out their memories, but they're not raging in my head."

Normally, when I feast on dark souls, they leave a headache behind.

But these spirits are quiet, almost subdued.

"They're still wicked spirits. The things they did..." I whistle. "Anyway, maybe it's this realm. Maybe it's Alina. Regardless, I'm thankful for the reprieve. I can actually hear my own thoughts for once."

And those thoughts are all focused on one very important person right now—our pet.

"What the fuck are you talking about? What exactly did you see?" Orcus demands.

I sigh.

Then I tell him about the event I attended.

How I found Cage and Sabre covered in blood.

Why I stayed to enjoy some delicious souls.

How I played with my scythe.

And provide a brief synopsis of my conversation with Cage.

By the time I'm done, Orcus is gaping at me.

"I guess this realm really is full of unique human mates," I conclude with another shrug.

Because it seemed Cage and Sabre had found one to share. *With Cain.*

"Long story short, the Strigoi Princes won't be returning to our realm." Morpheus is either going to be amused by the chaos or furious about it.

Regardless, I'll let Orcus handle all that.

I start toward the cabin again, only to be halted by Orcus's wing like before.

"Helia told me about your visits with Timothy."

I blink. That wasn't at all what I anticipated him saying. It's also completely off topic. "I didn't kill him."

"I know."

"So what's there to discuss?"

"Nothing." He smiles. "I just wanted to express approval."

I nod. "Did she give us permission to end him?"

"She gave permission for us to pass judgment upon him."

Oh really? I think, excited. "Does that mean I can bring his head to Alina? Or are we still giving her the first right to kill?"

"I don't know." He looks over his shoulder at the cabin. "We'll discuss it more later. I can feel her waking up."

A spear of jealousy kicks me in the heart. *He can feel our pet.* Because they're bonded.

I want that.

I want to feel Alina inside and out. Make her mine. Make me hers. Join her in the death plane and marry our souls for eternity.

We're almost there already, our spirits having been compatible from the beginning. I just have to finish the process with a blood vow.

A promise to worship her in life and in death.

Orcus turns, his wings vanishing into thin air.

I rip my shirt over my head as I follow him. The fabric flutters to the ground in my wake.

My hands are on my jeans when we enter, only for me to pause on the threshold. "Holy hell, Orcus. You turned this pile of rubbish into a Godsdamn palace."

That might be a slight overexaggeration. But the interior is all refined wood, carved poles, and finished floors.

There's a kitchen.

A dining area.

A living room.

And a massive fucking mattress resting on a wooden frame.

Our pet is in the middle of that bed, her body wrapped in a fluffy towel. Her hair is damp, as is Flame's, telling me he just rinsed her off in the shower.

"Did you set this place up with magical generators?" I ask Orcus.

"Something like that." He doesn't elaborate. As a God, I guess he doesn't have to.

Flame purrs, his fingers combing through Alina's wet hair as she stretches beside him. All three of us watch her, waiting. Adoring. *Plotting.*

Or maybe that's just me.

I've heard about this illustrious *heat* experience, of both the Shifter Fae and Mythos Fae varieties, and I'm very much looking forward to what's coming next.

Yet when Alina's eyes open, she simply blinks.

Then she smiles. "Hi." The greeting is for Flame.

"Hi," he replies, his gaze searching hers. "How do you feel, little panther?"

"Good," she replies. "Refreshed." She stretches again. "*Glorious.*"

Orcus smirks beside me, no doubt pleased by that adjective.

However, I'm... confused. "I thought she was going to wake up ready for fucking." I don't mind her being coherent and content. In fact, I love her being coherent and content. But I was under the impression that an Omega lost her senses entirely during a heat, turning her into a sex-obsessed Goddess.

Alina's gaze flies to mine, her pupils dilating. "*Reaper.*"

She launches herself at me, her arms flying around my neck as she hugs me tightly.

"Hmm," I hum, returning her embrace. This isn't exactly what I expected, but it definitely works for me. So I kiss her neck, ready to play.

However, she pulls back and clasps my face between her hands, searching my face. "You're okay." She hugs me again, my lips curling down as I glance at Flame and then Orcus.

They look as perplexed by this as I'm sure I do. "Yeah, I'm okay. Why wouldn't I be okay?"

"You were gone," she whispers. "I... I was worried about you."

I blink. "Worried? Why?"

"Because you went into the Elite City by yourself," she replies, a note of incredulity in her tone as she shifts to look at me again. "I... Maybe it's silly, but I was worried."

My eyelashes flutter once more. "You were worried." That's... that's an interesting concept. "I don't think anyone has ever worried about me before."

It's... it's kind of nice.

Flame and Orcus may be curious about my whereabouts sometimes, or even voice words of caution, but I doubt they've ever actually been concerned for me. Or maybe they have and just haven't told me.

However, Alina... I can feel her relief. It's written in the way her body clings to mine, like she thought she might not see me again.

I draw my hand down her back, my opposite palm going to her nape. "I'm okay, pet," I tell her again. "Thank you for worrying about me."

Her pupils flare as she stares up at me. "Is it silly to worry?"

I smile. "No. It's... refreshing." I draw my thumb up

and down her neck. "It makes me feel... cared about." Which is a very nice sensation, one that has me wanting to kiss her for entirely different reasons than before.

So I do.

I lean down and... kiss her.

Not passionately. Not hungrily. Just tenderly. Pleasantly. *Lovingly.*

It's a vastly unique concept, one I've never quite considered before. Kissing usually leads to fucking. But this kiss... this kiss is underlined in emotion.

Emotion I don't quite comprehend.

But I feel strongly for this female.

Because I care about her, too, I realize. Of course, I already knew that. However, I've been so caught up in the lust side that I haven't truly evaluated the compassion side.

Together... together it's... *flooring.*

Combustible.

Downright overwhelming.

The voices in my head are silent now, leaving me alone with my thoughts—all of which are consumed with Alina.

My intended.

My future mate.

My pet.

Her lips part as I slide my tongue inside, exploring her mouth and thanking her in my own way. Thanking her for this gift. For opening up my heart in a way I didn't know was possible. For providing temporary relief inside my mind. For *worrying.*

She's everything.

This is everything.

We are everything.

Her arms tighten around my neck, causing my grasp along her nape to flex as well. I want her. *Oh,* how I fucking *want* her.

It's so Godsdamn intense. And it's so much more than mere excitement to play during her heat.

I want to claim her. To voice the vows that will make her mine.

She lets me splay her across the bed, my jean-clad hips resting against her exposed center. I have no idea what happened to her towel. It probably fell when I tumbled her backward onto the mattress. It doesn't matter. I want her naked beneath me anyway.

"Alina," I breathe against her mouth.

"Reaper," she returns before nibbling my lower lip. "Kiss me more."

It's a request I can't deny. A request I happily fulfill.

She tastes so good, that sweet freshness that's all her consuming my senses.

I know the others are watching. Lusting. Wishing they were me. Waiting for their turn. But I don't care. I prolong every second of my time with our pet, laying claim to her mouth with my tongue while running my hands up and down her luscious form.

"I want to mate you," I tell her. "I want to claim you."

"Then claim me," she says, arching up into me.

My lips curl. "Oh, I want to do that, too. But a Death Fae's bond is created with a blood vow."

Her big midnight eyes lock on mine. "Okay. Mate me."

No hesitation.

No questions.

Just… acceptance.

I understand that immediate response because it's how I feel, too. I've known from the moment I saw her that there was something unique about her.

That feeling grew the second my spirit brushed hers in that hallway.

And my decision solidified by the time I finished devouring those bad souls.

It was instantaneous. A knowledge that just sort of clicked. My Death Fae soul had found his anchor in the world, allowing me to feel more alive. More... *sane*.

The darkness swirling around the edges of my mind has lessened, Alina's presence providing me with a renewed sense of purpose.

Because she represents creation and life, while my soul thrives in death and destruction.

She's an angel of vitality, pulling me from the depths of darkness and reviving my spirit.

Establishing balance.

Producing our very own version of utopia.

A blade forms in my shadows, the sharp instrument similar to what I used while playing with her and Flame.

Only this time, the dagger is for us.

For this moment.

For our vow.

Her pupils dilate when she sees the shiny tip, a kiss of lust pinkening her cheeks.

We'll come back to that, I tell her with a look. *But first...*

I twirl the blade between my fingertips, my gaze searching for an appropriate place to mark her. Lifting up, I can see where Orcus bit her breast.

Which gives me an idea.

My lips brush hers. "Stay calm for me, pet," I say before crawling down her body to the sweetest part of her.

Her breathing quickens with each passing second, her eyes widening. But she doesn't say anything.

"Tell him your new safeword, Alina," Orcus interjects softly. "Say it so Reaper and Flame are aware of the change."

I almost glance at him. *Almost.* But our pet has my sole

attention, my eyebrow quirking in curiosity. "You changed your safeword?"

She swallows and nods. "Chicago no longer works."

"All right." I rest the blade against her hip. "What's the new safeword?"

Alina clears her throat, a sense of boldness overcoming her features. "Monster."

My eyes widen.

"Tell them why," Orcus encourages her.

"Because you're fae, not monsters. And I know you won't do anything to make me feel otherwise." She shrugs. "I don't need a safeword. You won't hurt me. But if I have to pick one, I choose that word because I know I'll never say it when thinking of you."

Fuck. Hearing her faith in us, her *trust*, it makes me want to ravage her. To own her. To… to… *devour* her.

"You're so Godsdamn perfect, pet," I tell her, emotion thick in my voice. "I'm going to give you so many fucking rewards. But I have to claim you first. I have to pledge myself to you. Give you my soul. My very being."

And to do that, I have to mark her.

I draw the tip of my knife along her hip bone toward her mound. Then find the space I desire—an intimate spot situated right on her bikini line under her belly—and say, "Take a deep breath for me."

Alina does, her gaze on me the whole time as I press the sharp edge into her skin.

She releases a hiss, the bite of pain an aphrodisiac only because I know I'm the one causing it. And because I know what it means.

Soon, she will, too.

She fists the blankets on either side of her, then releases one side to grab Flame's hand as he offers it.

Fuck, that makes me harder. It's such a turn-on to see

that her instinct is to lean on him while I carve into her flesh. That reaction is part of what makes her ours. She simply knows what to do, just as Flame knows how to see her through it.

By the time I'm finished, her skin sheens with a thin layer of sweat.

But never once did she ask me to stop.

Because our mate is a warrior in disguise. *Our lethal pet.*

I kiss the mark I've created, her blood sweet on my lips.

Then I turn the blade on myself, drawing a different symbol on my palm. It'll forever remain there, just like the tattoo on my cock.

Forever Alina's.

Which is why the marking I create on my hand is an *A*.

And the one I left near her mound is an *R*.

When I finish, I lick the metal clean, then let it vanish into my shadowy strands. "Ready, pet?"

She's panting as she nods. "Yes."

"Good." Because there's no going back now.

This female is mine.

I just need to say the words…

CHAPTER THIRTY-THREE

FLAME

WATCHING Reaper carve that *R* into Alina's skin has my inner jaguar pacing inside. He's not upset. He's excited.

Because my animal knows I'm next.

The beautiful, naked canvas before me is my playground.

I can bite her wherever I choose and mark her for eternity.

Orcus chose her breast.

Reaper chose her pussy—or the area right above it, anyway.

And I… I'm going to choose… soon.

"Alina Everheart," Reaper says, his focus entirely on our mate. "I, Reaper of the Death Fae, choose you as my soul's mate. I vow to worship your mind and body, protect your heart and soul, and marry my spirit to yours for eternity. You are mine and I am yours. Until death do we prosper."

He presses his bloody palm to her hip, causing a shudder to roll through them both.

There are no words for Alina to say during the

ceremony. It's all about her soul's acceptance of Reaper's vow. And from what I can tell, the process has already begun.

She squeezes my hand, then reaches for Reaper with her opposite palm. He's there in the next breath, his lips crashing down on hers as energy hums all around them.

Orcus growls, the sound one of intense approval.

My jaguar responds in kind.

I want her. *We* want her. She's the key. Our heart. The middle to the circle we created long ago.

She moans as Reaper grinds himself against her, his jeans the only barrier between them. Alina isn't lost to her heat yet—something that surprised me when she woke up —but I can tell she's close.

Our girl is holding on for as long as she can because she wants to remember this. To experience us. To be able to consent to everything we want to do to her before she loses her mind to lust.

My sweet, beautiful panther, I marvel, loving that she's a fighter.

She showcases some of that fight now as she releases me to tussle with Reaper's jeans. He doesn't help her, the sadist wanting to make her work for it. It's not until she growls at him that he grins and lifts his body to help her with the process.

Then he grabs her thighs, spreads her, and thrusts right into her slick heat.

No foreplay. No warning. Just a feral claim.

My balls tighten at the display, my animal roaring with the need to do exactly that—to take, fuck, *please*.

Alina scratches her nails down Reaper's back, her mouth parted on a scream that he silences with his mouth.

It's a hedonistic display.

Rough. Angry. *Passionate.*

They're in each other's minds, feeling each other's emotions, and riding the high of their connection.

Orcus leans against a bedpost, his hungry gaze taking in their mating while I lounge beside them, waiting for my turn to pounce.

It's a gorgeous fucking view, one that has my hand inching down to stroke my cock in response. My thumb teases the ring in the tip—a ring I want Alina to remove.

Hell, I want her to handle the bar, too.

It'll be her way of saying she's ready for my barb.

Otherwise, I'll hold it back. Which won't be pleasant at all. But for her, I'll do it.

"Reaper," she breathes, her legs encircling his waist as she drives her body upward to meet his movements.

Fucking beautiful, I marvel. I don't know what his mind— or Orcus's for that matter—is teaching her, but she's a star pupil. *A wildcat.*

I grip my shaft a little tighter, giving myself a solid pump that inspires a growl in my chest. It must be louder than I anticipated because both Reaper and Alina look at me, their eyes glazed over with arousal.

"Fuck, pet, I think your jaguar wants a taste," Reaper says, his voice low and purposeful. "Should I come inside you first, let him lap it all up with his tongue? Or do you want to feel us both inside you at once?"

Alina visibly quivers, her legs seeming to squeeze around Reaper.

"Oh, do that again," he groans, his head going to her neck. "Yeah, pet. *Fuck,* that feels good."

Her nails dig into his shoulders, but her gaze goes to me. Then back to Reaper. "I…" She swallows. "When you say… both inside…?"

"I mean one of us in your pussy and one of us in your ass," he says, as straightforward as ever.

But Alina seems to appreciate his crass approach because the little panther licks her lips. "Both."

Reaper grins. "Excellent choice, pet." He starts to pull out of her, but her nails dig into his shoulders, her midnight gaze suddenly blazing like the stars on a dark night.

"*Both*," she repeats, drawing a growl from Orcus.

"There's my Goddess," he praises. "Reaper gave you a choice, but you're demanding *both* options."

Reaper's eyebrows lift.

Meanwhile, I groan. Because *fuck*, that's hot.

"Use her slick to prepare her, Flame," Orcus tells me. "Use your fingers on her while Reaper fucks her."

Shit, I'm going to come just at the thought of what he's telling me to do.

It doesn't matter that Alina sucked me off this morning; it feels like days ago.

I'm so pent up with need for this woman that I'm ready to combust at just the thought of *preparing* her.

But Reaper is already moving, the pair of them rolling as he places himself on his back and forces her to straddle him. "Ride me, pet," he tells her. "Ride me while Flame plays with your ass."

Her tits sway as she follows his command, her hands braced on his chest. I sit up, fist my hand in her hair and kiss the shit out of her.

Orcus told me to prepare her.

Well, this is my way of *preparing* her.

She pants against my mouth, her body moving, her orgasm mounting, all while I dominate her with my tongue.

My jaguar *purrs*, the sound rolling over her in a sensual vibration that makes her gasp.

Yeah, I'm going to enjoy the fuck out of this.

I nip her bottom lip, then use my hand in her hair to push her down to Reaper's waiting mouth.

He kisses her with a ferocity I can almost feel, my groin tightening with excitement.

So. Fucking. Soon.

But I have to prepare our mate first.

My fingertips drift down her spine, over her alluring rump, and toward the place she's joined with Reaper. She's so wet that she practically soaks my hand. "You weren't kidding about Omega slick," I say to Orcus.

"I only shared what I've been told by previously mated Alphas. Everything... *everything* is true." He sounds pleased by that last part, and I can tell without looking at him that he's smiling fondly at Alina.

She shivers, suggesting he just said something in her mind.

Then she moans as Reaper wraps his shadows around her in ribbonlike binds that hold her down so he can ravage her mouth.

I leave Reaper to his bondage games and focus on Alina's curved backside. Goose bumps pebble along her skin as I spread her cheeks to reveal her tight little entrance.

She's going to need a lot of prepping to take us all here.

Because that's exactly what's going to happen—we're all going to claim each of her holes.

Over and over again.

Once she's lost to her heat, she won't even notice.

But until that happens, she's going to feel every inch.

Just as she does now as I slide one digit inside her. She clenches down around me, her body reacting to the foreign intrusion.

"Relax, Omega," Orcus tells her, either having picked up on her thoughts or having noticed her physical reaction.

I use her arousal to slide in and out of her, slowly and purposely. She follows Orcus's command, her muscles gradually loosening until I'm able to add a second finger.

Reaper curses as she jolts forward, her hips bucking against him.

"Don't let her come yet," Orcus says.

Alina starts to voice a complaint, but Reaper cuts it off with his tongue, his dark tendrils seeming to pet her with his hands, which probably makes it feel as though she has multiple palms stroking her.

And it looks like some of those strands are between them, no doubt teasing her tits and clit.

She's a writhing mess.

Sounds escape her, only to be swallowed by Reaper.

She's breathing hard.

Sweating.

Ready to burst.

And Reaper is thrusting up into her from below.

He's close. I can tell by his movements, the harshness of his thrusts, the way he's clinging to her while I insert a third finger into her ass.

"*Now,*" Orcus demands, the word for Reaper. Or maybe for Alina. Or perhaps even for me.

Regardless, it's his way of commanding pleasure for his Omega. *For our mate.*

Oh, I might not have claimed her yet, but that doesn't make her any less mine.

Reaper growls.

And Alina screams, her back arching as her insides *squeeze.*

Fuck, I can feel her coming with my fingers, her

orgasm a vibration that reminds me of my purr. It's so alluring. So addicting. So *beautiful*.

I want to worship this woman for eternity. Draw those sounds from her every day. Make her fall apart on repeat until she begs me to stop.

Orcus's rumble of approval has Alina trembling all over again, her Omega soul naturally responding to her chosen Alpha.

I can't wait to ignite our connection, to let her *feel* my jaguar. It's going to be explosive. Emotional. And a little bit savage.

"Fuck, pet," Reaper groans, following her over the edge into oblivion. With her insides clamping down around my fingers, I can only imagine how tightly she's gripping him with her pussy.

It must be good because he shudders, his release long and hard and making her moan in response.

She's insatiable, just like a fae should be.

Which means she won't need long to recover.

Orcus was different, his Godlike prowess having knocked her out.

Oh, Reaper and I could do it, too. And we would.

But not yet.

This was just meant to take the edge off.

Because our mate wanted *both* options.

Which means it's almost time for me to *lick*.

My jaguar rumbles in excitement, eager to taste her. To claim her. To *fuck* her.

However, I hold him back, my fingers gently stretching her as she and Reaper come down from their high.

Her tremors slowly abate, her body going limp on top of Reaper. His strands run all over her in a tender caress as he kisses her, reveling in their new bond.

"Ready for Flame to clean you up, pet?" he asks softly. "Because I think he's eager to tongue-fuck you."

That I am.

I ease my fingers out of her and let Reaper roll her into position. Then I crawl between her legs to feast on her slick sex.

It's a unique smoky-and-sweet flavor that has my inner animal growling for more. I let Alina hear that hungry sound, wanting her to know what's coming for her. Because I'll be inside her next. And my jaguar isn't going to go easy on her.

I slip my hand behind her to keep preparing her backside while I lap up every inch of her cunt, just like Reaper said I would.

By the time I'm done, Alina's writhing in the sheets all over again.

I don't need Orcus to tell me to drag this out and deny her orgasm; I do that on my own. Because I want our mate wet and needy and begging.

She grabs my hair, trying to draw my tongue up to her clit.

I deny her and kiss a path downward instead, only pausing when my lips meet her thigh.

A protest escapes her as I withdraw my hands and mouth, her gaze flying downward. "*Flame.*"

I smile.

Then shift into my jaguar form, eliciting a shocked gasp from her.

Reaper chuckles. "Intrigued by the concept of bestiality, pet?"

Her eyes widen, her expression telling me she's nowhere near ready for that. Hell, she may never be into it either. And that's okay. My jaguar is content with me fucking her in human form.

But he's the one who has to claim her for our bond to snap into place.

Which Orcus explains for me now as he calmly says, "Flame's not going to fuck you like this, little one. But he is going to bite you."

Hell yes, I'm going to bite her.

And I'm not going to wait either.

Because I need to be inside this woman, not just physically but mentally, too.

My jaguar sinks his teeth into her inner thigh, claiming her intimately as ours.

The bond is immediate, the energy warming my blood as I shift back into my human form.

Alina's eyes are still wide when I crawl over her, my *mate* alarmed and impressed by the swiftness of my claim.

I... I can feel you, she whispers into my mind. *Fae, I can feel all three of you.*

I smile. *Just wait until all three of us are fucking you at the same time. You're going to be so fucking full that you won't even be able to think.*

She shivers, her irises almost completely overtaken by her pupils. *I... I think I'll like that.*

I press my lips to hers before whispering, "You'll fucking love it, little panther."

But there's one more item for us to cover before we begin again.

My barb.

CHAPTER THIRTY-FOUR
ALINA

MY BODY IS ON FIRE.

My mind is borderline delirious.

And my heart… my heart is *full*.

Three men. Three fae. Three perfect *mates*.

I can feel each of them inside me in unique ways, our bonds all different yet similar at the same time. It's… *amazing*.

My soul feels content, at home, perfectly at peace. All while I'm surrounded by my favorite scents.

Ash. Fir trees. Fresh air.

Reaper. Flame. Orcus.

I shudder, my insides burning with renewed need. Orcus's mind helps me understand the sensation, his Alpha instincts telling me my heat is approaching quickly now.

Part of me is already losing my mind to the lust. However, my mates are keeping me grounded, helping me be an active participant and to *consent*.

That word warms my mind as I hear it in each of theirs—they want me to want this. To want them. To want *more*.

Especially Flame.

He's staring down at me with his violet eyes, his panther lurking on the edges with a hint of black surrounding his vibrant irises. His thoughts are focused on his barb, not because he's eager to be inside me, but because he wants to know if I'll accept him completely.

His inner animal wants to breed me.

Just like Orcus's Alpha instincts desire to do.

Reaper is the only one who is content with pleasure. Though, he's not opposed to the concept of seeing me with child, either.

All three men want to create a proper nest, to make a family together. And my heat cycle will allow us to do that.

There's no longer any doubt in my mind regarding who and what I am—I'm an Omega. My soul seems to have joined my mind, my instincts renewed and refreshed with my Mythos Fae heritage.

I have no idea how it's possible. Orcus is just as bewildered. But both of us accept the miracle. More than that, we intend to embrace it.

And part of that comes with the natural desire to create a life.

Flame brushes his nose against mine. "If you want this, then I need you to free my barb," he whispers.

It's a final act of understanding, one he wants me to control so I can physically and mentally consent to what's to come.

I love that he cares so much, that they *all* care this much.

They never wanted to force me into our mating. Yet I can feel how, deep down, they all knew this was unavoidable, how their souls instantly recognized mine. It took effort for them to remain patient while my human mind accepted the inevitable.

But we're here now.

And I'm ready.

Very, *very* ready.

Flame smiles, clearly hearing that resolve in my mind. "Prove it," he dares me out loud. "Show us how ready you are, my panther queen."

I press my palms to his shoulders to nudge him off of me. He rolls to his back but keeps a hand on my hip to pull me with him. My legs straddle his on impulse, my core meeting his throbbing flesh.

And the piercings embedded there.

A tremble trickles down my spine, my insides pulsing with need. I rub against him, curious about the metallic ridges. His mind tells me what he wants me to do, but I counter that desire with one of my own.

I lift myself up and grab him by the base, wanting to feel the texture against my intimate flesh.

Flame groans as I place him at my entrance and slowly slide down, taking him all the way to the hilt. "*Fuck*, little panther… That feels… amazing."

It's a low growl of sound.

But it's punctuated with a hint of a plea in his mind, his inner animal begging me to release him. To let him be free for the first time in his existence.

Because Flame hasn't given his barb to anyone else. He's been waiting for his mate. *For me.*

I want to feel that part of him, to indulge in the experience and truly be his.

It'll be different from Orcus's knot, something the fae have already mentioned, but I can sense the difference in Flame's mind.

Now I just need to experience it.

I gradually pull myself off of his thick arousal and kiss

a path down his abdomen, the motions natural despite being mostly new.

However, everything feels intrinsic. Like I was born for this. Like these fae were made for me.

Flame's abdomen clenches when I reach his groin, his animal riding him hard. I can hear the fight in his thoughts, as well as see it in his stiff form.

He's trying to contain his feral needs, just for a little longer.

But once I remove these piercings, he'll pounce.

And then I'll be in for the ride of my life.

Because Reaper is going to join him.

I can feel the intention radiating from my Death Fae mate as he goes to his knees behind me, his heat blanketing my back as he leans down to kiss my shoulder.

"Free his barb, pet," he says, a hint of a demand in his voice. "Then I want you to take him inside that sweet pussy while I fuck your ass."

I shudder, my thighs clenching in response.

Focus on Flame, little one, Orcus whispers into my mind. *I want you to remember fucking him for the first time.*

I swallow, my neck twisting as I meet his gaze. He's still standing by the bed, almost like he's guarding us while we play. *You're holding back my heat.*

Not exactly, he says, his eyes flashing crimson at me. *It's more that I haven't issued my mating call yet. When I do, you'll fall into the full throes of your estrus.*

And if you don't? I wonder.

Then what's happening now will continue until your body overtakes your mind, he tells me. *Which will be very soon, Alina. So concentrate on Flame's cock. You need to feel his barb. And he needs you to feel it, too.*

Fae, he's right.

This moment, this bonding, this final step, means

everything. It's not just about us but about his jaguar, too. All that pent-up animalistic aggression needs an outlet.

And I'm that outlet.

I straddle his thick thighs, my hand once again on his base. Flame watches me from beneath hooded eyes as I bend to place a kiss against the weeping head. His arousal mingles with mine, tempting me into a lick that turns into an open-mouthed embrace.

A curse leaves him on a growl, his hands clenching the sheets at his sides.

But it's Reaper that fists my hair to push me down, forcing me to take Flame into the back of my throat. When I try to pull back up, he doesn't let me, his mouth suddenly at my ear again.

"You keep making him wait," Reaper says darkly. "So now you have to wait to breathe."

I squirm, something about that comment awakening a depraved need inside me.

"It hurts, doesn't it?" he continues. "Wanting something with your whole body and being unable to achieve it. That's how Flame feels right now. How he's felt since the moment he laid eyes on you. How we've all felt."

He slowly guides me back until I'm able to inhale, then roughly pushes me back down again.

Being connected to his mind tells me he's not trying to hurt me, but attempting to test my limits, to see what I like and don't like.

And, apparently, I like *breath play*—a term I learn from his mind—because his manhandling is making me burn even hotter inside.

He gently pulls me off of Flame, this time allowing him to completely fall free from my mouth. Then he kisses me hungrily and palms my cheek.

"No more teasing, pet. Free his barb," he tells me again. "*Now.*"

Reaper guides my attention back to Flame, his hand shifting from my face to my nape before moving down to my hip, all while he remains behind me.

The whole interaction leaves me panting, and the sight of Flame's straining cock has my thighs flooding with *want.*

It's intense.

Overwhelming.

A pang inside that makes me borderline impatient.

But I force my hands to remain steady as I focus on the piercings.

"Grab the metal ball and twist," Flame instructs me, his purr underlining each word.

A purr that's making me even wetter between my legs.

Fae, I'm... I'm going to explode the moment he's inside me, I realize.

Between his purr and Reaper's mental commentary—all of which is filthy in nature—I'm on the verge of climax without either of them truly touching me.

And that's *after* all the other orgasms.

This is crazy, I think as I unscrew the ball from Flame's bar.

This is being an Omega, Orcus corrects. *Now stop thinking and give Flame the attention he deserves.*

Fae, that demand makes me want to bend over and suck Flame's cock again.

But I know that's not what Orcus means.

So I do what he commands and remove the first piercing.

"Help her with the other one," Flame says, his eyes on Reaper.

My Death Fae mate grabs my hand and guides my fingers to the ring. "You have to pop out the bead in the middle there." He runs my thumb over it before grabbing my other hand and pinches the metal loop part between my fingers. "Hold here while you do it, then slide it off of him."

It's probably the most technical commentary I've ever heard from him.

"Good girl," he says as I follow his instructions. "Now crawl up there and mount him."

Only, Flame is already reaching for me before I can even attempt to move, his grip bruising my hips as he draws my lower half over his groin. "I need to be inside you," he tells me, the growl in his voice all animal.

He doesn't give me a chance to reply, just positions me and drives inside me in a harsh thrust that steals the air from my lungs.

"Fuck yes," Reaper says, his voice barely heard over Flame's aggressive growl.

I go to grab my Shifter Fae's shoulders, only to find myself suddenly being spun on the bed as he places his chest to my back and drives up into me from behind.

My lips part, my back arching at the impact.

Flame's palm is around my throat, his lips at my ear as his knees spread my legs even wider. "I'm taking you like this. Then I'm taking your ass. Reaper can watch."

My Death Fae grins in response, lounging on the bed beside us while he strokes his cock. "Fuck away," he says. "We'll tag-team next round."

"I call next round," Orcus interjects, his wings appearing at his back and stretching out on both sides. The sheer dominance in his voice and stance stirs a yearning deep in my soul, one I need to have fulfilled.

Then Flame drives into me again. *I'm inside you right now, little panther,* he growls into my mind. *Focus on me. My barb. Us.*

Fae, I breathe.

Flame's threatening to destroy me with his sharp movements, his jaguar roaring in my head.

"Grab the headboard," he demands.

I do.

And he truly starts to fuck me, his angle different from what the others have done. It's deeper somehow. More intense.

His pace is brutal, too. No gradual movements to prepare me for him. No tender strokes. Just unrestrained *thrusts.*

My nails bite into the wood as my head falls forward. Flame's inner jaguar is taking me now, driving us forward into a *rut.*

The word is one I hear echoing in Orcus's mind.

He fully intends to take me like this, too.

All three of them do.

To breed me.

Fill me with their seed.

Drive me to the depths of oblivion and drown me in their passion.

Fae, I'm... I'm lost. Swimming in the darkness. Reveling in the desires of three men. Floating in my own pool of need.

They're going to take me in so many ways. Destroy my senses. Repair my ability to breathe, just to cut off my air again.

It's going to be... a whirlwind of eroticism.

My inner walls clench around Flame, my mind slowly succumbing to my mating heat. That's the source of the fire inside me, the flames flickering through my veins and the inferno growing in my lower belly.

I'm nearly lost to the sensations.

Utterly engulfed by a sensuous blaze.

Flame's hands cover mine on the headboard, his lips

on my neck. "You're doing so well, sweetheart," he says. "Taking everything my jaguar has to give. *Fuck*, little panther. You feel so damn good. So fucking good."

I lean into him, the back of my head dropping to his shoulder as he kisses my throat.

He's not thrusting into me with the same vigorous pace anymore. He's doing longer, harder strokes that hit me so deep it almost hurts.

Yet it feels so, so good, too.

I can sense his pleasure mounting as well, his own warmth adding to mine and stoking my inner fire that much hotter.

"Touch her clit," Orcus says.

But it's not Flame who obeys that command; it's Reaper. And it's not his hand I feel, but his *tongue*.

Fae, I don't even know how he's doing that, but he's partially underneath me now as Flame rides me from behind, his hands the only things keeping me connected to the headboard.

My knees shake, my body weakening beneath my pending climax.

Flame must know because he pulls both my hands under one of his against the wood and wraps his other arm around me to keep me against him while he fucks me.

Hard.

Thoroughly.

Perfectly.

His name leaves me on a pant, my mind fracturing beneath a tidal wave of want and need. I want to fall into my heat. But I *need* to feel his barb.

"Please," I whisper. "Please, Flame."

His teeth sink into my neck, hard enough to draw blood, and I wonder if it'll leave a mark. I know the bite against my thigh will absolutely brand me for eternity, but this… this just feels like a jaguar trying to subdue his mate.

I buck back against him, needing him to give me his barb. To complete us. To properly mate me. To *join* us. *"Flame."*

He growls.

And I growl back.

Then I scream as Reaper bites my clit.

My orgasm is instantaneous, the pain inspiring an even deeper pleasure that has me convulsing around Flame's thrusting cock.

His fingers are suddenly in my hair as he tugs my head back and claims my mouth with his own. I nearly fall forward, but his arm is there, holding me, while my hands fall away from the wooden bed frame. He sits back and lets me ride the waves of my climax, his cock pulsing inside me with his restrained need.

"That feels so fucking good, sweetheart," he says against my mouth.

I shake.

Moan.

Blink in and out of consciousness.

And find myself on my back beneath him, my mind spinning with confusion as to how we've moved.

But Flame is there, mastering me, guiding me, pulling me into a rhythm that's becoming increasingly familiar.

My arms intertwine around his neck as he leans down to kiss me, the action soothing while his lower half drills into me.

So deep. So good. So intense.

I feel like I'm about to come again.

Except it's not me dancing along the edge; it's Flame.

White-hot sensation bursts through me as he explodes,

the force of his orgasm stealing all sense of reason from my mind.

There's just heat.

Vibrations.

Spasms.

Ohhhh… that last part… it's… it's unending. Like a volcano erupting all over my body, only instead of searing my skin, it's leaving pleasurable trembles behind.

Flame's barb, I realize. *Oh. My. Fae.*

It's… *wow.*

I… I don't know… I can't… There are no words. No thought. Just… *pleasure.*

He's whispering something in my ear, some sort of praise, but I can't understand it through the fog of rapture clouding my mind.

I no longer exist.

I'm simply… ecstasy.

Somewhere, Reaper chuckles.

And then Orcus *growls*. It's different from the others I've heard. This is deeper, more guttural, even more intense, and it rocks me to my very core.

The mating call.

I recognize it on a base level, my body instantly giving in to the need clawing at my insides.

Warmth floods my being, my lower half squeezing in a plea for more.

More sex. More seed. More pleasure.

"Fuck," Flame breathes as he pulls out of me. "Her *scent.*"

"It's fucking amazing," Orcus says, his big form suddenly climbing over me. "I want you on your hands and knees, Omega."

I hear him.

I understand him.

But I don't know how to move.

Except… except I do. Like I'm lost in a fog and my body is just his to command. His to *fuck*.

Which he does.

Hard.

My nails dig into the sheets, my body bowed as he masters me and envelops me with his wings.

More, more, more, I think at him, unable to vocalize the chant.

Only, no. I *am* saying the words. It's… I'm…

Fae, this is confusing.

It's erotic. It's perfect. It's… heaven.

All three men are surrounding me. Filling me. Kissing me. Loving me. Worshipping my body in ways I could never have imagined.

Orcus knots me while Reaper kisses me. Flame focuses on my breasts.

And then I'm suddenly between Reaper and Flame.

A scream rips from my throat as they take me together, Reaper buried in my ass while Flame's barb threatens to overwhelm my front again.

I'm no longer of sound mind. Simply lost to my lust. Completely at their mercy.

But I trust them.

They'll take care of me.

They'll protect me.

And they'll pleasure me.

Because they're my future. My circle. My mates. *My fae.*

CHAPTER THIRTY-FIVE
ORCUS

GODS, Alina is stunning.

I sit in a nearby chair, watching my naked little Goddess roll all over the bed as she fiercely rearranges the pillows and sheets.

Flame and Reaper stand nearby with piles of clothes and linen at their feet, waiting to be commanded by our furious mate.

She's been working on this all morning, her growls going straight to my cock.

I'm hard, just like I've been for the last five days.

Reaper and Flame are aroused, too.

It doesn't matter that we've basically fucked Alina around the clock for days; our little sex Goddess has put us in a constant state of arousal.

I've taken every hole, claimed her in the most intimate of ways, and still, I want to possess every inch of her all over again. Bite her sweet tits and redden those luscious nipples.

My crescent-like mark on her breast catches my gaze, making my lips curl. *Mine.*

Reaper seems to be staring at the *R* above her mound as well, his expression rivaling my own.

Meanwhile, Flame is just gazing at her with hearts in his eyes. He and his inner beast are completely smitten.

Our mate certainly looks adorable right now, though, growling and arguing with blankets as she punches the bed. "Stay," she snaps, causing me to bite my lip to keep from chuckling.

I know better than to upset a working Omega.

She's trying to build a nest, one meant to house all of us *and* the life growing inside her. There's no heartbeat yet, just the flicker of a soul. I felt it this morning, just like Alina obviously had as well—hence her urgent need to perfect her safe haven.

Fortunately, we preemptively brought most of the items from our room in Monster City, thus providing her with the base for her nest.

She growls again, the sound erasing my humor and replacing it with *need*.

I palm my shaft and give it a stroke. Once my Omega finishes her task, I can fuck her. Hopefully *in* her nest.

She's slowly coming out of her heat, her mind seeming focused on her other needs at present. But she's not quite done with our rut.

Once she finishes that nest, she's going to want to mark it with her circle's scent.

And the best way to do that is to fuck inside of it.

Her eyes narrow as she looks at Flame, her nose twitching.

He remains utterly still as she prowls toward him and sniffs his chest. A little moan escapes her, the sound one of approval. "*More*," she demands.

After a few trial-and-error moments, he now knows

what that means. With a swift shuffle through the fabric at his feet, he pulls out one of his shirts and hands it to her.

"Thank you," she says, kissing him on the cheek and crawling back across the bed.

Flame preens in response.

Meanwhile, Reaper narrows his gaze, clearly wanting to be *thanked* as well.

When Alina spins toward him, his glare melts into a hopeful expression. That expression morphs into pride when she scents him and issues the same command of "More."

But he doesn't hand her a shirt. Instead, he takes off the boxers he's wearing—boxers he literally only put on for her, as I know he prefers to go commando—and hands them to her.

She inhales deeply, her pupils dilating, and gives him a kiss on the mouth. There are no words spoken this time, but the kiss appears to be more than enough gratitude for Reaper because he's now beaming as well.

When Alina comes for me, I tilt my head and wait. She's already taken all the garments I have to offer her. There's only one item left I can give her, and that's my cock.

Or, more specifically, my cum.

Because that's what she said she wants in her nest. A sensual marking of sorts to chase everyone else away.

My mates are intimidating, that scent will say. *My mates are dangerous. My mates will do anything and everything in their power to protect me.*

She studies me intently, her gaze going to the hand on my cock while I continue to give myself a few slow, thorough strokes.

"See something you need, little mate?" I ask her.

She hums, her tongue sneaking out to dampen her lower lip. "Soon."

Her attention returns to Flame as she bends to sort through his garment pile herself. She finds a towel that she quickly adds to her nest, then another shirt. The process is repeated with Reaper's stack of fabric, her hands pulling out a robe and a pair of jeans.

All of it is carefully folded into the edges of her creation, leaving a large open space in the middle.

After a few more rounds of sifting through clothes and linens, she returns to Flame and extends her hand.

He happily accepts it and allows her to pull him into her nest.

Reaper is next.

Then she faces me. "Alpha."

"Omega," I return, my tone reverent. "Are you ready to play in your nest?"

She swallows and nods. "Yes. Scent the nest, then find my sister."

My brow furrows. "What?"

"Serapina," she murmurs, her expression shifting from dreamy to confused. "Sera…"

There's some thought trying to pierce through her Omega fog, one that's important enough to interrupt her heat.

Reaper sits up, as does Flame, all of us intently focused on our mate.

"Tell me about your sister," I say, all thoughts of fucking in her nest disappearing in the wake of this reveal.

"She… she left me a note." She seems to be trying to remember, her estrus having clouded her mind. When Omegas go into heat, they only care about one thing —procreation.

We've done that.

Which made building her safe haven her next task.

But it seems her sister is a competing priority.

No. Not just her sister, but *finding* her sister.

"What kind of note, Alina?" Reaper asks, his serious side obviously engaged.

Her nose crinkles. "I…" She swallows and shakes her head, almost like she's trying to clear it.

"Come here," I tell her, holding out my hand.

She obeys because she's still on the edges of her estrus, her body moving before her mind can stop her.

The moment she's close enough, I pull her into my arms and purr, my goal to soothe her enough for her to think.

That way, even if she can't voice what she wants to say aloud, I can catch her thoughts.

She buries her head against my chest, her body instantly relaxing into my hold while Flame and Reaper watch intently.

They're obviously trying to discern the same information that I am.

"Tell us about Serapina," I say softly. "What note did she send you?"

Alina is quiet for a long moment, her eyes having fallen closed. But she's not sleeping. She's searching in her mind, swimming through the memories of the last few days and trying to find herself.

This is going to pull her out of her heat, but that's okay. This is clearly important.

Why didn't she mention her sister before? I wonder. *Did she not trust us?*

She must hear the question because it triggers a memory in her mind—a memory of her deciding to ask for our help in finding her.

As soon as Reaper returns, I'm telling them, she thought then.

397

This was after feeling a hint of guilt at not having told us about her sister yet, followed by a realization that she was holding herself back.

But she decided to no longer keep the secret and to share it.

Right before the first wave of her heat began.

"Chicago," she breathes now.

There's an Elite City, she recalls in her mind, the voice not hers but presumably her sister's. Because she appears to be recalling what the note said. *Find an old map, Lina. Look for Chicago. I'll be waiting.*

"*Sera,*" Alina breathes, her eyelashes fluttering open as she looks at me. "My sister's in the Elite City."

"That's how you know about Chicago." It's not a question but a statement.

However, she nods anyway.

"Where did you find this note?" I ask, suspicious. Because from what Helia said, even humans in the Elite City are unaware of the former name.

So how does her sister know about Chicago?

And where would she have expected Alina to find an old map?

New York City no longer exists. The buildings of Monster City are new to this dimension, the technology and architecture inhuman. I highly doubt old maps exist.

And yet, the note told Alina to find one.

"In my room after last year's Day of the Choosing. Someone slid it under my door." She swallows. "I don't know how, but I know my sister's handwriting, and that note was written by her."

I nod. "I believe you, Alina."

Her eyes widen a fraction. "You do?"

"Of course I do." If she knows her sister wrote it, then her sister wrote it. The questions that remain are how she managed to slip the note into Alina's room and how Serapina knows about Chicago.

"You said she slipped you the note, and you're not sure how, so I'm guessing that means your sister no longer lives in your village," Flame says, his focus on our mate.

"She was an Offering two years ago," Alina replies, her expression turning distant as her mind pulls up the memory of the ceremony.

Her pain becomes my pain as she watches her sister walk down the aisle to her fate, knowing she'll never see her again.

"So maybe her mate or mates helped get that note to Alina," Reaper suggests, his focus on Flame and then me. "That would explain the mention of Chicago."

"As well as the comment about finding a map," I say, thinking it through. "Maybe her mate or mates know there are some in Monster City?"

"Possibly," Flame replies. "I didn't see any while we were there, though."

"Neither did I," Reaper admits. "But if Serapina and her mate or mates are living in the Elite City, then I imagine that Cain guy would know. He was very in charge during that massacre."

Alina stills. "Massacre?"

"Something to do with the Strigoi and their mate," I explain softly. "Reaper hasn't elaborated much."

The Death Fae shrugs. "Not my story to tell. Besides, I don't think it's relevant other than to say that if Serapina is in the Elite City, Cain can likely tell us where she is and who she's with."

I consider that for a long moment. "You think we can trust him?"

Reaper snorts. "Trust? No. But he has two of our Strigoi, and while they might be there willingly and happily, you're still a Mythos Fae from their home realm. That gives you political authority in this situation. Ergo, perhaps you can ask a favor in exchange for looking the other way."

"Not sure Morpheus will like that," I mutter.

However, Reaper has a point.

I could assert some dominance over the situation, demand a meeting, and request Serapina's whereabouts as a boon. In exchange, I would offer to not interfere with the Strigoi's choice to remain in this dimension.

As for Morpheus, I wouldn't be able to make any promises on his behalf.

The best I could do would be to not involve myself at all, which would include not dragging the Strigoi Princes back to the Morpheus Kingdom.

"I suppose you're right," I go on, looking at Reaper. "I could offer to look the other way in exchange for information about Alina's sister."

"You would do that?" my Omega asks, her gaze locked on me.

"Of course I would," I tell her. "I would do anything for you."

Her pretty eyes start to shimmer, the tears tugging at my heartstrings. "Thank you," she whispers.

"Don't thank me, Alina. You're a Goddess now." I palm her cheek. "It's my duty to serve you in all ways." And I mean it.

She's my heart.

My purpose.

My *future*.

"We'll find your sister," I promise her, my lips brushing over hers. Then I focus on Reaper. "Do you know how to find Cain?"

He considers it for a moment and nods. "I know a good place to start."

"Good enough." I look at Alina, her clear expression telling me that finding her sister has officially overtaken her need to finish her nest. "Would you like to go to the Elite City tonight?"

She gapes at me. "I'm going, too?"

"I assumed you wanted to go. Would you rather stay here?" I ask her, my thumb tracing her cheekbone.

"No, I want to go."

"Then we'll go together," I tell her. "And we'll go tonight."

Because I recognize the need inside my mate, a need she hasn't been able to fulfill since she found that note.

Tonight, we'll begin rectifying that need—by finding Serapina Everheart.

CHAPTER THIRTY-SIX

ALINA

THE ELITE CITY is nothing like Monster City. There are no giant trees or metal branches or jungle forests. Instead, it's mostly buildings. Some tall. Some short. And there appear to be various districts, too. Or that's my guess based on my current view.

We're high up in one of the Elite City's towers—one that appears to be the tallest in the city because it overlooks everything below.

The lights are what gives the illusion of districts. It's the way they're laid out more than their colors, the groupings seeming to be purposeful.

"It's terrible, isn't it?" Reaper says beside me. "No signs of old Chicago at all. It's all been rebuilt. But the worst thing? No Chicago pizza." He sounds very upset about this last part. "Whenever we go back to our home dimension, I'm taking you to our Human Realm for a do-over."

Flame snorts to my left, his long fingers wrapped around a crystal glass that holds a bubbly liquid. I can't remember what Prince Cage said it was called, just that it tastes similar to some mortal drink in their home dimension.

I opted for water instead. Mainly because of the life forming inside me. But also because my stomach has been churning since we arrived and a bubbly drink didn't appeal to me.

That queasiness hasn't improved, either. If anything, it worsened when we were escorted up to King Cain's penthouse. And standing here, staring out his floor-to-ceiling windows, just… intensifies the sense of unease.

It's likely related to whatever I might learn about my sister.

Or perhaps because I just spent the last however many days being fucked within an inch of my life.

Oh, or it could be pregnancy related.

It seems a bit soon for that, but it's not exactly a human baby growing in my womb—hence the reason I can sense the child's soul more than the physical entity.

I press my palm to my belly, my heart warming at the knowledge of the life growing there. It almost overshadows the sickly feeling threatening my insides.

"Gentlemen," a deep voice says as a large, elegantly dressed male enters the room. "And my lady," he adds with a slight nod my way. "Apologies for the delay. I wasn't expecting company, as last I checked, my schedule was clear this evening."

He casts a pointed look at Orcus.

"We're new to this realm and unfamiliar with your protocols," Orcus replies, his tone unapologetic. "As a Mythos Fae, I'm also unaccustomed to the concept of *scheduling* time."

Prince Sabre leans in to whisper in the newcomer's ear, then straightens and takes a sip from his glass. The deep red liquid reminds me of blood, making me not want to inquire about what he's actually drinking.

The man who just arrived clears his throat. I'm not sure what Prince Sabre said to him, but he instantly schools his features in a polite expression.

"Right, well, I'm Cain," the newcomer announces, his accent similar to Orcus's. "You obviously already know my bond-mates." He gestures toward the two Strigoi Princes, who are both holding glasses of red liquid.

"As they're from my world, yes," Orcus replies, his tone holding a hint of that Alpha dominance he favors. He's also purposely restating the reminder that he's a God, because that position demands respect.

"Of course," King Cain replies. "And I know you, as well as Reaper—although, we've not been officially introduced. Cage provided some details about you after the wedding last week."

Reaper cocks his head. "Do all your weddings end in massacres in this realm?"

King Cain smiles, but it doesn't quite reach his eyes. "Only the more entertaining ones."

"Noted," my Death Fae mate drawls.

How does a wedding end in a massacre? I wonder, shivering. I've seen a few in our village. They were boring affairs that the Viscount oversaw as the one blessing the union. None of those ended in bloodshed or violence.

"Hmm, yes, well, as I was saying, I've met Orcus and Reaper. But I have not had the privilege of formally meeting you"—his gaze is on Flame before returning to Orcus—"or your beautiful mate."

"Flame," my Shifter Fae mate says flatly. "And *our* beautiful mate is Alina Everheart."

King Cain nods. "Forgive me. I merely deferred to Orcus

since he seems intent on playing the God card today." His attention again goes to my Alpha. "That is the purpose of this impromptu visit, is it not? To assert your dominance?"

Orcus studies him for a long moment. "Actually, no. We're here to ask about Alina's sister."

The Elite City King blinks, his attention shifting to the Strigoi Princes. They appear as surprised as King Cain.

"Although, if you would like for me to play my *God card*, I can," Orcus goes on. "But I was under the impression my Strigoi are now your Strigoi—by choice. As far as I'm concerned, their safety is my priority. However, if you prefer that I return to my realm to discuss their fates with my cousin Morpheus, I would be happy to oblige."

My connection to Orcus's mind informs me of the threat underlying those words. However, I also heard it in his tone.

He's in Alpha mode.

"I don't think that will be necessary," King Cain says slowly, his gaze narrowing in a way that suggests Orcus has struck a chord—and it's not one he should have plucked.

Flame sets his glass down, his palm going to my lower back in a protective gesture that Reaper matches on my other side.

"Oh, I knew this would be fun," a feminine voice interjects as a screen appears on the wall that's adjacent to the windows. "I'm curious as to who has the bigger..." She trails off, her lips curling down. "Actually, I don't care. Which is a strange yet refreshing realization."

The dark-haired woman looks to the side then, her painted lips quirking right back up at whatever she sees off camera.

"Helia," King Cain says, his voice deeper than before. "How lovely of you to interrupt."

Helia, I repeat. *As in… the Queen of Monster City.*

Yes, Orcus replies, not that I needed his confirmation. I recalled her name from previous discussions. But I had no idea that *this* was what she looked like.

Gorgeous.

Dark features.

Long legs.

Wearing nothing but a silky robe.

And one of my mates met with her last week.

My lips curl down. I didn't like that realization one bit.

She does nothing for me, Alina, Orcus tells me, his mind confirming that to be the truth. But it only placates me a little bit, mainly because she appears to be eyeing each of my mates with interest now.

"It's not an interruption when one is invited to join a call, darling," she finally says, her striking face crinkled with mirth. "Or that's what Bernard said, anyway. Something about potentially being needed?"

King Cain glances at a door, his gaze narrowing. "I see."

"As does your assistant," she returns, the words not making sense to me. "Ravens are quite good for that, I hear."

"You two gossip entirely too much," King Cain mutters.

"Jealous he found out about my new mates before you did?" she asks, her eyelashes batting coquettishly at him.

"Not really, no. I've been too busy to care about anything other than my own mate."

Queen Helia smiles, her eyes creasing at the sides. "Right under your nose this entire time."

"Don't start with me," he replies.

She holds up her hands. "I wouldn't dream of it." There's a note of humor in her tone that has King Cain sighing in response.

He mutters something under his breath that I don't quite catch, but she somehow does because she laughs.

Then, louder, he says, "It seems Orcus would like to know more about Alina's sister. In exchange, I believe he's offering to leave my Strigoi alone." He looks at my Alpha. "Did I summarize that appropriately?"

"You did."

"Brilliant. Helia?" King Cain prompts, arching a brow at her.

"Why are you looking at me? This sounds like an arrangement between the two of you," she says.

"And yet you joined our meeting," he returns.

She grins. "Yes, and I've prepared popcorn as well." She stretches her long, dark-skinned legs out along her chaise, causing the robe she's wearing to inch upward on her athletic thighs.

The Elite City King gives her a look. "I think you'll find it to be a rather boring show, Helia." His focus shifts to Orcus. "I assume the human is from the same village as Alina, yes?"

"Yes," Orcus confirms. "Nightingale Village."

"I'm very aware of that part."

You are? I think, surprised by his comment. I assumed he had no idea who I was, but that statement made it sound like he might know more than I realized.

King Cain slides his hands into the pockets of his pressed slacks, giving nothing else away. He merely asks, "What's the sister's name?"

"Serapina Everheart," Orcus replies, causing my stomach to twist uncomfortably.

I would have expected my unease to abate now that I know the Elite City King has agreed to help us locate Sera. But for whatever reason, I feel worse. Like my energy is waning with each passing second.

Are you all right? Flame asks into my mind. *You look quite pale.*

I think… I think I'm just overwhelmed. I… I haven't seen my sister in over two years. I thought I would never see her again. But now… I swallow. *Now there's hope.*

But shouldn't that be making me feel better, not worse?

"Give me a moment to pull her file," King Cain says as he leaves the room.

Prince Cage clears his throat. "Did you mean what you said?" he asks, his attention on Orcus. "That you won't fight us on staying?"

"I wouldn't fight you in general," my Alpha replies. "But regarding staying, as long as it's a willing arrangement and you feel safe, I don't feel obligated to do anything at all."

"What about Morpheus?" Prince Sabre asks.

"I can't speak on his behalf," Orcus replies. "However, I can try talking to him when I return to our realm. But know that I have no control over his reaction. I can only make suggestions."

Prince Cage inclines his head. "We would appreciate that, God Orcus."

"Just as we appreciate you helping us to arrange this meeting so quickly, Prince Cage," Orcus replies, the words purposeful. Mythos Fae don't have to thank anyone for anything. But Orcus is showing respect now by acknowledging his gratitude.

Being connected to his mind affords me so much more knowledge and provides insight into fae mentality.

It's a… confusing world.

But I'm excited to learn more about it.

"There wasn't much of a choice," Prince Sabre says, his lips curling slightly. "Reaper told us to schedule the meeting or we would be shipped back to the Netherworld."

"I believe I used the word *might* somewhere in that sentence," Reaper drawls from beside me, his amusement warming our bond. "It's not my fault you mistook my request as a demand."

Prince Cage snorts. "Your first words were about how easy it was to enter our rooms without notice."

Reaper shrugs. "That was just a casual comment about the lack of security in this tower."

"And then you said Orcus would have no problem portaling into our chambers, too," Prince Cage goes on.

"Well, yes. I was determining logistics for our meeting." Reaper smiles and it's all teeth. "I don't scare you, do I, Cage?" His tattoos move along his exposed arms, the threat a stark contrast to the innocent tone he used to voice the question.

"Stop flirting with the Strigoi," Flame interjects. "You're a mated fae now." He tightens his hold around my waist, making me giggle. It's a nice distraction from the queasiness haunting my insides.

"It's a good thing Alina has three mates," Reaper replies dryly. "Because if you think that's flirting, then our girl is going to need me and Orcus to show her otherwise."

Flame grunts. "I'm more than capable of pleasing our mate."

"Pleasing and flirting are two entirely diff—"

"Here we are," King Cain interrupts as he reenters the room, carrying some sort of pocket device. "Helia, I'm going to split your screen."

The woman on the video sits up in her chaise, causing the light to create a unique sort of purple glow against her black skin. *Or is that her actual skin color?* I wonder, admiring the violet sheen.

However, her glimmer disappears as her screen is

moved to one side, her image smaller now as a document of some kind populates the space beside her.

"Serapina Everheart," King Cain says. "She was selected as an Offering two years ago but went to the Nightingale Compound, not Monsters Night."

The Nightingale Compound? I repeat in my head. *What is that?*

"The breeding compound," Orcus says, the words a statement, not a question.

Breeding. My stomach twists violently. *What...? What does that even mean? Bred by monsters?*

Bred for *monsters*, Orcus replies into my mind, his tone holding a dark note to it. *The Nightingale Compound is where humans go to procreate.*

CHAPTER THIRTY-SEVEN
ALINA

"Yes, the breeding compound," King Cain says, confirming Orcus's statement. "There were twelve Offerings that year from Nightingale Village. Only two went on to Monsters Night. The others were sent to the compound to create more ideal mates."

King Cain clicks his little device, bringing up more information. But I'm too lost in his statements—as well as Orcus's mental comments—to read the words on the screen.

My sister went to a breeding compound? To create… create more… potential Offerings. Is that… is that as bad as I think it is? I wonder, feeling deathly ill.

Flame's arm flexes around me, his voice suddenly in my head as he tells me it's going to be okay.

But nothing about this is *okay*.

My sister…

But how…? How did she…?

I don't understand.

This doesn't make any sense.

I… I…

"Indeed, that's where Alina and her sister were made, too," King Cain says, the mention of my name bringing me back to the conversation. "They were placed with humans in the village to be raised with greater care, as their genetics marked them as ideal Offerings."

"This is what I was telling you about last week with the placement program—ideal Offerings are given to certain humans for child-rearing," Queen Helia adds. "Some of those humans are later rewarded for their efforts as well by being given access to the Elite City."

"Yes, it seems that happened with Alina's guardians." Another screen pops up that shows my parents.

Except... except they're saying these are not my real parents. But my *guardians*.

"Their village death day was a little over a decade ago. They now live here in the city." The image he shows is of them on some sort of patio, dressed in similar attire from Monsters Night.

"I see." Orcus's tone gives nothing away, but I feel him in my mind, caressing my thoughts and assessing my emotional state.

I have no idea what he finds inside me because I'm not sure how... or *what*... I'm feeling.

Dizzy? Yes.

Nauseous? Also yes.

Confused? Absolutely.

Angry? A little. Or maybe... maybe *a lot*.

My parents faked their deaths? I wasn't even ten years old when they died. Serapina was only eight.

"As I told you, we don't govern the villages. The Elite families do," Queen Helia murmurs. "Whether we agree with the practice or not is irrelevant. But I will say it has worked well, as evidenced by your mating Alina Everheart."

Orcus says nothing. However, I can hear him conceding the point in his mind. But he hates that he agrees. Because nothing about this feels right to him.

And not just because I'm starting to scream in my own mind about the injustice of this insanity.

I was created in a compound.

My parents are alive… and they're not my real parents.

Sera is in the same compound now.

Being bred.

And creating…

More ideal mates.

Fae, I'm going to be sick. This is all too much. Too overwhelming.

"If she's in the compound, how did she send Alina a note?" Reaper asks, his question making me freeze. "I assumed she had mates who managed to magically place it in Alina's rooms. But it sounds like that's not the case at all."

"What note?" Queen Helia asks, causing my stomach to churn even more.

Flame squeezes me close. *It's all right, little panther. We need this information to find your sister. Something isn't right.*

While I agree with him, I… I still don't feel well. The world is starting to spin around me. Everything is upside down. *I—*

Reaper's voice interrupts my thoughts as he repeats the note aloud. But all I hear is my sister's words in my head, uttered in her voice.

There's an Elite City. Find an old map, Lina. Look for Chicago. I'll be waiting.

"That's how your mate knew about Chicago," Queen Helia says.

"Yes." Orcus's reply is flat.

"But it doesn't make any sense." Queen Helia's

statement is one I've been repeating in my mind for what feels like hours but has really only been minutes.

It's also not the same.

Because she's talking about the letter and I'm thinking about this situation.

"It's not only impossible for Serapina to have sent that letter, but it also doesn't serve a logical purpose," Queen Helia goes on. "Alina wouldn't have been able to get to the Elite City, even if she found a map mentioning the old Chicago name."

"If such a map even exists," King Cain mutters. "I haven't heard that name in over three centuries."

"Exactly," Queen Helia says. "So what purpose did this note serve?"

"We originally assumed it was to prompt Alina to rebel, to gain more entries into the Offering selection pool," Orcus says. "But I'm starting to realize that can't be the reason because it sounds like all the humans are selected based on genetics, not a random luck of the draw."

"Correct. Duke Nightingale always picks the Offerings ahead of the ceremony," Queen Helia replies, her words a punch to the gut.

Because that means I wasn't chosen randomly. I was chosen purposely.

And so was my sister.

"The Day of the Choosing is just an opportunity for the Village Viscount to assert authority and inspire fear," King Cain adds. "One of the former Nightingale Dukes believed fear was an excellent motivator to ensure the villagers cooperated and remained obedient."

"Again, it works," Queen Helia says. "Whether we agree or not—"

"Is irrelevant," Orcus finishes for her. "Yes, I've gathered that you don't actually care how the humans treat each other in this realm. It's an excellent way to disregard your responsibility as the higher species."

Queen Helia frowns. "We choose not to interfere with fate."

"Yet you profit from that same fate and reward the humans responsible for providing said fate," Orcus drawls. "But I'm not here for a moral lesson on right and wrong. We're here for our mate and her sister. You've mentioned Serapina is in the Nightingale Compound. I know that's near here. Where exactly is it?"

King Cain and Queen Helia say nothing.

"If you tell me we can't interfere with the Nightingale breeding process, then I suppose we will begin a conversation on moral ethics," Orcus says. "And as a God, I will win that discussion."

His mind tells me that *conversation* and *discussion* don't mean *talking*. He means *power*. He will fight for my sister's freedom because it's the right thing to do.

And he'll destroy a lot of infrastructure in place to make way for that battle.

For me, I marvel. *He's saying he'll destroy this world… for me.*

It's… a heady realization, one that has my heart skipping several beats in response. Because Orcus could follow through on his threat, and he will if Queen Helia and King Cain don't start speaking soon.

Reaper's mind tells me he's more than ready to watch Orcus in action, and he's prepared to fight alongside him.

While Flame has already decided he'll shift to protect me while the other two go to work.

These fae… they're everything. *My* everything.

King Cain's jaw ticks, his gaze meeting Queen Helia's on the screen. Then he pulls up another image with my sister's name scrawled across the top.

Serapina Everheart.

Nightingale Compound.
Second Floor.
Room 37.
Genetic Markers…

My mind skims over a series of codes, none of them making any sense, and lands on the photo beneath it.

I blink.

Then frown at the redhead with hazel eyes on the screen.

"That's not my sister," I blurt out, interrupting whatever King Cain was just saying—something about needing to go with Orcus to find out more about the letter.

But I don't even care about what that means or what he's implying.

Nor do I care about conversational etiquette.

Because that woman isn't my sister. "That's her name. But if that's supposed to be a photo of her, then that's not Sera's file because that isn't my sister."

I picture my sister in my mind, trying to show my mates what she looks like. Because I need them to hear me, to understand that this woman is not Serapina.

"She's… she's not my sister," I say again, even dizzier than before.

The world seems to be blurring before my eyes as I picture Sera. Her blonde hair. Bright blue eyes. Gentle smile. Petite physique that rivals my own.

I close my eyes, willing her into existence.

"Alina," I hear her say.

It's all so real.

Like she's standing right beside me.

I sigh, frustrated that my mates haven't replied. And irritated by the screen depicting a different woman.

Actually, no, I'm furious.

All this information. All these lies about the Day of the

Choosing, the unnecessary stress of the ceremony, the fact that my parents are not really my parents, that they faked their deaths and left me to grieve with Sera.

To create monster mates.

Everything… *everything* is for Monsters Night.

This world… it's a horrible place. I want to leave. For my mates to whisk me away to their home world, where humans are not subjected to such hideous fates.

But I need to find my sister first.

And that means opening my eyes and reengaging with this conversation. To demand that this *King Cain* tell me where to find Serapina.

My spine straightens, my mouth opening to issue an order as my eyes flutter open.

Only for that order to die on my next breath as I stare into the familiar eyes of my sister.

She's gaping at me.

Which makes me gape at her.

"Are you real?" she whispers.

"What?" I ask, glancing around the garden we appear to be in. *Did I fall and bump my head?* I wonder. *How…?*

"Alina," she says, making me realize I actually did hear her voice my name once before. Because she really was standing next to me when she said it. "Are you real?"

"Yeah," I tell her. "I… I think so?"

Unless this is a dream.

A very realistic, very messed-up dream.

Sera takes a tentative step forward, her hand lifting to brush my arm. When her palm makes contact with my skin, her eyes widen. "Oh my monsters," she breathes, yanking me closer. "You're here. You're really here!"

Suddenly, she's hugging me, her strength surrounding me in a way that can't be a dream. Because I can *feel* her.

"Sera…" I whisper, my eyes falling closed.

LEXI C. FOSS

"Lina," she whispers back, squeezing me harder.

I embrace her in kind, thrilled to feel her in my arms again.

My sister.

My family.

My *Sera*.

But something… something isn't right.

It's an intrinsic itch inside my mind that keeps me from thoroughly enjoying the moment. *I'm missing something.*

No. Not something.

Someones.

My mates. My eyes fly open again, my sister's light hair blending with the garden around us. *I can't feel my mates…*

LEXI C. FOSS

"Lina," she whispers back, squeezing me harder.

I embrace her in kind, thrilled to feel her in my arms again.

My sister.

My family.

My *Sera*.

But something… something isn't right.

It's an intrinsic itch inside my mind that keeps me from thoroughly enjoying the moment. *I'm missing something.*

No. Not something.

Someones.

My mates. My eyes fly open again, my sister's light hair blending with the garden around us. *I can't feel my mates…*

420

CHAPTER THIRTY-EIGHT
REAPER

WHAT. The. Fuck?

Alina was right next to me. My hand was on her lower back. And now... now she's gone. Vanished. Nowhere to be seen or *felt*.

I spin around in a circle, searching for her, while Orcus's growl shakes the entire damn tower. His anguish is a punch to the heart I don't need right now. Not when Alina just crushed it with her disappearing act.

Where are you, pet? I demand, my soul threatening to kill everyone and everything in this realm in its pursuit for her.

Flame is just as furious beside me—in the space our mate just stood—his beast positively feral.

I'm only mildly aware of the alarms blaring overhead. Just as I barely notice the fact that the Monster City Queen has somehow come out of the screen and entered the room.

It's chaos.

Everyone is shouting.

Orcus's leather jacket and shirt are in tatters on the floor, his wings having exploded from his back.

Flame is about to rip out of his clothes as well to reveal his beast.

And I… I'm twirling a blade.

All while focusing on our mate. Her essence. But I can still smell her. *Those delicious strawberries…* It's a thread in the air that I follow with my soul, causing me to go incorporeal as I wander the plane between life and death.

Where are you, pet? I wonder at her again.

She's still in this dimension. This *world*.

I float about the room, the knife still in my hand as I lurk in the shadows, utterly consumed by my mate's lingering presence.

She's not in this tower. Nor is she in the city. But there's a piece of her being left behind, a piece connected to a strand coated in unique magic.

I cant my head to the side as I kneel to inspect the strange ropelike spell. It's ethereal, like me. But definitely not Death Fae in nature.

Mythos Fae magic, I realize, recognizing the hint of a manifestation enchantment. It's similar to Orcus's portal magic, although it's very specific. Tailored to reach certain spirits. *Like Omega spirits.*

My eyes narrow. *What are you?* I reach to tug on the cord, only for it to zap my spirit and shove me back against a nearby wall.

A crack follows.

No. Not a wall. A window.

And I'm back in corporeal form.

Flame snarls, his beast shredding through his jeans and T-shirt as he takes on his jaguar form. The Strigoi beside me—Cage—ends up pinned beneath his massive claws.

Sabre darts forward, ready to rip the Shifter Fae off his lover, but I step in the way, blocking him from making a lethal mistake.

"*Stop!*" I shout, my deadly strands shooting out of my skin and wrapping around everyone near me. Including Flame.

Snarls erupt in response.

Snarls I respond to with a deadly one of my own as I *squeeze.*

"Everyone. Fucking. *Stop.*"

A few do.

But Orcus... he has his sights on Helia and Cain, his red eyes and splayed wings telling me he's about to do some serious damage.

He doesn't care that they're royals or powerful themselves. He's a God, and he's about to show them what that means.

So I do the only thing I can think of and shout, "*Monster.*"

He freezes, the safeword having been engraved into his mind by our mate. His Alpha side knows what it means. Knows he doesn't want to hear it. Knows that it's *important.* And it's just enough to make him pause to look at me.

"The magic is Mythos Fae," I tell him. "I can see it in the in-between plane. And it just tried to shove me out the fucking window."

He faces me fully. "Explain."

"I wish I could," I tell him. "But Alina is here somewhere. In this world. I can feel her."

"I can't," he says through his teeth. "It's like when the Omegas first disappeared."

"Because whatever this is, it's Mythos Fae related." I'm sure of it now. "I need everyone to calm the fuck down so I can focus."

I don't wait for them to agree, just blink out of existence again and start hunting.

It's only been two or three minutes since Alina disappeared, despite it feeling like longer due to all the emotions of everyone else. But my soul understands timelines better than most.

Everything is a ticking clock.

Life. Death. Afterlife. Rebirth.

It's all a cycle, one I'm *very* attuned to.

Souls are my purpose, and it's a purpose I tap into now as I track Alina's essence once more. She's almost entirely gone, but that strange magic is still hovering in the in-between.

Lingering. Waiting. *Observing*.

It's a bizarre incantation, one that has been here for a very long time.

Definitely manifestation magic, I decide as I cautiously move toward the subtle shimmer.

I wouldn't have even noticed its existence had it not been caressing the remnants of Alina's spirit. But now that I've sensed it, I can feel the hum of foreign energy all around this room.

No, I think, ghosting down to the street. *It's all over this city.*

Frowning, I take myself to the cabin Orcus built and study the in-between once more.

Nothing.

No strange sensation of being watched.

No sense of lingering.

Just... clean air and the scent of our nest.

Orcus's essence also resides here, his creation having required a lot of manifestation magic. But that feels new. Potent. *Masculine.*

I return to the tower, my nose twitching as I inhale the ancient spell tainting the in-between plane.

It's not overwhelming. Not new. And definitely not masculine.

So who put this here? I marvel. *And when?*

Because our worlds have never intersected, but the manifestation elements are clear in the way the spell seems to move. Very few beings can create such power.

Unless there's someone or something in this realm that's more powerful than a Mythos Fae.

I turn corporeal again, ready to ask the King and Queen about other entities, but pause when I see them all staring at the screen.

It appears to be some sort of footage. Orcus is the closest, his wings tucked at his back, his arms folded.

Flame is beside him with a towel around his waist—one I'm guessing was given to him when he shifted back into his mortal form.

Sabre, Cage, and Cain are all on the opposite side of the room where Cain is holding a remote.

And Helia is between them in the center of the room, her dark eyes scanning the screen.

"This is from the night Serapina Everheart arrived at the compound," Helia informs me, apparently having sensed my reappearance.

I'm not sure what she is, but power emanates from her. It's not as strong as Orcus's aura, though. So she can't be the one responsible for the manifestation spell. But she might be able to help us determine who is behind it.

Because I suspect that lingering incantation has everything to do with our girl's disappearance.

"All the compounds have surveillance," she continues. "The trains, too."

"Why does this matter?" I ask, confused as to why we're watching something that happened two years ago.

"Because I want to see which version of Serapina arrived at the compound," Orcus replies without looking at me. "Alina said the photo in the file wasn't her sister. So when did the switch happen? And is it related to what we just witnessed?"

I disappear for all of five minutes, and the Alpha regained his sense of control. It's impressive, given the circumstances. But it's also just like Orcus.

He's furious yet devastated. And those two emotions lead to a very important result—determination.

I understand that reaction because I feel the same way, and I'm sure Flame does as well.

"That's Duke Nightingale's son on the platform," Cain says through his teeth, his dislike of the man evident in his tone. "He used to be in charge of the Nightingale Compound."

"Used to be?" Flame echoes.

"He was recently removed from the position." It's a flat statement, one that has my eyebrow inching upward.

"Meaning he won't be available for a chat if we need to ask him some questions?" I ask.

"Something like that," Cage mutters, his distaste for the man rivaling Cain's.

There's only one reason these two men who hardly know each other could consider this *son of a Duke* to be an enemy—he hurt their mate.

I don't bother asking for details. They clearly handled the issue.

And I have a far more important one to handle now—finding Alina.

But I agree with Orcus that this information might be helpful, if the two are related.

Is the mystical energy there, too? I ponder while watching the train doors open just outside the compound gates. *Did the magical strand do something to Serapina as well? Make her disappear soon after she arrived?*

It's on the tip of my tongue to inquire about footage inside the compound—Alina's disappearance wasn't immediate, suggesting Serapina's won't be now either—when a group of humans step off the train.

None of them are the woman I saw depicted in Alina's mind, but I immediately recognize the woman from the photos.

"She was switched before she arrived," Orcus says, the words the same ones forming in my mind. "Who had the authority on that train?"

Cain doesn't immediately reply, his focus on the screen as he brings up old train records and routes.

"All humans selected on the Day of the Choosing from Nightingale Village ride the train to Monster City, but they're separated early on so the official Offerings can be properly groomed."

Flame snorts at the term, his version of *grooming* no doubt different from Cain's.

But the Elite City King doesn't comment. He just continues to scan records while explaining how the high-speed trains operate in this region.

I don't really care how many stops they make or the fact that there are over a dozen tracks that stop in various villages between here and Monster City.

"There's only one track that doesn't stop between the two cities," he says. "Which means all the others have to go back the way they came—through each of their respective villages."

"So Serapina went all the way to Monster City but didn't participate in Monsters Night. Then she went all the way back to her village and beyond it to Chicago," Orcus reiterates, applying Cain's explanation to the current mystery at hand.

"Is it possible a supernatural snatched her while in Monster City?" Flame asks.

I fold my arms while I wait for the answer.

"No." That comes from Helia. "I would have sensed it."

I eye the female with interest. "How?"

She shrugs. "That's a conversation for another day. I'm more interested in seeing the footage from the Day of the Choosing. Did she even get on the train?"

Cain uses his device to drag the train routes aside and begins searching through an archive of Choosing ceremonies.

My eyes are instantly drawn to Alina's form in the crowd. It doesn't matter that she's covered in a veil. I still know her on sight. And it's not just her curves I recognize, but her.

She stands absolutely still as a woman wearing a similar bridal gown approaches the stage. Her blonde hair definitely doesn't match the redhead in those photos.

We all watch as she's eventually escorted to the train, just like Alina would have been a few weeks ago.

An aristocratic male—one I recognize from last week —is waiting on the train and selects two numbers. They're apparently associated with humans because some guys in all-white military gear step forward to take the pair to another part of the train. Then the remaining humans are sent to an area with a communal shower and not much else.

Cain fast-forwards a bit to Serapina finally removing her veil to resemble the face I saw in Alina's mind. He freezes it there and looks at Orcus.

"That's her sister," he says. "What happens next?"

"She'll shower and then be escorted to the cargo hold. Unfortunately, that area isn't typically monitored by surveillance equipment. We rely on the Village Protectors to guard the cargo."

"You mean you rely on humans to act humanely when given power over others of their kind," Orcus corrects him. "Because that's been proven to work so well for you."

"We don't interfere—"

"I'm not interested in debating morals or hearing excuses, Helia," Orcus interjects. "I just want to know who had access to that *shipment* so I can find out how and when Serapina was switched. That'll help us determine where she is now. Because whoever has her might have Alina."

I agree with his plan. However… "Before we get into the identities of those on the train, I want details on exactly where that train stops," I say. "And I want to know where the Nightingale Compound is."

Because I want to see if that magical essence is haunting any of those areas. If it is, then it's entirely possible that no one on that train swapped out Serapina. Instead, a being of power similar to a Mythos Fae did.

And that being likely has our pet. Or, at the very least, will give us a good lead on where our pet might be.

Orcus frowns at my request but says, "Give him what he needs. But I still want that list of names."

"It would be faster if you just spoke to the Nightingale Viscount," Helia tells him, her tone flat. "He hires all the Village Protectors. He'll know who was on that train. Hell, he might even be responsible for the switch. He's the one who sent Timothy after Alina, yes?"

My spine straightens at the mention of the dark soul I left behind in Monster City. "I'll question Timothy," I volunteer. "I need to stop by the tower anyway."

Because I want to see if that mystical strand is in Monster City as well.

Orcus nods. "After they give you what you need, go do what you do best. If the human is worthless to us, end him." He shifts his attention to Helia and then Cain. "Now, which one of you can introduce me to this *Viscount*?"

CHAPTER THIRTY-NINE
ALINA

WHERE ARE WE? I wonder, looking around at the garden. *Why can't I hear my mates?*

It's like I'm in a bubble.

A very colorful, vibrant bubble filled with flowers.

The sun is warm overhead, which confuses me more because it was nighttime in the Elite City.

"I can't believe you're here," my sister says as she pulls back from our hug. "*How* are you here?"

"Where is here?" I ask her.

She frowns. "We're in Demeter's Gardens."

I blink at her. "Whose gardens?"

"Mine," a feminine voice says to my left as a woman with white-blonde hair dressed in white glides toward us.

Literally *glides*.

Like floating on air.

Because she's not walking at all. Her feet are about an inch off the ground, and her legs are not moving at all.

"Hello, Alina," the woman greets me, her arms spreading wide. "How lovely of you to finally join us."

I stare up at her—because she's tall, like Orcus-level tall. "I'm sorry; were you expecting me?"

"Yes. For a while now. But the Duke and those idiot Village Protectors all failed me." She rolls her eyes. "Men are predictably frustrating."

Her feet touch the ground before us, her hand stroking a nearby flower.

"It all worked out in the end, though." She smiles. "I knew you would understand and follow the note. You just needed a little push to grab the Duke's attention for the selection process. Of course, you did a little too well since he sent you to Monsters Night. Alas, it's fine. Because now… you're here."

"You sent the note?" I ask, confused. "I thought Serapina wrote it."

"She did," Demeter replies. "But I sent it to your room."

"Oh." I swallow. "And you did this so the Duke would pick me as an Offering." It's not a question since she's already stated that, but I needed to reiterate the words out loud. "Because you wanted me to come here," I add slowly. "Why?"

"To hide you, of course." She tips her head back on a sigh, the sun illuminating her otherworldly features. "It's very frustrating, honestly. Your mortal encasings, I mean. You all die so soon, forcing me to begin the hunt anew. Then I have to take on unpleasant roles to find you again."

I glance at my sister, curious as to if she has any idea what this woman is rambling on about. But she has this dreamy expression on her face like she's not even listening, her focus on the flowers to our right.

My brow furrows as she kneels to pluck a wilting petal, then she moves it to the ground and buries it beneath the dirt.

"I'm sure Persephone would love to introduce you to your new life here," the not-so-sane woman says. "Isn't that right, love?"

"Yes, Mother," my sister says, causing my brow to furrow even more.

Persephone?

Mother?

What the heck is going on?

"Excellent," Demeter says, clasping her hands together. "Show her how to make a flower bed as well. I'm sure she'll want to rest soon." Her bright blue eyes meet mine, a twinkle shining in their depths. "Welcome home, my darling. May your soul be at peace once more."

She reaches for my arm to give it a squeeze, and I nearly step backward, but a shock rolls through us both that causes her to stumble away in alarm, her eyes growing wide.

"That's not possible," she breathes, looking at her hand and then back at me. "*That's not possible.*" She charges forward to grab me again, but the same thing happens and she shrieks with rage.

Serapina immediately jumps to her feet, her expression no longer dreamy.

"No," Demeter says, her focus going to my belly. "*No!*"

She lunges for me, only for my sister to jump between us.

Demeter shrieks again, and the ground begins to shake.

What in the—

A large *boom* sounds above as the sky *cracks*.

I gape at it, then jump sideways as a shard of what looks like glass comes tumbling my way from above.

"Alina!" Serapina screams.

She darts in the other direction, her arm going up to shield her as more pieces of the sky fall all around us.

437

I duck around a bush and run toward her, then pull her behind a nearby tree while Demeter's screeches echo all around us. She's disappeared, but I can *feel* her just as well as I can hear her.

"What the heck is going on?!" I demand.

"I don't know!" my sister shouts back. "I—"

The path we were just on moments ago splits wide open, causing both of us to leap backward. The world is trembling all around us.

Flowers are dying.

The sky is crumbling.

The trees… are shifting colors and shapes.

Is this a nightmare? I wonder, spinning around in confusion. *It feels so real.*

But none of this should be possible.

Darkness swoops in as the sun blinks out of the sky, the greenery turning black. Serapina clings to me as others scream in the distance. I don't know who they are, or where they are, but their fear pierces my heart.

Where am I? What is happening?

Alina? Orcus's voice in my head makes me blink. *Alina, where the fuck are you?*

Alina! Reaper and Flame say at the same time. *Where are you, pet?* Reaper inquires as Flame asks, *Are you all right, little panther?*

I… I don't know, I reply, hoping they all can hear. *Everything is dark.*

But my sister is still here. Her arms are around me as the world continues to rumble.

I can feel her… and my mates.

Not a dream, I think. *Unless…*

It's not a dream, Alina. Now focus and tell me everything, Orcus demands.

I was in a garden, I whisper to him. *There was a woman. Or something like a woman. Blonde hair. Blue eyes. She said her name was Demeter, but my sister called her* Mother. *Then she touched me and...*

And I don't know.

I can't define what just happened.

So I show him instead.

His growl is furious in my head, making my legs quiver as I fight to hold myself upright.

We're coming, he promises me. *No matter what you do, do not let her touch you again. She might try to hurt the baby.*

My eyes widen. *What?*

Trust me, he says. *Wherever you are, I want you to hide. Do you understand me, Alina? You need to* hide.

His words send a shiver down my spine, my throat suddenly dry.

Because there's true fear in his tone.

And the warning about what Demeter might do to our child... is very real.

Okay, I say to him. *I... I'll hide.*

Only, I have no idea where to go because I can't see anything.

"Alina," my sister breathes.

"Shh," I hush her, needing to focus on my other senses.

Where to hide, where to hide, I think, closing my eyes to calm my mind.

We're somewhere dark.

Old.

Warm.

I inhale, my nose instantly curling at the familiar scent of burning. But underneath that, I recognize the hint of fir trees. Not from Flame, but from something else.

From home, I realize, my lips curling down. *It smells like the mountain side.*

Except it reminds me more of my cabin than being outside.

I toe the ground, my tennis shoes helping me to note the texture. Soil or carpet would have some give. Wooden floors or tile would not.

The latter applies here.

We're inside somewhere, I tell Orcus. *Maybe near the village. But I'm not sure.*

Swallowing, I open my eyes again.

There are silhouettes now. It's still dark, but not pitch black like before.

The trees... are now wooden pillars. Or maybe the better term for them is *support beams.* Regardless, we appear to be in a massive great room.

There are windows along one wall, allowing in a glimmer of moonlight from outside. But it's not much, which is why the majority of the room is cast in shadows.

"Oh, Alina," a voice tsks. It's not feminine, but masculine. "I knew something was different this time around, but I couldn't quite put my finger on it. Now... now I've *touched* it. A bond. A. Fucking. Alpha. Bond."

Goose bumps pebble along my skin at the anger underlining that voice.

It's familiar now.

A voice that haunted my nightmares until I met my fae. *The Viscount.*

I have no idea what he's doing here or how he plays into all of this, but I don't want to stand around and find out.

We need to hide. Just like Orcus told me to do.

"I have no idea how he found you or who he is, but I'll deal with him when he arrives," the Viscount continues. "Then I'll fix you, too."

My stomach twists at the notion of being *fixed.*

But I'm also confused as to how the Viscount thinks he'll *deal* with Orcus.

The Viscount is human.

Unless… I frown. *I was human… with an Omega soul.*

And now I'm no longer human, but a Mythos Fae.

A *mated* Mythos Fae with a life growing inside me.

None of that should have been possible, yet here I am.

Is the Viscount an Omega, too? I wonder.

The Viscount is Demeter in disguise, Orcus tells me, obviously having listened to my thoughts and perhaps even having heard what the Viscount said to me.

Demeter was a woman, though, I say, frowning.

Either she's disguised as the Viscount, or she's controlling him. Regardless, I need you to hide, Alina. Do not let Demeter find you. The urgency is back in his tone, making me want to move.

But I don't.

Because I don't want to make a sound either.

"Over two thousand years without an incident. But now…" The Viscount sounds disappointed. "Do you have any idea what this means, Alina?"

Sera squeezes my hand beside me, reminding me of her presence.

She hasn't spoken, but I can feel her tension. I have no idea what she's been through. Maybe Demeter kept her in that garden this whole time. However, she called her *Mother.*

What does that even mean? I wonder again.

But there isn't time to consider it now.

I need to focus on the Viscount and his voice.

He's talking about having to start over now, his irritation palpable.

"If the Alphas have found this dimension, it's no longer ideal," he's saying. "But it's going to take time to find a more appropriate place to begin anew. Not to mention the work involved in gathering all the souls hidden throughout this dimension."

I shift a little to the side, my night vision almost completely in focus now.

The Viscount doesn't appear to be in this room at all, his voice coming from all over. *A speaker system, perhaps?*

Regardless of *where*, Sera and I can't just stand here in the center of the room.

We need to go outside, I think, eyeing the windows. *Into the woods.*

Because we're likely in the Viscount Manor, which is high in the mountains, several miles from the village. But Sera and I grew up in that forest. If we get outside, we can run.

I take a tentative step, my breath holding in my lungs. When the floor doesn't make a sound, I exhale a little and move again.

Sera creeps along beside me, clearly following my lead.

It reminds me of how I used to lead Sage through the village to meet with the Protector to bargain for medicine. She used to mimic my movements, too, striving for quiet. Then mimicked my confidence when we bartered with the man.

"I'll be killing you last," the Viscount informs me flatly. "That way, you're reincarnated last. It's not that I want to punish you, darling, but I need to ensure your bond is broken. Like the others. It's the only way for us to hide."

Hearing the Viscount call me *darling* has me cringing. But the rest of his words make me frown. *Hide? Hide from what?*

"Has your Alpha told you our history?" he asks conversationally. "How the Alphas tried to enslave our kind to meet their baser needs? To force us to procreate against our will?"

My steps slow, my eyes blinking. *The Alphas enslaved Omegas?*

Don't listen to her, Orcus tells me. *Demeter is full of lies.*

What's she talking about? I ask him. *Why would she say these things?*

Because she hates the Alpha-Omega dynamic.

"There were more Alphas than Omegas. So their solution was to manufacture a system. One where Alphas created circles—or *packs*—and each pack was assigned a single Omega slave."

She's lying, Orcus insists. *You know me, Alina. You can hear my mind. See my memories. Use me to poke holes in her manipulation.*

"The purpose was to breed the Omegas in the hope of making more. But Alphas are far more common, so really, they just produced more monsters." The Viscount hisses over that last word, his voice full of distaste.

Sera and I have reached the windows now, but I don't see one we can slip through.

I'm also… listening.

I can *feel* Orcus's vow that Demeter is lying, and I believe him.

But the Viscount—*Demeter*—seems to believe this truth, too.

Almost like… it happened.

Orcus…

Hide, Alina, he demands. *I know she's convincing. I… I just need you to hide, little one. Please. We're coming.*

It seems strange to me that he's not already here.

He can portal at will.

Why isn't he here yet?

I almost ask, but a cold touch to my shoulder has me spinning around to find the Viscount standing right before me. His dark eyes burn into mine. "Hello again, Alina. Let's go teach that Alpha of yours a lesson, shall we?"

443

CHAPTER FORTY
ORCUS

"*FUCK.*" I can feel Demeter all around Alina now, telling me she's not only touching my Omega but also doing something to her.

Something deadly.

"Who is this bitch?" Reaper asks, a scythe in one hand and a sword in the other. "Tell us what we're walking into here, Alpha."

"She's an Alpha," I mutter. "A very possessive, pissed-off, insane *Alpha*. One who fancies herself to be the mother of all Omegas. That's why she acts as though she is one herself when she's very clearly not. She sees it as her duty to protect all of Omega kind."

"So she… won't harm Alina?" Flame hedges.

"If Alina's pregnant with an Alpha? Yeah, she'll harm her. And she's sure as fuck going to try to hurt me," I tell them. "She doesn't like competition, and she does not play well with other Alphas."

As evidenced by the fact that she apparently brought all the Omegas to this dimension. *And hid them.*

I overheard that part of her conversation with Alina.

445

Fuck, I overheard *everything*.

Because Alina was practically broadcasting the conversation to me as she puzzled over everything Demeter was telling her.

"She used to be part of an Alpha pack," I say aloud, still talking to Reaper and Flame. "They had a male Omega that managed to impregnate her. An Omega named Persephone was their child. Demeter developed an... unhealthy obsession with her daughter."

And from what I understood of the conversation, Serapina might harbor Persephone's soul.

Which further complicates matters.

If there was time, I would call my brother. But I need to get Alina back right fucking now before Demeter finishes doing whatever it is she's doing to my mate.

"Her focus is going to be on me," I think aloud, puzzling through what we should do. "Her primary goal will be to subdue me." Because killing me wouldn't be an option. Just like I couldn't kill her.

Mythos Fae don't die.

But we can be temporarily knocked out. *And trapped.*

"She's already weakened," I go on. "Whatever happened when she touched Alina destroyed the Omega prison she created here."

By here, I mean, the Viscount Manor.

Reaper and I were busy pursuing our own leads when we felt the bond snap into place again.

He immediately returned to the Elite City, where Flame and I were reading up on the Viscount. Cain was talking to the Duke of Nightingale about setting up a meeting.

Apparently, he lacked the contact details for the Viscount because he lived outside of the Elite City and was classified as a non-Elite human. It seems the village title means very little to the Elite City.

Regardless, the Viscount matters now.

Because he has a pissed-off Mythos Fae Alpha hiding inside him.

Hell, the Viscount may have always been Demeter. Who the fuck even knows?

"Did you catch any hints of Timothy being possessed?" I ask Reaper, wondering if perhaps Demeter is controlling him as well.

If my jumping topics bothers the Death Fae, he doesn't show it. He simply says, "No. He wouldn't need to be manipulated or possessed; he's a bad soul all on his own."

"Is he still alive?" Flame asks.

"Barely," Reaper says. "I was in the middle of sifting through his mind when I felt Alina. I left him to rot."

Which means he won't be alive for long.

"If Timothy wasn't possessed, then there's a chance Demeter hasn't possessed anyone else. Which means we should be dealing with just her, and maybe some misguided humans."

But I doubt that last part about the mortals.

Demeter would consider herself above humans and would only use them for menial tasks. Such as kidnapping another mortal, like Alina. Not battling a fellow God.

"How do you want to handle this?" Flame asks, his arms folded over his chest as he evaluates the forest before us. We're less than a mile from the manor, the three of us having arrived together once we sensed our mate's location.

But I didn't create a portal that would take us directly to her. I put us here instead.

A plan is needed.

A *good* plan.

Because we'll only have one chance to get this right.

I heard what Demeter told Alina about changing dimensions. Apparently, she's the one who made all the Omegas disappear over two thousand years ago. If she could do it once, she can do it again now.

"All right," I say. "Here's what I'm thinking…"

I quietly explain the idea formulating in my mind, the one involving the element of surprise.

Demeter is focused on me.

She doesn't know about Reaper and Flame. Individually, they might not be able to take her down. But if we work together as a mate-circle, we should be able to win the upper hand.

"You thought she was imprisoned originally," Flame says after I finish laying it all out—including the part about how to trap a Mythos Fae's soul.

Because we'll need to do that and then take her to my home realm to put her in Pandora's Box.

"How did she escape?" he presses.

"I don't know," I admit. "But I'm guessing it has something to do with breaking up her mate-circle."

There are four Alpha packs trapped in Pandora's Box. The very packs Demeter mentioned to Alina.

She didn't completely lie to my Omega, but she severely embellished her claims.

Alpha kind didn't agree to enslave the Omegas. A few ancient, insane Alphas *tried* to enslave them.

Twelve Alphas, to be exact.

One of whom was Demeter, but giving birth to Persephone changed her. She grew compassionate and later obsessed.

All while those packs continued to use and abuse their Omega mates. But soon, one Omega wasn't enough. They wanted more. Yet all the children were Alphas.

Except for Persephone.

She was a coveted Omega.

When one of those packs set their sights on Persephone, Demeter reacted, telling them they couldn't have her daughter. But they wouldn't accept her refusal.

Left with no alternative, Demeter turned to another pack—one that cherished and loved their Omega—and begged them to hide Persephone.

That pack was my mother's pack.

And my mother was the Omega in the nest.

She accepted Demeter's request.

Which was how my brother first met his Persephone.

But things soon went to hell after that happened, the four ravenous packs waging war on the other Alphas in an attempt to take their mates.

Then Omega kind vanished.

And the sane Alphas assumed the Fates had intervened to take the Omegas away as a result of their mistreatment.

Pandora's Box was created to imprison the offending Alphas, in hopes that the Fates would forgive the rest of the Mythos Fae by returning Omega kind.

Alas, that never happened.

And now I know why.

Demeter took them.

Either she was never put in Pandora's Box with the others, or she escaped.

The latter possibility concerns me because it means she could escape us now. Or maybe even possesses a talent that'll facilitate her ability to thwart us.

Which is precisely the point of Flame's inquiry and concern. He's basically asking, *If she escaped before, can she do it again?*

And my answer remains the same—*I don't know.*

But we're about to find out.

"Once she's subdued, we—"

The hairs along the back of my neck dance, alerting me to an incoming presence. Reaper straightens, his scythe lifted in a defensive pose as Flame takes the sword from his other hand, both of them battle-ready.

But the glass mirror forming before us isn't born of Mythos Fae magic. It's something else entirely.

Helia's face appears, her eyebrow arching at our display of aggression.

Then she casually steps through the glass with Cain following behind her.

"You didn't think we would let you fight a battle in our territory without a little assistance, did you?" she asks conversationally. "Now, bring us up to speed on this *Goddess*. And tell us the plan."

CHAPTER FORTY-ONE
ALINA

"WHAT ARE you doing to my sister?" Sera demands. "You're hurting her."

"I'm saving her," the Viscount hisses. "You have no idea what I've been through to protect you and the others. No idea at all. So just sit there and let me work."

"Protect us?" Sera huffs a laugh. "You pull our names from a Chalice once a year at the Day of the Choosing and send us off to Monsters Night. How is that *protecting* us?"

The Viscount huffs. "There's so much you don't understand, Persephone. So much I would teach you if you weren't going to just die in a handful of decades. Or years, thanks to your *sister* here."

"My name isn't Persephone," my sister tells her, the dreamy-eyed girl in the garden nowhere to be seen.

"We've been over this, dear. You're—"

"No longer under whatever spell you cast over me," my sister interjects. "Who the hell are you really?"

"Your mother," the Viscount growls.

My sister snorts. "My mother died over a decade ago."

I wince at her words because they remind me of what I learned today about the *breeding compounds*.

"Your mortal mother died two days after you were born," the Viscount informs her flatly. "And your father was a sperm donor." He sits back on his haunches to stare up at my sister. "And while we're on the topic, your *sister* isn't your real sister. She's just another Omega. An ungrateful one at that."

His eyes return to mine, and I can almost see the Goddess swimming in the depths of his dark irises, her power simmering just beneath the surface.

Is that the intensity I noticed during the Day of the Choosing? I wonder, viewing the Viscount through a new lens. *And again when talking to the Duke?*

"You just had to give in to the Alpha knot, didn't you?" the Viscount says to me, shaking his head. Then he sighs and cups my cheek. "It's okay, little one. I forgive you. I know how feeble and weak-minded your kind can be."

Feeble and weak-minded? I repeat to myself. *I am not feeble or weak-minded.*

Granted, I can't move at the moment because of whatever invisible rope the Viscount just used to bind me to this chair.

But that doesn't make me feel *weak* so much as *trapped*.

Something that causes my soul to growl with fury inside.

The Viscount did something to me the moment he touched me. Something that turned me into his personal puppet.

He told me to follow him and I did.

He told me to sit and I obeyed.

He told me to stay still and I didn't even think about moving.

But now that he's called me *weak*, I'm not so sure I want to stay still. Or obey. *Or put up with this.*

I'm not even sure why I did to begin with.

It's like I had a lapse in judgment, my body and mind trusting the being before me on instinct. Similar to how I felt around Orcus that night we first met when he held me and purred.

Only, the Viscount didn't purr.

The Viscount just... coaxed me with words. And touches.

But he disturbed my link to my mates again, making my mind go quiet. However, unlike when I was in the garden, I can still feel them.

They're close, I realize, the hint of their mingling colognes taunting my nostrils. *A beautiful summer's day.*

I close my eyes and inhale deeply, allowing their scents to claim me once more. *Mine*, I think. *My fae.*

The spark of life inside me gives a little pulse in response, pleased by their presence.

They've come to take me home.

I can feel their intentions, as well as their anger.

The Viscount took something that doesn't belong to him. Or rather, the Goddess inside him did.

And they've come to make that Goddess pay.

I can almost taste the plan in their minds, but a shriek from my sister draws me out of my connection and forces me to refocus on the room.

"Let my sister go!" Serapina demands.

I've missed something in their conversation because the Viscount now has my sister pinned against a wall.

"Stop it," he demands. "I need to focus, and I can't have you throwing a tantrum while I'm in the middle of ensnaring an Alpha."

"You're hurting her!" Serapina insists, making me frown.

Because I feel fine.

Except... except as I glance down... I realize the invisible binds have turned into something else. Electric currents zap across my skin as energy writhes around me, the tendrils a startling white color.

My stomach clenches in response, the life inside me flickering with panic.

The baby, I think, realization smacking me across the face. *She's... it's... whatever this is, it's trying to hurt the baby!*

Serapina screams as she falls to the ground. The Viscount is standing over her, growling out words I can't quite hear.

My world is swimming.

My vision going in and out.

There's an urgent sound in my head. Male voices. More growls. I... I can't...

I swallow.

My stomach aches.

My heart... it *hurts*.

And my soul... my soul is *snarling*.

Or maybe that's the men in my head?

It's hard to say where it's coming from, but I *feel* the rumbles vibrating up and down my limbs. Sense the fury deep inside. *Smell* the aggression.

The source radiates all around me. Within me. Outside of me. In the air. In my heart. Reverberating in my very spirit.

An instinct born of possession and protection tumbles through my being, making my limbs strain against the bindings. Pushing forward. Demanding freedom.

My child. My creation. My future.

The threat isn't acceptable. The power is foreign and obtrusive. The energy needs to leave me the fuck alone.

I shove the presence away from me. Fight the ropes surrounding me. And demand that the entity *release me*.

Someone bellows. It's a loud, masculine bark of sound that soon morphs into a feminine shriek.

I don't know what's happening. I can't *see*. Everything is white. Everything burns. Everything feels constricting. Like I can't breathe.

But I force my lungs to work, the hint of refreshing air helping to draw me from the dizzying fog.

Push forward, I tell myself. *Fight this!*

The life inside me is quivering, begging me to protect it.

I can't give up.

I can't allow this intense magic to win.

My purpose is to create life. To protect life. To thrive in a world of renewed existence.

My feet land on the ground with an unexpected thud, my spine straightening as the world blinks into view around me.

The Viscount—or what's left of him—is a bloody mess on the floor in front of me.

Serapina is gaping at his remains with wide eyes.

Then those eyes grow even wider as she looks up. I follow her gaze, my stomach twisting as the Goddess from the garden strides forward with a murderous expression.

Her focus is on me.

Her intent very clear.

I turn and run, my instinct to flee overriding everything else.

But just as I reach the door of the room, it bursts open to reveal my fae. Orcus leads the charge, his wings widespread. He looks at me, his expression melting into relief, only to realize I'm being pursued.

A roar rips from his mouth as he flies at Demeter, tackling her to the ground. Reaper is right behind him, a scythe in his hand.

But Flame comes for me.

He doesn't say anything, just scoops me up into his arms and starts carrying me away.

"No!" I shout. "I have to see. I have to... Flame!"

He's not listening to me.

But a shout of agony has him pausing, the sound having come from Orcus.

Flame looks down at me and I stare up at him. He's trying to make a decision. One I can hear in his mind. "Go," I demand. "*Go to Orcus.*"

He growls.

I growl back.

Then he sets me on my feet and runs back into the room.

I follow him, my mind racing as I search for Orcus. But it's my sister that catches my eye. She's on the outskirts of the room, watching the battle rage through narrowed eyes.

Orcus is missing a wing, the appendage lying on the ground near my sister's feet.

He's bleeding.

But all I really see is a blur of blood, black feathers, and blinding light as he and Demeter try to take each other down.

Reaper is nowhere to be seen.

And Flame is in his jaguar form, snarling as he tries to figure out how to join the fight.

Fae, this isn't good, I think, uncertain of how to help. I freed myself from the binds, did something to the

Viscount's form, but I... I don't know how I did that. Or even *if* I did that.

"This needs to end, *Mother*," my sister says coldly as a blade appears in her hand.

I blink at it, not understanding where or how the item materialized in her palm, but it's there nonetheless.

And she's lifting it toward her own neck.

"If I die, my soul will remain in this dimension," she continues, her voice eerily even. "And you know what that means."

The brawl ends as Demeter breaks free from Orcus, her bright eyes going to my sister. "Persephone..."

"He'll know I'm here, Mother. He'll come for me. He always does. He always *will*."

"Persephone," Demeter says again, her tone placating as she stretches out her arms and holds up her hands. "Don't."

"Why not?" my sister asks, the knife drawing blood against her delicate throat. "Maybe I'm ready to finally go home."

"You don't mean that," Demeter says, her face stricken. "You... you know what he'll do..."

"Do I?" Serapina arches a brow, her confidence in full force now. I've seen this side of my little sister a few times before. She's not the damsel many mistake her for. She might be tiny, but she's fierce underneath.

Just like me, I think.

"Maybe I want him to do those things," my sister goes on.

"Persephone, *no*," Demeter says as Orcus silently positions himself behind her. "He'll hurt you. That's what Alphas do. They take, take, and *take*. You can't want that. You *don't* want that."

"From what I can tell, Mother, you're the one who

continues to *take*. You kidnapped me. Brought me here. Force me to live and die on repeat, and for what? To stay with you for eternity? To hide from him? *My soul's mate?*"

I blink, not sure what she's talking about. But I can see the anger in my sister's expression, the inferno practically glowing in her liquid blue eyes.

All while Orcus works behind Demeter, his hand moving as he quietly creates one of his portal doors.

Demeter doesn't see it at all.

Her focus is entirely on my sister, her expression stricken.

"I've given up everything for you," she whispers. "*Everything*. Don't you see that?"

My sister tilts her head. "What I see is a selfish Goddess who doesn't trust her daughter to make her own decisions."

Demeter's lips part. "*Persephone.*"

"Serapina," my sister corrects, taking a step forward, that blade still poised at her own throat. "Your *Persephone* died long ago. Just because her soul might be inside me does not make me her. I'm my own person. I make my own decisions. And right now? I choose *this*."

I nearly start to run, worried my sister might actually slice her own throat.

But instead the knife whispers through the air.

And she stabs the Goddess in the chest.

Demeter gasps, her steps stumbling backward as a scythe appears out of thin air and lodges itself in her abdomen.

Then Flame pounces forward with his claws to shove the woman through Orcus's portal door.

My Alpha follows her, the mirror shattering in his wake.

I lift my hand to my mouth, my eyes blinking.

Reaper appears just as my sister's knees give out, his strong arm catching her before she hits the ground. And suddenly they're beside me, his shadowing ability having brought them to my side.

Sera collapses into me on a sob, her terror and confusion instantly washing over me. She was so strong, so *fierce*. But now... now her emotions are catching up to her.

"What did I just do?" she whispers to me. "What the hell did I just do?"

"Returned an insane Goddess to her box," Reaper replies.

"My... my mother?" she asks, shaking.

"That's what she thinks," Reaper tells her. "And you helped us play on that belief."

I blink, understanding suddenly piercing my mind. *You told her what to say*, I whisper to Reaper.

Yeah. Demeter believes your sister is her reincarnated daughter. It was Orcus's idea to use that against Demeter, to weaken her defenses long enough for him to get her back to the Mythos Fae Realm.

I swallow, my hand on my sister's head. *I-is she Demeter's daughter? This... Persephone?*

It's hard to say. Orcus says it's possible. But he also said your soul isn't one he's met before. So it's also entirely possible that the Omega soul isn't identifiable, just... reincarnated into someone different each time. He glances over at Flame as he approaches in his human form. He's shirtless but appears to have found jeans somewhere.

"You had one job," Reaper says to him. "To protect our girl."

"My job will always be to do whatever Alina tells me to do, and she told me to go back to Orcus. To help him." He shrugs. "I think I did my job well."

You did, I murmur into his mind, thankful that I can

hear and feel all my mates again without any intrusion. And that's not all I can feel.

The little life inside me is pulsing contentedly once more, protected in my womb.

Because we survived.

And my sister is here, too, I think, holding her close.

She's no longer crying, just shaking, like she can't believe everything that's happened.

"You're safe now," I promise her. "And I'm never losing you again."

Her arms tighten around me, but she says nothing. Just holds me. So I hold her in kind.

Everything's going to be okay, I think at her and the baby inside me. And I realize, deep down, that I don't just believe it's true; I *know* it's true.

Because my fae are my life now.

And they'll always do whatever it takes to protect me, our child, and our family.

Which also includes my sister.

I don't care what that Goddess said about our parents, or the fact that we might not even be truly related. What matters is our sisterly bond.

No one can take that away from us.

Not now. Not ever. We're in this together. *Until the end of time.*

CHAPTER FORTY-TWO

ORCUS

OVER AN HOUR LATER...

"WELL, THAT WAS ENTERTAINING," Helia says as Reaper and I step outside for some fresh air.

Flame is still inside with Alina and her sister, the two females deep in conversation about everything that's happened.

"I told you that you wouldn't be needed," Reaper drawls.

"Who do you think controlled the Village Protectors and kept them from hearing the fight?" she asks, arching a brow.

"I thought you didn't concern yourself with human affairs," I shoot back.

She shrugs. "Someone suggested that superior beings are morally obligated to handle human affairs in certain situations. I decided this might be one of those situations."

"Helia just wanted to teach some Nightingale Village Protectors a lesson after learning what they did to one of her mates," Cain interjects as he steps forward, his hands in the pockets of his dress slacks. "I basically just watched her work."

"He didn't want to dirty his expensive clothes," Helia returns.

But I'm still caught up on what Cain just said about her *mates*. "Your mates are from the same village as Alina?"

"Not only are they from the same village, but they were also selected for the same Monsters Night," she replies. "Perhaps that helps you understand why I needed to delay our meeting."

It does, I think.

"And maybe it also gives insight into why I requested a dinner," she adds, her lips curling. "Bartholomew and Miranda have been worried about Alina. I wanted to calm those concerns by showing them she's safe."

Bartholomew and Miranda? Alina asks into my mind. *Did I hear that right?*

I must have repeated the names in my thoughts, thus allowing Alina to catch that part of the conversation. *Queen Helia just mentioned them. Apparently, they're her new mates.*

Surprise trickles through our bond. *Really?*

Do you want proof? I ask, curious. *Because I can demand it.*

Her amusement shines through with a hint of exhaustion. *Honestly, I just want a nap.*

Hmm. Back at our cabin? In the tower? Or... would you like to go home?

She doesn't immediately respond, her mind processing her options. Then she chooses the one that warms my heart the most. *Home, please.*

"We may need to postpone that dinner," I tell Helia. "Our mate says she wants to go home."

Reaper's lips curl. "Fucking finally. This dimension leaves a lot to be desired."

Helia and Cain just look at him.

"What?" he asks. "No Chicago pizza. New York City looks like a metallic jungle. Your humans use the word *monsters* in reference to supernaturals in this realm. Which is fucking rude, by the way. And you have all these rules that just don't make any sense. *Keep the dark soul alive. Stop stealing cupcakes. Don't shadow into the dungeon to torture humans. Blah, blah, blah.*"

The not-so-great feminine tone Reaper used on all those rules has my lips twitching at the sides. He's clearly trying to imitate Helia.

"Say what you want about our dimension, but you found your mate here," Helia reminds him, yet her eyes are on me while she says it. "And all those Omegas are here, too. Assuming I understood that conversation right, anyway."

She was obviously eavesdropping when I gave Reaper and Flame an update after returning to this dimension.

"Well?" Reaper prompted the moment I appeared.

"As I expected, Ares felt my arrival," I said. "He's taken Demeter into custody and is handling the imprisonment of her soul." That was his primary role as the Warden of the Mythos Fae Dungeon. "I think he was excited to have something to do."

Of course, his interest was almost immediately piqued by the Omega scent covering both me and Demeter. Which naturally led to a conversation about the new dimension.

I informed Reaper and Flame of the development and ended with, "A Mythos Fae liaison will need to be appointed. The Alphas are going to want to hunt down the missing Omegas."

"What about the ones from Demeter's garden here?" Flame asked, referring to the handful of scared humans he found huddled in another room.

"The appointed liaison will be managing that." It'll require several delicate conversations, similar to the ones I've had with Alina. Only, these Omegas will likely be taken to the Mythos Fae Realm for their introduction.

"A Mythos Fae will be in touch," I tell Helia now. "I don't know who it will be, but I imagine the new liaison will be decided very soon."

"And he or she will be coming here?"

I nod. "I gave someone instructions." That *someone* being Ares. He would have followed me back, but he can't leave the dungeon.

"Then I suppose I'll stay here to greet the new arrival," Helia replies.

I'm about to say that I'll check in with Ares on our way back—since we'll be heading through the dungeon again—when I feel the arrival of another Mythos Fae.

Helia must sense it as well because her eyebrow wings upward again. "That was quick."

Yes, I think, my eyes narrowing. *Too quick.*

Reaper stiffens beside me, suddenly on alert. Likely because he can sense my mounting unease.

I know that aura. I turn to head inside, the presence near my Omega.

But Alina doesn't appear to be in any distress.

Actually, she seems… calm. *Too* calm.

Alina? I breathe into her mind.

I'm fine, she promises me.

Still, I can't help taking on my Alpha form as I prowl toward her. My wings, both of which are fully functional again, take on an ethereal state, similar to when I first arrived in this realm. Usually, I prefer to let them free—which requires losing my shirt. But something about this aura has me feeling… less on edge. More *soothed.*

There's only one being in the world who has ever made me feel that way.

"Mother," I breathe as I round the corner and see her standing beside my mate.

It's not her soul reincarnated, but her. *Rhea*. The Omega Goddess who birthed me and Hades.

She turns toward me, her long brown hair braided with golden ribbons down her back. "My son," she says, tears pricking her eyes. "You found them. You found the Omegas."

I rush forward to pull her into a hug, my arms shaking as I feel her embrace me in kind.

She's alive. My mother's alive.

Alina's emotions trickle into me, her heart exploding at the sight of me seeing my mother for the first time in over two thousand years. She can feel what I'm feeling and hear what I'm thinking. Just as I know she can see the memories in my mind, including the day I lost my mother.

Despair unlike anything I've ever felt before pummeled my soul. It was a sensation I never wanted to experience again.

Yet I did.

Last night—since it's nearly morning now—when I thought I lost my mate.

But not only is Alina okay, my mother is, too. "Where have you been?"

"Hiding," she whispers. "Waiting."

"Why?" I ask, flabbergasted. "Why didn't you come to us? Why didn't you *tell* us?"

"I tried," she replies. "But this dimension is so different from our own. And I couldn't risk returning without Demeter noticing. So I stayed, hid, and did my best to guard them all in my own way."

"So you've been here," I realize. "In this realm."

She tilts her head back and forth. "Sort of. I've been… all over." It's a cryptic response. "But I felt your brother recently, and I knew either he or you would come. And now that you have, the true hunt can begin."

"What?"

"There are so many more Omegas here," she tells me. "Thousands of them, my son." She turns then, her eyes landing on someone behind me. "Hello, Queen Helia."

"Rhea," she returns, a note of familiarity in her tone. "I should have known you had something to do with this."

My mother simply smiles. "I suppose you won't mind me being the liaison between dimensions?"

"Like I could stop you from coming and going even if I wanted to," Helia drawls.

"My thoughts precisely," my mother muses, mischief dancing in her eyes. "Well, I have a lot of work to do. And so do you." That last part is for me because she's looking at me once more. "Your Omega is pregnant, Orcus. She needs a nest. Why are you still here?"

Leave it to my mother to go two thousand years without a word, just to turn around and make demands of me within minutes of seeing each other again.

Of course, this is a demand I very much want to follow.

Whatever the story is between her and Helia, I'll discover it later.

For now, I have a mate to protect and to cherish.

As well as a brother to update, I think, exhausted already.

I'll meet with him after I secure Alina in a new nest.

"Can Sera come with us?" Alina asks, her gaze hopeful.

Only it's not me she's addressing, but my mother.

"Of course, dear. If that's what Serapina desires?" Her dark eyes—the same color as my own—go to the petite

470

blonde female curled up into Alina's side. "Would you like to go with your sister?"

Serapina nods. "Yes, please."

My mother smiles again. "Good choice." Her focus returns to me. "Well, don't just stand there, Orcus. Your mate just ripped herself out of an intense binding spell and forced Demeter to lose her human shell. Create a portal and take her home."

Cain snorts behind me.

Which promptly earns my mother's attention. "Don't even get me started on you, Dream Eater. You have a new mate at home, and you're here doing what exactly? Planning who will take over as the new Village Viscount?"

He takes a step back as my mother moves toward him, his expression holding a touch of dismay.

Yeah, my Omega mother has that effect on Alphas, too, I think at him. Not that he can hear me. Besides, he's a bit too busy trying to avoid my mother's finger that she's now waving in his direction.

"Just pick one of your friends—not a human, but a *monster*—and overhaul the hierarchy," she goes on. "Demeter chose a man because only men seem to have power in this realm. Imagine how different your world would be if women were in charge, hmm?"

He blinks and clears his throat. "I'll… take that under advisement."

Helia huffs. "Goddess has a point, Cain. Maybe pass that point on to Scarlett's father."

He doesn't agree out loud but nods, probably to get both women off his case.

"As entertaining as this has been, I'm ready to go," Reaper says as he plucks our mate off the ground. "Make the portal, Orcus. Our pet needs orgasms, cupcakes, and rest."

Flame smirks.

Serapina looks a tad alarmed but slowly stands.

Alina just stares at Reaper and gives him a small smile. "A cupcake actually sounds pretty good right now."

"I know," he murmurs.

That tone suggests it's not the cupcake he's referring to, but the process of *earning* the cupcake that appeals to him. Since he seems to use them as a way to thank her after giving her pleasure.

Flame joins them, his fingers combing through Alina's hair. "How about a warm bath, too?" he offers her. "I'll brush you afterward."

Her cheeks turn pink. "Okay."

He leans in to run his nose along her jaw, then whispers something in her ear that has her skin reddening even more.

My lips curl at the display of care, my inner Alpha pleased.

Our mate is alive.

Our future child is okay.

And soon, all of us will be safe.

"Good luck," I tell Helia and Cain. Because if my mother is the new liaison between the dimensions, they're going to need it.

Rather than wait for them to reply, I open a mirrorlike door and step through it. Once I'm sure it's safe, I signal for the others to follow.

Then I lead our mate to the Netherworld Kingdom.

Where she'll be able to create a new nest.

In our forever home.

EPILOGUE: ALINA

"Are you sure you're all right?" I ask my sister.

She's lying in her new bed, admiring the view from her open balcony doors, while I sit beside her.

We're in Orcus's palace in the Netherworld Kingdom. It's not at all what I pictured when Reaper and Flame told me about their home. I expected crypts and graveyards. Darkness. Deadly tones.

But we're high up on a mountain overlooking the gothic-like city below.

There are black structures, inky ponds, leafless trees, and smoky ravines. But overhead, three moons shine brightly, illuminating the remarkable view.

So I suppose it does have *some* deadly tones since everything is primarily obsidian in color, but it's still stunningly beautiful.

At least to me.

I'm not sure how my sister feels, though. She's been quiet since we arrived early this morning. I've spent the day with her, despite Reaper's request for orgasms and cupcakes. I just wanted to make sure she was okay.

She watched quietly as various fae came and went in the room, bringing her new furniture, decorating her wardrobe with clothing, and even installing a few enchanted devices designed to create any food item she might be craving.

I tested the device by making her a strawberry cupcake.

She didn't seem as enthused by it as me.

We repeated the process with a cappuccino—something I enjoyed and she... didn't.

Now, she's just staring wistfully at the view, like she's contemplating flying.

"Sera?" I prompt her.

"Hmm?" she asks, the dreamy quality of her voice reminding me of when we were in Demeter's Gardens.

"I asked if you're all right."

Her lips quirk up. "You've asked that seven times today. Now eight. Or maybe it's technically *nine* since you had to repeat yourself."

"Maybe I have, but that wasn't an answer."

"No, I suppose it wasn't," she replies, still smiling. "But I'm fine, Lina. Just tired. It's been... a unique two years."

"Do you want to talk about it?" I ask her.

"Not right now, no," she murmurs. "However, I may at some point. If I do, I'll let you know."

I swallow, wishing there was more I could do.

But if my sister doesn't want to talk about her experience and whatever actually happened in that garden, then that's her choice. And it's a choice I have to respect.

"You really ought to get back to your mates," she goes on. "Reaper is growing antsy."

I frown. "How do you know that?" She's not wrong. I can feel him in my head, patiently waiting for me to finish my conversation with my sister.

Flame and Orcus exude similar thoughts of patience. However, all three fae want to introduce me to my new room, to our future *nest*. But I wanted to see to my sister's comfort first.

"He's pacing over there," she says, gesturing with her shoulder to a space on the other side of her bed—away from the balcony doors.

"He's... what?" I glance at the empty room around us. "There's no one here but us."

"Technically, that's not true," Reaper replies as he materializes by the nightstand. "It's strange that your sister can see me in the in-between, while you can't."

"The in-between?" I repeat, my brow furrowed. "What...?"

"The space between life and death," my sister whispers. "That's how Reaper told me what to say to Demeter."

"When I realized she could see and hear me, it made our plan a lot easier to execute," my Death Fae says conversationally.

"So you... you can see the in-between?" I ask my sister, unsure if that should impress me or concern me.

She shrugs. "Apparently."

I look at Reaper. "And you go to the in-between?"

"Often," he replies. "In fact, that's how I found the spell Demeter used to yank you into her Omega prison. She cast it over the entire Elite City, which is pretty fucking impressive. That's why she sent you the note to go there— she knew the magic would eventually ensnare you."

Yeah, I more or less figured out the latter part of that when Demeter mentioned the note earlier.

Still, it's strange to me that my sister can see the in-between plane. *Is it related to whatever Demeter did to her?* I wonder.

Alas, I know now isn't the time to ask.

Something my sister confirms as she says, "As I said, I'm fine. Go be with your mates, Lina. I'll still be here tomorrow. And the next day. And the day after that. We can talk then, okay?"

The last time I saw Sera, she was eight-and-ten and somewhat frightened by her first Day of the Choosing as an eligible Offering. I'll never forget the way her shoulders caved in when the Viscount called her name or how my heart broke to watch her stumble up those stage stairs.

But seeing her now, I realize the sister I knew is no longer here. This is Serapina the survivor. The woman who drove a knife into the heart of a Goddess.

A Goddess who may or may not be her mother.

I swallow down that thought, determined to worry about that another day.

For now, I need to give my sister her desired space.

And go properly thank my mates.

Because they've given me everything, including providing this lovely room for my sister.

Not to mention saving me on Monsters Night, gradually introducing me to their lives and desires, and basically rescuing me again from a crazy Goddess.

They're the kind of "monsters" a girl wants to dream about. The ones that are actually heroes in disguise. Angels when one needs them. And feral… *in bed.*

My heart skips a beat at the prospect provoked by that last bit.

"Okay," I say, standing and clearing my throat. "We'll talk more tomorrow," I promise my sister.

She nods and reaches for my hand to give it a squeeze. "Thank you for finding me, Lina."

"I'm just sorry it took me so long," I admit.

"I'm not," she replies. "You found me. That's what

counts." She releases my hand and closes her eyes. "See you tomorrow, sis."

"Tomorrow," I agree.

Reaper leads me into the hallway without a word, his tattoos writhing up and down his arms along the way. Once we've moved about ten paces away, I ask, "Does she seem okay to you?"

He snorts. "No. She seems irritated that you keep repeating that question."

I glare at him. "She's my little sister. I'm allowed to worry."

"She's twenty years old, Alina. All she wants is some space to heal." He cups my cheek, pulling me closer to him. "And strawberry cupcakes are *our* thing, pet. Pick another dessert to give her in the future."

"Just how long were you watching us?" I ask him, more amused than annoyed.

He shrugs. "A while." He looks a little sheepish now. "I… I feel better when I'm around you. Like I can actually focus and hear myself." He tilts his head a bit, almost as though he's trying to find the right words. "Your presence quiets the dark souls inside me."

"Oh." That… that seems rather sweet. Especially coming from Reaper.

I can feel his vulnerability via our bond, his admitting the words out loud the equivalent of him expressing deep emotions.

He isn't the type for fluffy comments or romantic devotions.

But he is sensitive in his own way.

Just like Flame and Orcus—they all have their own varying degrees of emotional displays.

Flame shows his affection through grooming.

Orcus proves his devotion through protection.

And Reaper demonstrates his admiration through gifts, while also expressing gratitude through truth.

I press my lips to his, suddenly feeling the need to show him my own version of loyalty by initiating contact with my tongue.

It's always him seducing me.

Now it's my turn to seduce him.

He growls in approval, his arms encircling my waist as the world melts away around us. *Literally.* I can feel his smoky tendrils pulling me into the shadows as he takes us somewhere new. I'm still kissing him when my feet touch the floor, my heart hammering in my rib cage because I want more.

But I'm suddenly distracted by a familiar scent.

My perfect day, I think, surprised to find it here in this new room.

My eyes open and my attention shifts to a massive bed, one that's exceedingly familiar to me.

Because it's the bed from the cabin.

The bed holding my nest.

I gasp and move toward it, shocked to see that almost everything is already in the right place. "How…?"

"Orcus and I have been working on it all day," Flame says softly. "I'm sorry if it's not perfect. We tried to put it back together just like you had it, but…"

"We're not Omegas," Orcus finishes for him. "We need your magical touch, sweet Goddess of ours."

"More than you know," Reaper adds as he pulls his shirt over his head and holds it out for me.

I take it on instinct, my soul instantly knowing exactly where to put it.

This intrinsic need is slowly becoming more normal and less foreign, my mind having chosen to give in to the nesting inclination instead of fighting it.

I'm an Omega, I acknowledge. *And these are my fae.*

I press my palm to my belly, feeling the life we've created there, and smile. Because I can't imagine a better fate.

Who knew Monsters Night would end like this? I marvel. *Offering Nine. Claimed and mated by three gorgeous fae men.*

Now that's what one might call a happily-ever-after.

Thank you for Reading *Their Lethal Pet*!

If you're curious about Serapina's story, flip the page for a sneak peek at *Bride of Death…*

BONUS EPILOGUE:
SERAPINA

"YOU JUST LIED TO YOUR SISTER," a deep voice says from the shadows, stirring goose bumps along my neck. "You're not fine at all, *Persephone.*"

I shiver, the name one that haunts my dreams. It's always *his* voice that whispers it, too.

The voice I'm hearing now.

Only this isn't a dream.

This is real. *Very. Fucking. Real.*

"Two thousand years," he continues, a slight admonishing lilt underlining his tone. "That's how long I've searched for you, my darling soul mate. Two thousand years, each passing second infuriating me more and more."

I swallow, his quiet fury resembling a hot wave against my exposed skin.

"That's a long time to plot revenge," he goes on. "To consider all the ways to torture your betrayer." He sighs, his features still hidden by the shadows. "I chose this kingdom for you, darling. Or rather, *because* of you. I needed a place to sharpen my skills, to master the art of death. Because I can't have you dying too quickly, now can I?"

He finally moves, his black robes blending with the darkness of the room as he steps into the moonlight. His chiseled cheekbones are the first attribute I see, the hard lines of his face giving him a lethal vibe that has my blood running cold.

Only for my belly to flip as I meet his dark, intense eyes. The color matches his hair, the strands floating down around his alluring face to rest against his broad shoulders.

He's sinfully handsome. Almost too perfect in appearance.

And glaring at me with hatred in his gaze.

"I'm going to make you suffer, my darling little flower. Break every stem inside you. Tarnish your petals. And bury you in the fucking ground just so I can resurrect you to do it all over again."

I swallow, my heart skipping several beats.

He's threatening me.

Saying *awful* things to me.

Yet… I don't fear him. I'm… *intrigued* by him instead.

It's the most intoxicatingly idiotic reaction, one I don't understand at all.

However, I can't help but ask, "Who are you?" Because I need to know his name. To know *him*. He's magnetic. Imposing. *Dominant.*

And something inside me also thinks he might be mine, too.

"You're going to feign innocence? Pretend you don't remember me?" He chuckles, but the sound is too deadly to be amusing. "How sweet." He saunters forward to sit on the edge of my bed, right where Alina sat just minutes ago.

"I don't remember you," I promise him, speaking the truth. "But I sometimes hear you in my dreams."

He arches a dark brow. "Oh, do you? And what do we do in those dreams, hmm?"

I bite my lower lip, not wanting to answer that question.

Because after he whispers that name—*Persephone*—we engage in… sensual behavior. Do wicked things. But before I can thoroughly enjoy the experience, I always wake up. Yet I never know his name.

"Will you please tell me your name?" I ask again, needing to know.

He considers me for a long moment, his full lips curling on one side. "A game, then, little betrayer?" he asks, sounding indulgent in a sinister way. "All right, my darling little broken flower. I'll play." He leans forward, his face suddenly close to mine. "But you should know there will be consequences when I win."

I swallow again, not sure what he means by *playing a game* and *winning*. Yet I feel myself nodding in understanding anyway, my body seeming to do whatever it wants in his presence.

Or maybe it's just doing whatever *he* wants.

He pulls back a little, his dark eyes searching mine.

Then he smiles again.

"My name is Hades," he tells me, his name striking a chord somewhere deep inside my mind. "And I've just become your worst fucking nightmare."

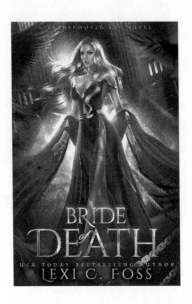

BRIDE OF DEATH

A Persephone & Hades Retelling with a "Why Choose" Twist

"Hello, Persephone."
The voice that haunts my dreams is standing at the edge of
my bed, his face covered in shadows.
"Welcome home."

God Hades thinks I'm his soul mate. The same one who
betrayed him over two thousand years ago. And he's hell-
bent on making me pay for my former sins.

"Guard her," he tells his two best friends. "Don't let that
little trickster out of your sight."

Maliki and Onyx take the demand seriously.

They're my constant shadows, just like Hades. Following me everywhere. Staying in my room. Guarding my bed at night.

"I'm not who he thinks I am," I promise them. "I don't even know him."

But no one seems to hear me.
Because I'm all alone.
Lost in this Netherworld Kingdom.
And destined to become Death's future bride.

Author's Note: *Bride of Death* is book one of the Netherworld Fae trilogy and ends on a cliffhanger.

THEIR BLOOD QUEEN

Three sexy vampires haunt my dreams and they love to make me scream.
For all the right reasons.

The nightmares started on Monster's Night. I figured my overactive libido was just tripping out because of all the literal monsters on the news. Some portal opened up and they were terrorizing women, in particular.

But seriously, what female hasn't thought about that monster under the bed once or twice in a sensual light? There's just something about danger, about fangs, about long tongues...

So, I let the dreams happen. I ***invite them in.***

But one night, when I open my eyes and they're literally feasting on me... I realize it's no dream.

This is real.

"Get off me!" I scream, not because it doesn't feel *good* what the one with an unnaturally long tongue is doing, but because this was supposed to be a dream.

"Not a chance, sigil."

Why do they always call me that?

I move to push the one between my legs away, but I realize I can't. My muscles don't comply.

Red eyes glow at my right. Eyes that belong to a face crafted by a master sculptor, but his fangs dripping with my blood suggest he's anything but a benevolent being. *"You're far too delicious to release now. Plus, you invited us into your mind. You told us to play."*

Yes, but that had been when this was all a fanciful dream full of orgasms and forbidden desires.

I opened my mouth to say as much, but the creature on my right groaned at the sight. "Yes, open that mouth wide, our sigil. We're starved for more of your screams."

Their Blood Queen *is a standalone paranormal romance with three monstrous vampires that feed on blood and dreams from their chosen mate. There is NO OWD and always HEA.*
Triggers: Explicit content, somnophilia, blood play, overstim, and others. Please check the full list on the trigger page inside the book.

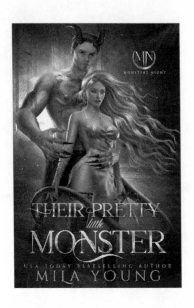

THEIR PRETTY LITTLE MONSTER

In their arms, danger becomes desire.

Every year, monsters demand their Offerings—women like
me. This year, I thought I escaped. I thought I was safe.
Then he arrived.
The Viscount.
Dangerous and ruthless, he declares me a late Offering.
Swept into the deadly realm of the Shadowfen, I realize
I'm not here by chance.

They want to rule, and I'm their key. My reality crumbles,
and as much as we act like enemies, they refuse to let me
go. Their touch ignites a fire I can't resist, fueling desires I
never expected.

They call me their little monster.

Maybe they're right.
Because when everything is stripped away, a fiercer side of
me no one expected—not even me—emerges.

You see, in the shadows, temptation and peril collide.
So, ready or not, the monster within is about to be
unleashed… and these three Shadowfen are eager to claim
their prize in the Monster Bride Trials.
Me…

Their Pretty Little Monster is a standalone
paranormal romance with darker themes, enemies to
lovers, a sassy heroine who comes into her own power, and
three stubborn Alphas who aren't releasing her.

USA Today Bestselling Author Lexi C. Foss loves to play in dark worlds, especially the ones that bite. She lives in Chapel Hill, North Carolina with her husband and their furry children. When not writing, she's busy crossing items off her travel bucket list, or chasing eclipses around the globe. She's quirky, consumes way too much coffee, and loves to swim.

Want access to the most up-to-date information for all of Lexi's books? Sign-up for her newsletter here.

Lexi also likes to hang out with readers on Facebook in her exclusive readers group - Join Here.

Where To Find Lexi:
www.LexiCFoss.com